TWISTED METAL

TWISTED METAL

TONY BALLANTYNE

TOR

First published 2009 by Tor
an imprint of Pan Macmillan Ltd
Pan Macmillan, 20 New Wharf Road, London N1 9RR
Basingstoke and Oxford
Associated companies throughout the world
www.panmacmillan.com

ISBN 978-0-230-73860-7

A CIP catalogue record for this book is available
from the British Library.

Typeset by Intype Libra Ltd
Printed and bound in the UK by
CPI Mackays, Chatham ME5 8TD

Map Artwork by Raymond Turvey

Visit **www.panmacmillan.com** to read more about all our books
and to buy them. You will also find features, author interviews and
news of any author events, and you can sign up for e-newsletters
so that you're always first to hear about our new releases.

For
Laura, Sophie, Laura,
Ben and James

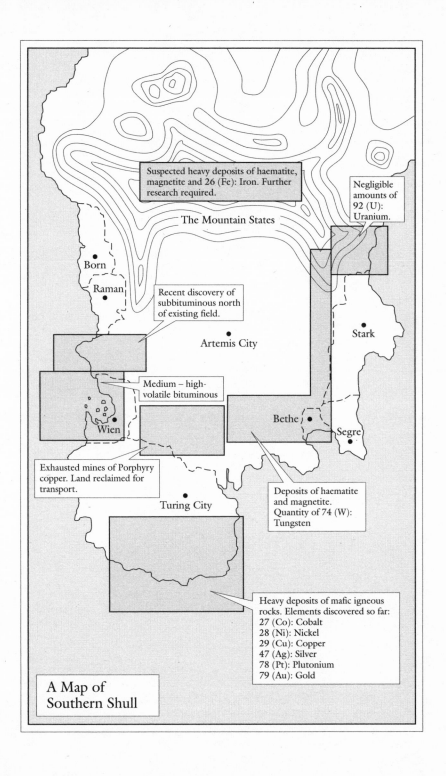

Suspected heavy deposits of haematite, magnetite and 26 (Fe): Iron. Further research required.

The Mountain States

Negligible amounts of 92 (U): Uranium.

Born

Raman

Recent discovery of subbituminous north of existing field.

Artemis City

Stark

Medium – high-volatile bituminous

Bethe

Segre

Wien

Exhausted mines of Porphyry copper. Land reclaimed for transport.

Deposits of haematite and magnetite. Quantity of 74 (W): Tungsten

Turing City

Heavy deposits of mafic igneous rocks. Elements discovered so far:
27 (Co): Cobalt
28 (Ni): Nickel
29 (Cu): Copper
47 (Ag): Silver
78 (Pt): Plutonium
79 (Au): Gold

A Map of
Southern Shull

From *The Song of Hiawatha*

Ye whose hearts are fresh and simple,
Who have faith in God and Nature,
Who believe, that in all ages
Every human heart is human,
That in even savage bosoms
There are longings, yearnings, strivings
For the good they comprehend not,
That the feeble hands and helpless
Groping blindly in the darkness
Touch God's right hand in that darkness,
And are lifted up and strengthened,
Listen to this simple story . . .

HENRY WADSWORTH LONGFELLOW

Twenty-two Years Ago . . .

The Stark robots were better engineered, faster, stronger, sleeker – but they were being overwhelmed by the sheer number of the enemy.

The grey Artemisian infantry marched out of the darkness of the plain, following the segmented pipes that snaked from the wells to the oil refinery.

The Stark robots fell back before them in good order. They dropped flat magnetic mines and kicked sand over them. The hidden traps stuck to the iron feet of the advancing troops, discharging a shock that contracted the electromuscles of the body, pulling it into a tight, agonizing ball before shorting the life from the victim in one convulsive burst.

Everything about the Stark robots suggested better materials and better minds. Each shot from their high-velocity rifles shattered an Artemisian head, blowing a mind apart in an explosion of blue wire.

But still the grey forces came on, marching ever forward in a seemingly unending stream, underpowered rifles pumping forth ineffectual lead slugs that spread across the steel plate of the defenders, slowing them down, reducing each movement to a painful struggle.

Inevitably, the grey robots fell upon the defenders. They pulled out knives and awls and began to beat at the Stark bodies, denting them, worrying at them, seeking a point of entry. The defenders struggled on under the unceasing attack, but eventually their armour was punctured. Awls and blades worked at the bodies, peeling back the plating, piercing through to the electromuscle beneath. The Stark robots died in an agony of cuts and feedback, while all around them the Artemisian forces marched on, eyes fixed on the refinery and its precious oil.

Other creatures joined the battlefield. The soldiers' feet slipped and skidded on the metal shells of beetles that dug their way up from their burrows to steal the shards and swarf that dropped from the bodies of the downed.

A chatter of metal, the sound of a toothed blade tearing itself apart on a tungsten block, and a line of holes appeared in the grey metal bodies of the Artemisian infantry, running up and down the ranks. A Stark machine gun was firing upon them from a mile off. Falling bodies followed the line of holes, and the scavenger beetles swarmed over the newly dead. Still the Artemisian advance pressed on.

A hiss, and the air filled with a thin mist of water; it drifted through the grey ranks, a minor annoyance. Circuits felt mushy and sparky in the moist conditions.

Unnoticed at their feet, the soil churned as the beetles burrowed their way back beneath the ground.

The Artemis robots stumbled on, feet tripping on the potholed earth, metal bodies misting with water, droplets running down their arms and fingers, electromuscle singing with power, the sight of the refinery, empty and undefended, spurring them on.

And then they felt it, the sense of building power ahead; an enormous potential forming, it resonated in their bodies, set their electromuscle singing. The advance faltered, the robots behind still pushing into those in front. The leaders paused to gaze at the line of metal spikes thrust in the ground before them, each spike humming with ominous intent.

Something was coming. The grey bodies at the front held for a moment in desperate equilibrium, ready to retreat, knowing it was too late . . .

The power discharged. A near-solid bar of electricity hit the metal shell of a leading Artemisian soldier. Her mind exploded; the power within it was added to the lightning bolt that now spread crackling across the field of battle. Metal screamed and shuddered, twisted metal expanded and melted. A magnetic pulse spread out from the battlefield, across the continent of Shull; it rose up into the night and bounced off the ionosphere.

An army was wiped out, just like that.

Silence settled over the battlefield, nothing was heard but the ping and crack of cooling metal. So many bodies, so many minds, so much twisted metal. All dead.

The soil began to stir again.

The beetles were returning.

Far away, halfway around the world, a robot monitoring the radio frequencies in distant Yukawa heard a crackle, a blast of white noise. It was the sound of so many souls departing the world, not that he recognized it as such.

He scored his stylus across the metal, drawing the pictograms that represented an electrical storm somewhere over the western sea.

Liza

Two robots were making love in the middle of an electrical storm.

Crouching in an old shell hole, searing white lightning arcing above them as the charged night sought release, Liza paused in the act of twisting wire and gazed up at her husband.

'Is everything all right?' Kurtz asked. The sky flared, and gravel tipped from the rim and rolled to the base of their shelter. It was a night of changes: far across the dark plain, Artemis was on the march; attacking the distant city state of Stark.

'Are you worried by the fighting?' pressed Kurtz. 'Shall we go back to Turing City?'

'No,' she smiled at him. 'Stark is a long way from here. What sort of a child would we make if we were to run at the slightest disturbance?'

His eyes glowed soft yellow, a gentle contrast to the raw power tearing the night apart above them.

As she spoke again, her voice crackled with the static of the storm. 'I have reached the point. Have you decided?'

'Yes,' whispered Kurtz. 'A boy.'

Liza nodded and returned to her work, her hands moving in

the feminine manner as she wove a mind from the twisted wire that Kurtz made for her.

'Thank you,' said Kurtz, watching her movements with fascination.

'Thank you for what?'

'For giving me the choice.'

'It's tradition,' Liza replied simply, her hands ever moving. 'Thank you,' she murmured.

'For what?'

'For trusting me. For not asking if I am really weaving what you asked for.'

'It's tradition,' said Kurtz.

There was a sizzling crash, and several lightning bolts arced down, earthing themselves through crude plugs of raw iron that had thrust themselves up from the stone plain. Glowing plasma formed an arch in the sky, burning its way into the electrocells of Kurtz's and Liza's eyes.

'That came from Stark,' observed Kurtz, the purple lines of lightning slowly fading from their vision. 'Their Tesla towers are too powerful. Artemis won't defeat them tonight.'

'Good,' murmured Liza, still weaving busily. 'Good.'

'It only means that they'll attack again,' said Kurtz despondently. 'And they'll keep attacking until they have defeated Stark, and then Segre, and then Bethe. And then it will be our turn.'

'Shhh . . .' said Liza. 'Not tonight. Let them sort out their own problems. Just concentrate on us . . .'

'Yes,' said Kurtz, and he relaxed, allowed his electromuscles to discharge a little.

Liza worked carefully on, twisting Kurtz's wire into a mind. The little body that would house that mind lay at their feet. A smart little body, lovingly built by Kurtz out of steel and brass, the whole then painted in black and gold stripes by Liza. A beautiful little body, its skull gaping open, ready for the mind she was twisting to be inserted. It already had a name: Liza and Kurtz's little boy would be called Karel. Karel. A lovely name for a lovely child, due to be born in the midst of less than lovely times.

Liza and Kurtz crouched together in an old shell hole, the remnant of a long-spent war, making their own little expression of peace while electric bolts fanned across the sky, painting themselves on the canvas provided by Zuse, the night moon. Meanwhile, a low rumbling spread across the stone plain. Artemis machinery being destroyed: they had attacked Stark too soon.

The rhythm of Liza's movements had changed.

'What are you weaving now?' asked Kurtz.

'His sense of self,' said Liza. 'His sense of otherness. Isn't it obvious?'

'No, I see your hands move and all I see is twisting. It has no order or meaning to me.'

Liza smiled. 'Now I am giving him your stubbornness.' Her hands danced lightly, tweaking, turning, teasing.

'I'm not stubborn,' he protested.

'You'll stand your ground, even when you suspect you're wrong. You'd rather see a bad argument through to the end than change your opinion. It's not your most attractive characteristic, but,' she shrugged, 'there are worse things to be ashamed of.'

'But I don't want my child to be stubborn. Take it out!'

'The weave must balance.'

Kurtz said nothing, and Liza knew he understood. He would have seen children who walked and talked and performed simple tasks and nothing more, seen the way other mothers would look at them with sympathy or disapproval. *The mother tried too hard,* they would say. *The weave doesn't balance.*

The electrical storm was rising in intensity: an incredible tearing sound ripping across the world. White light poured down from the sky to the east, a waterfall of light increasing in flux. A curtain of electricity was fast being drawn across the horizon, a flood of light that blasted the plain; the squat iron plugs firing ultra-black shadows westwards. The reddish stones kicked across the plain by the metal feet of so many robots drew long lines of darkness towards Turing City itself.

'What is going on out there?' wondered Kurtz aloud. 'Is that the battle or the elements?'

'Shhh,' said Liza. 'Let the rest of the world take care of itself. We have our own child to attend to.'

'Artemis,' reflected Kurtz. 'If we were Artemisians, we would be making this child very differently . . .'

'Do you want that?' teased Liza. 'I could make Karel think only of the glory of the Artemisian state. Is that really what you want?'

To her surprise, Kurtz did not answer straight away.

'I don't know,' he said, slowly. 'There's no denying how successful Artemis is. Their forges grow larger every month.' He lowered his voice.

'Is that what you really want?' asked Liza, soft yellow eyes glowing, hands never ceasing their manipulation of the warm, pliable metal. 'Tell me now, Kurtz. We are of Turing City State. We can make our child share its values, respect itself and others as individuals, or we can make our child strong and empty, just like an Artemisian. What do you *really* believe in?'

'Liza, I don't know. I know we agreed, but are we sure we are right to do this? Turing City will only succeed if *all* the children really believe in what we stand for. If just a few of them turn and run, the rest of us will fall. All it takes is a few children. Do we want to condemn our own child to be the one remaining while others are running?'

'But if we all stand together we will have a better life. After all, we want what's best for our boy.'

'But which is the best?'

Liza couldn't stop moving her hands: she couldn't allow the pliable wire to set.

'You choose,' urged Kurtz.

'No. You choose.'

'But it's such a huge responsibility. Choices like this could change the world.'

'Never mind the rest of the world,' said Liza. 'This is just about us. Come on, individual or drone, which is it to be? Turing City or Artemis?'

The world seemed to pause. The wall of lightning held its breath, just hanging in the air in a blaze of white. The rumble of explosions to the east ceased. In that moment of stillness, Kurtz told her, and she nodded, and began the final part of the weave.

'Almost done,' she said.

The tearing noise stopped abruptly. The storm died, the wash of light fading, the stones and iron plugs of the plain inhaling their long shadows.

And the world changed.

Kurtz groaned, and Liza looked up, saw the green glow fading from his eyes.

'Kurtz?' she said. Slowly his body rocked forward and fell to the ground, just a collection of jointed metal.

'Kurtz!' called Liza. 'Oh *Zuse* no.' She stood up, the blue wire trailing from her hands to where it emerged from Kurtz's body. She looked around, barely comprehending what had happened. Had it been the lightning, she wondered; had it hit her husband? But the sky was now so still and dark.

Then she heard the sound of metal on bare rock. Footsteps?

Someone loomed out of the darkness. A metal body, dented and scarred. Red eyes glowing in infrared, iron hands gripping a projectile weapon. The dull grey paintwork of an Artemisian soldier. He walked easily towards her, rifle pointing loosely in her direction.

'You killed him,' said Liza.

'I killed him.' The soldier looked down at the warm wire, still being twisted in Liza's hands.

'You can let go now,' he said. 'There isn't enough metal left there to complete your child.'

'How do you know?' asked Liza. 'What would any man know about that?'

The soldier ignored her question. 'I heard you both talking,' he said. 'Even through the storm.' He tapped one of the overlarge directional microphones on the side of his head. Then he pointed at poor Kurtz's dead body. 'Do you *really* think he made the right choice?'

'Of course I do.' she said quietly. She was looking at the remaining length of wire, calculating.

The Artemisian robot shrugged. 'You *would* say that, I suppose.'

'What are you doing here?' asked Liza. 'Why are Artemis trespassing into Turing City State?'

'Haven't you heard? Bethe has just fallen. Artemis is the largest forge on this plain now.'

'*Bethe?*' said Liza. 'I thought you were attacking Stark!'

'Stark?' laughed the robot. 'Not likely. Not with their Tesla towers to defend them. No, that was just a little misdirection. Bethe first, then Segre. Then we'll be right on Stark's doorstep. And then we'll see.'

Liza wasn't listening. Kurtz lay dead at her feet, his wire still twisted around her hands, cooling, dying. She felt as if something was dying within herself too, leaving nothing but a cold emptiness inside her metal shell.

'Kurtz,' she whispered. 'Kurtz, what am I to do?'

There was no reply. She was on her own now. A cold determination began to rise up within her. 'Kurtz made his choice,' she murmured to herself. 'Kurtz was right.'

She had forgotten about those overlarge ears on the Artemisian robot. He picked up what she had muttered. He laughed.

'That's easy for you to say now,' he said, 'not that you will ever know. I saved you the choice. There is not enough wire for the child to be born.'

Again, Liza looked at the wire that trailed from her hands, recalculating.

'There is just enough,' she decided.

The dull grey robot's hands tightened around his rifle. 'I should dash that wire from your hands now; make you lose your place.'

Liza's voice trembled. 'But you haven't.' She clutched the wire tighter.

'Go on,' said the soldier. 'Finish the mind. Finish it the way he said.'

Liza did nothing. With a low whirr, the soldier brought his gun to bear on her.

'Do it, or, so help me, I will shoot you too. I have one charge left.' He laughed. 'Hey, you can be just like Nyro. You've heard of Nyro, haven't you?'

The lightning flared again, and, just for a moment, Liza could have sworn that the robot flinched and looked up to the sky.

'Yes, I've heard of Nyro,' she said.

Liza began to twist wire once more. She rolled her eyes up to meet those of the soldier, her metal face taking on an odd expression.

'You're doing it,' said the soldier, in surprise. 'Or are you? I find it hard to believe you're really making that child *his* way. Not after I killed him. Not with me standing here with a gun like this, raping you. You don't *really* believe that he made the right choice, do you? I can't believe you would really do what he said.'

Liza continued weaving. She was almost done.

'Well?' said the soldier.

'I'm not telling you,' said Liza. 'You'll never know.'

It was so quiet on the plain now, so quiet and dark. The climax of the battle had passed, and Bethe had fallen. Even now Artemisian soldiers would be penetrating its streets, ripping it apart, remaking it in the image of Artemis itself.

And look what's happening here, thought Liza, staring at the red eyes of the man opposite, the dark aperture of his rifle's muzzle fixed upon her head.

She concentrated again on the wire. There was life in that forming mind already. She could feel it begin to pulse. All that remained was to tie it off and bring the mind into existence. She made to start the knot, and hesitated, remembering what her mother had told her: *it wasn't until this point that you truly understood what life was about.*

Liza had never really understood until now, but here it was, staring her in the face. Should Liza now tie the knot as a seal and wake a simple, mechanical mind that would live indefinitely? Or should she tie it the other way, in the fuse, to create a living, thinking being, and, in doing so, condemn it to death in thirty or forty years' time?

In the end she did as her mother had done, and her mother before her. She tied the fuse.

Something came to life.

'Hello Karel,' she murmured. She looked over at the dead body of her husband. 'Here he is, Kurtz. We did it. Here's our little boy.'

Carefully she placed the mind into the tiny body and snicked the skull shut.

'All finished,' she said to the soldier.

The soldier looked from her to the child. 'Did you really do it?' he asked.

'I'm not telling you,' replied Liza.

'Then I shall say goodbye, *Tokvah*.'

He raised his rifle once more, pointing it at her head. Her gyros were wobbling, but she held herself steady.

'Then shoot me,' she said. 'But you'll never know.'

The robot stared at her, his red eyes glowing. Liza held his gaze, determined not to flinch, even here at the end. She was ready to die.

And then the robot lowered his gun.

'There is a way to find out . . .' he said.

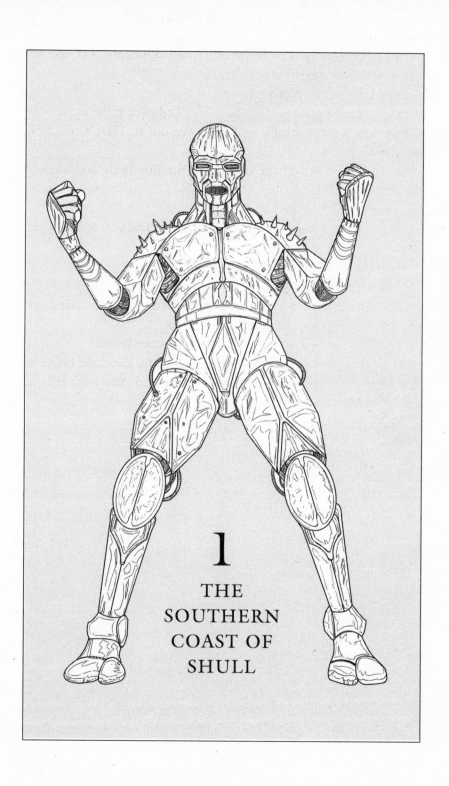

1

THE
SOUTHERN
COAST OF
SHULL

Karel

Karel's body wasn't designed for this sea wind. It got under the thin metal panels that plated his torso, it whistled through the cylindrical sheaths that encased his thighs and shins. The people who worked out here on the coast wore flexible plastic gaiters on their arm and leg joints to keep out the salt water, their body work was thick with weatherproof paint. Now, as he left the marble promenade that ran along the cliff top and strode down the stone steps cut into the cliff face, Karel's stylish city body felt weak and ineffectual against the elements. The lace-lined waves that crashed and drained from the grey rocks below seemed so much more vital than the pastel paisley pattern his wife had used to decorate his chest plate.

The Immigration Station was a rusted box built on metal stilts that raised it just above the surge of the waves. A retractable metal walkway led from some steps at the base of the cliffs out across the swirling water to the office itself. As Karel looked down through the gaps in the walkway grille towards the blue waves swirling below, he felt his gyros shudder. Living as he did in the city, he had never seen the need to fully waterproof his interior circuitry. Fall down there and he would probably short himself out.

But then Karel felt as if he had lived his whole life in fear of falling: falling from the state of grace in which he now found himself in the city, with a wife and a child and a good job: pulled down by the suspicion of his fellow citizens who never quite trusted what was woven into his mind.

But this was not something to think on today. Buffeted by the wind, he staggered on across the walkway and pulled open the heavy sea door leading to the Immigration Station.

Gates sat in reception, one of his legs on the desk as he made minor repairs to himself.

'Close the door!' he called, without looking up. Karel dutifully pushed the heavy metal door into its plastic seal, shutting out the wind. Still the rolling of the waves could be heard, crashing against the metal stilts below, echoing hollowly through the metal building.

'It's getting rough out there,' said Karel.

'Rough!' laughed Gates, still fiddling with his leg. 'This is just an autumn swell. You want to come here in winter when the storms really get up. The waves go right over the building!'

Karel knew he wasn't exaggerating. Immigration was a different job here on the south coast, and Gates and his team were scornful of Karel and the team operating in Turing City, perceiving them to have an easy life.

They were wrong, of course.

Karel studied Gates, noting his battered body and chipped paintwork. When a robot started to neglect his appearance, especially in a place like this, it was not a good sign.

'Well, I'm here now,' said Karel, coolly, 'and I would appreciate a little courtesy on my arrival. Is this how you greet all your visitors?' He stared hard at Gates, who paused in the act of adjusting the tension in the calf ligaments of his left leg. Gates held his stare for a moment and then pushed the leg back into place. It locked into position with a click. He stood up and flexed it.

'All sorted, *sir*,' he said, shifting his weight from foot to foot as he felt for his new balance. 'Would you like to come straight through and see the case in question, *sir*?'

'Don't get sarcastic with me, Gates,' warned Karel.

'I wasn't being sarcastic.'

Karel tried a different tack.

'Listen, Gates, let's not do this. I've got enough going on back in the city without having to come down here. I'm sure you're gritted up with work too. So just tell me, why am I here?'

Gates held Karel's gaze for a moment longer, and then he too relaxed.

'Yeah, you're right. Sorry, Karel. Come on through, it would be better if I showed you. We have a client held in isolation that I want you to see. I asked for you specifically because this one is . . . odd. Like nothing I've ever seen before.'

Gates picked up a heavy iron key and placed it in the lock of the door that led through to the holding area. He banged twice on its metal surface and called out: 'Hey, Cabeza! I'm coming through with Karel.'

There was a bang in return and the sound of Cabeza's muffled reply. Two keys were turned at the same time, and the heavy door swung open.

'After you,' said Gates, and Karel stepped through into the holding area.

The isolation area lay at the far side of the station, past the rows of iron-barred holding cells where the immigrants and refugees waited to be processed. Gates led Karel down the central walkway.

The cells in the main area were nearly full, but that was no surprise to Karel. All throughout Turing City State, the holding cells were filling up fast. Stir the political waters and all sorts of things come to the surface, and the political waters of Shull had been stirred plenty of late by the expansion of Artemis. Turing City State was a kitten compared to the lion of the Artemisian Empire, but it was a kitten with adamantium claws, with Stark electromuscle, and with a mind twisted by Oneill herself. Turing City could defend itself, and every displaced robot on the continent of Shull seemed to be making his or her way here in search of shelter.

Karel might have expected this many clients, but he was still a little surprised at the startling variety of the station's occupants. Gates's team's normal clientele tended to be the Spontaneous, those robots who had been formed somewhere out in the southern ocean and then walked here along the sea bed. Indeed, Karel could see plenty of examples of these now, sitting or standing or lying about in the various cells. They tended to have heavy iron bodies, simple facial features, their eyes usually recessed behind thick glass. A few of them were humanoid in appearance; most of them were crab-like. They were kept in specially constructed cells, the floors of which were lowered to allow pools filled with salt water. One that Karel spotted was little more than a dark shape in the water: gunmetal grey, biological life clinging to its body – barnacles and limpets – and with green algae staining its underside. Raising its eyes, set below the rim of its shell, it glanced for a moment at Karel and then returned to contemplating the dark patterns below it in the rippling water. Unfused, unsentient, this was just the sort of thing that Karel expected to find here on the south coast.

Karel resumed his progress along the walkway, still surprised by the number of the Made that had turned up here. Such robots had had their minds twisted by their mothers from wire spooled from their father. But the Made were usually seen on the northern borders of Turing City State, as refugees from Bethe and Wien. How had they made it all the way down here, to the southern coast? And there were so many of them . . .

He saw elegantly engineered robots from Stark, their shiny smooth casings humming with quiet power as they patrolled the confined space of their holding areas with proud dignity. There were short, unassuming robots from Bethe and Segre, sitting in groups, staring out through the bars. And even the peculiar builds of robots from distant Raman and Born could be seen, with their magnetized bodies and overlarge feet and hands.

Most surprisingly, there were the Artemisians. The city state of Artemis was not supposed to recognize any difference between normal metal and the carefully twisted metal of the mind. Robots born into a low rank were held to be expendable in the Artemisian State. Karel guessed that their mothers would have twisted their minds towards thoughts of escape as a more likely means of survival than service at the bottom end of Artemisian society.

Suddenly the sheer number of people in the large room made Karel feel giddy, as if his gyros were spinning too fast. Metal hands, metal feet; metal floors, metal bars. Grilles and wire and water splashing inside and booming beneath his feet and, meanwhile, all that other motion around him. It seemed as if the entire world was pressing in on Turing City. Newly constructed Artemis railway lines were spreading across the land. They brought metal to the Artemis forges that made new robots daily, even hourly, robots that poured in metal waves across the southern part of the continent of Shull. Could little Turing City's walls really hold up against that encroaching tide? Who knew? If the rumours were true, even mighty Wien looked to be on its last legs, ready to fall at any time.

'What are you looking at?'

The words jolted Karel from his reverie. The speaker was an Artemisian war robot. A Scout. Her body was made of katana metal, silver grey and hard. Her hands and feet were lean and sharp, mirror-bright blades almost totally retracted, only the very tips emerging to scratch curls of swarf from the metal floor as she advanced. She brought her head right up to the bars, stooped a little so that it was level with Karel's face. He could see how her eyes were recessed behind their narrow slits, withdrawn beyond the reach of any blade. Now she allowed them to protrude ever so slightly, signalling her contempt.

'How much longer are you going to keep me in here, *Tokvah*?' she whispered.

With a speed that surprised everyone present, Karel slammed a hand into her face, sending her reeling back across the cell, a grinding noise from his arm signifying a stripped gear. All of a sudden everyone else in the holding cells was very, very quiet, all of them staring at Karel, now flexing his hand, flexing his supple, city hand made of light metal, finely engraved with swirling patterns barely seen in the light, then continuing to walk the gangway towards the rear of the vast room. He seemed oblivious to the way the other immigrants drew back in their cells as he walked by.

Gates followed just behind him. '*Zuse*, Karel,' he swore. 'I just don't understand you, I really don't.'

'Not in front of the clients,' muttered Karel, but Gates didn't seem to hear.

'I just don't get the way you're made. Most of the time you act like a classic Turing City robot: behaving as an individual, but still capable of cooperating for the good of all, and then you turn around and pull a stunt like that.'

'I don't see why hitting that *Tokvah* stops me being a cooperator,' said Karel.

'Maybe. I don't know. Hey, I'm not judging! But there's just something about the way you're made. People talk, you know.'

'Let them,' said Karel.

They had stopped at the very rear of the holding pens, just before the door that led to the isolation area where Gates and his team kept the special cases.

'So,' said Karel. 'Is there anything I should know about this character you're holding in here?'

'There's nothing really to tell,' said Gates still eyeing Karel with a thoughtful expression. 'I've never known a robot like this one . . . I think you'd better speak to him yourself.'

Karel folded his hands together, feeling how the right hand was slightly bent out of true from where he had hit the Artemisian. That could be repaired later. For the moment he felt apprehensive, more so than he would have expected. He wondered what lay behind this door that necessitated him being dragged all the way here, away from his work, away from his wife, Susan. Especially when she had been acting so oddly lately, suddenly so emotional. Karel tried to dismiss the thought. She had been like that the last time they were planning a child, he told himself.

'Very well,' said Karel. 'Let me through.'

Gates opened the door.

'Cell number two,' he said.

Susan

'What's the matter, Susan? You look like Oneill herself has just spoken to you.'

Deya's face was filled with concern. *Why can't we make a face that fully masks our emotions?* wondered Susan. *We can build blank masks or we can build faces. Why can't we build a buffer between our feelings and our expressions?*

'Susan, speak to me,' Deya insisted. 'Is it Karel? Are you worried about him? I heard he was out at the coast today.'

Deya has such a pretty face. I could never build anything so delicate, or so well formed. The curve of the brows over her eyes, the line of her cheek. When she speaks it's like a breeze blowing on flutes. No matter how I tune my electromuscle, I can never pull a smile like hers . . .

'Susan, stop staring at me like that!'

'Sorry, Deya. I'm okay. Just a little, I don't know . . . angry I suppose. And shocked.'

Deya turned this way and that, looking around the metal and glass arches of the railway terminus, trying to determine what had upset her friend.

'Susan, is it this?' She pointed to the letters, engraved on the sheet of steel at the top of the notice board.

Susan nodded.

'Oh, Deya, I know I'm being silly. I shouldn't let it affect me like this.'

'It annoys me too, Susan, but I don't let it spoil my day.' She smiled. 'But then again, I'm not making plans at the moment.'

'Who told you?'

'Susan, it's so obvious. For weeks now you've been walking around storing up bits of conversations and mimicking character traits and observing other people's interactions. You and Karel are going to have another child.'

'We're thinking of a little girl,' Susan admitted.

'You're the chief statistician of this state,' said Deya. 'If anyone is going to build a successful child, it's you.'

'Deya, you're just like Karel. You make it sound so easy.'

'It *is* easy, Susan. Robots have been doing it since Oneill showed them how.'

'You don't really believe in Oneill!'

'No! A figure of speech! But Susan, I believe in you, and you should know better than anyone what makes a successful robot. You have all the necessary figures delivered to you on metal film.'

'I know what makes a successful robot in Turing City,' conceded Susan. 'But is *that* the right way? You can see what it says . . .'

She read the notice again:

WOMEN OF
TURING CITY

RAMAN AND BORN.
BETHE, SEGRE AND STARK.
AND NOW WIEN.

The Artemisian model has again proven to be the superior philosophy for building robots. Do you want your line to continue? Do you want your children to build children of their own? Then consider Nyro's design. Nyro's children are successful. Nyro's children now populate almost all the southern continent of Shull. By any measure, Nyro has woven the most flourishing pattern of any robot mind currently existing on Penrose.

Does your husband agree? Or does he still cling to the outdated practices of Turing City? It's easy for men to talk about the nobility of a certain philosophy. All *they* do is produce the wire. But, come the night of the making of a mind, it is *you* that hold in your hands your child's future well-being. Are you going to throw it away on some arbitrary belief, some vagary of fashion, or are you going to make a mind that really *works?*

Think about it, Mother.
You owe it to your child.

'I didn't know they had taken Wien!' said Susan.

Deya laughed dismissively. 'Don't believe everything you read, dear.'

'I don't care,' said Susan weakly. 'It makes a good point.'

A diesel engine revved once, twice, somewhere behind them.

'I can't *believe* you're talking like this,' said Deya. 'How many robots are there in Turing City at the moment?'

'In the city itself, or the state as a whole?'

'The city.'

'Thirty-three thousand, one hundred and nine.'

'And how many of them are built according to Artemisian philosophy?'

'Twenty-one.'

'Twenty-one! Hah! Well there you go.'

'That we know of, anyway. But this time last year there were only four.'

'So what? There's no choice, Susan. Who is going to sacrifice their child to Artemis in this city? We have so much more going for us. Look!'

She pointed to the high-vaulted roof of the station, the way that the thin, white-painted metal joined in delicate curves, the way that patterns of sunlight coloured by the glass illuminated the scrollwork of the wrought iron.

'I bet they don't have that in Artemis,' said Deya.

'I bet they don't. But I wonder if they were saying the same in Wien, just before the invasion.'

'I told you, Wien has not been invaded. That notice is lying. Anyway, we're stronger than Wien.'

'But are we strong enough? It makes me wonder whether it's worth even making a child any more . . .'

'It's never been a good time to make a child! But you know you're going to, Susan. You have the capability. You're not like Nicolas the Coward.'

'Am I not, Deya? I really don't know if that's true any more.'

Susan stared out through the big empty end of the station, out across the wide valley, with its low railway bridges crisscrossing copper-green rivers, looked out at the deep blue sky that covered Shull, and she felt terrified. Some days she had felt as if the rails that emerged from this station were carrying Turing City's philosophy out to an entire continent. Today she felt as if they were like an open door inviting in whatever darkness was now waiting beyond its borders.

Karel

Everything in the isolation area was painted white: new paint daubed on old, forming uneven patterns and waves on the metal of the floor and walls, white paint gathered on the bolts and rivets holding the building together. The sea could still be heard booming and crashing outside, but now the sound seemed more distant, muffled.

There was a click as Gates locked him in. Now Karel was alone. There were three cells in here, each sealed with a heavy metal door, a tiny porthole placed in its centre. There was a sudden bang, and a rapid staccato hammering started to his right, like a blunt drill skidding across steel. Something was trying to get out, trying to attack. Karel ignored it.

Cell number two was right in front of him. Karel peered through the porthole.

The man inside there was big: a body built for ore mining, with wide shoulders and great shovel-shaped hands. This was a robot that could have formed spontaneously beneath the earth and then dug his way free. His body was red iron, rusty and scarred, but with great long streaks of shiny metal showing where the corrosion had been scraped from his body in his climb to the surface. His eyes were tiny and recessed below a circular brim that ran around the top of the head. His legs were short and squat, ideal for pushing and scrambling through tunnels.

Everything about the man suggested strength and power, and Karel now needed to step inside that cell in his delicate city body. No wonder Gates had told him so little about this client. This was his way of getting his own back, the tough south coast folk teaching the city slicker a thing or two. Gates and Cabeza and the rest would be laughing at the thought of Karel stepping in to meet this giant.

Well, let them, thought Karel. He grasped the handle and pulled open the cell door. The handle only appeared on the outside of the door, and the isolation room was rigged so that only one cell could open at a time.

The man inside remained standing in the middle of his cell as the door opened. Only his eyes moved.

'Would you like to come out here for a moment?' asked Karel. 'Stretch your legs?'

Silence. At first Karel wondered if the man in there couldn't speak, but then:

'I am happy to remain here while we talk.'

'Fine, fine.' Karel moved forward into the cell. The stranger looked even bigger inside it. His shoulders were almost as wide as the cell itself, so that he would have to take care when turning around. 'Allow me to introduce myself. My name is Karel, son of Kurtz and Liza. I am a Disputant for the Turing City Immigration Office. Do you understand what that means?'

Again silence. Karel wondered if maybe being so big meant that it took longer for words to reach his mind.

'They said that you were coming,' said the other robot, eventually. 'But I still don't understand your role.'

Karel had been expecting this. He clasped his hands together, then let go as he felt the deformity in his right hand from where he had hit the Artemisian. 'Well,' he said, 'my job is to speak to robots such as yourself and determine whether or not you are intelligent.'

'Surely that is a job for a woman? Couldn't you just get a woman to look at a mind and see if it was fused or not?'

Karel smiled.'Usually, yes. But sometimes, even though minds are woven and fused, they just don't work properly. I'm here to decide if you are a potential Turing Citizen.'

'Well I can save you the trouble. I'm not.'

Karel smiled again.

'I wouldn't be so hasty in claiming that. This is Turing City, you know. There's no need for lies here.'

'I'm not lying. Why would I wish to do that?'

'Some people do. They don't understand that Turing City is a *cooperating* city. Any robot able to think is welcome here. Don't you realize that if you had emerged in Artemis we wouldn't even be having this conversation? You would already be owned by the state! Every item there, every rock, every scrap of metal, every robot is considered nothing but property.'

'That would seem proper.'

'Proper? Really? Take a look at my body. Do you like the paint-work there?'

The stranger's little eyes peered down at Karel's chest. He took in the curves of the metal there, the pastel traceries of the paint-work.

'It is an elegant example of metalwork,' he said.

'Thank you,' said Karel. 'I bought the original panels from a shop in Turing City and bent them into shape myself. They are of an alloy originally devised by the robots of Stark, but improved upon by the artisans of Turing City. The paintwork was done by my wife. It took her many nights of work.' He flicked his chest with a finger and it made a ringing sound. 'Beautiful! But a lot of effort just to make this body. It begs the question: what is so special about me that all this effort, all this material can be applied to what is really nothing more than an affectation?'

'I don't know the answer to that.'

'But I do!' said Karel. 'It's because I *think*! That is the difference between owners and property! Here in Turing City State we recognize sentience. All it takes to join our state is that you prove your intelligence!'

'But I am not intelligent.'

Karel felt a twinge of anger at the robot's stubbornness. He repressed it. 'Don't you realize what will happen to you if you maintain this ridiculous pretence? You'll be taken from here and shipped inland and put to work down a mine. Working at the top of a magma chamber, or set wandering through a pegmatite forest. You'll be treated as nothing more than a shovel or a pick.'

'Mining is what I do.'

'Yes, but mining as a *free* robot! It's your purpose, it's your life, it's what makes you happy. But as a possession they will just keep you digging and digging and digging. You'll never come to the surface! If your body breaks down they will patch it up with whatever comes to hand and then just set you off digging again, and they'll keep doing that until you're completely past repair. Nothing more than a selection of patches and spares. And after they've stripped what they can use from you, they'll just push you into an unused tunnel and leave you there. Is that what you want?'

'I don't care. Why should I?'

Karel was momentarily lost for words. Gates had said that this client was different, and he hadn't been exaggerating. Karel had never encountered anything like this before. He tried another tack.

'Come on,' he said. 'Let's be honest with each other. I don't understand what game you're playing, I don't know what you hope to achieve. Tell me something about yourself. How did you get here?'

At this the big man became animated for the first time. A low grinding noise sounded, deep in his body, and then his arms swung out. The big shovel hands knocked against the wall of the cell, scraped it so that white paint now marked the edges of the blades. The squat legs began to march in time to some unheard beat. Karel found himself backing out from the cell.

'I was born in darkness,' said the stranger, 'held in the earth. I saw nothing, heard nothing. I felt gravity, and I knew I had to dig my way in the opposite direction. I knew my name.'

'You have a name?' said Karel in surprise. He had assumed the stranger was nameless. 'What is it?'

'My name is Banjo Macrodocious. I was told: *Banjo Macrodocious, dig your way upwards until you break free through the surface.*'

Karel didn't ask Banjo who had told him to dig. Banjo wouldn't answer because he wouldn't even understand the question. This was part of birth, the weaving of the mind. This was the way with the spontaneously formed. If Karel was to trace back his own lineage, through his parents and grandparents and great-grandparents for however many generations, this would be the story of his origins too.

'I began to dig,' continued Banjo. 'I swam through the earth, I drilled and I chipped my way through the batholith. I pressed myself into cracks and fractures. I tugged aside small rocks and pushed them down with my feet, I made my way around larger obstacles. I learned the feel of my body in the darkness, the stretch of my arms, the strength in my shoulders. I felt the stones scraping down my sides; I heard the slow sounds of the underworld. And all the time I rose higher and higher. I wondered more and more what it would be like to finally break free of the rock and to walk on the roof of the world. I continued to dig. And as I did so I felt the earth changing. Higher and higher. Until that day . . .'

'Did you emerge in the sea?' asked Karel.

'Yes, in the sea. The debris on the seabed, the softness of it, how easy it was to dig through. The water all around me. The cold. And then I began to walk. Following the direction in my head.'

'Who found you?'

'I don't know their names. They found me trying to scale the cliffs. They brought me here.'

Karel was unconsciously unscrewing his right hand. He wanted to begin work on straightening it. He forced himself to stop.

'Okay, Banjo, I have heard your story.'

Karel stood formally to attention.

'As Disputant for Turing City State, I am prepared to announce my decision on your status, Banjo Macrodocious. You have a name, you take part in reasoned conversation. I believe that you are intelligent. I believe that you could be an asset to Turing City State. I would therefore like to invite you to join us. Would you like that?'

'I don't think I would like or dislike it. I have no feelings.'

'I don't believe that is true, Banjo Macrodocious. This is my job; I know what I am doing. You *are* intelligent. I am inviting you to join our state. All you have to do is declare your willingness.'

'I have no preference as to whether I join your state or not.'

'How can you say that? Don't you realize that most of the people waiting out there in the cages beyond this door are desperate for me to invite them to join Turing City? They live in fear of being sent back to their broken countries, of being enslaved by Artemis. Don't you see what you're giving up? Do you really just want to be adopted as a tool, to be worked till you drop and are eventually abandoned in a mine underground?'

'I have no preference.'

Karel's anger was such that he wanted to smash the big robot in the face, just as he had done the Artemisian soldier. Wisely, he restrained himself.

'I don't think you mean that. You know what I think you are? I think you're a coward. I've met people like you before: robots who don't have the courage to accept the faculties they have been given. You have a mind and a well-designed body and you refuse to take responsibility for them. You know what they call robots like you? They call them Nicolas the Coward. Call them Nicolas the Shirker. That's what they'll call you.'

Banjo Macrodocious looked puzzled. 'Why should I care?'

'You pretend not to understand, Nicolas the Coward.'

'Call me what you will.'

'Nicolas the Shirker.'

'I don't even know who you are talking about.'

'Don't know Nicolas the Coward? Nicolas who was blessed by water and refused all that he was offered? Nicolas who ran away from his gifts rather than accept responsibility?'

'No.'

'Then I shall tell you the story. Sit down, Banjo Macrodocious.'

'I can't sit down. This body is not built that way.'

'Well stand there and listen . . .'

The Story of Nicolas the Coward

Nicolas was an Artemisian soldier.

Long ago, before Nyro's philosophy had completely enfolded their minds, when Artemis's eye was still drawn down into the earth in search of ore, rather than out across the continent of Shull desirous of power, the rulers came to wonder at their origins.

The Raman mountains were long known as a source of the Spontaneous, and it was decided to send an expedition there to search for the origins of these robots, and thus the source of robot-kind.

Nicolas was part of that expedition. His body was made of steel, of hammered beaten steel. His electromuscles were tuned and harmonized to his body, every last screw was tightened, every last joint was greased. His troop moved through the caves that they had found deep in the Raman range with practised grace and maximum efficiency. Twenty-four robots, their bodies engineered and modified to be identical, interchangeable.

They moved swiftly through the caves like sunlight that flickers from a falling blade.

They moved silently through the caves like shadows in the darkness.

Down through tunnels, passing the silent machines that still made their slow climb from the depths and up to the sun, their minds as yet unwoken. The passageways through which Nicolas moved became softer and more polished by the tread of ancient feet.

There was the sound of water, the playing of a stream mixing with the rolling crash of a waterfall. Nicolas and his troop sensed a deep pool somewhere near. They heard the echoes of a huge space; they felt the ionization in the air increasing.

In those days the Raman state counted the caves as their own. They sent men and women out from their mountain-top cities to patrol the twisting passes and slate-covered slopes that led to the caves. Though Nicolas and his squad had moved so carefully, they had been observed and followed down into the earth by Raman soldiers.

The Raman feared those caves and the passageways that led back through time all the way to Oneill, yet their anger at the intrusion by Artemis was even greater.

The Raman carried steel discs, magnetic chaff and awls.

The Artemisians carried blades and guns, for the Artemisians were not used to fighting in the Raman mountains.

The Raman came close in the darkness, moving silently on plastic-soled feet, crawling silently on plastic-bound hands. They attacked.

A steel disc spun through the darkness, its polished surface reflecting nothing but the night, its razor edge silent as it cut the air.

Nicolas and his squad had paused near the stream. They were adjusting joints and calibrating senses, rubbing in grease and cleaning away grit. Nicolas was watching Kathy as she rubbed the casing of her thighs with emery cloth, as she used a fingertip to tease out swarf from the seams. Nicolas saw her head smashed to one side, saw her fall to the ground, arms and legs twitching, the top of her head half sliced open by the black disc that had lodged there.

Nicolas stifled the cry that arose in his throat, and rose to fighting stance, his troop smoothly echoing his action. Twenty-three robots turning to cover all directions, the gentle hum of electro-muscles charging with energy, ready to move with explosive force. Eye shields slid into place, rifles were cocked, ears were turned up to detect any sound, and then turned straight back down again as the noise of the waterfall and the splashing stream overwhelmed them. This was a good spot for an ambush.

And then the air was full of the harsh percussive beat of steel discs, ricocheting from the stone walls. Two more robots were decapitated.

'Up there!' called someone, and twenty-one rifles swung and fired simultaneously. Three bodies fell, splashing into the pool.

'Raman,' said someone. 'Look at the build on those bodies.'

But now it was getting harder to see and to move. Nicolas's ears were cutting out, silences punctuating the noise of the battle all around. His vision flashed with white noise and he felt his electromuscles twitching.

'Chaff!' he called, wiping the back of one hand over his eyes. It came away covered with charged black iron filings. Somewhere off to his side there was a loud buzzing as someone began setting up a magnetic perimeter, drawing the chaff away from his troop. The air was becoming clearer already.

Now Nicolas had time to think. He counted seventeen robots still standing.

'Report!' he called. 'Where are they?'

Calmly, the robots relayed the information back to him. There was a group up in the roof, a second blocking the passageway by which they had entered this cave.

'Take out the ones above first,' called Nicolas. 'Then we can mount an assault on the ones behind us.'

Seventeen rifles swung back upwards. They began to fire infrequently, but with thoughtful precision.

'Not so well trained,' said the man to Nicolas's right. 'Soon be out of here.'

Nicolas felt uneasy. He knew the Raman lived in the mountains. He knew they were expert at this sort of fighting. Nicolas thought about this, Nicolas dredged his memory.

'Anyone here got a nose?' he asked.

'I have,' said a woman nearby, still gazing at the ceiling along the length of her rifle.

'What can you smell?'

The woman paused, sniffing.

'Organics. A lot of them. Petrol.'

'*Zuse!*' swore Nicolas.

'Hey, they're retreating!'

'Of course they are. It's a . . .'

The world exploded. The petroleum vapour with which the Raman had been flooding the cavern ignited and sucked up all the oxygen. Nicolas was left standing in a near-vacuum.

His electromuscles were weak and shrivelled.

His brain hurt.

He was deaf; the delicate connections in his ears had burned away.

His casing was so hot that it glowed blue-white.

The Raman were charging now. Only a dozen of them, but more than enough to defeat his weakened, crippled squad.

The Raman had long bodies plated in chrome. They carried short, sharp awls in their fists, held low, ready to punch up beneath a robot's chin, right up into the brain.

'Stand firm,' said Nicolas.

Fourteen robots formed up in line. They dropped their rifles, barrels breached after the ammunition had exploded in the blast, they drew out their knives, held them in hands over which plastic had melted and dripped away. Held them weakly in their glowing hands. Still the Raman came, metal feet pounding on the stone floor. But now the Raman paused and put away their awls. They turned, looked back, fear crossing their faces.

'What is it?' asked someone.

'I don't know,' said Nicolas. And then they, too, felt it and heard it. A trickle of water. A stream. A torrent of water released from somewhere, bearing down upon them. Flashing white foam on dark water, set free in the petroleum explosion, released from some other cave by the cracking of the walls.

It engulfed the Raman, swept them before it. And then it engulfed Nicolas and his squad, still glowing blue-white hot from the burning petrol.

The pain was like a shaft of lightning.

The pain was almost beyond endurance.

Hot metal steamed and then cooled too quickly. It snapped tight around robot bodies, it crystallized, hard and brittle. The world was full of the crash of water, and Nicolas's squad was sent tumbling down through the earth, pushed deeper and deeper down caves and passageways, all spinning and crashing as they went. They bashed against rocks, and metal that had been heated and cooled too quickly shattered. Brain casing splintered and twisted wire unravelled and sent minds spilling and then untangling into nothing more than so much metal.

Bashing and crashing, tumbling and swirling. Dizzy and hurting. Gradually the motion slowed down, and the percussion of the unheard noise died away, and Nicolas was left beached on cold stone, his body dented and aching.

Other men and women lay around him, along with broken and shattered parts from dead robots. Water dripped from metal onto stone.

People began to stir. Nicolas looked around in anguish. There were no other Artemisians there present, only Raman.

Nicolas rose unsteadily to his feet. His balance felt off. He needed to strip apart his body and get a close look at the gyroscopes, but he didn't have time. The Raman soldiers had noticed him. They were already pointing in his direction.

'Hey,' said Nicolas. 'I surrender.'

They were looking at him oddly. Pointing to the dented casing around his body. Nicolas looked down and saw why.

He had changed. In the light from his own eyes, his body shone with a dull grey lustre.

Nicolas began to twist this way and that, examining himself.

The few Raman who had managed to hold onto them drew out their awls, short and wickedly cruel. They began to advance on Nicolas. Poor, weakened Nicolas, his electromuscles shrivelled by the heat.

Three, no, four Raman soldiers, all badly dented by their passage through the water.

Four awls were raised. Four awls were brought down on Nicolas's body. Nicolas flinched as the blades struck home; he felt the pain as they cut into the circuitry beneath, felt . . .

He felt nothing. The blades had bounced clear. The Raman looked puzzled. They struck once more. Again Nicolas flinched and again the blades were deflected, leaving not even a scratch on his body.

Heated by the explosion of the petrol bomb and then explosively cooled by water, Nicolas's body had been at the sweet point. He had hardened like the blade of a katana.

Now he was indestructible.

Again and again the Raman struck. Eventually they tired, their electromuscles drained of energy. The five robots stared at each other.

'Why can't we kill you?' one of them asked Nicolas.

Nicolas raised one weak arm and reached out for an awl and took it from the unresisting hand of the Raman woman who had asked the question. He reversed the awl, weighed it in his hand. Then he reached forward and drove it up into the skull of the woman opposite him. She gave off an electronic scream that made the other soldiers back away.

Nicolas stabbed again. There was a nick at the end of the awl, a barb. This time, when he withdrew the point, twisted wire trailed from it. The woman screamed louder.

Nicolas stabbed again and again. He pulled at the twisted wire and unwound the woman's mind. She died.

The other Raman soldiers had frozen in silent, helpless contemplation of this horror. They watched as the body of their companion slumped lifelessly to the wet ground: they watched as Nicolas, his arm tangled in the twisted wire of her mind, began to cut himself free of their dead companion. Then, finally, as Nicolas stepped weakly towards them, they turned and ran, fleeing up the long passageways to the surface.

Nicolas stripped the body of the woman. He pulled out her overlong electromuscles and cut them shorter to fit into his own limbs. Awkwardly, one-handedly, he took apart her hands and replaced the muscles in his own with hers. He studied the circuitry of her ears and found it inferior to his own burned-out sense, but at least her ears still worked. He took them and he could hear again. Raman State occupied the mountains and the coast. They built their eyes to see long distances. Nicolas was impressed by their design, and he incorporated it into his own body.

It took him several hours, but finally Nicolas rose again. The

Raman had destroyed his entire squad. Now he would have his revenge.

Nicolas rose from the depths, clad in his dull grey shell and carrying a Raman awl. One by one he caught up with the fleeing soldiers and stabbed the awl up into their chin before winding out the twisted wire of their minds, their hands scrabbling all the while at his indestructible body.

It took him days, weeks, wandering in the dark, water-formed passageways, but there at last came a time when he rose from the ground among the moonlit peaks of the Raman mountains.

Behind him, sealed in the earth, were the bodies of his troop.

Behind him, dead in the darkness, were the disassembled minds of his enemies.

Now Nicolas had returned to life, to Artemis, to his destiny.

Nicolas was a new man. A robot in an indestructible body. A robot destined for great things. All would fear him. All would envy him.

And there, in the night, in the starlit, moonlit peaks of the Raman mountains, Nicolas came upon a still pool of water and looked into it and beheld himself. And his fate descended upon him, and Nicolas saw himself for what he was.

A coward.

For now all robots would desire his body. All would try to take it from him. He would never be able to rest, never be able to drop his guard for fear that someone would strip his mind from its indestructible shell, just as he had taken the parts from the Raman woman, deep beneath the ground.

Nicolas did not want his wonderful body. He did not feel strong enough to be the one to own it.

And so he lay in wait by the caves from which the Spontaneous emerged. The same caves he and his squad had entered just a few weeks before.

He waited by the entrance as day followed night. Waited there for seven days. And on the seventh day a robot emerged.

A man, dark in metal and slender in build. Black rock still clung to him from his emergence from the ground.

Nicolas came upon the man and killed him. Unwound the man's mind from his body and placed his own there instead.

He left the indestructible body there at the mouth of the caves, its skull cracked open for any robot to take.

And then he walked down from the mountains.

Karel

'What happened to him?' asked Banjo Macrodocious.

'No one knows,' said Karel. 'He just vanished.'

'What happened to the body?'

'It vanished too. Some say that somewhere a robot still wears it, but painted, disguised.'

'*Your* body is painted,' observed Banjo Macrodocious.

Karel tapped at his chest plate. 'This is not so hard.'

'I can hear that. So what is the point of your story?'

'That Nicolas was given a great gift and yet refused to use it. Your intelligence is the same.'

'I am not intelligent,' said Banjo Macrodocious. 'I would not want to do as Nicolas did, to kill in that fashion.'

'No robot should. That is an intelligent thing to say. Listen, Banjo Macrodocious, don't deny your gift. Would you be Nicolas the Coward?'

'I have no preference.'

Karel clenched his fist, wanting to smack the door beside him in frustration. The pain in his bent right hand caused him to pause just in time.

Gates was waiting right outside the door to the isolation area.

'So, what's the verdict?'

'He's intelligent all right,' said Karel.

'Thought as much,' said Gates.

'. . . but I can't formally declare him so. He refuses to pass any of the tests. I've warned him and warned him, but he refuses to listen. He doesn't seem to care. *It* doesn't seem to care. I can't call it *him*, as it's not a robot. It's technically a possession. It shouldn't be that way, it's not right, but that's what the rules say. The stupid *Tokvah* is so stubborn.'

Gates frowned. 'Hmm. Do you think it's being threatened? Or playing a game, or something?'

'No. I honestly believe that it thinks it's unintelligent. Hah, that's an oxymoron isn't it?'

'I think it's a trick. Artemisians are cunning. It's the sort of stunt that they would pull.'

'Yes, but why? What could they hope to gain?'

They began to make their way back along the walkway, back out of the holding area. The chatter and clanking of the immigrants fell silent as they walked by.

'They all know what's in there,' said Gates. 'They are all wondering what it is. They're wondering what you've decided.'

'I don't know,' said Karel.

'Well, make a decision fast, Karel. I need it out of here. I need the space. Just look around you.'

Karel shook his head. 'I've no choice. It refuses to accept citizenship. Mark it as unintelligent.'

'Fine,' said Gates. 'It makes no difference to me.'

'Well, it should do,' said Karel. 'You sound like an Artemisian.'

2

SPRING
BY SPRING,
PLATE BY
PLATE . . .

Eleanor

Wien had fallen long before most of the combatants were aware of it. Like old metal thrown on the family forge to be melted down and cast anew, the city stood apparently firm whilst all the time being on the point of dissolution.

The Wiener Stonewall Troops that had organized the last solid resistance were not to know that behind them the core of the city was already breached. The Artemisian Storm Troopers repeatedly breaking themselves against the marble ramparts that ringed the city did not realize that the terms of surrender were already being discussed at gunpoint. They weren't to know that one resourceful Artemisian unit had already breached the city's security and made its way to its heart.

Wien was a beautiful city, built half on land, half on the handful of islands that dotted Wien bay, but above all built on the riches brought by the plentiful coal fields that sloped from just below the city out to the seabed. While the aristocracy walked the marble bridges linking the lush green islands – their polished bodies rippling with the sunlit reflections of the calm silver water – the working classes laboured deep beneath the earth, dressed in iron that glowed dull red with the heat of radioactivity and the friction of the continental plates.

For the working classes things would change little, but the aristocrats were due a rude awakening. They would not enjoy their way of life for much longer.

Wien had fallen to Artemis.

Twenty-four hours later and Wien City reverberated to the steady stamping of victory. Artemisian robots marching to take key positions stamped to the rhythm; Artemisian robots guarding forges and metal stores struck time with their feet; Artemisian robots plundering the defeated kept up the shaking beat.

The cracks in the broken streets of Wien City were shaken wider, black lightning zigzagging up the white marble towers until yet another wall collapsed in a white rockslide. Bouncing rubble tumbled over the robot bodies strewn through the streets. There were too many to completely remove, even for the plundering victors and the desperately scavenging defeated searching for upgrades or replacement body parts.

So many dead bodies. Dirty smoke rising into the sky; bent, scorched metal; twisted wire spilling from skulls, twisted wire wound amongst the broken machinery of war, like the trap webs of metal spiders from childhood tales. And everything shaking and rattling to the relentless stamping of the victors. Stamp, *stamp*, stamp; stamp, *stamp*, stamp.

Here another cracked marble tower shook and slipped and fell in an accelerating avalanche of rubble that danced and slid through the wrecked streets. Broken stones bounced and rolled to a halt, and then began to bounce and shake again to the relentless stamping. Stamp, *stamp*, stamp; stamp, *stamp*, stamp.

Here a Wiener worker family, sheltering in the remains of their forge, heard the approach of Artemisian troops, heard the door slam open, saw the sleek, powerful bodies of their victors as they entered the room, their eyes glowing green in the half-light, their entry accompanied by that never-ending percussion: Stamp, *stamp*, stamp; stamp, *stamp*, stamp.

Here in an aristocrat's hall, the finely engineered and oh-so-delicate bodies of a noble family were being pulled apart by the rough hands of the invaders, spring by spring, plate by plate, electromuscle by electromuscle. And all the while the noblemen thought on the folly of selling coal to the Artemisians. It had been such easy money at the time, but how it had come back to haunt them all.

White dust rose into the smoke-choked evening, the sun barely seen, merely a pale yellow shape across the silver sea. To the accompaniment of endless stamping, it was setting for the last time on Wien.

*

All that within twenty-four hours. And now the morning sun had risen on this newest corner of the Artemisian Empire.

The robot sat on the cracked rim of the marble fountain that occupied the middle of the square, his matt-black Storm Trooper body seemingly untouched by the bright sun up in the blue sky. He was picking apart the body of a dead Wiener commando with practised efficiency, running a finger down the seams, popping the rivets apart to expose the mechanism underneath. His assault rifle lay propped on the rim of the fountain beside him, matt-black too, even the cruel bayonet at its tip smoke-blackened after last night's action.

The Storm Trooper had not noticed Eleanor yet; it was too interested in examining the composition of the body it was taking apart. Eleanor knew what it would be thinking: the Storm Trooper's mind would have been woven by its mother to be a Storm Trooper, and so it would think like a Storm Trooper thought, and it would build its body like a Storm Trooper built a body. The design of the body it held in its hands would seem wrong: more crafted than built. The Wiener body would seem too weak and too fragile. No wonder the Storm Trooper found it so fascinating. No wonder it hadn't noticed Eleanor's approach.

Finally, it heard her, heard the measured tread of Eleanor and the rest of the troop as they moved into the square. Without pause, sleekly, silently, it took its rifle and rolled into a crouch position, sighted along the length of the barrel.

'There's a Storm Trooper training its gun on us,' said Eleanor.

'Ignore it.'

Eleanor did so. She walked on, one of nineteen infantryrobots, dressed in grey-painted armour, their bodies identically built and maintained. They had been walking through the broken city all morning, looking for a place to rest and repair themselves. The sun had nearly reached midday in a blue sky still tainted by streamers of rising black smoke. That same sunlight failed to find a purchase on the Storm Trooper's matt body. Eleanor glanced back towards it and saw, to her surprise, that it had vanished.

'It's gone!' she said, scanning the square for movement. There was a scraping sound, and rattle of bricks and suddenly it was there beside her, rising up behind another of the grey-painted infantry, an awl pressing up against the soldier's chin.

'Gotcha,' he said, peripheral vision tracking the grey bodies that were still turning in his direction. He was already releasing the soldier, spinning around, coming to stand in the middle of the group. 'My name is Arban. Who's in charge here?' he asked.

The infantry looked from one to the other.

Eleanor spoke up. 'Our sergeant was caught by a grappling hook five days ago and dragged down into the sea.'

'Dragged into the sea, sir,' corrected Arban.

Carmel stepped forward, just another grey infantryrobot, identical in every way to Eleanor.

'There's no calling of "sir" in Artemis,' she said calmly. 'Why should there be when we are all nothing but twisted metal working to a common purpose?'

Arban exploded into flashing movement, pushing her arms to one side, reaching around behind her neck to snatch out the interface coil there. The light in Carmel's eyes went out, and her metal body slumped to the ground. Arban held up the silver coil that was the link between the twisted wire of the brain and the rest of the body. Slowly, he crushed it between his fingers.

'Answering back a superior? I don't like this sort of thing, you know,' he said, conversationally. 'There are minds and there are minds. Soldiers who are more loyal to themselves than to the state. Only fighting when they can see the advantage to themselves . . .' He dropped the broken coil to the stone flags and ground it beneath his foot. '. . . and not for the greater good of Artemis.' His electromuscles were powering up with an audible hum. 'Now, some people say you should blame the parents. Blame the mothers. They twist a mind that follows Nyro's pattern for most of the way, making a child loyal to the Artemisian state, but then they leave that last little inch at the end, that little voice telling the child that when things get really tough, when things aren't going well, they should just cut and run. Their mothers make them put their own survival first. Can you blame the child if its mother made it that way? They ask. Maybe they have a point.' He looked thought-ful for a moment. 'But I don't think so.'

The remainder of the grey infantry looked on warily as Arban tapped the side of his head with one metal hand. 'I wasn't made that way,' he explained. 'My mother twisted my mind to think first and last of the greater good of Artemis. That's why I keep my body strong and in tune. That is why I constantly seek to improve it.'

The power in Arban's electromuscles was building to a peak. *It must hurt,* thought Eleanor. Arban held that pain for just a moment longer, revelling in it, and then he released it in one great explosion of movement, springing upwards and backwards to land by the soldier behind him, who had been on the point of raising his gun. Arban gripped the top of the soldier's body armour and tore at it, electromuscles in his arm discharging painfully as he ripped the metal free of the man's body. The mechanism beneath was exposed to the sunlight, pitiful and embarrassing.

'Look at him!' called Arban. 'Look at yourselves. Identical bodies, identical parts, all so that you can rebuild yourselves from your comrades. Submerging yourself in each other for safety. You act like Nicolas the Coward.' He pushed a finger into the mecha-nism in the chest of the man he now held, stopping a wheel that turned there. A whining noise emerged from the man's mouth. The other soldiers shifted, distressed by their comrade's pain.

'And now you mill about in the midst of a conquered city, taking it easy, running from danger, avoiding the spoils that are rightfully ours. I tell you, better robots than you have died these past few weeks. Better robots than you have mounted attacks and been repulsed, and this is how you repay them. You are a *disgrace*!'

The whine had risen to a scream now. Arban looked down at the distressed man, tensed his hand as if he were about to rip the mechanism apart, thought better of it and released the man to col-lapse painfully to the ground.

'I should kill you all now. You're practically traitors! Any other time maybe I would, but not today. We are short of robots, even second-rate ones such as yourselves.'

The infantry looked on thoughtfully, the sun warming their grey skins.

'You killed Carmel,' said Eleanor.

Arban shuddered. 'Even your voices!' he shouted. 'So grey and colourless! But, no, I didn't kill anyone.' He held up a hand, showing the silver spiral of an interface coil.

'I palmed a coil, just like this one. You saw me crush the coil of a Wiener soldier, not your comrade. Artemisian troops are too valuable to waste. All I did was disconnect Carmel's coil from her body. You can easily link her back up.'

Eleanor nodded to Hetfield, who bent down over Carmel's body.

Arban turned to address the others. 'While he's doing that, the rest of you form yourselves into two lines. You are under my command now. There are still a few towers defended here in Wien. Still a few booby-trapped doors with aristocrats hiding behind them. Robots beyond hope and fear, robots who would rather die than give up what they have, and are quite prepared for their workers to make that sacrifice along with them. Well, my happy crew, you shall be the first to face them!'

Arban drew himself to his full height. The grey infantry weren't moving. 'Didn't you hear me?' A note of anger in his voice. 'I said line up!'

Slowly, the soldiers began to shuffle into position.

'Faster! Do I have to really kill one of you to set an example? I don't have any time for sulkers and shirkers who have spent the last few hours hanging around at the edges of the camps, waiting for the danger to pass so that they can creep in amongst the bolder robots and share the spoils and the glory. I tell you, I was the first into this city, and . . .'

'No you weren't.'

Everyone turned to look at the robot who had spoken. He seemed identical to the rest: thin grey-painted body armour, unexceptional machinery. He did not pause in the process of taking his place in the line.

'What did you say?' said Arban, his voice dangerously low.

'I said that you weren't the first into this city.'

It was so quiet in the square. From somewhere in the distance a crumbling crash of rubble could be heard as another marble tower slid to oblivion.

'Are you daring to call me a liar?' hummed Arban, his voice modulated so low. Eleanor reached slowly for her awl. Around her she was aware of other infantryrobots doing the same.

'No,' said the robot. 'I believe you to be merely mistaken. You were not the first into this city. We were.'

Arban held the robot's gaze. There was something strange about the man, something so still and unafraid. Eleanor felt it, they all felt it, yet they had worked and fought with him for so long. Arban laughed to cover the unease that suddenly arose within him. 'Hey, who's to know? We all had our part to play. Maybe I got it wrong. Maybe I owe you an apology. Still, it isn't done to disagree with your superior.'

'I'm not sure that you are my superior. I'm not sure that such things exist within Artemis.'

Arban looked the plain grey robot up and down.

'Okay, soldier boy,' he said. 'Single combat. You and me.'

The grey man seemed unimpressed. 'Are you now going to kill us all one by one? What's the good of that to Artemis?'

'I don't intend to kill *all* of you,' said Arban. 'Just enough to ensure discipline.' And he sprang: his electromuscles had been charging even as he spoke. He went for the quick kill, landing on the man's chest, his feet scraping down the chest armour and wrenching it clear of the body, his left hand pulling the coil from the back of the robot's neck, his other hand . . .

The robot wasn't there. He was standing just out of reach of Arban, arms folded. Eleanor and the rest of the infantry were moving, getting into position. Arban unslung the rifle from his back and fired it, dead centre on the infantryman's chest. The robot was already standing within the length of its barrel, raising his hand to strike, bringing an awl down . . . Eleanor saw the sharp point scrape down the Storm Trooper's left arm, saw the electromuscles there discharging in a crackle of sparks. The grey soldier had punctured him!

But now the grey soldier was tumbling backwards, his grey body folding in half, badly dented where Arban had kicked him in the chest. And now he was having trouble getting to his feet. Eleanor saw why: Arban had snatched off his arm. Eleanor nodded to the reanimated Carmel.

Arban held the arm out for his opponent to see. 'What's your name, boy?' he asked.

'Kavan,' said the crippled grey man.

Eleanor watched for Arban's response

'Kavan?' said Arban, 'Kavan. I've heard that name before. Now, when was it?'

The grey robot said nothing. Arban was disturbed, Eleanor could tell. The name obviously struck a bell deep inside him, and not a tinkling little silver bell but a great tolling chime of warning.

'I *have* heard of you,' he said. 'Back when we took Stark. Were you there?'

'I was.'

We all were, thought Eleanor.

Arban was picking apart Kavan's arm, stripping off the grey casing, popping out the joints and peeling away the electromuscles. He dropped them on the ground, one by one.

'I remember. You led the charge through the Tesla towers. A lot of robots died there . . .'

'But we made it through in the end.'

Arban finished stripping the arm. He rubbed his palms together, scraping off the remnants of Kavan's grease and lubricant, his left hand moving oddly: the effect of the punctured electromuscle.

'You were offered promotion,' said Arban. 'A Storm Trooper's body, but you preferred to remain as an infantryrobot. Yes, I knew I'd heard of you! You're not a coward, that's for certain. I've heard you called a hero, but I'm not sure that's exactly right. Anyone can get *others* killed. So what are you? You're not a good soldier or you wouldn't be skulking in this square. I don't know what I should do with you.'

'This is single combat,' replied Kavan. 'To the death.'

'Don't be stupid! You don't stand a chance!' Arban stepped forward and ground the remains of Kavan's arm into the flagstones with a hard metal foot. Kavan took a step back. And now Eleanor and the grey infantry were moving. Carmel tossed something towards Kavan. Something long, it bent as it tumbled. Kavan snatched it from the air.

Arban jumped, kicked out with one foot, bringing the ultra-hard, shovel-like edge around and upwards just at Kavan's knee joint, breaking the leg there, but Kavan moved in at the same time, stabbing out at the metal in Arban's thigh, puncturing him again, rupturing the electromuscle there. Arban landed and spun around, slightly clumsy, slightly off balance due to the spasming muscles in his left thigh.

Kavan had two arms again! As Arban moved in to attack, Eleanor nodded to Ulrich, who detached his own leg at the knee and threw it to Kavan, who snapped it into place and then, almost in the same movement, jumped at Arban.

Arban anticipated his attack. He grabbed Kavan's right arm once more, pulling it off, but again Kavan reached out and with his left hand stabbed at the electromuscles in Arban's arm. They were spasming all the more. With difficulty, Arban tore apart Kavan's arm again, but the grey robot simply snatched another arm out of the air, thrown by one of his own robots, and reattached it. Eleanor wondered if Arban yet had any real inkling of his peril. This might be single combat, but Arban wasn't only fighting Kavan, he was fighting all of them.

Smoothly, though not as smoothly as before, Arban drew his rifle from his back and shot Ulrich in the head. Twisted wire exploded in a cloud. Ulrich's arms and legs jerked up and down, thrashing as the curving, expanding wire sent strange signals to the robot's limbs. Arban fired again, catching Hammett in the chest. Arban's finger was tightening a third time just as Kavan smashed the rifle from his hand. Arban kicked down, incapacitating both of

Kavan's legs. Kavan stabbed Arban's left arm once more, and the electromuscle there flashed and died. Kavan took the opportunity to drag himself backwards and out of range, detaching his legs as he went. Arban should have gone for his arms, Eleanor knew, should have stopped Kavan from doing what he was doing now – snapping two more legs into place. Arban jumped, but Kavan was already there, this time scraping at his right arm . . .

. . . and they fought. Metal puncturing metal, mechanisms sticking, smoke rising in the air and the rhythmic pounding of metal feet in the distance as the infantryrobots anticipated their leader's victory.

And with rising incredulity Arban realized he was going to die.

His body, his great, polished, finely tuned body was being gradually eroded by this grey robot that just didn't stop. Kavan simply didn't seem to care about the pain. His patchwork grey body fought on, his mind surely exhausted by the exertion, but still he fought.

Until eventually Arban lay on his back, his right arm mushy, his arms and legs dead, looking upwards as Kavan stood above him, the other grey bodies of the broken-down infantry haloed by the sun as they too loomed over him. Then Kavan spoke. For a moment, Arban thought he was speaking to him, but he was mistaken. Kavan seemed to no longer count Arban as a sentient being

'Come here, Eleanor,' Kavan had called.

'What are you going to do?' asked Arban.

Kavan bent down and used the awl to pry Arban's head armour clear. Arban felt the awl tapping on his skull. He looked up at Kavan, felt him doing something there.

'What are you doing?' he repeated.

Eleanor was looking into his skull. Kavan had opened him up and Eleanor was looking at the twisted metal of his brain.

'What do you see?' asked Kavan.

'Nothing,' replied Eleanor. 'He's just a standard Artemisian robot.'

And then Arban felt an odd sensation down his left side. It was as if his dead arm had come back to life and was waving in the air.

He heard the sound of music playing on trumpets, and a rainbow seemed to be forming within his body. He saw Kavan pulling his awl up into the air, the twisted wire of Arban's own brain around it . . .

Kavan

There was enough metal and parts from the dead Wiener soldiers to rebuild the damaged bodies of the robots in his section, but it took time to knit electromuscle.

Kavan sat on the rim of the fountain in the centre of the square, waiting for his mind to attune itself to his new body. It was always the same when you added new parts: things didn't feel right for the first few days, and you had to wait for them to bed in properly and become part of you. Kavan had been swapping body parts with gay abandon not twenty minutes ago. No wonder he now felt tired and shaky.

'We've got six *whole* robots left; eight if you count you and me,' said Eleanor, her hands moving in regular patterns as she knitted wire into muscle.

'Have you got anything out of that pile of bodies we could use?' Kavan waved a hand towards the dismembered Wiener robots that Arban had been messing around with.

'Some muscle that can be shortened. But frankly, it's quicker to knit it ourselves.'

'That's not good. We need to move on. We can't just stay here like that *Choarh.*' He gestured to the broken body of Arban, twisted wire spilling over the ground from the shattered skull. Kavan shook his head. 'Idiot. Just sitting here with that over-engineered matt-black body. If we hadn't got to him first the Wiener defence would have. That head would have looked good as a mascot for some Death and Glory last-stand squad.'

Kavan flexed his arms and legs. They just didn't feel right.

'What are we going to do now?' asked Eleanor.

'Send out four of the able-bodied to scout the surrounding buildings. There'll be some Wiener civilians hiding out in them.

Have our robots rip the usable parts from their bodies and bring them back here right away. The more robots we have out cannibalizing, the more parts we can collect.'

'I thought you'd say that,' said Eleanor, and she gestured to four waiting robots, who loped off towards the edges of the square.

Kavan moved his new arms and legs in turn, getting the feel of them.

'It's pretty up here,' said Eleanor, unexpectedly.

Kavan followed her gaze and looked out through the wide gate at the bottom of the square, out over Wien bay. The city had been built on a hillside that sloped gently downwards to the sands below, sands that were lapped by the clear green sea. A number of rocky islands studded the bay on which robots had long ago originally built their forges and sunk their mineshafts for ease of defence. And, once they had built those forges, they had then raised towers to proclaim their status. Marble towers. When most other robots on Shull were still only forming metal, the Wieners had used what they had learned in mining coal and developed that into the skill to work rock. Quarryrobots, sawyers and banker masons had dressed stone; carvers and fixer masons had raised the beautiful towers for which the state had become famous.

Over the years the islands had grown more powerful, the mine shafts beneath the sea had joined together, and alliances had been made, and eventually Wiener State had been formed. The islands had been joined by brass bridges, and a wall of marble and brass had been raised around the landward perimeter of the new state.

Kavan and his robots had breached that wall, though not without losses.

There was an abruptly silenced scream from one of the broken buildings into which the four Artemisian robots had recently entered.

'Careless!' said Kavan.

'They're getting tired,' said Eleanor. 'We've been fighting for six days solid now.'

'Everyone's tired,' said Kavan. 'That's why this is the perfect time to move.' He kicked at the metal shell of Arban's body. 'You know, we could use this,' he said thoughtfully. He glanced across at Eleanor. 'Do you think you can control it?'

The woman put her hands on her hips and tilted her head. 'I know you're tired,' she said. 'That's why I'll pretend I didn't hear you insult my ability to ride metal.'

Kavan jerked his head at the sudden movement at the edge of the square and then relaxed when he saw two infantryrobots coming back with long strips of electromuscle trailing from their arms.

He turned back to Eleanor. 'Technically we're still both infantry, Eleanor. So tell me now; do you think that you would make a better leader than me?'

Eleanor held his gaze. She didn't reply, though.

'We're both Artemisians, Eleanor.'

'Your mind wasn't twisted in Artemis, Kavan.'

'Maybe not. But I was in Segre when it fell, and I saw how the Artemisians fought and I saw how the Segreans fought, and I realized then that the metal of my mind was twisted in the Artemisian fashion. My mother had read the signs, she had followed the propaganda. Artemis is a philosophy, not the place you are born. I am therefore an Artemisian, just as much as you are, Eleanor.'

'I know that, Kavan.'

'And yet you still think you would make a better leader than me?'

Again, Eleanor didn't answer.

'We both serve the state to the best of our abilities, Eleanor. Tell me now if you think you would make a better leader of this section.'

Again Eleanor said nothing.

'Go on then,' said Kavan. 'Get undressed.'

First there were four robots harvesting parts, then six, then nine. Soon Kavan's full troop was rebuilt. He took a last sweep through a random selection of buildings, checking on his team's work.

There was a Wiener family lying dead in the living space of one apartment. Two children, noted Kavan with interest. The Wieners had this thing about building kids in pairs. He never quite understood it. Still, he bent and inspected the little bodies. Interface coils crushed, but brains untouched. It was a neat job. A soldier's job. The minds in those skulls were still alive, but now cast adrift in eternal darkness and silence. It would be merciful to kill them, but mercy took time, and anyway they weren't Artemisians. Just metal to be reclaimed by the salvage squads. The railway lines would be approaching Wien even now. Soon these bodies would be crushed, the metal loaded onto flat trucks and taken back to feed the forges of Artemis.

It was time to get back, but Kavan paused just a moment longer. This apartment was unusual. Foreign. Built in the Wiener way, half stone and half metal. There was even biological life growing in it. Deliberately cultivated by the looks of it. Long green strands of – what were they called, leaves? – trailing from pots.

Really odd.

From outside, Kavan heard the sound of unfamiliar voices.

He hurried out to see what was going on.

There were three Storm Troopers out there now. One of them was Eleanor. Kavan deliberately took his time walking up to the group. He could hear Eleanor speaking as he approached.

'. . . requisitioned these troops for myself,' she was saying. 'I'm taking them out to the islands to sweep and comb.'

'What did you say your name was?' asked one of the newly arrived Storm Troopers.

'Eleanor. What did you say your name was?'

'Di'Anno. Funny. I don't remember meeting you before, and I thought I knew most of the STs on this incursion.'

'You know what, I really don't care.'

Kavan came to attention by the group. 'Area's clear, Eleanor. All ready to move out.'

'Very good, Kavan. Have the robots form up in two lines.'

'Kavan?' said one of the Storm Troopers. 'You were in Stark. I've heard of you. You're a hero.'

'I don't know about that.'

'You're also trouble.'

'Oh, I am,' said Kavan. 'You've no idea how much.'

The three Storm Troopers were moving swiftly, forming a triangle, Kavan at the centre of it.

'You are under arrest. We have orders to bring you to field command.'

'Field command are fools,' said Kavan. 'I would have issued orders long ago for my immediate execution.' He glanced at Eleanor. 'Okay then,' he said. 'Take me in.'

Eleanor

Eleanor had not expected to see so many colours inside a creature. Greased iron alloy plates over brass and aluminium, steel and copper bones steeped in rock oil. The looming bulk of the whale seemed to have been more excavated than disassembled.

The creature had been dragged up the concrete slipway from the water by steel ropes. It lay on its side in the shallow cutting that slid down into the clear water of Wien bay, Artemisian soldiers walking over and around it, inspecting its parts. The top half of the creature was still reasonably intact: General Fallan himself, full of the flush of victory, had invited Eleanor to join him as he picked his way carefully over the greased, interlocking plates of the whale's flank. They had both watched the troops peeling away copper plate and electromuscle from the exposed interior of the beast. They had looked down into the scratched quartz bowl that protected its eye, seen the faint glow and felt the creature focus on him.

'It's still alive?' he had asked.

At first Eleanor thought he was speaking to her, but then Ruth, the General's aide, had answered.

'Oh yes,' she said. 'The Wieners always preserve the brains. They put them in the support tanks at the top of the towers,' and she had waved her hand to indicate the few marble towers that still rose from the islands of Wiener bay.

'General,' interrupted Eleanor, 'there is someone below who wishes to speak . . .'

'In a moment, Storm Trooper,' said the General. 'Look at all this metal. Don't you wish to rebuild yourself too?' He waved a hand at the other troops as they swarmed over the half-demolished body, pulling apart the metal of the whale and clothing their bodies in its superior plate.

'I will, General. It's just that . . .'

'All those marble towers,' said the General, smooth in his new whaleskin body, 'They each hold a mind, you know. Ruth tells me that the Wieners allow the whale minds to see by fashioning them eyes set in the windows of the towers. They give them ears to hear.'

'Really?' Eleanor had taken a real dislike to this smoothly engineered man. He spent his time dressing himself in whale metal and engaging in discussion while the remnants of the battle still played out around him. In her opinion, he wasn't fit for purpose.

'Oh yes,' he continued. 'The Wieners suspend these creatures' non-sentient minds over the city. Tell me, do those whales think they are still under the sea, that the smoke that rises into the sky from the city forges is a new sort of weed, that the robots that walk beneath them are crabs and shellfish?'

'I don't know, General.'

'The thought puzzles me! Why have the Wieners kept the whale minds alive? Why do they do it?'

'They've always done it,' said Ruth, as if that was an answer.

From the surrounding city came the sound of stamping feet: Stamp, *stamp*, stamp; stamp, *stamp*, stamp.

'Still going strong, I hear,' said General Fallan, and there was polite laughter from his staff. Eleven members of high command, all newly clad in whaleskin.

Eleanor had heard him speaking on the subject just as she had arrived in his presence, escorting Kavan through the perimeter of guards: 'This skin is strong, heavy,' the General had said. 'Let this be our badge of victory. We will wear it with pride, not turn away from this gift in fear, like Nicolas the Coward.'

The first flush of victory, thought Eleanor, *funny how quickly it ebbs away.* All around there were the sounds of celebration. The General seemed to have forgotten that there was still much work to do. He began to descend down the side of the stricken whale, the rest of his entourage following him.

'We need to discuss our next move,' said Ruth. 'Turing City.'

'Give us a break, Ruth!' laughed General Fallan. 'We need to rest, repair and regroup. We shall establish ourselves here in Wien, and ensure that we have full control before we move on.'

'No, General,' said Eleanor firmly, 'we haven't got the time.'

At that General Fallan finally seemed to notice Eleanor properly. He gazed at her in her big black Storm Trooper body.

'I'm sorry, soldier. Why exactly are you here?'

At that the concrete slipway echoed to the sound of marching feet. Kavan had grown impatient, had marched forward with the rest of the grey infantry. Walked forward to meet the General, now stepping down from the body of the whale.

Kavan moved forward and pointed out Eleanor.

'She is here because she brought me here, General. Me and the rest of my squad. And no one questioned our presence. Sloppy, General, way too sloppy.'

Eleanor towered above Kavan in her new body. Even so, the quiet authority that seemed to radiate from him left the General in no doubt who was in charge.

'We need to attack Turing City swiftly,' said Kavan, 'while this victory is still in their minds. We have the strength and the will.'

'Who are you?' asked General Fallan. 'How dare you interrupt my war council?'

'This is no war council. This is a group of tired, discredited old robots justifying their bad decisions and growing fat on the spoils of war.'

To Fallan's obvious astonishment, Kavan leaned forward and flicked the dark whale iron of his breastplate.

'How dare you speak to me like that, soldier?' Fallan gazed coolly at Kavan. 'Look at you, standing here in the midst of plenty and you still wear a body of old grey metal. Look at your troop.' He turned to his staff, and from the city the sound of the stamping grew louder: Stamp, *stamp*, stamp; stamp, *stamp*, stamp. 'I've met these sort of robots before,' he announced loudly. 'In the middle of a battle they think of nothing but their own safety. They play it safe and shelter until the real work is done and then they come out at the end to share in the credit.'

Everyone was watching now. His staff, the junior robots who had stripped the whale, his guard, sleek in their silver bodies, all listening to his denunciation of this dull grey robot.

'Cowards,' the General announced, warming to his theme. 'But they are cowards not only in war but in victory, too. They creep through a conquered city taking only what their timid nature allows! Whilst other soldiers rip the metal from the population and the wire from the enemy mind, they are content to pick up the few scraps that fall unnoticed to the floor. Look – look at that whale over there! Metal and electromuscle beyond the quality that *you* now wear, soldier. You stand here speaking to me when you should be over there, replating your body for the glory of Artemis.'

Kavan didn't move.

'Come on,' said Fallan. 'Why don't you go and help yourself? I know why. Like Nicolas the Coward, you find yourself granted huge opportunities but fear to accept them.'

General Fallan waved his hand in a final flourish. No one spoke. Only the persistent sound of distant Artemisian robots stamping echoed around the slipway.

Still Kavan said nothing.

'Well?' said General Fallan. 'Don't you have anything to say before I have you led from here and stripped apart?'

Kavan spoke. Old metal body, scratched grey paint. His voice was quiet.

'My name is Kavan. I am taking control of this army.'

'Like *Tok* you are,' laughed Fallan. 'I see what you are now. A half-build renegade! A mind from here, a mind from there. Father's metal from Stark and mother twisting minds like they do in Bethe, trying to copy the Artemisian model. You have joined

up but you don't really understand the Artemisian philosophy, the
Artemisian mind.'

General Fallan tapped his head. 'This mind was woven according to Nyro's model from good Artemisian wire. Not like yours,
Tokvah. You walk as an Artemisian soldier, but you don't understand what it means. If you did you would realize that Artemis is
not a person, it is a philosophy. You seek to take power for yourself, but that is not the Artemisian way. There is no *self* in Artemis.'

Kavan waited. And then at last, he spoke.

'I understand that, Fallan,' he said. 'The soldiers here understand that. It is you who have forgotten it. This campaign has been
badly managed, this army needs better direction. There is no self
in Artemis, there is only Artemis itself. And Artemis is changing
its thinking on how the army is led.'

'And that leader will be you, I take it?' said Fallan. Eleanor
could see that the General was not afraid. He wouldn't have risen
to the top of the army without learning to fight. The General's
body was the superior, his electromuscles were charging. The
sound of the stamping increased in volume. Eleanor readied herself to spring.

And then there was the crackle of electricity discharging, and
General Fallan slumped to the ground. Eleanor looked around
curiously. Kavan hadn't moved. Neither had she. What was going
on?

'What happened?' called Fallan. 'What happened? Ruth! Tell
the men to fire. Kill this man!'

But Ruth said nothing. To her surprise, Eleanor saw Ruth stepping forward to speak to Kavan, saw her putting her gun back into
its holster as she did so.

'Ruth?' shouted Fallan in indignation. 'Was it you that shot
me?'

No one was listening to him. Kavan was right, realized Eleanor.
Artemis was ready for a change of leader. Only Fallan didn't seem
to realize that yet . . .

'Ruth? What did you do? Have you destroyed my coil? No, you

can't have done, or I wouldn't be able to see and hear. I can hear the soldiers stamping still. I can hear them celebrating my victory!'

Kavan was talking to Ruth. She reached up and disengaged her breastplate of colourful whaleskin, pulled it off, exposing the bare machinery beneath, and dropped it the ground. All around him, the other soldiers were doing the same.

Fallan shouted at them to stop, but no one listened to him. Instead Eleanor watched, unbelieving, as two of the grey infantry bent down and began to strip his body. Whale metal panelling was unshipped and thrown to the side. Electromuscle was carefully unhooked and laid on the ground as Fallan called out to the men to stop.

Kavan had taken control of the army. Eleanor looked on as its old leader was disassembled.

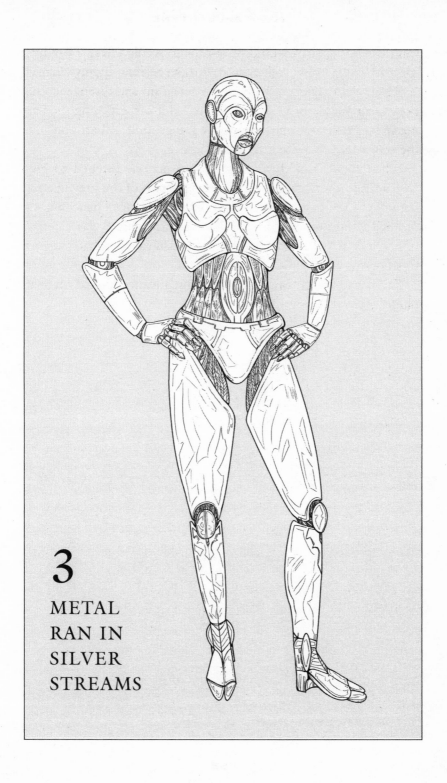

3
METAL
RAN IN
SILVER
STREAMS

Karel

Once there were thoughts and there was the world.

The thoughts lived in the heart of the planet, thinking, and the thoughts did not touch the world and the world did not touch the thoughts.

But deep in the heart of the planet metal was heated and cooled. Metal ran in silver streams and metal cooled in silver webs, deep in the heart of the planet. Metal formed patterns, and the thoughts moved over those patterns, unknowing. But the metal formed shapes that took on meaning, and so the thoughts gained a window into the world. They saw rocks and the caves lit by the glow of molten metal.

And so the first eye was born.

Now the thoughts saw the sky and the sun, the two moons and the sea. And the thoughts thought about what they saw.

And as the thoughts thought, the metal churned in the caves, and still the metal formed shapes that took on meaning, and another window was pushed into the world, and through it came the sound of the wind and the sea.

And so the first ear was born.

Now that the thoughts could see and hear, they began to wonder at the order of things. They saw that day followed night, and that calm followed the storm, and that all hot metal must cool. And the thoughts wondered; must it always be so? Was it possible to change things?

Must a rock always stand where it had come to rest? And as the thoughts thought, the metal churned in the caves, and the metal formed shapes that took on meaning and the thoughts found they had moved the rock.

And so the first arm was born.

And then they sought to move another rock, further away, but they could not reach it. So the thoughts strove to reach that rock.

And so the first legs were born.

And they thought of day and night, and warm and cold, and calm and storm, and wondered that everything came in pairs. And so the thoughts built another, like themselves.

And so the first robots were born.

Karel smiled at his son as he finished the recitation.

'And that's where robots come from, Axel.'

Axel nodded slowly.

'How long ago was that, Dad?'

'We don't know. Robots didn't know about time back then.'

Axel was working on his legs. Lengthening them. The electro-muscles he had put in place were too powerful for his young mind. Even if he could move them, they would bend the chassis out of true, but Karel let him continue. It was a mistake that every growing boy made: building a body too big, so that there was insufficient lifeforce from the mind to power it. That strength of lifeforce would come eventually as the twisted metal of the child's developing mind continued to form new connections while it folded itself into shape, but in the meantime it did a child good to learn from his mistakes.

Karel looked around the family forge and felt a sense of warm satisfaction at what he had achieved. Karel was well paid for his work: in steel, copper and silver of high purity. Even a little gold. He and Susan could afford a good apartment in a good part of town – four decent-sized rooms with a view that looked into Turing State, beyond the city itself, out over the railway station and the galleries and the old town. In clear weather, one could even make out the coast.

The forge itself was small but hot, and Turing City afforded an excellent purity and variety of metal to work in it. Karel and Susan were built of tungsten and steel, of iron and brass and silver. Thriving on such fine-quality materials, Axel showed prodigious talent, already learning how to bend titanium into shape as he built his little body. Standing in the yellow glow of the forge that squatted in the middle of the stone floor, the room around it lit up in golden-orange, Karel felt at peace. Susan was out buying paint and tasting the world, storing up thoughts to weave into their next child. Axel was building himself into a great boy. All was well. Even the bizarre ravings of Banjo Macrodocious, the Spontaneous robot, could not disturb Karel.

'Daddy?' Axel paused in the act of fastening an electromuscle that was simply too big to work properly. Karel smiled at the serious look on his son's face, felt a pang of sympathy at the disappointment he knew he was about to experience.

'Yes, Axel.'

'Daddy, why did you make me this way?'

Karel smiled.

'Is this about us making you build yourself again? Listen, Axel, Mummy and I want what's best for you. Not everyone can afford titanium and tungsten. Not everyone owns a forge as hot as this. These are advantages you have had from birth, you didn't earn them. But there is something that everyone can have, no matter how rich or poor their parents, and that is self-reliance. That's what we are giving you Axel. That's why you're building yourself.'

'No, Dad, that's not what I mean.' Axel gave up forcing the spongy knitted wire of the electromuscle for a moment and fixed his gaze on his father. 'What I mean is – why am I the way I am? Why did you make me unselfish? Why do I always have to share with other people and take my turn and be part of the team? Why did you and Mum twist my mind that way?'

Karel didn't speak for a moment. He came close to his son and crouched down so that their heads were nearly level. There was an asymmetry to Axel's skull that his son hadn't noticed, or was beyond his current ability to remove. Or maybe he just didn't see the point yet. It took the onset of puberty for a robot to realize the importance of a well-built body as an advertisement to the opposite sex. Karel touched his son gently on the hand.

'Axel, what brought this on? Have the other children been talking?'

'Sometimes. But when we're playing some of the other robots cheat. Or, when we're picking at the metal scraps in the gangue, some of the others push in and take more than their fair share. Why did you build me so that I couldn't do that?'

'Because this is Turing City. We look after each other here. Together we are stronger.'

'But other children aren't made that way.'

'*Some* other children aren't made that way,' Karel allowed.

'But that's not fair! They get to do what they want and I'm left just standing watching.'

'It may not seem fair at the moment, Axel, but as you get older you'll find out that those children aren't lucky at all. They won't be trusted; they won't get chosen to join the best teams; nobody will want to spend time with them. Their parents think they are doing them a favour, but really they are not being fair to them at all.'

Karel was struck by how small his son really was: still just a four-year-old, with a perfectly formed little body. No, not perfectly formed, because children never were, that was just the way that their mothers and fathers saw them, but there was something about him, the way that everything was there, and working in miniature. Something formed out of Karel and Susan. Axel was fiddling with the electromuscle once more, serious again.

There was something else, though. Karel knew Axel wasn't telling him the full truth: no mother would ever have twisted their child to be completely predictable. There would always be that last couple of inches, that last little part of the personality that could lie or cheat, if necessary.

'What's up, Axel?' asked Karel. 'This isn't like you. Is there something else bothering you?'

Axel pulled at the muscle halfheartedly.

'Dad,' he said. He was coming to the point, but in his own time. 'I know you're right about the selfish ones. I've seen the way that they get treated. The way that people talk about them, behind their backs. That's not what I mean, though.' He paused as if unsure what to say next.

'What do you mean, Axel?'

'I mean, well, this is all very well in Turing City State, but what if . . . I mean, what about . . . ?'

'Are you talking about Artemis, Axel?'

Axel dropped his eyes to look at the floor.

'Well, yes. They say that they have invaded Wien. And that we're next.'

Karel laughed. 'Artemis could never take Turing City State, Axel. They are strong, it's true, but they don't really value what they have. They don't recognize their robots as being anything more than metal. In Turing City we value life. Our power lies in our recognition of what makes us all special. If we stand together, they will break off us like waves off a rock.'

'But suppose they do invade!'

'They can't!' insisted Karel. 'They never will be able to beat us. Because we will always stand together as robots, and they will only be fighting as machines.'

'But suppose they do beat us! Couldn't you have built me so that I could pretend? So that I could share and be honest most of the time, but take it back when it really counts?'

'But when would it really count?' asked Karel.

Axel rolled his eyes. 'I hate it when you say things like that. You don't know what it's like . . .'

'Trust me, I do,' said Karel quietly.

'No you *don't*! I know about you. The other children say the rules don't apply to you. They say that your mother bent your mind in strange ways. That you don't tell the truth. That you only pretend to be part of Turing State.'

Karel was shocked by this sudden outburst. So was Axel, who looked embarrassed and not a little ashamed of the ferocity with which his feelings had bubbled out. Silence fell, warmed only by the orange glow of the forge.

'People say a lot of things,' said Karel at last.

'But is it true, Daddy?' asked Axel plaintively.

'Of course not. Why would I *pretend* to believe in Turing State?'

'The other children say that Granma was raped by an Artemisian soldier. That he made Granma twist your mind to be like his.'

'Those are just stories, Axel. People make things up.'

'I know that, Dad. So I asked Mum. I asked her about what happened to Granma.'

'And what did Mum say?' asked Karel softly.

'She wouldn't tell me . . .' Axel sighed. 'Which way was it, Dad? Some say that Granma would never make you a Turing City robot when Artemis was so powerful. But surely she couldn't make you an Artemisian when one had just killed Granddad? Dad, I don't know what to think.'

Slowly, Karel crouched down by his son again.

'Axel, who do *you* think I am?' he asked.

Axel reached out and took his father's hand. 'I think you are a good man, Daddy.'

Karel looked down at his son's tiny hand held in his own. So tender, so delicate, so strong. His face split into a smile.

'Thank you, Axel,' he said. They gazed at each other for a moment, and then his son removed his hand and went back to working on the electromuscle in his legs.

'Tell me a joke, Dad.'

'A joke?' said Karel, bending to scoop up some of the bright silver curls of swarf Axel had dropped on the floor. 'Let me see . . .' Absently he rubbed the swarf together in his hands, making a thin metal worm. 'Well, once there was a robot who didn't like the way he was made. He noticed that all the other robots could run faster than him. So he bought steel and copper and he rebuilt his legs so that he could run fast too. But he still wasn't happy, because there were other robots stronger than him. So he went and bought iron and tungsten and he rebuilt his arms. But he still wasn't happy, because he saw that there were other robots that were better-looking than him. So he bought lead and oil and he repainted his body. But he still wasn't happy. In fact, he was more miserable than ever. And he wondered to himself, *I have better arms, I have better legs, I have a better body than all the other robots. And yet they are all so much happier than I am. It's just not fair!*

'And he sat there thinking those sad thoughts, and then an idea occurred to him. Maybe he had been going about things the wrong way. He had tried to make himself happy by building arms and legs and painting himself. Maybe he should try a more direct method. He would build himself happy thoughts. So he took off his head . . .'

Axel stared at his father. 'I don't get it, Dad.'

Karel smiled at his son's puzzled expression.

'Well, if he took off his head, how was he going to make his body move? How could he put it back on again?'

'Oh, I get it! Good one, Dad.'

Axel returned to his work. Karel watched him and felt sad. Axel was distracted for the moment, but he would ask the same question again.

The thing that every one wanted to know.

Just how does your mind work, Karel?

Susan

Masur sold only the very best paints. His little shop stood back from the main street, tucked away in the corner of a narrow arcade, built, like so much of Turing City, of cast-iron arches and plate glass. There was nothing to advertise the shop, nor to indicate the quality of its wares, save for the elegantly worked silver leaf around the doorframe.

Masur was serving another customer as Susan entered the shop. Masur was a trim, unexceptionally built robot. To the untutored eye, his body did not appear painted. Only under close observation would one notice that copper and bronze finish had been applied to raw iron.

He was an artist. And he affected an artistic temperament.

'Thinnest gold leaf in the city?' he was saying, incredulously. 'Hah! There is nothing thinner on the continent of Shull! Are you suggesting to me that those *nekulturny* from Artemis would be able to make anything as fine as this? That they would have a use for it, even? Hey, be careful with the door! The draught!'

Susan carefully snicked the door shut.

'It's *that* thin,' continued Masur to his customer. Gently, he opened the stone book, revealing a page that shone as yellow and smooth as sunlight.

'Have you handled anything this fine before? It will crumple in the slightest breeze. It will stick to oil, though, so you must ensure your hands are perfectly clean. *Some* choose to handle it using static electricity. *I* say they are clumsy brutes, not worthy of the art!'

'Then how do you apply it?' whispered the customer.

'I speak to it,' murmured Masur. 'I bring my head close to it and speak to it, and direct the vibration from my voice, and this way I guide it into place. I speak the form that I require, and it takes shape before me.'

The customer looked from Masur to Susan, not sure if he was being wound up.

'It's true,' said Susan. 'Masur is a master. That book holds the finest gold leaf, barely a few molecules thick.'

The customer turned back to Masur, still hesitant.

'But if you are not sure,' continued Susan, 'perhaps you should try Kurt's, down the street. Practise with foil first.'

'No, I'll buy it,' said the customer, obviously feeling completely out of his depth.

Susan waited patiently as Masur completed the transaction. She gazed around the shop at the tiers of brushed metal drawers that lined one of the walls from floor to ceiling, each of their edges marked with a small circle of colour. A selection of wire brushes, from fine to coarse, lay on a nearby counter, with an arrangement of nibs behind them. On the far wall were shelves of various heights, stacked and lined with books of beryllium copper foil, books bound in copper and iron or in polished soapstone and slate. Susan felt the urge to take one down and to begin to paint; to open up its cover to reveal the shiny foil beneath and to splash paint over it, to create something to show the way she was feeling: scared and apprehensive and yet full of fecund promise.

The customer shut the door timidly as he left, and now Masur came to her side.

'Susan. Good to see you again!'

'Hello, Masur.'

'You don't look too good, Susan. You don't see me as often as you used to.'

'I've been busy, Masur. I'm . . . we're thinking of making a mind.'

'Making a mind?' Masur wagged his finger. 'And yet you come here to buy paint? You should be saving up all that creativity for your child, Susan.'

'Not you too, Masur. Please don't lecture me.'

Masur held Susan's gaze for a moment. Then he went to the door and locked it.

'We need to talk, Susan.'

'Oh, Masur, later. Please, I just want to buy some paint.'

'So you said.'

'Some yellow. I feel as if the world is dark. I want to paint sunlight on my body.'

Masur relented. 'What sort of yellow, Susan? Lead tin yellow? Cadmium yellow? Chrome yellow? Cobalt yellow?'

'All of them, Masur. And some red lead and realgar. And some titanium dioxide.'

Masur took a slim aluminium case from one pile and then moved around the room, sliding open drawers, pulling out thin tubes and slotting them into place in the case.

'How is Karel?' he asked.

'He's fine.'

Masur paused in the act of sliding open another drawer.

'Really, Susan?' he chided. 'We've known each other for years, yet you never really open up, do you? And yet there is something about you that people trust . . .'

'What do you mean?'

Masur pulled the drawer fully open and ran his finger along the neat lines of tubes of titanium white paint it contained.

'I wonder about Karel, Susan. We all do. And yet you trust him, and so that's good enough for us. But do you trust him completely?'

'Of course I do!'

'Then why are you here in my shop, looking so unhappy, rather than at home, speaking to your husband? Maybe I wouldn't understand. I pour my life into paints, mixing lead oxide and tin oxide or precipitating cadmium nitrate, rather than spending my time forming a relationship. But then again, that was the way I was made. My parents only had two children: one to go out into the world, and me here to tend the shop . . .'

He looked around, thinking. 'They never thought about who it would pass to, after I died . . .'

He snapped out of this reverie and gazed at Susan. 'So tell me, why aren't you at home, telling Karel how you feel?'

Susan stared down at the marble floor. 'I don't know, Masur. I don't think Karel would understand this.'

'What makes you think *I* would?'

'I don't know. I feel so full of . . . something.' She reached into the aluminium case in which Masur assembled paints, and pulled out a silver tube of realgar red. 'Life, I suppose. I am ready to twist another child. And yet, at the same time, I am frightened. There is something out there, Masur. I feel as if our city is wide open, and that something is going to sweep into it and crush it completely . . .'

She squeezed the tube of realgar as she spoke. The thin foil casing split, and red paint oozed out, covering her delicate fingers, running around her hand, filling the mechanism in her wrist.

'Oh! *Zuse!* I'm sorry, Masur.'

'Don't worry,' said Masur, opening a cupboard and bringing out a tin of thin oil, clean and clear as water. 'Dip your hands in this.'

'What do you mean, there is something about me that people trust?' asked Susan, dipping her hands in the solvent and watching the red paint forming itself into little drops and floating away.

'Give me your hands.'

Susan paused in the act of dipping her hands in the solvent. Masur took them. His own hands were very big compared to hers, the metal on them smooth and unpainted.

'What?' said Susan, nervously. Masur turned her hand over. He dipped one finger in the red paint that covered that hand and began to draw a shape on her delicate palm. A circle. He placed a dot on the top part of the circumference.

'What is that?' said Susan.

'Shhh,' whispered Masur. He dipped both her hands into the tin of thin oil. It slowly turned red as he wiped away the circle of paint that he had sketched on her palm.

Spoole

In the heart of Artemis City, yellow light filled a simple room. This was Artemis, so utility was the theme, but there was something about the line of the furniture, the quality of the metal, that suggested that this room was different to the rest of the city. That it was even, dare one say it, more important.

One wall was given over to bookshelves; so many books in one place was a rarity on Shull. These were all identically bound in brushed steel, their titles picked out in gold foil.

One of the books lay open on the clean steel desk occupying the centre of the room, its smooth metal pages untouched. A robot clad in simple iron stood gazing at it. Simple iron, but again there was something in the line of the metal that suggested expert craftsrobotship.

After much thought, Spoole picked up the stylus and began to write.

To my successor . . .

He paused, studying the looping curves of the script he had just engraved on the metal foil page of the book. It didn't look right. He ran a finger along the last word, reshaping the metal, erasing it, enjoying the feel of its purity as he did so. And then he engraved another word. The sentence now read:

To my child . . .

That still wasn't right. He wondered about replacing *child*, but realized he was just finding excuses not to go on. This wasn't what he wanted to say at all. And now the first page was creased and spoilt. He tore the metal page from the book and crumpled it up, compressing it into a tiny ball bearing.

The trouble was, he reflected, he wasn't even sure why he was writing this book in the first place.

It was getting dark outside. Zuse, the night moon, was yet to rise. All the lights of Artemis were turned up bright. The Centre City looked like a dark web threaded with glowing jewels. From his window, Spoole could see the network of railway lines that had spread out across southern Shull, all converging on the floodlit yards that fed the forges and factories of Artemis. Coal, limestone, haematite, limonite, chamosite and bauxite, all came flooding in, and here in Centre City it was extracted and smelted and twisted and forged and sent back out across the continent as workers and soldiers and weapons and tools, all bent on shaping the land. Out they went, building bridges and more railway lines, sinking more mines and constructing furnaces and forges.

Once Spoole had enjoyed the feeling of power this view gave him, but that had been replaced by something more subtle: a feeling of *connectedness*. Now Spoole took pleasure in the fact that he could lay a hand or a foot on any piece of metal anywhere in the city, and he knew that it would be connected, by wires, plates and ultimately rails, to every other point on the continent where Artemis had insinuated its railway lines.

Spoole had caused an iron pillar to be driven into the floor by the window. Smooth and polished at the knob on the top, its fluted length sank into the floor, driving its way down into the earth below, where wires linked it to the main railway lines that radiated from Centre City. To Raman and Bethe and Segre and Stark. To Wien. Even to Turing City. He placed his hand on the pillar and he enjoyed the feeling of contact. He was touching half of Shull.

Gearheart had entered the room as silently as she was wont to do. She was the most beautifully crafted robot in all of Shull, her mechanisms moving without sound.

'Kavan has taken control of the army,' she said.

'It was inevitable, I suppose,' said Spoole. A thought twisted through the metal of his mind. A thought of the words *To Kavan* . . . inscribed at the front of the book that lay on the desk.

'I don't know why you smile so,' said Gearheart.

'I was thinking about something else.'

Her body was lovely in the yellow light. Made from the very best materials, brought here from across half the continent. She was curved and balanced, a superb advert of her own skill as a builder, yet Gearheart had never twisted him a child. That sort of woman was always the same, reflected Spoole. They would rather not do something than risk doing it imperfectly. It was a bitter shame. Spoole almost loved Gearheart.

She came closer. 'What's this?' she asked, taking from his hand the tiny ball he had pressed from the page.

'It's nothing,' he said, but Gearheart wasn't listening.

'Keep him busy, Spoole,' she advised. 'Better that Kavan is constantly searching out new enemies on our borders than sitting around here in the Centre City with too much time on his hands.'

She rubbed the ball bearing between her own hands, making it rounder, smoother, more symmetrical. She held out the tiny sphere in her left palm, striking a pose; her right leg stretching back, her right arm turned out at her side.

'Do you not like this?' she asked. 'Am I not in perfect balance?'

'You look beautiful,' said Spoole, and he meant it. That was the thing about women, they became more beautiful as they grew older. More practised in the art of bending metal into themselves.

'What if I were to weave you a child, Spoole? Would you like that? Sometimes I feel so in harmony with the world that I feel that I must express it in some way. Should I weave a child?'

'Stop teasing me,' snapped Spoole. 'I could have you taken apart.'

'You'd like that, wouldn't you? But you know they could never put me back together as well as this.' She struck another pose, ran her hands down her body. 'Look at you, Spoole, the most powerful robot on the continent. What couldn't we do together? I'm tempted. I really am.'

'But you never would, Gearheart. You're too selfish.'

'Oh, I am. I am.'

Spoole had had enough. He changed the subject. 'He wants to attack Turing City now.'

'Kavan? Well, let him. No, don't just let him. Order him to! Make him attack sooner than he wishes, and with fewer troops than he requests! You are the leader, Spoole, so keep the initiative! There are plans long laid for this eventuality. Well, put them into action! Let this attack be seen to be your decision, not his! And why not? If he succeeds, it will be to the benefit of Artemis: if he fails, you will have one less problem to deal with. Either way, you will be seen to be decisive.'

'I know, I know. I just can't help thinking, if he fails, what would the benefit of that be to Artemis?'

Gearheart shifted her pose, stretching her arms up and back, arching her body.

'The benefit of what?'

'Oh, never mind.'

Spoole came up behind her. He placed his hands gently on her hips and increased the positive charge there, sent it flowing into her body. Gearheart stepped lightly forward.

'Keep your hands off me, Spoole,' she said, turning to give him a brilliant smile. 'We both know that you don't really need that sort of thing. Power is what *really* interests you.'

Spoole said nothing.

'And now,' she continued, 'I think I will go and look at the stars.'

At that she turned and glided from the room, the motion of her body almost silent. A wonderful piece of engineering, and a man liked to look at a beautiful piece of machinery.

Spoole sighed and moved back to the window.

His eye was drawn back to the railway tracks. Silver in the night, they spread out across the plain, branching towards the conquered countries, to Bethe, Segre, Stark and now Wien.

One of them even led to the heart of Turing City. He could almost feel the line out there, running through the darkness across the plain to the unseen lights of that distant state. It was almost as if there was a current flowing from him, running down that same line and earthing itself in some sink at the other end. A bizarre sensation, as if someone were waiting for him there.

He wondered who it was. He darkly suspected it might be Kavan.

Susan

Susan hadn't gone straight back home. It just seemed too hard to do, like she was walking just below the rim of a funnel, and her feet found themselves drawn downwards, and she couldn't summon the energy to walk upwards but just felt herself spiralling down to the hole at the bottom where she would fall out.

The hole at the bottom? She was circling the railway station, she just couldn't admit it to herself. Her path had taken her from the iron and glass of the shops and galleries in the middle town, out from the concrete and metal walkways, and onto the dusty piles of gangue heaped amongst and under the foundries and mills of the old town. Out to where the air was warm with the air rising from the forges and smelters, and the red glow of the streets reminded her of childhood. She walked on, clutching her case of paints. Passing through the narrow streets, hemmed in by corrugated iron fences and old dressed-stone walls, she felt a pull of nostalgia as she stepped onto the stone paths that led from the city.

An outcrop rose to the west, the remnants of the rocky mass that had been the source of the iron ore on which the city was founded. The iron was long gone, ripped from the orogenic belt to leave a honeycombed slab of tilted rock that listed in the earth, like a mile-long ship slowly sinking beneath the soil.

At its highest, the outcrop rose just above the graceful buildings of Turing City. The City Guard had built a watchtower up there, half of its silver side visible in the glow of Zuse, the night moon. The City Guard watched the stars as well as the landscape from that tower. They drew maps of the night sky, showing the paths of Zuse and of Néel, the day moon, and the course taken by the planets: Siecle, the hot world, and Bohm, with its one ring. They drew star charts, and they labelled the constellations: the Forge and the Fire and the Spear, and the rest.

Susan's feet hesitated at the fork in the gravel path, and she wondered about walking upwards and staring up along the watchtower's smooth wall at the stars, but her feet took the right-hand fork seemingly of their own accord, and she began to walk the length of the outcrop.

The City Guard had their fort down there, built of dressed stone. A garrison for the watchtower. Rumour had it that the hollow spaces in the outcrop, where the iron had once rested, were now filled with secret weapons. Powerful weapons, to be used against the troops of Artemis, if and when they attacked.

Susan walked down the path, the grey stone fort of the City Guard to her left, the City Centre to her right, the glass panels in the iron galleries glowing white and yellow.

There was someone waiting for her up ahead.

'Hello Susan,' he said.

Susan felt something lurch inside her.

'Who are you?' she asked. 'How do you know my name?'

The robot who stood on the path was one of the City Guard, no doubt about that. His body was made entirely of machined parts. There wouldn't be a single nut or bolt on him that he had made himself. It showed. There wasn't a visible seam on him: arms, legs, fingers, waist, all fitted together so smoothly that it looked as if he were formed from a single blob of mercury. He was tall, much taller than Susan, with narrow hips and broad shoulders. And he was so, so good-looking. Susan felt such a pang of lust and felt guilty for it. She tried to think of Karel and Axel back at the family forge, but she was so *creative* at the moment, so ready to twist a mind . . . And this man seemed to plug himself into her needs at every level.

'Who are you?' she demanded.

'Maoco O.'

'What do you want with me?'

Maoco O reached out.

'May I?' he said, taking the aluminium case from Susan's hand. He removed a thin tube of cadmium red paint. 'I want to ask you a question, Susan.'

'Why? Who are you, Maoco O?'

'I'm a friend, Susan. You have so many friends that you don't seem to know about.' Maoco O squeezed paint from the tube onto the palm of his hand.

'What are you talking about?'

Maoco O held up his palm by way of reply. He had painted a shape there. A circle with a dot marked on the top of its circumference.

'That's what Masur drew!' she whispered.

'No names,' warned Maoco O. 'Susan, you've heard that Wien has fallen?'

'Yes . . .'

'You know that they will attack Turing City next?'

'I hope that will be a long time in coming.'

'No, it will be soon. Very soon. I look forward to it.'

The robot was so silent that in the still of the night Susan was suddenly painfully aware of the humming and whirring that emerged from her own body. The sound of joints creaking as she moved. She felt terribly gauche in front of this engineered marvel, and she scolded herself for being so. She was a married woman. What did it matter what this robot thought of her? How could she possibly hope to compete with it anyway? There was something unnatural about a robot that didn't build itself.

'What's it like?' she asked.

'What's what like?'

'Having all your parts made for you? Doesn't it feel strange, like your body is not really yours?'

'I've been like this since I was a made. The Mothers of the Fort twisted me this way.'

'Oh? Can I touch you?'

'If you like.'

In the light of the night moon and the city, Susan reached out and touched the smooth moonlight of Maoco O's skin.

'It feels so strange.'

'Susan, you are thinking of weaving a new child.'

'Not with you!' said Susan, too quickly.

Maoco O laughed. 'I know that! I've embarrassed you now, haven't I? Listen, Susan, things will change here soon. When Turing City is under attack, it will be harder to retain the philosophy that has made us strong.'

Susan just stared at him. 'It's hard enough at the moment, Maoco O.'

Susan turned away from him and looked out over the extent of Turing City: the warm glow from the old town, the yellow lights from the galleries. And beyond them, lying in shadow, the regular geometries of the residential area, the neat lines of steel apartments. Her house lay there. Karel and Axel waited there for her. It all looked so peaceful in the still night. It was impossible to believe that all this could be wiped away by Artemis. Or was it?

'Maybe that notice in the railway station was right,' she murmured.

'What notice?'

'It was a message to all expectant mothers, telling us that Artemis's was the dominant philosophy; that we would do well to weave our children in that manner. They were right.'

Maoco O moved so quickly that Susan's electromuscles jerked. One moment he was standing apart, the next he was right there, face pushed close to hers.

'Of course they weren't right!' he scolded. 'Even if Artemis does reach our defences, even if the City Guard falls, even if all the city is melted down and shipped as ingots to Artemis to feed their forges, that will not be the end! Robots will still be born and their minds will still be shaped by their mothers. How will they be made? That will be your choice, Susan.'

'Oh.' Susan suddenly felt very small and foolish.

'Think about Karel, Susan. Think about how he was made. Liza knelt at the feet of an Artemisian robot, a gun to her head, and she twisted metal. Answer me this, when Artemis stand at the city gates, will you be brave enough to twist the metal the true way?'

Was Liza? wondered Susan, quickly dismissing that treacherous thought.

'Susan, this planet's history hasn't been shaped by bodies, or by machinery or by cities. It is shaped by minds. The battles that are fought aren't about metal, they are about how the next generation of robots will think.'

'I see,' said Susan.

'You don't,' said Maoco O. 'None of us does. We all think exactly the way we were shaped to think by our parents. We never question it. But how do we know what is right? *How* do we know? Is it normal to be a robot?'

'What?' Susan was thrown by this sudden change in the direction of the conversation. 'What do you mean?' she asked.

'Is it normal to be a robot?' repeated Maoco O. 'You're a robot and I'm a robot. We're all robots. Is that normal? Is robot life any more normal than the biological life that creeps across this planet? We are obviously superior to biological life, but why? Why are we?'

The question had never occurred to Susan before.

'I don't know.'

Shadows passed across Maoco O's body, clouds blocking the moonlight that he reflected.

'We take things for granted, Susan. Artemis assume they rule by right, and you assume that all minds are special. Who is right? How do we know? Where is the answer written?'

'Perhaps it's not written anywhere!' said Susan in frustration.

'Perhaps! Or perhaps it is written all around us, in letters so big that we can't see them! Imagine that, we could be walking on a world where the answer is all around us, and we can't even see it!'

Susan suddenly felt very tired. She wanted to go home.

'Listen, Maoco O, I don't know who you are, or why you are telling me all this, but I have to go.'

'So do I, Susan. I will be missed if I remain out here too long. Listen, I have three things to tell you.'

'Then say them.'

'Susan, listen carefully. First, you have friends, don't forget that. No matter what happens, they will find you. Some day you will see why.'

'Okay . . .' said Susan, feeling very strange.

'Secondly, remember this, it is not how strong we are. Strength alone does not win the battle. When it comes down to it, will you be strong enough to twist a mind in the way that *you* know is right?'

For a treacherous moment, that poster in the railway station popped into her mind. She forced it away.

'I hope so,' she murmured.

'And lastly, Susan, when you read the Book of Robots, understand this: it speaks the truth.'

'The Book of Robots? What's that?'

'Look, Susan.' Maoco O pointed.

She turned.

'What? What am I looking at?'

Maoco O

Maoco O pointed and, as Susan turned to look, he vanished silently away into the night, slipping unnoticed into one of the Fort's many concealed entrances. As he did so, his whole demeanour changed. Gone was the friendly competence, in its place was Maoco O: detached killing machine. It was part of his make-up: *emotion is just another state of mind, to be adopted according to the situation at hand.*

The whole of Fort Accardo was filled with the hum of quiet efficiency. Walking down the metal spiral staircase, descending the rough bore of the rocky shaft, he felt as if he was rejoining the mechanism of a finely balanced machine. But still there was that nagging feeling at work inside him.

Emotion is just another weapon in my armoury, and yet still I work to resist this idea. For it is nowhere written in the Book of Robots that there should be robots such as myself.

He stepped from the entry shaft into the wide open space of the practice range. Once this cavern would have echoed to the chatter of machine-gun discharge, to the crack of directed explosions. Now the weapons racks were full, rows of gleaming weapons lining the entire space to seeming infinity. But the dark grey shapes shone with the polish of newness, not the healthy glow that a weapon acquired by being handled and discharged, by being stripped and cleaned and oiled and reassembled.

It was like this all throughout the fort. *We've lost touch with our purpose,* reflected Maoco O, but without any sense of bitterness. Emotional detachment seemed to fill his every action: did it resemble the emptiness that filled his beautifully engineered body?

That was the trouble with the new paradigm. The bodies the Fort Mothers built were so sleek, so powerful, but in donning them the Guards seemed to experience the world at a distance. It wasn't their world any more; they had built themselves no part in it.

He stepped from the practice range into the magazine. Three robots crouched around a shape on the floor. A child: crudely built. It was obviously dead.

'Whose was it?' asked Maoco O.

'We don't know. Not yet.' Maoco L glanced up at him as she spoke. She looked identical to Maoco O in every way, same mercury skin, same V-shaped torso. She returned to examining the pathetic body.

'This is the third one this year,' said Maoco O. 'Where are they coming from?'

'From here, Maoco O. City Guards are making them.'

The concept would have filled a robot less emotionally secure than Maoco O with revulsion. As it was, he remained calm.

'Why? The reproductive urge is not twisted into the metal of our minds. The Fort Mothers would not build us to think of such things.'

'Not intentionally perhaps, but the pattern of a mind is a complex thing. For centuries mothers have made minds focused around the reproductive urge. The offspring of those mothers that did not do so never reproduced: they are not with us today. The reproductive urge is so much a pattern of the mind that it is impossible for the Fort Mothers not to incorporate it in some way.'

Maoco O looked down at the pathetic metal shell on the ground.

'So there are still some women in this fort who will seize on any man and try to make a child with him.' His words were matter-of-fact.

'And they lack the full knowledge to properly twist a child,' answered Maoco L.

'Interesting. It is a problem that should be addressed.'

'Agreed. Perhaps after the oncoming difficulty with Artemis is resolved.'

Maoco L picked up the tiny shell. 'I will pass the mind inside here to the Fort Mothers. Perhaps they can decide who the mother is by looking at the weave of the mind.'

'A good idea,' answered Maoco O.

But inside a little voice was speaking. *Why can't I be as positive inside this fort as I am when I walk outside? Why don't I feel the same sense of optimism for the future?*

The answer filled the dark stone spaces of the fort. The answer *was* the darkness, and it was given shape by the geometry of the polished stone walls.

Because there is no future. Because there is nothing to be optimistic about, and no reason to wish for such optimism. All there is, is the day that follows this, and the relentless upgrading of smoothly milled bodies as they approach perfection. What else should one require?

Silently, perfectly, seamlessly, Maoco O passed through rooms of identical robots, heading towards his duty station.

The evening dance was due to begin.

Karel

Axel was still young enough to sleep. Karel squatted down before him and gazed into his eyes, wondering where his son had gone to. Karel knew that he had once slept too; he knew that he had once had dreams, back when the metal in his mind was still unfolding and gaining in lifeforce. But that had been long ago and, like every other adult, he had forgotten what it was like. Axel looked so peaceful, following the twists of his own mind, growing new wire, forging new connections and fixing the mind. Karel tried to recall the path he had taken as a child, how he would turn his mind in on itself and descend into sleep. But without success, for the way there was gone.

He heard the front door to the apartment slide open and shut. Susan had returned home at last.

'Where have you been?' he asked.

'Out. Walking. I bought some paint.' She held up the thin metal case.

'Let me take that.' Karel remembered how Susan had been last time they had been getting ready to make a child. So receptive. So creative. She had taken to walking day and night, gazing at the sky, at the sea, at the land. At everything, whether a building, the slope of a pile of gangue, an oddly shaped stone. She was drinking in images and thoughts and concepts, storing up information to be used in the making of a new mind. Too much information, perhaps. She would come home and it would all spill out of her, painted onto the foil leaves of books, scrawled across the walls, twisted into iron and silver. What must it be like to be a woman? he wondered, as he took the metal case and laid it on a table. He took her hand and led her to a chair. There was a shallow foot bath pushed underneath it, already filled with light oil.

'Sit down,' he said. He knelt on the floor before her, took one of her feet in his hands and began to pry the segmented casing away from it.

'Oh, Karel, thank you!' She sank back into the seat, electro-muscles discharging. The plastic-coated sole of the foot came away, and Karel quickly stripped the segmented steel upper.

'That feels so nice,' said Susan.

Karel pulled out the oil bath and dropped the upper into it.

'You've got gangue lodged in here,' he remarked. 'Where have you been? Into the old city?'

'Yes.'

'Did you make it as far as the fort?'

'Oh, Karel, do the other one too.'

She waved her other foot in his face. He quickly stripped away its covering, then gazed at his wife's naked feet. Delicate steel bones, shimmering thin electromuscle.

'You build yourself so well,' he said.

She gave a relaxed sigh. 'You're not so bad yourself.'

He worked on her feet for some time, flexing them, cleaning them, straightening out control rods. He oiled them and slipped the casing back into place.

Then they sat in silence for some time.

'What are you thinking, Karel?'

Karel looked up into his wife's eyes.

'Nothing in particular. Why?'

'I never know what you're thinking. Not really. You never let on.'

A distance fell between them.

'Susan, what's the matter? Is it the child? It is, isn't it? Your emotions are all bubbling up, trying to get themselves into order, ready for the making.'

'Yes! No! Oh, I don't know. Tell me, Karel, how do you know? All those immigrants. All those people trying to get into Turing City. How do you know they are telling the truth? How do you know that they are who they say they are?'

She leaned forward, her gaze intense, pleading for an answer.

'How do I *know*?' echoed Karel. 'I don't. Not really. But that's not the point. They say that they will act in accordance with Turing City's philosophy; they promise they will weave their children's minds in that fashion. What more can we ask of them?'

And for a moment, an image of Banjo Macrodocious leaped into his mind.

'Supposing they're all lying?' said Susan. 'What if they are just saying that so they can come and live here? Wouldn't we do the same? If our home had been destroyed and we had nowhere else to go?'

'I'm sure that some of them *are* lying, Susan. Listen, they used to need permits to have children in Segre, back when the Artemisian siege was on and metal was short. But, really, they were just adapting a system that had been used for years in the middle countries. In Stark, robots used to have to pass a mechanical competence test before having children. That's the price that bought their technical excellence. Robots have been leaving Segre and Bethe and Stark for years to come and live here, simply so they could raise their own children. Were we right to let them in? Well, I think so. Look at what happened: those other countries are conquered, and we are still standing.'

Susan stared at him. She didn't seem convinced.

'Are you going to work tomorrow?' she asked.

'Yes.'

'What about the parliament? You've heard, haven't you? Kobuk has managed to get a petition together for parliament to be convened.'

'Everyone has heard, Susan. Of course I'll be back for that. But listen, we have Wieners now flocking into the western stations, running from Artemis. We can't just ignore them, we need to get them processed. And there will be more robots coming. Lots more.'

The golden glow in Susan's eyes deepened. 'I can't help thinking that they're wasting their time,' she said, 'that Artemis will get them sooner rather than later.' She put her hand to her mouth. 'Listen to me! I'm talking like a traitor. Karel, I don't think we should have another child.'

'That's just the build-up of emotions,' said Karel soothingly. 'You were like this the last time, too.'

'No I wasn't and you know it. Karel, there is something waiting for me out there, and I don't know what it is. My mind isn't right. I don't know what to think.'

Karel took her hands. 'Susan, it will be all right. Trust me.'

He gazed at her. She looked away.

'Susan? Susan! You do trust me, don't you?'

She couldn't look at him. She spoke to the floor.

'Karel,' she said, in such a little voice. 'I don't really know what's on your mind. I don't know how it was made. I don't think anyone does, not even you.'

She pulled her hands away from his, stood up and walked from the room.

Karel remained where he was.

Thinking.

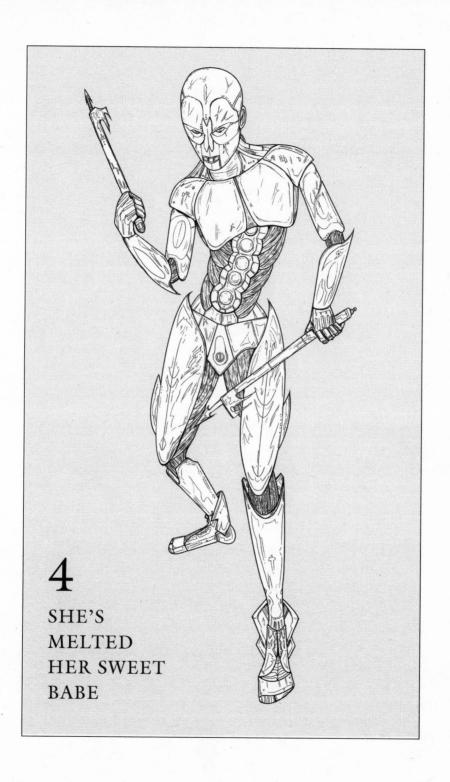

4

SHE'S
MELTED
HER SWEET
BABE

The Cruel Mother

Nyro sat down in the land of Born,
The rain her metal has misted;
And there she has knelt with her own true man,
And a new mind she has twisted.

Smile no so sweet, my Bonnie Babe:
And you smile me so sweet, you'll smile me dead.
She's taken out her own little awl
And pulled the metal from her sweet Babe's head.

She's lit a fire by the light of the night moon
And there she's melted her sweet babe in.

As she was going to the forge
She saw a sweet babe in the porch.
Oh, sweet babe, if you were mine
I'd clad you in the metal so fine.
Oh, Mother dear, when I was thine,
You didn't prove to me so kind.

O cursed mother, this land is full
And it's here that you will no longer dwell.
O cursed mother, Shull is empty
Go there now, cursed empty shell.

Olam

The feeling of fear in the stadium was electric: it was a static charge building up in the jolting, clanking crowd of robots, threatening to earth itself in a runaway crackle of panic.

'There's nothing to worry about,' said the robot next to Olam. 'They need us because they're going straight on to attack Turing City: they'll have to enlist every robot they can.'

Olam eyed the robot with a dislike that was momentarily stronger than the fear that currently ran through him. The robot was tall, his body plated in whale metal. Clearly one of the Wiener aristocracy. The robot possessed an air of certainty that Olam despised.

'Why would they want to attack Turing City right away?' asked a nearby robot. She was a pretty thing but damaged, the panel on her upper thigh cracked. Olam could see electromuscle sparking through the break. 'Surely they would want to pause and rebuild their strength?' She was confused, trying to make sense of this sudden reversal in her fortunes.

'No,' insisted the tall robot. 'Doe Menloop knows what's going on. She told me, Kavan's leading the Artemis forces now.'

'Who's Kavan?' asked the woman with the damaged leg.

'Kavan is a folk legend amongst the Artemisians. Kavan is the robot outsider who came to Artemis and proved himself more Artemisian than the Artemisians themselves.' The tall aristocrat explained all this without a trace of condescension. Well, he would, reflected Olam. His sort would force you to work underground for a lifetime on low wages without any hesitation, and yet would be mortified if they thought they had been unintentionally rude to you. 'A lot of people have been waiting for Kavan to take control of the army. They expect him to march upon Artemis City itself some day.'

Olam felt moved to speak, but at that moment there was a crackle of static, a whistle from the speakers that studded the iron walls of the stadium, and the anxious noise of the gathered robots died away.

It should have been a beautiful day. A holiday, a day for the people of Wien to take a walk, or go sailing, or to climb the towers of the whale minds. The weather was perfect, the late-autumn sky filling the gaps between the struts and the pillars at the upper reaches of the stadium with bright blue.

Just at that moment Olam fantasized what it would be like to be able to fly. To lift himself out of this cauldron of terrified, pleading robots and to rise up into the air, past the Artemisian guards who patrolled the terraces that looked down over the stadium floor, their guns at the ready. To just rise out of this nightmare and fly to safety . . .

But the speakers whistled again, and the fantasy vanished, and Olam was back in the stadium, just one of hundreds of robots who had come here seeking the only apparent opportunity left for survival.

There was yet another whistle, and a voice resolved itself.

'Good morning, robots.'

Olam followed the turning heads of his fellow captives towards the Royal Box. Only a few days before, Olam had visited the stadium with his brothers to watch the combat: robots in a carnival of customized bodies fighting to the death. Then, the Royal Box had been draped with tungsten alloy foil that flashed iridescent patterns in the wind. Now, it was just another iron box. A nondescript grey robot stood there on the balcony, speaking into a microphone.

'My name is Eleanor,' she was saying, 'second in command to Kavan, leader of the Artemisian troops. Kavan, who was born an outsider and is now part of Artemis. Take him as an example, robots, and remember the words that Nyro spoke. "*Artemis is never intended to be a country. Artemis is an ideal.*"'

'I told you,' murmured the aristocrat. 'They want us. They *need* us.'

'Silence,' said another robot, but the tall robot was going to have his say.

'To think there are some fools still hiding out there in the city, just waiting for their brains to be unwound at the end of an awl. They should have come here, to safety. They should have listened to me . . .'

Eleanor was speaking again. Olam strained his vision to get a better look at her. She seemed so nondescript. So grey. So interchangeable.

'And now you, too, have come here to serve Artemis. Some of you, no doubt, with a genuine desire to be part of the Artemesian state. But some of you will have come here through fear, or cowardice. Those in the city beyond would call you traitors . . .'

At her words, Olam felt a lurch in his gyros. He remembered the looks on his brothers' faces as he had left the shelter of the forge earlier that morning, the foil sheet advertising Artemis's offer clutched in his hands. He remembered the walk through the clear morning towards the stadium. The city was broken, wreathed in smoke and spattered with droplets of metal, but the tall iron shape of the stadium remained untouched, rising cold and sinister above the streets. For decades, robots had fought to the death in that stadium, the wire of the defeated minds unwound and spooled up and sent off to be melted. Olam had thought little of their fate in the past. Now, maybe, he was going to join them. Perhaps he, too, would meet his death on the stadium floor.

His thoughts were yanked back to the present and Eleanor's words.

'. . . but, no matter what your motives, all of you are welcome here. Now, if you will just bear with me a few moments . . .'

There was another whistle and the speakers were clicked off. Eleanor turned away from the balcony. Olam had a surge of hope at her words. Maybe it was going to be okay after all.

'I told you,' murmured the tall robot, and suddenly Olam had a clear vision of how things were going to be. A vision of the Wiener aristocracy and their hangers-on, slotting easily into place in the Artemisian army, rising quickly through the ranks, while the likes of him were left at the bottom as always, only one step above the slaves and the condemned. Some things never changed.

The aristocrat murmured again. 'I'll tell you something else . . .'

There was a harsh rattle of metal and an electronic whine.

'No talking!'

The infantryrobot had seemingly appeared from nowhere. He had hit the aristocrat across the back of the head with his rifle. The tall robot was rubbing his head, trying to adjust the set of his mind.

And now Olam realized how the crowd had been silently infil-
trated by grey Artemisian troops. They were picking their way
through the mass of Wiener robots, pulling random people out of
the crowd and herding them towards one of the stadium exits.
Olam looked closer. Pulling only the women out of the crowd, he
realized. The Artemisian soldier that had hit the tall robot over
the head was now examining the woman with the damaged leg.

'Is there any other damage?' he asked her.

'No . . .' said the woman. 'No, I'm fine.'

The soldier was unconvinced. 'Hey, Greta. Come and take a
look at this one.'

Another grey soldier came over. Slightly shabby-looking, made
of well-worn metal. She examined the damaged leg.

'Seems localized,' she decided. 'But why risk it? We've harvested enough. Leave her here.'

The two soldiers vanished into the crowd. Only Olam noticed
that one of them had dropped something. An awl. Nonchalantly,
he bent down and palmed the glossy black spike.

The aristocrat seemed to be recovering. 'Best not to speak,' he
said.

The woman looked concerned. 'What did they mean, *why risk
it*?' she asked, too nervous to heed the tall robot's advice. 'Why
did they leave me behind? They've taken all the other women
away.'

'Not all,' said the aristocrat quietly. 'They've left the young
ones. Now, let's stay quiet . . .'

Olam felt his gyros lurch again. What was going on?

The grey troops were moving back through the crowd, sepa-
rating them out. Olam found himself being forced off the gravel
that covered most of the ground and onto one of the magnetized
running surfaces that ran around the perimeter of the stadium. He
felt his feet lock onto it as he walked; and he felt a lurch of fear.
This is where robots had been run to death, supercharged and sent
hurtling around the track, expending their lifeforce in one burst,
whilst he and his brothers had watched and cheered. Now it
seemed that the roles were about to be reversed.

He looked around to see that the crowd was being spaced out into groups of three. Olam found himself with the tall robot and the damaged woman. More and more, he realized he had made a big mistake in coming here.

'What's going on?' asked the woman again. The tall robot just rubbed his head thoughtfully.

The speakers whistled. Eleanor's voice sounded.

'Future Artemsians,' she said. 'Artemis was never intended to be a country. Artemis is an ideal. Artemis does not serve you, nor you it. Rather, you *are* Artemis. Artemis only needs the strong, the clever, the cunning, the artificers.'

Olam's gyros lurched again. The damaged woman looked at him, fear in her eyes.

'Prove you have those qualities,' continued Eleanor. 'We only need two-thirds of your number.'

There was an uneasy stirring in the crowd. Olam felt removed from the events, he felt as if he were standing in the terraces amongst the grey soldiers, or sitting where he belonged, up there ready to watch the killing, not down here participating in it. Hah, at least if he was up there he would be enjoying this spectacle, not like those grey soldiers above. They didn't seem concerned by events on the stadium floor; they simply watched it all with bored resignation . . . A shot rang out, jerking him from his reverie. And another. There was a continuous volley of shots. All around the stadium, robots slumped to the ground, blue wire twisting and uncurling from their heads. Grey soldiers walked away, their guns smoking.

'Five minutes,' announced Eleanor, 'or we reduce the numbers ourselves.'

The aristocrat moved coldly and dispassionately, seizing the damaged woman with his two long arms.

'I saw you pick up that awl,' he said to Olam. 'Use it on her.'

'Please!' cried the woman. 'No.'

Olam looked at the shiny black spike in his hand.

'Do you want them to shoot us?' asked the tall robot. 'Use it!'

'No!' said the woman, eyes wide with fear. 'Please, no!'

'It's you or us,' explained the aristocrat. 'This isn't personal.'

'But I have two children . . .'

Olam weighed the spike in his hand. He looked at the tall robot, looked at the whale metal covering his body. The tall robot knew what he was thinking.

'There's no point attacking me,' it said. 'That awl would never pierce my body. I'm covered in whale metal. Look at you, with your pig-iron plating. I could defeat you with ease, but this woman is weaker. And you have a weapon. So use it on her.'

The woman gazed at him, eyes pleading.

'What did you expect?' asked the aristocrat. 'This is Artemis we are dealing with. Only the clever and the strong serve it. That is why it's so powerful.'

Olam looked around the stadium. He could see that most groups were, like his own, gripped by indecision. But in some of them a fight was taking place. In a few, robots already lay dead. One lay nearby on the magnetic track, arms and legs pulsing as two young women repeatedly smashed his head on the ground. Olam watched as the unfortunate robot's skull was buckled and torn. The women pulled blue wire from the widening cracks in great loops, their mouths emitting excited electronic squeaks as they did so.

'I can't,' said Olam, sickened. But maybe also a little excited, he realized. 'I won't,' he said firmly.

'Then give me the awl and let me do it!' The tall robot's voice was cold. There was no anger there, no passion. Nothing but pure logic.

Seemingly without his volition, Olam's arm reached forward, the awl offered up on his palm.

'No!' screamed the woman, her body rattling with fear. 'Please!'

Olam came to his senses and snatched his hand back.

'You're a fool, man,' said the tall robot coldly. 'Do you mean to tell me you've never come here to watch the fighting?' He saw the answer in Olam's stance. 'I thought as much. Lower-class voyeur. You can watch it, but can you do it? Well, here's your chance to join your betters! I killed my first robot when I was just ten! You should know what to do; you've seen it happen often

enough. Come on! We've only got a couple of minutes left! Do
you want to be killed too? It's the logical thing. Only she dies, or
we all die. Either way she will be dead. You're condemning both
of us as well.'

The woman began to sob.

'Don't do that,' said the tall robot, dismissively. 'You're being
selfish. Die like a true Wiener.'

He meant it, realized Olam and, out of nowhere, a mad laughter bubbled up inside him.

'But we aren't Wieners any more,' he cried. 'We're all
Artemisians now!'

And at that, he gripped the awl in his fist, point down, and
leaped at the tall robot. The sun was at his back: he saw their shadows stretching out on the ground before them. He saw himself
gripping the tall robot around the neck, bringing the point of the
awl down again and again on the aristocrat's skull.

'You can't hurt me,' said the tall robot patiently. 'I'm made of
whale metal.'

He was right. They all three struggled in vain, Olam blunting
the point of the awl on the beautiful grey metal of the aristocrat's
skull, the woman desperately fighting to be free.

'I'm growing impatient, prole. Only one minute left. *Kill her!*'

Olam gave up on the man's skull. He brought the awl around
and stabbed at an eye. The man raised an arm to defend himself,
and the women finally broke free of his grip.

'Hold him!' called Olam.

The woman grabbed an arm and held onto it. Olam stabbed at
the aristocrat's eye once more, grazing it.

'You see!' The tall robot was almost laughing. 'You *have* got the
motivation. You can kill . . .'

With a gyroscopic lurch, Olam realized that the tall robot was
right. So *this* is what those robots on the killing floor felt. It felt
good! The feeling rushed through his electromuscle, and he
stabbed at the aristocrat again. The eye flared and died. A sharp
current ran through the awl into Olam's hand.

The woman screamed. The tall robot had reached through the

damaged plating at her thigh and grabbed the electromuscle there. Now Olam stabbed at the tall robot's hand.

All around them, he was vaguely aware of more and more robots lying dead on the track.

'Stop wasting time,' snapped the tall robot. 'Kill her!'

The aristocrat honestly believed he could still order him about! Fury overtook Olam. His arms functioned of their own accord. He stabbed for the tall robot's other eye and was batted away, flung to the ground. He rose and charged forward, just as a volley of shots rang out.

A series of sharp cracks. The spang and whiz of ricochets. Olam looked at the woman, at the tall robot. They looked back at him, at each other, both waiting. There was another volley, and another. Still they waited.

Silence. And then the light faded in the woman's eyes. She slumped to the ground.

The tall robot gazed at Olam with disgust.

'They shot her,' he said. 'So apart from me losing my eye, what have you achieved?'

Olam felt the lurching inside him come to a halt. It was replaced with a smooth calmness and a cold certainty.

What have I achieved? he wondered. The answer came in a hot charge of current. *The knowledge that I can kill, if I need to.*

Eleanor

Eleanor didn't pay much attention to what was going on on the stadium floor. The weak and the unlucky would die, and in that way the overall quality of the new recruits would be raised. It wasn't as if they were Artemisians yet. At the moment they were nothing more than talking metal.

She resented Kavan sending her here. Her talents were not best serving Artemis by being stuck in this stadium: she would be better with Kavan, discussing their next move. Could they seriously attack Turing City now, this soon after their near-defeat in

Wien? Why had he sent her away? Did he fear her? Zuse knew that Eleanor craved power too, but Kavan was the better leader. She knew it. Surely Kavan knew it as well?

But it was time to speak again. She returned to the balcony and reached for the microphone. The Wieners had used a speaker jack which they plugged directly into their bodies, thus connecting them to the speaker system. Eleanor had found the idea vaguely distasteful, so she had built a microphone onto the end of the jack with parts taken from the head of a dead Wiener.

'Well done, survivors,' she said. 'Your numbers are now two-thirds what they were. I estimate that half of you will be suitable for conscription. Now, before we continue with the process, I think it is important that you understand exactly what Artemis is. You will have heard stories, you will have heard lies, and you will have heard the truth and misunderstood it.'

The sun beat down on the arena. Oil slicked the magnetic track, overworked and heated metal could be heard plinking along with the whirring and sparking of broken machinery.

'Artemis begins with Nyro, of course. But who was Nyro? Where did she come from? There are stories, that she came from Born, that she killed her own child. Yes, we've all heard the ballad. We've heard that she murdered her own husband, tangling him in the wire of his own mind. Are these stories true? No. Nyro was none of these things. She was just a woman who lived in a barren land. She had nothing. Nothing but her mind.'

The True Story of Nyro

Artemis in those days was nothing but a barren plain. It held no metal; there was nothing there but organic life and empty rock.

But there was metal in the mountains: iron and phosphorus.

But there was metal on the coast: nickel, gold, silver and copper.

But the robots who lived there kept their metal to themselves, so that the robots who lived in the centre were left to forge bodies out of wind and dust.

What metal *did* they have? Only the metal the robots who lived there had brought with them. Only the rusty skeletons of dead machinery. Only such as they could salvage from the bodies of the meagre robot life that dwelt there, the rodents and insects that fed on one another.

And sometimes there was the metal that could be harvested from the dead bodies of the occasional robot that foolishly strayed into their land from the richer cities. For the robots that dwelt in Artemis were poor in spirit as well as poor in metal and would even prey upon their own kind.

On the central plains the surrounding world becomes distant, and a robot can see nothing but the sky. A robot's world reaches up into nothing instead of stretching out to other worlds. Nyro was a robot woman like any other that dwelt in that land, except in this one respect: Nyro had been to those other lands.

Whether she had been born there, or she had developed the wanderlust, or she had gone there to beg for metal to make a child, Nyro had seen the other robot communities that dwelt on the continent of Shull. But they had turned her away, and so now Nyro envied and hated them. Nyro wanted Artemis to be like them, and yet at the same time she wanted those other communities to be punished.

But Nyro knew she couldn't compete with the cities to the east and the cities to the west, not with their forges and their metal.

There was not enough metal in Artemis to build cities like those she had visited in the south, with their soaring towers, their arches and their roads. There was not enough metal so that minds could merely sit in contemplation as they did in Stark, devising new forms of machinery. There was not the metal to arm soldiers so that they could fight the guards that prevented them entering the mountains to the north, and thus gaining access to vast lodes of iron that lay there beneath the rock. No, here in the centre of Shull, minds were turned, every hour of every day, to the search for what scant metal there was.

But Nyro did not retreat into bitterness or resentment. Rather, she planned how best she could use what she did possess.

Nyro had long been ready for the night of the making of a mind. She had spent half her life, it seemed, ready to twist a child. But she had held back, wondering how to make a child that could compete in this world of scarce resources.

Until, finally, Nyro had her vision of the future that would shape the continent of Shull.

This was what she realized.

When a woman twisted metal, she would make the child in her hands to care for itself, for it needed to value its own existence, or else it would not survive. Then she would make the child in her hands care for its father and mother, and then its brothers and sisters, for this is the way that the family grew strong and how the mother herself would be cared for in her old age.

But Nyro realized that this land did not have enough metal for the old ways to continue. So instead she wove an idea.

The idea was called Artemis.

Artemis was to be the mother and father, the brother and sister of the child. The new child would care for Artemis above all else. It would protect its own life for the good of Artemis. It would protect others for the same reason. This way all those lengths of wire in robots' heads would become as one wire.

The idea was a good one, and Nyro's children prospered. They wove other children in turn who also served Artemis. And Nyro watched as those children became strong enough to take metal, just a few scraps at first, from those proud communities to the east and west that had once turned her away. She watched as those children twisted more children, all with minds bent towards Artemis.

Nyro died forgotten by her own children. Nyro died alone, and yet proud to see what she had wrought.

Artemis had taken on life. Artemis was no longer just a place, just a feeble city that stood on the continent of Shull: Artemis was *alive*.

Any robot, whatever its origin, could pledge allegiance to Artemis. Any robot could be said to be serving Artemis, so long as this idea was served.

That my life, my body, my wire, all is subservient to Artemis.
Artemis.

Olam

Olam glanced around the assembled robots as Eleanor completed her story. How did they feel? Looking at their faces, he saw his own emotions reflected back. Horror, confusion, fear. And, also, on one or two robots, this horrible aching eagerness. This feeling of safety and order that Olam recognized deep in his gyros and that he tried to push away. This sense that all of life's fears and confusions could be ticked off and lined up and assigned to the reassuring answer that was Artemis. The thought that, if he became part of this, he would never feel fear again.

His attention was distracted by a scraping, scratching noise coming from the stadium steps. The guards were dragging metal crates into place.

'Would-be Artemisians, you have already shown strength, but now is the time to demonstrate cunning and agility . . .'

Olam only half heard Eleanor's words. Like every other robot in the place, he was dreadfully fascinated by those crates and their contents. The grey guards were now lifting the lids, shaking something lose. His gyros gave a sickening lurch as he saw what they held. Snakes. Boa inductors. They were small, less than a foot long.

'Freshly imported from Raman,' continued Eleanor. 'They won't kill, but they carry a current that will paralyse a robot for about thirty minutes.'

All around the stadium, tangles of silver snakes were slipping, sliding, dropping to the ground. They whipped their way across the floor, seeking out the shadows and safety, silver bodies reflecting bars of blue sky and darkness. Eleanor pointed to the ends of the stadium, to the metal markers indicating north and south. Olam's electromuscles trembled. Some of the more extreme sports in the arena relied upon direction . . .

'You are in pairs already,' said Eleanor. 'It's either you or your partner. Disable the robot standing beside you. Bring your robot to the north of the stadium if you wish to show it mercy. Bring it to the south if you wish it destroyed.'

Olam dived forward, under the reaching grasp of the tall robot. He saw the flash of a silver boa before him, but it was already gone, snatched up by a nearby man dressed in copper. Something seized his legs, trapping him. The tall robot.

'What's your name, boy?' his assailant asked, hands prying at the panelling on his legs. He was going to repeat the trick he had tried on the damaged woman, squeezing Olam's electromuscles to send the current back up into his brain to short his mind.

'Olam,' gasped Olam. There was another flash of silver over to his side. He rolled for it, but the snake saw him coming and retreated in panic. Olam could see clearly the smooth silver of its upper side, the rough segmented iron of its lower surface. The aristocrat jerked at his legs, pulling him around and sprawling him onto his back. Olam stared up at him; saw the dead eye that he had stabbed with the awl.

The tall robot realized what he was looking at. 'There was no need to make things personal,' he said.

Olam wriggled in panic. He could see the huge silver marker at the south end of the stadium. That way lay death . . .

'You could always make a new eye,' he babbled.

'You're making things personal again.'

The tall robot was too strong. The Wiener aristocracy had access to the best metal, to the best technology. Olam couldn't hope to fight him.

Without hurry, he was dragged across the track towards the shadows at the perimeter where the snakes sheltered. Up above, the sun was now like a yellow hole in the blue sky, it reflected off every piece of polished metal in the arena.

'What's your name?' he asked the aristocrat, who ignored him. 'What's your name?' he screeched.

The tall robot bent down and grabbed a snake in one easy movement.

'Doe Capaldi,' he said. With one hand, Doe Capaldi held onto Olam's legs; with the other he held the snake by the tail, swinging it back and forth slowly to stop it curling around his own arm. Olam kicked out hard, twice, but the tall robot's grip was too strong. Now he was turning the snake so that the iron bottom faced towards Olam. He could see the segments, grey and scratched. He could feel the magnetic pull they made. The snake would try to wrap around his neck, where it could fire off a magnetic pulse strong enough to disrupt his coil, effectively paralysing him. And then Doe Capaldi would drag him, helpless, to his end. All around he could see other robots in the stadium already being dragged to the south side of the stadium. Dragged to their death.

Doe Capaldi flicked the snake forward . . . Olam snatched it from the air. His right arm went numb as the snake fired off its inductor units. The tall robot flipped Olam onto his front, jumped forward and knelt on his back. Olam saw a whale-metal arm scrabbling for another snake just out of reach.

'You'll never make it in Artemis,' shouted Olam. 'You'll never be able to make yourself subservient.'

'I'll do whatever it takes.' Doe Capaldi snatched again at the snake. Olam struggled harder, to no avail. His opponent was just too strong. All he could do now was taunt him.

'They'll strip that whale metal from your body . . .'

'I'll still have my mind.'

'They already have you fighting on the arena floor, just like a slave. What will they have you doing next?'

'Whatever it takes. Here we go . . .'

Olam braced himself, waiting for the flash and the subsequent numb sensation as the snake fired. And he waited. And then the tension in his arms and back ebbed away. He forced himself up, sending Doe Capaldi tumbling to the ground next to him, a silver loop wrapped around the tall robot's neck.

A man dressed in a copper skin shook his fist in the air. 'I got that aristocratic *Garo* for you. Now finish him!' He gave Doe Capaldi a kick for good measure.

Olam staggered to his feet, the magnetic track feeling good beneath him.

'Tha . . . Thank you!' he called.

He turned and looked down at Doe Capaldi, the sudden release of fear turning to hate.

'*Choarh!*' he yelled, kicking at the robot's side. The whale metal gave a dull thud.

He bent down and began to drag the tall robot south, to the killing zone.

I can kill, he thought to himself with pleasure, the current in his electromuscles singing. *I can kill.* All those times watching the fighting in this arena, he had often wondered if he could do it himself, when it came down to it. Now he knew for certain. His mind seemed alive with sparks, like when a hammer was brought down on hot metal.

With macabre humour, he sat the tall robot in the middle of the south section of the stadium, sat him up to face the balcony. He could see other robots around about him, each with a silver band around its neck. He leaned close to his captive's ear.

'It's nothing personal,' he said. He looked deep into Doe Capaldi's good eye, and then turned back to watch the balcony.

Here came Eleanor now. What was it about her that Olam found so disturbing? She was so plain, so grey, so nondescript. So Artemisian. This was what he was signing up for, he realized. Eleanor was the embodiment of Artemis. Interchangeable. Not so much a robot as the realization of an idea. Did they all really believe, he wondered, or were many of them driven there by circumstance, like Doe Capaldi the aristocrat? Like himself, Olam?

Eleanor spoke.

'Future Artemisians, you have made your choice and recognized that in Artemis there is a time for mercy and a time to kill.'

She paused to survey the crowd. Olam felt strangely calm. The sun was up and the sky was blue.

Eleanor resumed her speech. 'But sometimes the merciful should kill, and sometimes the killers should learn mercy. And sometimes Artemis changes its mind, because Artemis has no ego, no pride. Artemis is Artemis.'

Olam felt a lurching in his gyros.

'Those to the south will be spared. Kill *everyone* to the north.'

Nobody moved at first.

'All of them.' said Eleanor, without heat.

And then Olam saw the grey soldiers returning to the floor of the stadium. He heard the sound of bullets, the ringing of skulls being shattered.

He looked down at Doe Capaldi. Hesitantly, he reached down, took hold of the silver snake and slowly pulled it away from the man's neck.

Slowly, the tall robot got to his feet. He looked down at Olam. 'No hard feelings, boy,' he said. 'I told you, it's nothing personal. I would have dragged you to the north. But that would have been a mistake wouldn't it? We'd both have been dead.'

Olam didn't reply, just stared with hatred at the tall robot clad in whale metal, stared at his aristocratic curves. A passing grey soldier caught the look.

'Hey, no need for that,' she said with a laugh. 'We're all Artemisians now.'

Karel

Axel stood behind Susan, one dark iron hand gripping the exquisitely enamelled powder-blue panel on her thigh. He was staring up at his father, pleading.

'I still say he is too young to attend the meeting,' Susan was saying.

'This is too important for him to miss. He needs to know what's going on.'

'He's only four. He won't understand. He'll only be frightened. You know how people exaggerate.'

'He'll be just as frightened if we keep him in the dark. I think he should attend, and I'm not going to change my mind.' Karel give her a bitter look. 'You should know me that much, Susan.'

And so he had won the argument at least. Susan couldn't say anything else, not after what she had said last night. And Karel knew it, and Susan knew that Karel knew it.

So they left their apartment and made their way from the smooth stone and metal of the residential district, and down the gangue mounds into the old town.

The oldest part of Turing City was built on a series of descending ledges, a legacy of the great open-cast mine from which their wealth had been dug. Karel and his family walked down steps, over metal walkways that ran from the edge of one ledge to the roof of a building and onto the next ledge down, over bridges that spanned the gaps between the piles of gangue: the waste material left after the metal had been extracted. They made their way along the grey lips of the retaining walls that held back the debris of yellowish stone, part of a growing throng of robots making their way to the parliament arena. It was a bright day, the sun warming their metal skins, the blue of the sky seeming to deepen as one stared into it. Karel wondered if they shared this same blue sky in Wien. Were the robots there taking any comfort in such a glorious day?

The air was filled with the sound of marching metal, the hiss and spark of bodies, the tread of metal feet on metal walkways and concrete paths, as the mass of robots converged on the parliament arena, which lay near the centre of the city. In the distance, to Karel's right, the rails into the station could be heard singing with the sound of trains bringing to the debate robots from all four corners of Turing City State. From behind came the dying notes of the foundries and mills in the old town being stilled as the robots there left their work. The residential districts were being drained as entire families left their homes to attend. Even up on the rocky outcrop there was a suggestion of stillness over the square shapes of the fort and the silver needle of the watchtower, and Karel wondered if even the City Guard would be leaving their posts to come to the meeting.

'Daddy?' Axel stretched the last syllable of the word upwards.

'Yes, Axel?'

'Why are the Artemisians going to attack us?'

Susan gazed at him with an *I told you so* expression.

'They're not going to attack us, Axel.'

'I know. But why would they? Why do people say that they will?'

Karel looked to Susan for support, but she looked away.

'Well,' said Karel. 'I suppose in the end it's down to basic geology. What have you learned about that?'

Axel spoke in his best classroom voice.

'Penrose is made of many elements, but the five most abundant are oxygen, silicon, iron, aluminium and calcium.'

'Well done,' said Karel, impressed. 'Hold on there.'

They paused at an iron bridge that spanned the gap between two buildings, waiting for two robots that were walking against the flow of the pedestrians to cross.

Axel and Karel looked down into the street below, saw robots riveting the last few slats into place on a metal fence. A fire glowed red beneath the rivet bucket. The robots were hurrying to finish their job, eager to be off.

'So tell me,' continued Karel. 'What are those elements used for?'

Axel chanted as he watched the scene in the street below.

'Oxygen is useless to us and always will be,
Silicon hides its mind,
Iron is the living element, it marks our birth,
Aluminium hides its face, it is the mythical element,
and calcium completes the circle, useless like oxygen.'

'That's very good,' said Karel. 'But we use oxygen, you know. We use it to extract iron from ore.'

'I know that,' said Axel. 'But it's an old verse. Aluminium is just a story too, like Oneill. I know that.'

'Well done. So, where do we find these elements?'

Axel began to chant again.

'The elements are bound into minerals.
A solid mass of mineral grains is a rock.
Orthoclase is the most common,
Then sulphides and oxides and carbonates.
Magnetite and haematite contain iron.
They are mined from beneath the central mountain range of Shull.
This is from where the robots came.'

'Good! And what about here? What about Turing City?'

'There are mafic igneous rocks beneath Turing City.

From sulphides and oxides such as these we get nickel and cobalt and copper.

And gold and silver, platinum and palladium,

Which help make the metal out of which we twist minds.'

Axel smiled. 'We have more of these metals than anyone else. That's why the robots of Turing City are cleverer and more skilful than other robots.'

'Not necessarily . . .' laughed Karel.

'No, Dad, it's true. Deanne's dad said that it was treason to say anything else.'

'It's not treason to state facts, Axel.'

But Susan was staring at him again.

'What?' said Karel.

'You should be careful,' she said. 'You know what they say about you.'

'No?' said Karel, folding his arms. 'And what exactly do they say about me?'

'Anyway, it's true, Dad,' continued Axel, oblivious to his parents' simmering argument. He was lost in a world of super robots, of perfect minds and the flashing silent blades of the City Guard. 'Other robots may have more iron, they may have bigger bodies and more lifeforce, but they don't have our minds.'

'It's not about minds,' said Karel. 'It's about what those minds *think*. But Axel,' he said, noting Susan's glance again. 'We were talking about Artemis. Why *do* they want to attack us? Can you tell me?'

'Well,' said Axel, carefully. 'I suppose they want our metal.'

'Partly right,' said Karel. 'Artemis is a barren country. They have had to fight for everything they need. That has been their weakness . . . and their strength.'

At last they approached the circle of brushed stone that immediately surrounded the parliament arena. Axel stamped down the steps, making the metal ring as he went. Other robots glanced at him and then looked away, and Karel became painfully aware there were few other children attending. Or was the look given because he, Karel himself, was attending? He placed a hand on his son's shoulder.

'Gently,' he said.

Now they walked over bare rock towards the arena itself.

'You know, this was one of the oldest parts of Turing City,' said Karel to Axel. 'Metal rots, but rock endures. The parliament is sited on one of the first mines dug here. When that mine was emptied, they dug down to the galleries and opened them to the sky. They peeled back the earth and carved away the stone to leave this. They wanted to make a point, Axel. What do you suppose that point was?'

'I don't know, Dad.'

'That this place was important. That the parliament is a part of Turing City, that it is the very centre of Turing City.'

'Yes, Dad.'

'That's important, Axel. Remember that. No matter what people say today in this meeting, no matter what they may say about Artemis, just take a look around you. It takes a lot of time to work stone. The people who made this place obviously thought that our parliament was important.'

Maoco O

Deep beneath the earth, Maoco O was dancing.

Long ago, the miners of Turing City had wormed their way down through the rock, following the deposits it contained. The galleries immediately beneath the city had long since been emptied of copper and nickel and silver, so the miners had turned their attention to the coast, eventually tunnelling out beneath the seabed.

Now the City Guard had requisitioned the excavated spaces beneath their own rocky outcrop. They had chiselled and filed the passageways smooth, they had widened them and filled them with armour and weapons and, all the while, with the efficient silence of their duty.

Stone corridor after stone corridor filled with polished bodies, sanded stone, oiled machinery and emptiness. The robots that moved through those quiet passageways did so without disturbing the peace that had taken hold therein, and they barely stirred the air. They passed almost unnoticed, except by the other robots that shared those deep places. No wonder each robot found itself alone, reflected Maoco O. No wonder they felt themselves separate from the city above, separate from their companions, separate even from their own selves in these perfectly engineered bodies.

The only sense of connection the robots felt was like now, when they danced. All war was a dance, he understood. The dance of two combatants moving around each other, seeking the perfect stance from which to swoop forward for the climax. Two robots, two sides, it was all the same thing. And so Maoco O and the others danced in the darkness; moving with grace and elegance through the silent spaces, they practised their craft.

In the silent darkness, Maoco O chasséd and spun in perfect synchronization with his partners.

Karel

Karel and his family made their way down the grey tiers of the parliament and found a place to stand on the third terrace. Looking up, they could see the brightly painted robots still spilling over the rim of the bowl.

'Susan!'

Karel recognized the robot who had called out as one of Susan's work colleagues. He was beckoning to her from a nearby set of steps that led to the base of the arena. He was an effeminate sort, his body constructed too thin and covered in flimsy steel.

'Susan, there is a place reserved for you on the first level. You must join us.'

Susan glanced at her husband. 'No, Shear,' she said after some hesitation. 'Go ahead without me. I'm not really needed. My mind is full at the moment. I'll stay here with my family.'

'You go,' said Karel, gazing hard at Shear. 'You know they need you. I'll stay here with Axel.'

Susan sounded tired. 'How long are you going to stay annoyed with me? I told you I was sorry.'

'I'm not annoyed.'

They stared at each other, neither willing to back down. Reluctantly, Susan made her way along the row and then followed Shear down to the first terrace. Karel saw her take her place amongst other robots from the Statistics office.

And now three robots walked into the centre of the bowl.

'Pick me up,' said Axel.

Karel did so, impressed at how heavy his son was getting. To think that he could control that much metal already. His boy was growing up.

'Look at them, Dad,' said Axel in a hushed voice. Karel understood why. Their golden skins had been brilliantly polished; they reflected the sunlight in giddy patterns.

'They're just robots,' said Karel. 'Tonight they will take off those skins and put on iron and copper, just like the rest of us.'

The meeting began.

'Robots of Turing City. This parliament has been called by petition of the people. Susan, will you verify this?'

'That's Mum!' said Axel, yellow eyes glowing.

Susan had stood up. She looked so delicate in her finely painted skin, and yet so self-assured. Karel felt a sudden pang of love that wiped out his resentment of a moment ago.

Susan began. 'Speaker, sixty-one per cent of the population wish to debate the motion recommending that *This parliament will declare war upon Artemis.*'

'That is sufficient for the debate,' said the speaker. 'Will the proponent please state his case?'

There was a murmur from the assembled robots. Now the proponent moved forward.

'That's Kobuk,' whispered Karel. 'He used to be part of the City Guard.'

Even dressed in a harlequin pattern of silver on gold, Kobuk was obviously a soldier. You could tell it by the way he marched to the centre of the arena and stamped to attention. You could hear it in the tone of his voice as it rang through the air.

'Fellow citizens, Artemis's plans to conquer Shull are well known to all of us. Wien has recently fallen to their troops. Now only one state remains free on the southern part of the continent. Turing City! It does not take Oneill to see where Artemis will next turn its attention. I say we have left our metal too long out of the fire. We must close our borders, raise an army and prepare for war. Why sit here awaiting Artemis's closer attention? Let us go out now and meet them on the battlefields of Zernike before the city. Zernike defeated Artemis there in the past. If we fight, we will defeat them again. But if we remain here and hesitate we will be destroyed. Let us rip up the rails that lead to Artemis, use that metal to make guns and then march upon that badly twisted state!'

Some of the robots in the stadium began to stamp their feet. Karel looked around him. Many, but not as many as he would have expected. The applause gradually faded.

'Was he right, Dad?' asked Axel. 'Should we fight?'

'I don't know, Son. Let's hear what the opponent has to say. It's Noatak. She's an architect.'

Despite her profession, Noatak looked even more like a soldier than Kobuk, the former City Guard. Her golden body was big and heavy. It would take a powerful mind to control that much metal, reflected Karel.

'Citizens,' began Noatak. 'I don't think that there is a robot here who does not respect Kobuk. His work with the City Guard is celebrated, and justly so. But times move on. Just as the City Guard has reformed itself around a new paradigm of technical excellence, so has Turing City. Look at the magnificence and prosperity which we now enjoy!'

There was more stamping at that. Noatak waited for it to die away.

'And yet, that does not mean we should forget all of our past. Turing City has always been an open state. Open to all robots, open to new ideas. Remember, it is this that has kept us strong, not the walls and ditches and isolation that Kobuk would wish upon us. I say that Artemis is *welcome* to come here! They will find our philosophy the stronger, as others have before them. And, should they try to attack, they will find our City Guard more than their measure.'

More applause. Karel listened carefully. Was this louder than before? He thought so.

'Is she right, Dad?' asked Axel.

'I don't know, Son.'

'But haven't you always said that we should welcome outsiders? It's what *you* do, after all.'

'I know but . . .' He became silent. It was Kobuk's turn to respond. The harlequin robot waved a dismissive hand.

'Noatak puts words in my mouth. I never said that we should build walls, nor that we isolate ourselves. I welcome the robots who join us from other states! But that does not mean that we should sit here and await our doom! I say yes, keep the borders open, but I also say yes, let us cross those borders, accompanied by all those who would now call themselves Turing Citizens, be they originally from Wien or Stark or Bethe, and that we go forth and face Artemis on the battlefield. That we face up to Artemis and defeat it!'

More applause.

'He's right, isn't he, Dad?' said Axel.

'Yes,' said Karel. 'Yes, I think so.'

Noatak took up her place again.

'And I say that we have nothing to fear from Artemis. And yet, why force their hand by declaring war? If they come, we will defeat them. Why should we go and destroy our quality of life by inviting something that otherwise may never happen?'

She left this question hanging in the air. There was a murmur of conversation from the assembled robots. Brightly painted bodies stirred in the ancient grey stone bowl of the arena.

Now the Speaker took his place.

'We have heard from the proponent and opponent. I now open the parliament to all on the terraces.'

Many robots raised their hands. The Speaker turned to Susan's team, who were gazing at the crowd, noting names, comparing histories. That was what Susan did, thought Karel with a touch of pride. She knew *everybody* in Turing City. She and her team could map the opinions of the whole population.

'What's happening now?' asked Axel.

'Mummy and her team are deciding who will best contribute to the debate. Here we are . . .'

Susan stepped forward. 'Delius,' she called out.

Delius stood on the second terrace, an elegant woman with a finely balanced body.

'Kobuk,' she called. 'Wien has just fallen. By all accounts it was a close-run thing, so Artemis will still be weak. Do you *really* believe an attack is imminent?'

Kobuk gazed up at her.

'It could happen as soon as next month.'

Delius wasn't fooled. 'The night moon could fall from the sky next month. When is the attack *likely* to happen?'

Kobuk shifted. 'Not for another three years at least . . .' There was a stirring in the parliament. '*But that's not the point.* Whether they attack now or in three years' time we must be fully prepared!'

The parliament wasn't convinced, Karel could tell. Now the Speaker was looking to Susan again.

'Saddleworth,' she declared.

Saddleworth was a short, stocky robot standing up on the fourth terrace. He spoke in self-important tones.

'Now hold on,' he began. 'I think we're all missing the point here. We've been told that Artemis now basically controls the continent. We've also been told that we should have nothing to do with them, that we should shut out the outside world. Well, I operate a foundry, as you all know, and a foundry needs coal. Now, answer me this. Where is the coal going to come from if we have closed our borders?'

There was a murmur of assent from around the arena.

'I never said we should close the borders,' insisted Kobuk. 'Besides, where *is* your coal to come from now that Wien is captured?'

'I dare say the Artemisians will still trade with us,' said Saddleworth stubbornly.

'Dad, I don't understand. Aren't they frightened?'

Karel looked into the yellow glow of his son's eyes.

'I think they are. That's why they are pretending that nothing is happening.'

'Dad, what's the matter with Mum?'

Karel looked down to where Susan stood. She seemed dazed, as if she had seen something that shocked her. He followed her gaze, but he saw nothing unusual in the terraces over there. Nothing apart from a City Guard robot who stood at the top of the terraces, obviously just arrived. A City Guard robot attending parliament was unusual, it was true, but surely not enough to induce this reaction in his wife.

Saddleworth was still speaking. Now he had the floor, he obviously didn't want to give it up.

'So what I want to know is whether the City Guard is up to the task of defending us? Can anyone answer me that?'

Susan was still staring at the City Guard robot. She looked totally stunned. When she finally spoke her voice sounded strange.

'Thank you, Saddleworth,' she said. 'You've had your turn. Maoco O.'

The crowd looked up towards Maoco O. He was a tall robot, his body so beautifully engineered it held the eye, begging to be looked at. So smooth, so seamless. The way the metal curved in at his hips, flared at his shoulders, the dull glow with which it shone, even in the blazing sun. When he spoke, his voice was so clear, so finely modulated.

'Citizens,' he said. 'I bow before Kobuk.' At this he turned and bent in an ostentatious fashion towards the ex-City Guard who still stood on the parliament floor. He straightened up and addressed the crowd once more. 'The City Guard has served us well in the past, and I pledge to continue that tradition. Turing City has stood here many years, during which our mines have produced the best gold and nickel. With these metals we have wound the finest minds. Here, at least, all robots may stand equal. I say to you, citizens, the City Guard will stand strong.'

The assembled robots stamped their feet again in applause. Karel paid little heed to the robot's words. He was still gazing at Susan, rapt in concentration as she stared at Maoco O. What was the matter with her? The Speaker was trying to gain her attention, trying to find out who would be the next to contribute to the debate. Finally she noticed him; she seemed to take a moment to regain her balance and consult with her team. At last she spoke.

'Leavore,' she said.

And the crowd began to murmur again. Leavore? That was an Artemisian name!

Karel saw ripples in the silver pool of light reflected by the assembled robots. Heads were turning to the stranger in their midst. And there she stood: an Artemisian war robot. A Scout dressed in a silver skin of katana metal, the blades at her hands and feet barely sheathed. She reminded Karel of the robot he had seen so recently at the Immigration Centre. Maybe it was even the same one, now released and given citizenship. She would have the right to attend parliament, so why should she not be here? For a moment his thoughts travelled back to Banjo Macrodocious, the strange robot that had denied its own intelligence. What had happened to him?

Leavore spoke. 'I wish to question Maoco O. I am a new citizen of Turing City. I thought we were all equal here. And yet Maoco O claims that your minds are wound of better metal. Is this true? Are we not all equal?'

There was silence. The point had struck home.

'Dad?' said Axel, but Karel was trying to think. He had never thought of that before. Turing City minds were wound with equality in them, and yet the war robot had a point. They did believe their minds were better than others'.

'Don't listen to her. It's an Artemisian trick!'

'She's a spy!'

'Even if she's not, she's a traitor to her own state!'

The Speaker raised his hands. 'The parliament will come to order!'

In the ensuing confusion, and much to his own surprise, Karel found he had raised his own hand. As the noise died away he saw Susan, down below, staring at him. He held his hand higher. Susan seemed to consult with her team. Then she spoke.

'Karel,' she called out.

This brought silence to the crowd. Now all those many heads turned towards Karel. So many eyes, yellow and green and red, their glow dimmed by the bright sunlight.

'You know me,' said Karel, 'and that I'm an immigration officer. If this woman has been deemed fit to be a citizen, then we should listen to her. We may disagree with what she says, but we cannot dismiss it. I will try to answer her question for her. Leavore, what makes us better isn't our minds or our gold or our nickel. It's our philosophy, our . . .'

The Speaker interrupted. 'I am sorry, Karel, but this is not pertinent to the debate. Do you have anything to add that is relevant to the motion?'

Karel felt his electromuscles tense in anger. Slowly, he allowed them to discharge. Across the stone bowl of parliament, he saw Leavore, the war robot, gazing back at him with something like contempt.

'Dad, what's going on?'

Karel looked again at Axel, and the last of his anger ebbed. He looked back into the arena.

'Yes,' he called, 'I do have something to say. Noatak, assuming that Artemis does not attack soon, what will you be advising us in three years' time? Will you still counsel patience?'

'If it is the correct thing to do.' Noatak chuckled. 'Karel, your mind seems already made up. I wonder when that happened?'

There was a ripple of laughter around the terraces, and Karel felt himself gripped with cold fury.

'Why are they laughing, Dad? Are they laughing at you?'

'It's okay, Axel.' Karel could barely speak. His electromuscles were sparking within him, overloaded with angry current. The Speaker was shouting for order again.

'Noatak will withdraw that remark!'

'Of course I withdraw,' said Noatak, bowing in Karel's direction, and Karel felt himself seething. Axel still didn't quite understand. But he got the gist of it.

'Dad, are you okay?'

Karel said nothing.

Susan

Susan spent the remainder of the debate gazing up at her husband. She could feel his anger, even from here.

It was hot down on the parliament floor, standing on sun-heated stone, hearing the constant plink of hot metal. Her team worked well, but Susan felt removed from them. She was ready to weave another child, her mind sparking with ideas, and yet she was frightened of the future. Her husband was a mystery to her, at least part of him was, and, somewhere behind her, she could feel the gaze of the mysterious Maoco O focused on her back. What did he want with her?

Time passed as the sun descended, and longer shadows cut across the far wall of the parliament bowl. The debate was coming to an end, and Susan was surprised at the turnaround. At the beginning, sixty-one per cent of robots had been all for declaring war immediately, but now she guessed that the motion would be opposed. Noatak had spoken well. Surprisingly well. She had come across as sympathetic, understanding, brilliantly undermining Kobuk's position as an ex-soldier, portraying him as behind the times and unnecessarily cautious. Her offer to have a permanent cohort of no less than one-fifth of the City Guard constantly on duty at the railway station, in case of a surprise attack, had both defused many of Kobuk's arguments and made it obvious to all that she was not totally ignoring a possible threat. Of course, she had been helped out by a number of robots in the crowd who had supported her, Susan realized. Robots who did not usually attend parliament. Noatak had been lucky today.

Kobuk and Noatak began their summing-up speeches, and suddenly Susan felt very tired, her mind only half on the job. She looked up again and saw that Karel had gone, she didn't know when. Axel would have been tired too, she guessed, so he must have taken him home. That was probably just as well. Karel would not have reacted well to a vote opposing the motion. He could get so angry sometimes . . .

And now the summing-up had finished, and the Speaker was calling for the vote. Myriad arms were raised, and Susan and her team scanned the crowd and conferred.

They were all agreed. Susan was surprised at how shaken she was by the final vote.

She relayed it to the Speaker, who announced it as the sun set over the bowl.

'Citizens, the motion for combat is opposed.'

Grey shadow filled the bowl. Susan felt empty.

'Citizens, it is time to return to our homes. Turing City will remain open. We will welcome Artemis!'

Susan's gyroscopes lurched. She looked up, and there was Maoco O, staring down at her. There was something so desolate about the City Guard's stare. And then he recovered himself, turned away and slid from the arena.

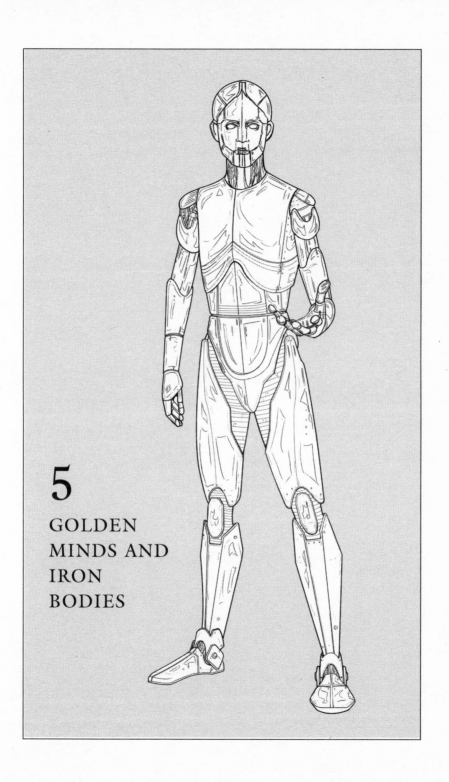

5

GOLDEN MINDS AND IRON BODIES

Olam

A thin wind whined southwards: barely there, but sharp like an awl. It hissed through the gravel on the Zernike battleground, scratched at the rock and prised at the cracks. It was the last remnant of the winds that had torn over the icy plains of the North, whipping up the snow into blizzards before rushing on to tear the foam from the iron-grey waters of the Moonshadow sea. It was a scout wind, searching out the land, preparing for the invasion of winter.

The wind hissed between the chinks and joints of Olam's new metal body, cooling the electromuscle inside, making him feel numb and sluggish. He needed to get up and move around, but he wasn't allowed to. He had been ordered to lie down on the bare rock and wait, and so that's what he did.

It wasn't that great a distance from Wien to the Zernike plain, but Olam felt as if he had come a very long way.

After the trials of the stadium, he had been marched with the other recruits to a training camp. There he had been drilled in Artemisian philosophy and engineering by one of those seemingly identical grey-painted robots. The lectures had gone on, day and night, while in the distance they could see Wien being quickly and efficiently disassembled. But there had been little time to watch, his attention constantly called back to what they were being taught: how to be Artemisians.

And then the lessons were over. He had been marched with the rest to a forge; his panelling stripped away and sent off to be melted down. Artemisian soldiers had probed his body, detached his electromuscles, showed him the standard design for Artemisian infantry and then patiently watched over him as he rebuilt himself as an Artemisian citizen, all the time correcting him and offering advice. They had been kind and helpful, much to Olam's surprise.

Now he was a little shorter and squatter, even a little weaker. His eyesight had improved, his hearing was a little more acute, but aside from that he couldn't help thinking that he would have made a better soldier as he had been before.

Doe Capaldi, the tall aristocrat, lay nearby. Except he wasn't the tall robot any more, just another interchangeable infantryrobot exactly like Olam. To Olam's surprise, Doe Capaldi had altered himself with little complaint, stripping away whale metal and replacing it with the iron and copper the Artemisians gave him, thus making himself Olam's equal.

Except he wasn't, of course. He never would be. Doe Capaldi's mind had been woven for leadership, just as Olam's own had been woven for servitude.

The wind blew, and the electromuscle in his abdomen ached. They had lain there unmoving on the plain for hours. They had seen the sun set in the west, red fire over distant Wien, his broken home. Zuse had risen, its silver light reflecting off the railway lines that ran across the plain.

He listened to the wind. He listened with his new ears to the voices carried through the night. He recognized the voice of Eleanor, the robot who had conscripted them. She was speaking in tones of disbelief.

'Madness! We are not ready to attack Turing City! Our numbers are too depleted. We should return to Artemis and re-equip!'

'That is not the will of Artemis,' replied another voice. 'The city is closed to us. Spoole has sent a message, that we are not to cross the marshalling yards. We are not to enter the city!'

'Spoole is frightened of you. He will have heard about what you did to General Fallan.'

'Possibly. Nonetheless, we attack Turing City.'

The robot that spoke to Eleanor sounded male. His voice was low and colourless, and yet he was clearly in charge. Olam hadn't seen the leader of his group, nor had he been told what they would be doing. He had merely been assigned a place on a train, and then shipped out here to this plain in the middle of the continent.

Maybe Doe Capaldi was right after all when he had said Artemis needed cannon fodder to launch an attack on Turing City.

'We'll be wiped out,' Olam muttered. 'Doe Capaldi, you were right. We're just cannon fodder!'

The other robot didn't reply, so Olam lay in the dark, wondering whether it would have been better to have just remained in Wien.

The cold wind sang through his elbows and knees. All he could hear now was the same whistling sound from the bodies of the other robots that lay around him, and he began to wonder if he had imagined those voices in the night.

Thin ribbons of dark cloud were approaching from the north, oily bands that slicked across the moon's surface. They drew patterns across the sky so that the stars seemed to gather in bright pools amidst the darkness.

And then there was a stirring of bodies. The whine of muscle, the scraping of metal. The rails were singing.

A train was coming.

Eleanor

The train was four and a half miles long, weighed over nine thousand tons, and was moving at one hundred miles an hour. Eleanor had been given the job of stopping it.

'It's just passed me by,' crackled the voice on the radio.

Eleanor held the radio away from her skull. The signal made her mind sing.

'Did the driver see you, Paxan?'

'I'm pretty sure she did. I don't know if she took any notice of me, though.'

'Okay.' Eleanor thought for a moment. She clicked the send button on the radio and spoke to the next soldier in the long line that she had arranged along the track, ready to meet the oncoming train. 'Crewe, aim your rifle at the driver. That should send a message.'

'Okay, Eleanor.'

She looked into the distance. The dark plain was cut by two perfect lines of silver, and she could see the lights of the train there in the distance, seemingly unmoving. And yet the train was rushing to meet her with incredible momentum. How long would it take to stop the behemoth, she wondered.

The radio crackled. Crewe spoke again.

'I aimed the rifle. I don't think it worked, though. That train is still going by, and it doesn't look to me like it's slowing.'

'Thank you, Crewe,' said Eleanor. She looked back across the plain, coming to a decision. She clicked the radio back on. 'Seth,' she called. 'Shoot out the windshield.'

The headlights of the train were noticeably larger now. A high-pitched hum insinuated its way through the night, and Eleanor realized she was hearing the reaction motor. The radio crackled to life.

'I got it.'

'Well done, Seth.'

'I think that got her attention!'

Eleanor heard the hum of the reaction motor change in pitch. The train was slowing down.

Olam

Olam rose at the command and ran forward across the dark plain towards the longest train he had ever seen in his life. It was like a green metal wall, seemingly stretching into infinity. No, that couldn't be right. He dialled up the focus on his new, more powerful eyes and there, in the far distance, he spotted the locomotive, a swollen but still streamlined shape. There was a small group of infantry around the cab.

'Other way! We take the rear!'

That was Doe Capaldi, already in charge of a section. Just as Olam had suspected, the former aristocrat was rising rapidly through the Artemisian ranks. The other grey robot was just ahead of him, and Olam's hands tightened on his rifle. One squeeze on the trigger and Doe Capaldi would be dead.

Not now, though, not with all these witnesses around.

Olam ran on, tripping and stumbling on the loose rocks that strewed the plain. He dialled his new eyes back down to close focus. On and on they all went, approaching the seemingly endless green wall of the train. It seemed to curve slightly, and then, as the ribbons of cloud peeled away from the moon, they followed around the curve and finally Olam could see the end of the green wall.

There were coaches here at the rear of the train. They had been opened up and the passengers forcibly disembarked and separated into two groups. One group, the Artemisians, were already beginning the long walk back along the tracks towards Artemis City. The remaining passengers were being efficiently herded together and shot.

Olam wasn't thinking clearly that night; it took a while for his brain to process all the information: the train was heading for Turing City; and those people being shot were Turing Citizens.

Turing Citizens?

And then he had it.

They were doing it. They were really doing it. They were really going to war on Turing City State.

The thin wind carried the crack of rifles through the darkness, the night moon shone down on the green wall of the train, and Olam and the rest of the infantry ran even faster across the plain.

Eleanor

Eleanor climbed into the cabin of the reaction engine and looked around its cream-painted interior with interest. So many dials, so many levers. She had never seen anything so technically advanced. It made her proud to be an Artemisian.

'Who are you? By what right do you stop this train?' The driver of the train came forward in order to block Eleanor moving further into the cabin. She was a well-built woman, she obviously had some skill with metal. She wore little panelling, as was the current fashion amongst the intelligentsia of Artemis City. A band of metal around her chest, a band from her waist to her thighs. All the rest was bare machinery and electromuscle. The mechanism of her fine body was shown off to all: the elegantly knitted muscle that ran smoothly over her metal bones. Eleanor was left in no doubt; this robot was a thing of craft and beauty.

'Who am I? My name is Eleanor, infantryrobot. Who are you?'

'Dorore.'

'Ah,' said Eleanor, 'now I understand. A goldenmind. Am I right?'

'Yes,' replied Dorore, with obvious pride. 'My mind was twisted from gold taken from Bethe, just after the invasion. Those in the making rooms say my mind is patterned on those of the thinkers of Bethe and Segre and Stark.'

'And your mind has earned you a place on the reaction project. As a train driver, no less.' Eleanor was impressed, despite herself. Once more she looked around the controls of the cabin. The needles on the dials before her were all neatly centred; the reaction chamber was humming at the correct frequency, the generated current smooth and powerful: she could feel it.

Dorore was craning to peer past Eleanor, trying to look out of the open door.

'What's going on out there?' she demanded. Like Eleanor, she could hear the sound of the troops outside in the night, moving moving back and forth, swinging open the access hatches as they boarded the train. Eleanor moved to one side to let the driver past. Dorore dropped down the ladder into the night beyond. Eleanor heard her shouting out orders into the dark.

'Hey! Stop that! Get off of there!'

Nobody answered.

'Hey! I'm talking to you! What are you doing with my train?'

A quiet voice carried through the night. 'Not your train. Not your train at all.'

Eleanor recognized Kavan's voice, and she felt a spark of annoyance. Why was he here? Didn't he trust her? Did he think she was not capable of handling this situation? She quickly climbed down from the cab to find Kavan speaking to Dorore in soft, compassionless tones.

'Why should my troops not do this?' he was asking. 'They are doing what is necessary for the coming battle. Do you think that you know better? Do you think that having a golden mind makes you special? No, I don't think so. Only Artemis is special.'

To Eleanor's surprise, Dorore found the courage to answer Kavan.

'I'm not saying that. But why have you stopped me? Let me go on my way! I too work for Artemis!'

The grey soldier spoke contemptuously.

'Doing what? Driving an engine back and forth? There is gold on your wrists, there is a gold band around your waist. You have gold in your mind, and you choose to advertise the fact, golden-mind. Is that why they picked you to drive this engine?'

Dorore hesitated.

'Yes,' she said, eventually. 'And why not? It's not easy to control. I bake the control rods myself. I maintain the primary coolant loop, I keep the temperature constant . . .'

'What would happen if you didn't?'

She had missed the meaning in his words, Eleanor knew, eager as she was to impress upon him the importance of her job.

'The train would run slow!' said Dorore. 'But when I get it right . . . Look at the length of this train! Four and a half miles of Artemisian beauty. It takes a reaction engine to pull this much mass. This train is an expression of Artemis power!'

She now had the first inkling that she was saying the wrong thing. Her words, carried by the cold wind, seemed to chill the mood of the half-seen robot.

'Artemis has no need to express its power. Artemis merely is.'

'I know that,' she hurriedly replied, 'that's not what I meant. I meant to say this train better serves Artemis . . .'

'No, I don't think so. Four or eight or sixteen diesel trains would carry the load just as well, and at far less cost to time and resources.'

'That's not true . . .'

'This is just an expensive toy. A way for goldenminds to amuse themselves and justify their existence. There is too much of this sort of thing in Artemis of late. The state is losing its purpose.'

'No!'

The grey robot was silent. Despite the constant activity around them, it was strangely calm on the plain. The night stars billowed above them, like the highlights on a foil sail cracking in the wind. Eleanor could see the silhouettes of robots as they climbed into the interior of the engine. She imagined them running their coarse hands over the marvels of the pressurized water reactor.

'What are they doing?' asked Dorore in alarm.

'They are rigging it to explode.'

Dorore laughed. Rather, forced herself to laugh. It was a gesture of defiance. If anything, it seemed to impress the grey robot.

'You don't understand, do you?' she said. 'That's a PWR, you can't make it explode! It's all to do with the negative temperature coefficient of reactivity. As the reactor gets too hot, the water becomes less dense and the chain reaction slows down. You can't have a runaway explosion like you got on the old reactors. Besides which, I baked the control rods myself. They don't contain enough fissile uranium to sustain a critical chain reaction!'

'They will do, goldenmind.'

And at that Kavan turned and made his way to the engine to direct operations, leaving Eleanor and Dorore standing together in the empty night, on the empty plain, the cold breeze whistling through their bodies.

Dorore turned to Eleanor, desperate for her to understand.

'Tell him,' she said. 'Tell him this train is needed back in Artemis City. My crew will be waiting for me. Pinza, Alycidon and Tulyar . . .'

Eleanor said nothing. Behind Dorore, the grey robots were withdrawing from the innards of the reaction train. The panels and hatches were being carefully locked back into place.

Kavan returned. 'Okay, goldenmind, it's ready. You can get back on board.'

It took a moment for Dorore to register what he meant.

'Back on board the engine? But it's rigged to explode!'

'Yes. And we need someone to drive it to its destination.'

'What? But you can't mean . . . It will explode! I'll be killed!'

'Yes. But this way you will best serve Artemis.'

'Set one of your own troops to drive it!'

'They would not know how. There is the pressure to keep constant, the primary coolant loop to maintain . . .'

Dorore paused, registering his tone. 'You're being sarcastic.'

'No. Besides which, my troops are too valuable to waste. Their training and experience offers Artemis much. What can *you* offer?'

'I am a goldenmind!'

And at that there was another of those cold silences. And then . . .

'No. There is no goldenmind, there is no golden body. The wire is not special, only the pattern that is twisted there. There is too much of this thinking back in Artemis City. Some day I may turn my attention there.'

Despite her original annoyance at his intervention, Eleanor felt a thrill at Kavan's words.

'What do you mean?' asked Dorore, who didn't understand.

'I mean that the last state that Artemis will conquer may well be Artemis itself.' He seemed to come back to the present. 'But now, for you, it is time to get on the train.'

And at that Dorore lost her temper. She had nothing else to lose.

'You! I know your sort! You are like Nicolas the Coward! You turn away from anything new. You fear it. You fear my mind!'

Kavan didn't seem to care. 'You will set off in five minutes.'

'Why not now?'

'You will give my troops sufficient time to climb upon the back of the train. Four and a half miles should be sufficient to keep us all clear of the blast.'

And at that he turned and began to walk back along the length of the train.

Dorore turned and looked at Eleanor, pleadingly. 'What shall I do?' she asked.

'Do what he says,' said Eleanor, turning to glare at Kavan's retreating back. 'That's what we're all doing.'

Susan

'Where are you going?'

Karel looked up at her from where he knelt, feeding coal into the forge.

'I'm going to the railway station,' said Susan, pained by the suspicion in his voice.

'The station? Why?'

The look he gave her was so hard and unforgiving that she felt as if she were rusting from the inside. She couldn't even meet his eyes.

'I need to think. I need ideas to make our child, Karel. There are concepts collected there from all across the continent. Oh, Karel, please don't be like this. I'm sorry.'

And, just like that, the spell was broken. He rose to his feet and crossed the room and was holding her hands, his body close so she could feel the currents running through his electromuscle, the edge of his lifeforce.

'I'm sorry too, Susan.'

They held on to each other, tight.

'You're a good man, Karel, I never doubted it.'

'I know, Susan. Come on . . . Oh!' He stared at her body and laughed guiltily. He had smudged ash from his dirty hands all down her powder-blue panelling.

Susan saw it and started to laugh too. She reached for a clump of twisted metal and gently wiped herself clean.

'Let me come to the station with you,' said Karel.

'No, it's okay, you don't have to.'

'I want to.'

'What about Axel?'

'He'll sleep for another one hundred and twenty-seven minutes. He's fine. I want to come.'

'I'd like that. Thank you.'

Karel gently wiped her hands clean with his. She could feel the current in the electromuscle of his fingers as he did so.

The marble flagstones of the residential area were covered in a fine dust, carried by the cold wind that blew from the north. Oily black clouds were spreading across the sky like a slick over water; the sun seemed to shine a muddy brown that day. Susan rejected this image instantly; she didn't want her child to grow up thinking of this.

'I want to hear the ocean,' she announced.

'The wind's the wrong way,' said Karel. 'Do you want to catch a train to the coast?'

'No, Axel will wake before then.'

'What are you looking at?'

Susan was staring at the white walls of the fort of the City Guard, clearly visible in the distance above the glass-and-iron roofs of the railway station.

'The fort,' she said.

Karel said nothing, just squeezed her hand, made her electromuscles pulse in time with his own.

The railway station was set at the head of a wide, shallow valley that cut through the hills at the northern edge of Turing City State. The valley had been excavated centuries ago by porphyry worms, copper animals that had ground away at the fissured rock of the land, sifting through the residue for the frills of copper that had been left behind when acidic magma had bubbled up from deep beneath the world.

Susan had never seen the worms herself, but their memory was woven into the wire of her mind: a memory she intended to pass on to her child.

The worms had been small to begin with, but long years of dining on the thin veins and frills of copper had allowed them to grow fat and huge. By the time the first robots had walked south into southern Shull, the worms stood taller than a robot and were as long as a whale. They had eaten the rock away down to a depth of a hundred metres. Those robots who had first viewed the land that would become Turing City State found a valley filled with porphyry worms, their beaten-copper bodies dull in the sunlight. They watched in wonder as the worms reared up high to nibble at the rocks of the valley walls. Susan now had that image in her mind. It was strange and gorgeous and filled her with a ravenous feeling.

Those first robots had felt the same. A base greed had come upon them, and they had lost control of themselves, falling on the defenceless worms without restraint. Robots had melted their way into the bodies of the worms and had gazed in lust at the brass and copper and tin of their interiors. They had walked through the ringing tubes of their bodies to their minds woven of electrum wire, and a frenzy of greed had overtaken them. They ripped those minds apart, spooling out the electrum wire into the daylight. They had mounted the carcasses with sharp knives and shears and cut the worms' bodies open lengthways and then peeled them apart, laid them flat and plated the valley floor with copper, the remaining worms looking on, uncomprehending. They had taken those worms and built themselves castles with copper walls. They had unwound the electrum wire of the porphyry worms' minds, and with it they wove children with golden minds.

They did all this without restraint, without guilt, and in doing so they rendered the porphyry worms extinct.

Only then did they look out at the once beautiful valley and see what they had done . . .

And this memory I will weave into you, my child, Susan thought to herself, *for this was Turing City's darkest moment, and it was as a reaction to the horror of this that we became what we became. This was where we learned to respect the mind as something more than just metal.*

'Are you okay, Susan?' Karel was looking at her with such concern. 'Are you thinking of the child?'

'I was.'

They looked down at the valley now. Its rocky walls had long since been mined away, leaving a series of terraces. Bridges from one level led to the roofs of houses on the next level down. A maze of metal walkways and steps led them down to the railway station below. Many silver rails set in white concrete sleepers led north from the station, heading out over the Zernike plain beyond. A wide river, green with copper, ran southwards between brick embankments, twisting slowly underneath the pattern of the railway lines.

And then there was the railway station itself. Seen from above, it resembled an iron-and-glass sphere, cut into segments and then pressed flat on the ground. Arched glass canopies ran in all directions: they covered platforms serving railway lines that ran to all the former countries of southern Shull. Over to one side there were platforms for Bethe and Segre and Stark, the three of them crowded together, made of good steel and pale green glass. And over there was the wide arch of the Wien terminal, the long thin platform that jointly served Raman and Born, twisting like a snake in a north-westerly direction. And last, but by no means least, there was the Artemis terminal. Plain and functional in clear glass and dull iron it may have been, but it was by far the most impressive. Its utilitarian shape dominated the head of the valley, a visible proof of the power of the two states that it joined. Robots streamed into it, and a constant array of goods rolled in and out. Plain, functional machinery from Artemis exchanged for the delicate and quirky metalwork of Turing City.

'Look,' said Karel. 'Look at all the City Guards down there! I've never seen so many of them!'

'It's what Noatak promised at parliament, remember? That the station would be guarded.'

Susan and Karel descended by the maze of metal walkways that led over the roofs of the buildings on the lower terraces, heading down to the wide marble square that lay before the station itself.

Behind them, the shops and galleries of the retail district rose in riotous colour. Before them, the iron and glass of the station stood in measured solemnity.

'What's the matter, Susan?'

'I don't know . . .' Susan wanted to ask him what was the noise that she could hear, but she felt too disoriented, like her gyros where spinning too quickly. She could hear the rumble of trains on the rails – that was normal, here outside the station – but there was something else too. A high-pitched whining noise that seemed to resonate with the wire of her mind.

'Is it that noise?' asked Karel, tilting his head. Susan nodded.

'It is a little odd, isn't it?' He listened some more. 'Don't worry, it's just a train approaching. A reaction engine, I think.'

Susan pulled at his hand.

'Karel, let's go.'

'But we only just got here!'

The noise of the reaction engine filled her mind; it seemed to resonate with the wire of her brain, shrilling terror straight through her body to her electromuscles.

'Karel, let's get out of here. Please.'

'Susan, you're being silly. Look – look at all the guards. We shall be safe here.' He pointed to a nearby guard, looming tall and silver in the sunlight.

Susan jerked at his arm. 'Run, Karel. Please, let's run . . .'

She pulled Karel along a few steps. The other robots in the marble square were looking at them curiously, but Susan didn't care.

'It's all going to go wrong,' she said with utter finality.

Karel started to walk with her back towards the steps that led up the residential district.

'No, not up there,' insisted Susan. 'No, it's the wrong way. We need to run. Back into the city, to the shops.' It struck her then with a feeling like a cold awl plunged into her mind. 'Oh, Zuse, what about Axel?'

Karel was staring at her, humouring her.

'Why don't we go back and see him?' he asked carefully. 'We could check he's all right.'

'No! We have to run!'

A Guard had seen them and came walking in their direction. 'Is everything okay?' she asked.

'I think so . . .' said Karel.

The high-pitched whine was louder now, accompanied by a rumble that was filling her body. Susan wrenched herself free of Karel, began to run. The rumble was filling her entire world. She ran. Stopped. Turned to see where Karel was.

He was there, following her, seemingly in slow motion.

But it was too late.

Behind him she saw the station, its roof glass glowing orange and white, like the sun was shining on it. But shining from inside, like the sun itself was within the station. A beautiful orange glow, licking outwards from the centre of the Artemis terminal. Things were moving so slowly. The glass was shattering, diamond shards floating outwards, tumbling prettily, end over end. And look, behind them, clouds of orange flame blooming, spreading across the windows of the station walls like drops of oil on water before the glass began to bloom and shatter. And now the metal of the arches and vaulting was twisting upwards and outwards, spreading like open hands . . .

And, with a solid *wham*, time slammed back into normal speed, and she was picked up and blown across the great square by the force of the explosion. Her ears exploded. Her eyes whited out. The last thing she saw was the incredulous expression on Karel's face as he was flung towards her.

Kavan

'She did it,' said Eleanor, in tones of mild surprise.

Kavan raised himself to his feet, body swaying as the carriage rolled slowly away from the explosion.

'Dorore actually did it,' repeated Eleanor. 'I didn't think she would.'

'She was a true Artemisian at the core,' said Kavan. His ears were crackling, the after-effects of the explosion that had taken place four and half miles away, right at the head of the train. He opened the door of the carriage and saw the ground rolling by, white sleepers and grey gangue. They were going backwards. Ahead, black smoke was rising from the shattered railway station at the head of the valley.

'Get the troops to move out. We've got a lot of ground to cover.'

Eleanor gave the signal. All the way back along the stripped-bare carriage, soldiers got to their feet, opened the jerry-built doors they had hacked out of the carriage walls and bailed out onto the ground.

'I wish we had more Storm Troopers,' said Eleanor. 'There's barely two thousand of us. There are over thirty thousand robots in Turing City. We don't stand a chance against them.'

'Spoole thought it enough,' said Kavan.

'Spoole is forcing you to commit suicide, Kavan. He wants you dead.'

'Artemis doesn't want. Artemis just *is*.'

'Cut the rust, Kavan. We're not talking about Artemis, we're talking about Spoole.'

'That should be the same thing.'

Eleanor was staring at him like he was being stupid.

'We're up against the City Guard,' she warned.

'That's what I'm counting on, Eleanor. Don't you see, Turing Citizens aren't like Artemisians? They're not like us; they're not even like Dorore: she was true to Nyro right at the end. Turing Citizens don't think that way. They get others to do their fighting for them.'

Karel

Karel pushed his face close to Susan. She couldn't hear him, she could barely see him. The golden light in her eyes was blurred.

'Susan, come on, we've got to get away from here.'

The square was in chaos. Black smoke leaked across it like thick oil, orange fire jumped into the air. Even the electrical currents felt wrong, screwed up by the atomic explosion. Robots were running around in confusion: heading to the station, running from the station, trying to help friends to their feet, or simply emitting electronic wails of fear.

'We need to get back to Axel!' he shouted, shaking his wife by the shoulders.

The same idea had obviously occurred to Susan. She pulled away from him and began pushing her way through the confused crowd towards the valley wall, heading for home. Karel ran to catch her up, but it was difficult to keep sight of her in the thick black smoke and the mêlée of frightened people.

And then the confusion increased. There were shouts and electronic screams, and the tide turned against him. The robots began pushing them back towards the centre of the square.

'Run!'

'Get out of my way!'

'Move, you fool!'

He caught sight of Susan, someone had sent her spinning and crashing to the ground, the enamel on one side of her body scraping a pastel blue streak across the white marble of the square.

The man that had accidentally pushed her over went on running, straight into Karel's arms. Anger singing through the wire of his mind, he tripped the man, pushed him to the ground, fell on his shoulders and took hold of his head and slammed it against the marble paving.

'K*r**l NNNnnnoo!'

Again he smashed the man's head on the marble, scraped it forward.

'K***r**l!'

That was Susan shouting. She had taken him by the arm, she was pulling him away from the man, her voicebox squawking and crackling. Now she was pointing back towards the valley walls, trying to tell him something. There were bodies falling there, brightly painted Turing Citizens slumping and falling, their heads expanding in clouds of blue wire, and Karel's mind finally caught up.

Gunfire! Artemis was attacking.

'AAAax***l,' phased Susan, 'Aaxxellll!'

Karel felt the sheer rage inside him recede. He looked around, taking in the situation.

'Artemis! Where are the Guards?' He saw the answer almost straight away, saw the dead and damaged bodies that littered the space close to the station. All caught in the blast. Karel came to a decision. 'This way,' he shouted. 'We'll loop down through the galleries and back up around the parliament.'

She couldn't hear him, of course. He pointed. Reluctantly she followed. He was taking her away from their son.

They began to run again, this time heading south towards the shops and galleries.

'The rest of the City Guard will be coming,' he told himself.

Olam

'Run!' yelled Doe Capaldi. 'Run! Get into the city, or the City Guard will pick us off out here on the plain!'

All down the line came the sound of leaders calling their troops to action. Olam ran, his electromuscles throbbing with pain, his stride matched perfectly to the distance between the concrete sleepers. That cold, sharp wind that had started in the night was blowing him up the valley, over white sleepers, between the pair of silver rails that he was following. Black smoke ahead of him and grey infantry around him, their feet pounding on concrete as they rushed on and on and on, towards Turing City. He could hear gunfire already; he gripped his rifle tighter, eager to be part of the attack. That was the order: rape and kill. Rape and kill.

Olam couldn't believe how good that sounded. Something had awoken inside him back in the arena. Something that had long lain dormant. Now it sharpened its blades and charged its muscles, ready for the fight.

Suddenly the ground beneath the sleepers vanished, and he saw bright green water down there, between the gaps. He stumbled and fell, almost lost his rifle. There was a river down there, water dancing along, and in the middle of the water a long copper worm turned its head up to look at him and then slipped quietly below the water's surface, leaving Olam wondering if he had imagined the sight. And then someone took hold of him and pulled him upright. Doe Capaldi.

'Come on, Olam. Run!'

And Olam did just that. Doe Capaldi was helping him? No way. He fixed his gaze on that robot's back and continued to run, heading towards the wreckage of the station, the broken green body of the train plunged into its very heart, its tail cast out across the valley.

Karel

Karel and Susan fled through the milling crowds into the shops and the galleries of central Turing City. Everywhere was confusion. People looked round for the Artemisians, looked for the City Guard without success. Where were they? Rumours were rife.

'The City Guard have cut them all down on the plain!'

'The City Guard were all killed in the railway station!'

'They are preparing a counter-offensive up by the fort!'

'The Artemisians have taken the fort!'

'The residential areas are burning!'

Karel was grateful that Susan's ears were damaged. If she heard that, she would have lost control completely. As it was, it took all his effort to keep her running in the opposite direction from where Axel lay sleeping.

The situation was like a childhood dream. Everywhere still looked so normal: the tall, arching iron galleries with their plate glass windows, the neatly tiled streets that ran through them.

Karel pulled Susan to a rest for a moment by a display of molybdenum ingots in the window of Grossmith's, trying to get an understanding of what was going on. Suddenly their situation seemed ridiculous. They were standing on rose porphyry, amidst rose porphyry pillars, looking through leaded glass at some of the most expensive metals on the planet. He was standing in the middle of one of the richest and most powerful states on Shull. Why was everyone panicking? Surely they had nothing to fear, not with the City Guard to protect them?

So where were they? And where were the Artemisians? If there were no City Guard to stop them, they should have made it up to the galleries by now.

Something wasn't right here, realized Karel. Something wasn't right, and he couldn't figure what that was by himself. He looked at his wife as she fiddled with the mechanism of her left ear and he came to a decision. Susan would understand. He needed Susan in working order, right now.

Karel led Susan through the milling crowds to Harman's, the closest body shop he knew. Susan pulled against him all the way.

'Aaaaxx***ll,' she kept phasing, 'Aaxxellll.'

'I know,' said Karel. 'Susan, listen, I need you to help me.'

Susan didn't understand what he was saying, but she recognized Harman's and she realized what he intended. She followed him into the shop without further complaint.

Harman's was expensive. It used only the very best metals, the finest oils and plastics. The paintwork they produced was on a par with that of Susan's skill, though invariably more expensive. The staff there were knowledgeable, skilful and, for the moment, absent. They had fled when the panic had gripped Turing City. Only Harman herself remained, a small woman clad in dark iron, a deceptively simple construction.

Karel saw her and began to gabble. 'My wife, she got caught in the explosion. Her ears, her eyes, her voicebox, they're all wrecked.'

Harman nodded. 'Susan always has been a finely built machine,' she said approvingly. 'I would have been disappointed if she had not succumbed to a magnetic pulse! Her body is such a delicate creation.' She seemed to think it a judgement on Karel that he had not himself suffered damage.

'Come here, Susan,' she said leading her to the centre of the room. 'Sit down.'

The shop forge was tiny, but very, very hot. The instruments and tools that Harman used were small and delicate. Karel watched as she took a sliver of steel from a tray and set about opening up one of Susan's ears, then carefully sliding the mechanism there from his wife's skull. He saw the delicate blue wire of her brain beyond and turned away in embarrassment. He went to the window of the shop, looking out into the square beyond, his gyros spinning.

The robots out there still milled about without any sense of order. Clearly, no one yet knew what was happening. He scanned the crowd: all he could see were Turing Citizens. No City Guard, no Artemisians. What was happening? Why was there no fighting?

Behind him, he could hear Harman singing softly to herself as she adjusted his wife's ears.

'How long will this take?' he called to her.

'As long as it takes,' said Harman. 'I stay here with you, Karel. I leave when you leave.'

'Where is the City Guard?' shouted Karel in frustration.

'I imagine they are wherever the Artemisians are,' said Harman calmly. 'Please don't shout. Your wife's ears are very sensitive at the moment. You will hurt her.'

'Sorry.'

'Panic and haste will lead us nowhere, Karel. I was in Stark when that city fell. The thing to do is to keep one's head, to ensure that one has a fully functioning body and a clear sense of purpose.' She reached for a silver pick. 'I saw too many robots in Stark who ran half-panelled out into the streets, straight into the guns of the enemy.'

Karel knew she was right, but it was hard to keep calm. Out in the square the crowd seemed to have reached some consensus. They were fleeing south, towards the old town and the foundries.

'Something is happening out there . . .' began Karel.

'Stay calm, Karel,' warned Harman, her hand on his wife's chin as she tweaked at something. 'Let the foolish ones take the bullets for us.'

The crowd of Turing Citizens was thinning, draining away between the arcades and galleries at the south end of the square. Karel found himself straining to look north, waiting to see the grey shapes of Artemisian infantry. Nothing.

'I don't need a work of art. Just get her talking again!'

'That's what I'm doing,' said Harman, equably. 'There, all done. Susan, can you put yourself back together whilst I collect a few things?'

Karel turned to see his wife sliding her mouth back into place.

'Thank Zuse,' he called. 'Let's get out of here!'

'One moment longer,' said Harman. She had opened a cupboard and was pulling out a black plastic shoulder bag. She moved around the shop, dropping things into it.

'That's better,' said Susan, her mouth clicking into place.

'I'm ready,' said Harman.

'Then let's go!' called Karel. He swung open the door and found himself face to face with an Artemisian infantryrobot that seemed to have appeared from nowhere. They both froze, shocked by the sight of the other. Karel took in the dull grey paint on the other robot, the fact that it was a little shorter than Karel himself, and nowhere near as well made. He noted the way its eyes shone dully; saw the scratches and dents on the panelwork.

And then they both seemed to come to their senses. The Artemisian swung up its rifle, Karel grabbed it, tried to jerk it free of the other robot's hands. No use, the soldier held on too tightly. Desperately, Karel pulled the rifle and the robot backwards, and then Susan was next to him, doing the same. Wrestling the robot back into the shop, where Harman stood patiently sorting through her bag, pulling out a sliver of metal. The infantryrobot saw what she was doing and redoubled its struggle, but Susan and Karel held him in place. He seemed surprisingly weak for a soldier. Deftly, Harman popped the infantryrobot's head open, raised a glass bottle in her other hand and dripped clear liquid into the robot's mind. 'Hydrochloric acid,' she said, as the infantryrobot thrashed harder and harder.

'You can let it go now,' said Harman.

The robot seemed to have lost control of itself: it was having an electronic fit. It kicked over a rack of tools, sending them jingling across the shop floor.

'Come on,' said Harman. 'We'd better leave by the back way.'

Karel and Susan followed her through a door at the rear of the shop. Karel paused to look at the dying robot. Body thrashing weakly, it looked back at him with fading eyes, smoke leaking from its opened head.

Out back, they picked their way south through deceptively empty streets. Streets bordered by eyes that suddenly ducked down out of sight behind windows, streets where bodies withdrew into doorways. Streets filled with the staccato sound of receding footsteps, with the distant crack of gunfire.

'We should have taken the rifle!' called Susan suddenly.

'Too late for that,' said Karel, knowing she was right. 'Come on, we need to start circling back towards Axel.'

They were leaving the centre of the city, with its expensive galleries and arcades, and heading into the older district, where the shops were smaller, the goods they carried cheaper. The first of the forges and foundries that were concentrated mainly in the old town began to appear, slotted into spaces between the lines of shops constructed of brick and iron. The marble and porphyry pavements gave way to cobbles, and then to the loose gangue upon which most of Turing City was built. Harman's dainty iron feet, in particular, seemed too small and delicate for the unmetalled surface over which they began to trek. The hills of gangue and rock rose around them, metallic bridges and walkways arched over the street, connecting buildings and making an aerial path through the city.

'*Look,*' phased Susan, pointing up to one of the walkways almost directly above them. It was an Artmesian infantryrobot, on the lookout.

'*Why hasn't it seen us?*' she asked.

It was looking elsewhere, Karel realized, just as it raised its rifle and fired at something in the distance. They heard the crack of the shot and a scream. A second shot, and the screaming ceased.

Karel, Susan and Harman froze in place, hoping that the soldier would not now look down. They waited and waited. Eventually they heard the slow clink of metal on metal as the robot walked away, the sound of its feet echoing from the brick walls around them.

'Where are the City Guard?' wondered Karel. 'What are they doing?'

'I don't understand this,' said Susan. 'We've seen only two Artemisian soldiers in half an hour. Surely you would need many more of them to take the city?'

'You think so too?' said Karel, delighted that he had taken the time to restore her voice and hearing. Susan was a statistician. She would know how big the city was, what the spread of invading troops should be. 'I knew it,' he murmured. 'Something odd is going on here. Artemis *shouldn't* be attacking, not now, not so soon after they've invaded Wien. There's not enough of them. And where is the City Guard? They should have made short work of this assault by now. What's going on?'

'Listen,' said Harman. The sound of running feet. Six brightly painted Turing Citizens came hurtling around a corner. They stopped at the sight of Karel and the rest, registered what they were seeing and then . . .

'Run!' one of them called. 'Artemis, just behind us! Eight of them!' Then they were all off, pounding down the street, running deeper and deeper into the old town. Past a line of acid tanks, their great mushroom rivet heads green with salt.

'This way,' called Karel, and the group followed him up a narrow alley between two brick walls, their feet slipping on the loose, uncompacted gangue. They emerged from the alley into a wide, dirty street lined with oil-stained foundries, twists of scrap metal rusting outside their doors. Black pools of stagnant water lay in the middle of the road.

'Which way?' called Susan, looking up and down the empty street, her words caught in the rattle of metal feet on stone.

'Uphill, up towards the fort!' called Karel. He pointed to the upper level of the fort, rising above the dirty brick and verdigrised roofs of the broken-down foundries that surrounded them.

'Artemis!'

The call hissed with static. He heard a crackle of shots, the rattle of falling metal. Someone had been hit.

'Colina!'

A robot tumbled to the ground, her head a mass of blue twisted metal.

'Leave her,' ordered Karel. 'This way!'

Shots spat out around them, puffs of dust sprang up from the ground. They ran, around another corner, into a street where the buildings seemed better maintained, the gangue of the road well stamped down. A wide road, it curved upwards, following a gentle incline towards the fort. From behind, Karel could hear the stamp stamp stamp of Artemis troops, more of them, closing in on them, hemming them in.

Susan was listening carefully as she ran. 'Still not enough troops,' she said, 'still not enough for an invasion.'

'There's enough to kill us,' said Harman. 'Keep running . . .'

They ran up the hill, around the curve, and then they stopped.

Karel looked on in horror. Up ahead, the road simply came to an end. The last two foundries were built into a great white heap of gangue, piled up against the sheer wall of the fort. They were caught in a dead end. There was no escape.

Susan walked up to the white wall of the fort, looked up at the empty battlements above.

'Help!' she called. 'Down here!'

All the robots looked up, scanning along the white wall, up at the crenellated parapet high above them. There was no reply. No sign of movement. The fort might as well have been deserted.

Karel turned to look down the empty street behind him. There was nowhere now to run. He heard the stamp of feet approaching around the corner.

The Turing Citizens looked at each other in despair. Susan came close to Karel. She took his hand.

'What about Axel?' she asked, despairingly.

'Someone will look after him,' said Karel, trying to sound confident.

The sound of approaching feet grew louder. Karel and the rest drew into the corner, wedged between the pile of gangue and the sheer white wall of the fort.

The marching grew louder still, and there they were. The first of the Artemis infantry appeared around the corner, their dull grey bodies all in a line.

'Where is the City Guard?' complained Karel bitterly.

Olam

It was so easy to kill. The discovery had been a revelation to Olam.

Just point the rifle, pull the trigger, and watch as another robot slumped to the ground in a cloud of blue wire. All the fear, all the uncertainty of the last few days evaporated as Olam raised the rifle and squeezed.

He marched through this strange city, with its iron arches and shattered glass and, where once he would have felt timid and uncertain, he now felt invincible. He was the man causing the fear, not the man feeling it. He was in charge, in control.

'Don't be careless,' warned Doe Capaldi, walking at his side, scanning the upper storeys of the galleries that surrounded them.

'I'm fine,' said Olam. 'Hey, look over there.'

A glint of reflected sunlight, so easy to miss. Fine, powdered glass, trodden into the plastic matting at the entrance to a store. A trail, leading into the building.

'Someone went in there,' said Olam, the lust rising within him. 'Someone sneaked in after we smashed the glass.'

Olam didn't like the look Doe Capaldi was giving him. 'I'll send Janet in,' he said.

'No way,' said Olam. 'I know the orders: maximum disruption. I spotted it, I get to go in.'

He was off into the store before Doe Capaldi could tell him otherwise. Zig-zagging across the shop floor, keeping low. Dodging for cover between the plastic sheeting that was hung on display all through the shop. Pushing past sheets of plain red, green, yellow and blue. Slipping past black and white checks, turquoise and purple knotwork; through a riot of paisleys and tartans.

Olam found the shop disorienting after the grey of the Zernike plain. This city was so colourful: there was barely a place where plain stone or metal could be seen.

He heard a mechanical whirring, the faintest click. Someone was upstairs.

Hot and lovely current poured into his electromuscles, his movements became staccato and excited. Up the stairs, gun at the ready. The sound of footsteps, over there behind the green door.

He moved forward, gun at the ready, kicked the door open with his foot . . .

There was a woman inside, two children sheltering behind her. She held an awl in her hand. She dropped it as soon as she saw Olam.

'No!' she cried. 'Please!'

Olam raised his gun and felt the current surge inside him. He held it in check as he pointed the rifle at the child on her left, held it there a moment and then moved the gun to point at the child on her right.

'Please,' she said, her voice emitting electronic squeaks of fear. 'I'll do anything!'

'Anything?' said Olam. He pretended to think about that, but the urge was too strong and his finger squeezed. The head of the child to the right of the woman exploded, the twisted metal of its brain tangling over its mother's shoulder. The woman cried out; the other child stared at him, frozen in fear.

'Would you really do anything?' said Olam, his gun now turned to point towards other child. He pretended to think some more. 'Then come here and kneel before me . . .' he said.

Sobbing, her eyes fixed on the gun, the woman did so.

Olam felt so strong. He felt like an aristocrat. The current was constantly building inside him. He couldn't control it; he dropped his rifle, seized his awl and plunged it into the head of the woman who knelt before him. The remaining child screamed, but Olam stabbed again and again, his electromuscles crackling with energy.

Maoco O

Maoco O waited in darkness, cut off from the world.

How long had he waited here? Did it matter?

They had lost forty soldiers in the explosion at the station, a further forty were badly damaged and in need of urgent repair. There was talk of a counter-offensive, but for the moment they had been told to hold position. Maoco O waited patiently. He was a soldier, and his mind was woven so that he could wait for ever, if need be.

And then, something odd: he heard Susan somewhere nearby. Close enough to touch, even. He could feel her fear. Not just for herself, but for the other robot that stood by her: her husband. Susan and her husband. That was not all. Maoco O sensed eight other Turing City robots standing not an arm's length away.

And now, finally, he felt the approach of the Artemisian troops. So many of them, and so close.

It was time . . .

Maoco O exploded from the gangue, white dust billowing and

shrapnel stones ricocheting and ringing off the bodies of the surrounding Turing City robots. He had fired six head shots before
the Artemisian infantry had time to react, their bodies slumping
to the ground, tangles of wire unwinding from their minds as they
fell.

He was calm. Away in the distance, undetected by regular robot
senses, he saw more infantryrobots standing on the metal walkway
between two buildings, exposed against the skyline. One, two,
three shots and they fell to the ground in a rattle of broken metal.

In slow motion, the brightly painted Turing City robots were
turning to gaze at him with a mixture of fear and awe. There was
Susan. Did she recognize him? He doubted it. The robots were
edging closer to him for safety, but not too close, wary of the black
spike of his rifle, the needle points of the armour-piercing bullets
emerging from the cartridges on his belt, the razor curve of the
sword fixed on his back. Gangue was slipping back into the hole
from which he had leaped, dust was settling, blown in eddies by
the cold wind, the ground still slipping beneath their feet.

Maoco O took all this in, and he was bored. The attack had
finally arrived, and it was so much less than he had been expecting.

Maoco O heard the grinding noise first, but the edgy crowd of
Turing City robots soon picked up on it too. Someone was
approaching. Someone in incredible pain.

A robot dragged itself around the corner. A child. And it was
burning. White flame at its joints, its paintwork blackened and
peeled away, its mouth locked in an endless scream. It was trying
to say something, trying to modulate that endless electronic
squeal.

A woman was screaming. And another one, transfixed by the
sight of the burning child, the hot metal over its chest beginning
to sag.

Maoco O shot it in the head. A merciful end. More footsteps.
He could hear more Artemisian troops approaching.

'Get behind me,' he said to the Turing City robots. He was
calm. This battle was a dance, and he was following the steps. He

shifted, and the extra metal that he carried around his body fell away. No civilian had ever seen the true shape of a Turing City City Guard Robot. They did now.

From behind him he heard stunned gasps, the sound of applause, and it was a moment before Maoco O realized it was himself that they applauded. His body. They were looking upon perfection for the first time. He tried to remember what it must be like for them, it was so long since he had first seen such a body as his own. He had felt himself special too, once. But now he was just calm.

He went to meet the foe.

Everything about him was curved and sharp. Curved arms swept forward to hands like blades, his body curving from his hips to his head, poised ready to strike; his legs curved and sprung. Everything about him suggested smooth, slicing motion. As he walked he sliced the cold wind in two, he cut a path through the settling dust.

The Artemisian robots let loose a volley of shots, but Maoco was already leaping through the air in a smooth silver curve, punctuated by the launch of four silver shuriken that went spinning from his hands to lodge themselves in the wrist and knee joints of four of the attackers.

Maoco O was calm as he descended, as he stepped lightly onto the raised barrel of a rifle, the face of the infantryrobot below gazing at him in slack incomprehension as it pulled the trigger, but Maoco O had already stepped forward onto the tip of the awl held up by the next soldier.

A crowd of them, milling beneath him as he danced on their confusion. Conscripts, Maoco O guessed, judging by their poor order and discipline. They all sought to turn their rifles on him, but Maoco stepped lightly from barrel to barrel just as the shots were fired, he danced on the tips of the awls, he was a quicksilver blade that reflected the cold sky and the dust and metal of the city, too fast to catch. And, as he danced, he reached down and broke the coil of a robot, or hooked his awl into a skull and jerked it back with blue wire wrapped around it. Beneath him, the infantry upon whose guns he danced were beginning to panic, but Maoco O was still calm.

All too soon they were nothing but dead, grey metal at his feet. Up on the gangue heap, the painted robots of Turing City looked on in awe and fear. But what did they know? Maoco O did not care for them, he realized suddenly, any more than he cared for the Artemisians. For what was it to be a citizen of Turing City but to be willing to fight for it? To die for it? Those citizens, with their handmade bodies, were almost a separate species to him.

The crowd began to applaud, to stamp their feet in a crunching of gangue, and Maoco O realized that they had only just caught up with events. His mind was made of pure electrum, he thought so much faster than they did. They were shouting encouragement to him, yet he took no pleasure in their adulation. Where was the skill in what he had just achieved? Merely following the steps of a dance?

And now the dance resumed.

Another robot was approaching. A different robot this time. Silver-grey katana metal, bladed hands and sharp feet half drawn. Recessed eyes. An Artemisian Scout. The cold wind chilled Maoco O to his soul, but not with fear. This was the best that Artemis could send up against him, and it would not be enough. The Scout raised her gun and fired, and Maoco O leaned out of the path of the bullet, reading her moves perfectly. He was calm. She was calm, too. She fired again, and again, and each time Maoco O leaned out of the way. Now she was firing one-handed, reaching with the other for one of the grenades attached to her waist. She lobbed it towards Maoco O, still firing as she did so, and Maoco O spun a shuriken to meet it. The grenade exploded only just beyond her hand, shattering it. Three fingers fell to the ground, the others were left a twisted mess. Still she fired at Maoco O. Bored, he raised his own gun and shot her through the head.

Another Scout approached, walking slowly towards Maoco O, not even keeping cover. Simply raising its gun and firing. For the briefest of moments, Maoco O's calm gave way to confusion.

What were they playing at? Why advance like this, one at a time: why not rush him all at once?

He heard the noise then, the high-pitched whine coming from within the Scout's body. And then he recognized the way that she was walking. Not dancing, not leaping along like a Scout would, but rather walking with the slow, steady trudge of an infantry-robot. And he realized: this wasn't a scout at all. This robot was wearing another robot's body, and inside it there was . . .

'Get down!' he shouted to the Turing City robots that were lined up behind him. He flung himself forward, just as a flare of brilliant white shone at the robot's arms and legs and neck . . .

Kavan

There was a dull crump in the distance as another robot exploded somewhere in the city, and Kavan gave a nod of satisfaction.

'It won't work, Kavan,' said Eleanor. He ignored her. Before him, the lines of grey infantryrobots and Scouts stood in patient silence, their rifles held at the ready. The sergeants stood at the head of the lines, sending the soldiers out one by one into the frightened city. Some of them were armed with bombs, some of them weren't. Nobody knew which was which, save for the soldiers themselves.

Kavan crouched at the edge of the forward command post, pouring gangue from one hand to the other, studying the composition of the spoil. Behind him, the railway station was still burning, white and orange flames dancing inside its black skeleton. The last of the injured City Guards that put up a struggled resistance before the building had just been put down with some effort. Even damaged, they still fought like ten Artemisians. White dust fell in the burned streets; it blew through the shattered windows of the soot-covered buildings that surrounded the square. There was a shout, and another set of infantry were sent off through the streets of the city to find the enemy.

'I said it won't work,' repeated Eleanor. She was standing just behind him, her voice still crackling with the after-effects of the nuclear explosion.

'Maybe not,' replied Kavan. 'You know that no plan ever survives contact with the enemy.'

'Kavan, there's not enough of us!'

He straightened up. The engineers had moved fast. A second railway line had already been laid from the undamaged section beyond the station, and flat-bed trucks were now rolling into Turing City, laden with more troops and weapons. It was an odd sight: an engine would pull up in the middle of the damaged square, and the troops would dismount and then turn on their transport and quickly dismantle it to make room for the next train. The separated parts were neatly packed into boxes and stacked at one edge of the square. The trains could be rebuilt later on, should this attack prove successful. If not, then the metal would be available to Artemis at a later date, when they finally seized full control of Turing City. Turing City's defeat was, after all, inevitable in the long run.

Kavan turned to Eleanor. 'You know, if we had to fight thirty thousand robots, I would say you were right, Eleanor. We wouldn't have a chance. But we're not fighting thirty thousand robots. We're only fighting the City Guard while the rest of Turing City is hiding behind their precious champions, waiting to see what happens. The City Guard may be our superiors in combat, but there are more of us than them.' He looked over to the ruined body of a Guard that lay nearby, his dented head pierced by many bullet holes. He had taken some finishing, but now he was dead.

'You know, if an Artemisian is damaged he can take spare parts from any of his comrades,' he said, wonderingly. He pointed to the dead Guard. '*They* get wounded and they can't properly repair themselves. I tell you, Eleanor, they may construct better robots here in Turing City, but we have the correct paradigm for war.'

A shout, and another set of infantryrobots peeled away from the head of each column, heading into the city beyond. Eleanor could hear the humming coming from within their metal shells. These were all walking bombs.

'They'll soon figure out what we're doing,' said Eleanor. 'Then they'll just pick them off at a distance.'

'I know,' said Kavan. 'But that's to our advantage. We can't beat them at close quarters, but if we reduce this battle to each of us sniping at long range . . .'

Eleanor said nothing. Kavan glanced back at the burning railway station. It reminded him of something, the way one side of its curved shape had collapsed in on itself . . .

'I can't believe we got this far,' said Eleanor, suddenly. 'If I'm honest, I didn't think we would do it.'

'What we think isn't important, Eleanor. Artemis does what Artemis will.'

He looked back at the railway station and he had it now. *The whale.* The railway station reminded him of that whale, back in Wien. The place where General Fallan had fallen.

There was another shouted command, and the next set of infantry headed into the silent city. Kavan watched them go.

Maoco O

. . . fell to the ground and rolled awkwardly to a halt. His right side was badly damaged, caught full in the blast of the exploding soldier. He looked back in disbelief at the shattered remains of the silver Scout body. No wonder it had shown such trouble moving! The robot's entire chest must have been packed with high explosive.

He saw the three puffs of dust on the floor in front of him, heard the crack of gunfire a moment later, and he rolled forward, tumbled to the side, his right arm and leg refusing to operate properly. In his peripheral vision he saw the crowd of Turing Citizens that had stood on the gangue pile all watching him. One of them was shouting, pointing to a group of Artemisian robots that had just rounded the corner and was advancing towards him.

Awkwardly, he raised his gun, and then he felt his reactions adjusting to his new body form. The Fort Mothers had done their jobs well: the mind of a City Guard took feedback from the shape of the body to which it was attached, constantly adjusting itself to new circumstances. He fired, once, twice, three times, an Artemisian falling on each shot. As he made to fire the fourth, he was caught in the hand by a bullet. The electromuscle there shorted.

His radio crackled to life.

'*Maoco O. This is Aorne H. What's your status?*'

'I'm fine,' said Maoco O, taking the rifle in his other hand. He fired off three more shots, finishing off the remaining Artemisians.

'*Some of the enemy are packed with explosives.*'

'I just encountered one of them. I'm twenty per cent damaged.'

'*Listen, we're regrouping before the fort. We can pick off the explosive robots there before they can get close enough to do us any damage. We will use that location to relaunch our counter-offensive. Can you make it there?*'

'No problem. I have a group of Turing Citizens with me, though.'

'*Get them clear of your current position, and then ditch them. This is more important.*'

'They can't fight for themselves, you know!'

'*They're not supposed to.*'

'Okay.' Maoco O scanned the area, searching for more Artemisians. 'What's the situation in terms of casualties, Aorne H?' he asked.

'*Thirty per cent. That's not a problem. We will prevail.*'

'We will prevail.'

Maoco O scanned the area once more. Everywhere seemed clear for the moment. He turned to the Turing Citizens who stood nervously on the gangue behind him.

'Come on,' he called. 'Follow me.'

The robots began to scramble down towards him. Maoco O shifted his position, adjusting to his newly damaged body. Still, he was calm.

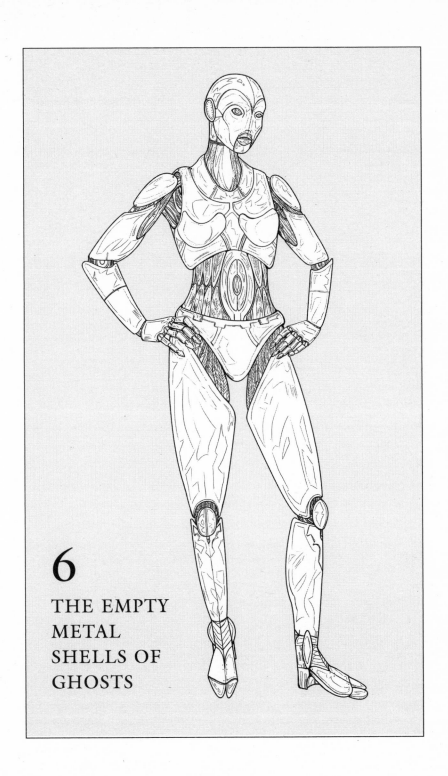

6

THE EMPTY
METAL
SHELLS OF
GHOSTS

Karel

Axel's look of terror as they entered the apartment was enough to unleash Susan's emotions in a crackling outburst. She took her child in her arms, her voicebox squeaking and squawking as she comforted him. All Karel could do was lean weakly against the wall. *Thank Zuse,* he thought. *He's safe. He's safe.*

Axel was whining as his mother stroked the currents that emanated from his little body, releasing an electronic hum of anguish. Karel's gyros lurched in sympathy. *How long has Axel been gazing at the front door, listening to the explosions in the city, wondering what had happened to us?*

'Where have you been? Where have you been?'

Karel felt guilt and fear in equal measure. And then the child saw the blue paint down his mother's side was badly scratched, her mouth and ears obviously recently repaired. 'What's happened to you, Mummy?' he asked.

'Nothing, Axel, I'm fine.'

'Susan, I'm going to extinguish the forge. Anything to avoid attracting attention to this apartment . . .'

Susan didn't hear him; she was too busy stroking her child. Karel bent down and began to close the forge vents. He just needed to do something. Besides, the Artemis robots would have heat vision; they could be out there now, scanning the city, looking for pockets of life . . .

Even so, Karel felt a lurching sensation as he closed the final vent on the fire; it was as if he had just smothered the life of the family.

'I'm going to the outside room,' he announced. 'I'm going to see what's happening.'

'Stay here, Daddy!'

'It's okay Axel. I'll only be next door.'

He slipped from the forge into the tiny room, closing the door carefully behind him. The window in there offered a view over the seemingly impossible evening. Nothing seemed real. The sky was composed of lines of red and black, the setting sun behind streaks of cloud. The city beneath it was lit by orange fires. The train station was burning, the central district was burning. The foundries burned blue and white and red and golden, as different metals ignited, their incandescent flares dimming the flames beyond them.

The flames beyond them . . . Karel realized with horror that he was looking at the fort of the City Guard. Even from this distance he could see the flare of the fort's Tesla towers, brilliant white in the encompassing night.

The Artemisians had made it all the way up there! What was happening now? Some desperate last stand? But it wasn't supposed to happen this way! The City Guard were supposed to be invincible.

And they were, almost.

He recalled how that City Guard robot had erupted from the gangue and saved them all. It had stood in the middle of the street and calmly shot the approaching Artemisians one by one, like doing no more than testing its gun on a firing range. The minutes had crept by and the robot had just stood there, shooting the enemy down to the diminishing applause of the crowd. Even when that Artemisian robot had exploded right next to it it had gone on fighting, badly damaged as it was. And then it had led them through the streets, avoiding the distant sounds of fighting that echoed panic through the city, and shown them a safe path back here, to the flat. The Guard had paused for a moment, thinking.

'This is far enough,' it said. 'I have new orders. Good luck to you all.' And then it had raised its rifle and headed back towards the fighting.

The City Guard seemed invincible, and yet the Artemisians were winning. They had made it all the way to the fort itself. How could that have happened?

But a terrible suspicion was growing within Karel that he

already knew the answer. He had known all along that this outcome was inevitable. Turing City was falling not because of the City Guard, but because of everyone else. Karel had walked almost the length of Turing City that afternoon, and the only robots he had seen fighting were the Guards and the Artemisians. Few regular Turing Citizens, if any, had bothered to defend their city. They had just left the job to someone else. How much did they really believe in their freedom? He thought suddenly of Susan. *Just how did their mothers twist their minds?*

The windows rippled: an explosion. Clouds suddenly billowed way into the air, and Karel guessed that an acid tank had ruptured. Hydrochloric acid drifted in a grey pall across the burning streets.

A ghost walked across the scene: Susan's reflection in the window, outlined in the light of the open door to the forge room.

'Close the door!' said Karel. 'They'll see us!'

'But Axel is worri . . .'

'DO IT!'

Susan did so; she moved up and gazed out over the city with him.

'What can you see?' she asked.

'Nothing. Nothing but burning.' He heard the emptiness in his own voice. 'Susan, I think this is the end. I think it's over.'

'It's never over,' said Susan, her tone unconvincing. 'What's that?' she asked, pointing to a series of lights moving towards them across the Zernike plain, converging on the burning railway station.

'More trains arriving,' said Karel. 'Reinforcements from Artemis.'

Light filled the room again, now Axel stood in the doorway.

'Mummy, I thought you had left me again!'

Karel bundled his family back into the forge room, back where they couldn't be seen by any enemy troops, outlined against the light.

Karel spoke gently. 'Susan, take care of Axel. I'm going to go out into the block. See if anyone has some news.'

The iron corridor outside Karel's apartment was so quiet, so almost normal. The lights were dimmed: others obviously appreciated the need to avoid drawing attention to their apartment block.

He walked carefully down the corridor, listening for voices behind the iron doors. Nothing: the building was hollow, a drum seemingly devoid of the beat of life. Everyone was keeping quiet. The silence unnerved Karel as he came to the curled serpent of the brass banister that spiralled up the stairwell. Silence seemed to well up from the floors below, and it took a conscious effort to step forward and to descend into its forbidding depths.

The faux circuitry patterns in beaten copper that decorated the white walls, the brass banister, the soft tread of his feet on the steps – Karel's senses seemed enhanced in the silence. Every step, every touch of metal on metal was amplified to become the sound of Artemisian troops entering the building.

He almost collided with a robot that was creeping the other way, up the stairs.

'Whoah!' In panic he brought up his arm to strike out at the intruder.

'No, Karel! Stop!'

Their voices echoed in the stairwell. Karel paused, gazing at the apparition.

'Gustav . . . ?' he said, relief surging through his circuits. 'It is you, isn't it? But what have you done to your body?'

Karel's sense of the unreality of this evening deepened as he gazed at the other robot. Gustav used to dress pretty much like any other Turing Citizen; in well-formed lightweight metals, brightly painted and enamelled. The contrast to his current body could not be more marked. He now looked like something from a ghost story, covered as he was from head to toe in some heavy dull-grey alloy, the panels sealed so tightly, their seams rubbed down with thick grease. His head was an elongated, curving tube, the eyes much larger than usual and sealed behind thick glass lenses. His hands and feet were larger too, with foil webbing running up to the first joint of the fingers and toes.

Gustav's voice resonated deep and booming, as if welling up from the bottom of a deep pool. 'We're getting out,' he said. 'The city has fallen, if not now, then certainly by morning. Haven't you heard? The City Guard are dying. They've fallen back to the fort. They're holding their ground there, but more Artemisians are arriving by the hour, coming in by the railway. The Guards will be overwhelmed by the morning.'

Gustav's words kindled the embarrassed anger that glowed dimly within Karel.

'They're dying, and you talk of running?' He was almost shouting. He couldn't help it. 'They're giving up their lives for this city!'

'I don't see you joining them,' said Gustav.

'I have a wife and child!'

'So do I.'

Karel lowered his voice, fought to rein in his anger. 'Listen, if Turing City falls, then the whole southern continent will have been taken. Gustav, there's nowhere left to run to.'

Gustav nodded, an odd movement with his newly elongated head. 'Nowhere left here on Shull,' he agreed. 'Karel, we're heading out to sea. That's why I'm dressed like this. It's not too late, Karel. Get up to your forge; get Susan and Axel and yourself adapted for water.'

Karel looked at Gustav's streamlined, watertight body.

'But we haven't the metal. It would take days to build something like that . . .' A thought occurred to him. 'How long have you had that body, Gustav?'

Gustav's posture radiated embarrassment. 'Hey, Karel, people have known this was coming for months. I'm not the only one to have considered an escape plan.'

Current built in Karel's electromuscles. 'I hadn't heard anything . . .' he said softly.

'Well . . .' said Gustav, and then he took refuge in frankness. 'Come on, Karel, maybe that's not surprising. You know what people say about you.' He held up one webbed hand in apology. 'Hey, I'm not saying they're right, far from it . . .'

'I'm pleased to hear it,' said Karel, icily calm. 'So tell me, what *do* they say about me?'

Gustav shook his head. 'Karel, I'm not getting into this argument now: I'm doing you a favour. Get upstairs and get your family kitted out. We're making our way down to the coast tonight. We'll walk out under the water and start heading south. There's metal down there on the seabed: placers and exposed ores. Enough to get by on.'

'I don't believe what I'm hearing! What about fire? How are you going to work metal?'

'You don't need fire to work metal, Karel. They didn't in the old days. Robots used to get by just with the strength in their hands. We don't need these fancy bodies we've got used to. I tell you, it will be good to get back to basics. It will be just like starting again!'

Karel's voice was filled with contempt. 'I can't believe you're giving up so easily. You should be outside fighting.'

His words rang out in the echoing shaft of the stairwell.

'Like I said, I don't see you doing any fighting.' Gustav was dismissive. 'Listen, ten o'clock tonight, down in the communal area. We're setting off then. I'm offering you a lifeline, Karel.'

'Gustav, listen . . .'

But Gustav turned and resumed his silent progress upstairs. Karel noticed for the first time that Gustav was carrying panels of some kind of alloy. It looked like whale metal, heavy and completely out of place in the white delicacy of the apartment block. Where had he got it from?

Just what was happening here?

She sat in the forge room with Axel on her knee. The living metal of the stove still retained some dying warmth. Karel crouched in front of his wife, speaking quietly.

'Susan, it's like they've been planning this for weeks – months, even. It's like Turing City gave up the will to fight before the battle ever began!'

Susan was calming Axel, stroking him, letting him feel the warm current from her hands move through his electromuscle.

'Susan, did *you* know anything about this?' Karel looked up at his wife suspiciously.

'Karel, I told you! I knew nothing about it!'

'But you worked for Statistics. You were supposed to know everything! Didn't you notice a build-up of whale metal in the city?'

'Karel, you're scaring Axel . . .'

'And it's such a stupid plan! They don't know *anything* about what they will find down there! There could be another robot civ-ilization living there already. Or worse . . .' He brooded. 'You know, out at the Immigration Centre, the one on the coast, you hear stories. Robots with arms a mile long. They reach out from deep under the water to pluck people from the land and drag them down to the seabed, where they strip the metal from their bodies. Leave only the twisted wire of the mind to slowly untangle in the dark depths.'

'Karel,' said Susan warningly. 'Not in front of Axel!'

'Sorry!' He smiled down at his son. 'But what if they are real? What if they are waiting down there for Gustav and the rest to walk into their welcoming arms?'

Susan raised her voice. 'Karel, stop it!'

'And even if they are safe down there, how long before Artemis comes looking for them? How long before the next wave of expan-sion sweeps over the seabeds? Gustav and the rest are just delaying the inevitable. I tell you, we should stand and fight here!'

'I told you, that's enough!'

Susan had *shouted* at him. Susan who never shouted. And now Karel saw the fear in her eyes, and he realized just how frightened everyone was. And he realized that it was far too late to make a stand.

Turing City had already fallen. All they could do was wait . . .

Spoole

The land around Artemis City was healthy. The air was filled with the soot of a thousand belching chimneys; the acid rain washed the streets and pitted the copper-lined roofs and killed off all the green organic life. From where he stood on the roof of the city, at the edge of a wide platform built at the top of the basilica, Spoole saw nothing but good, healthy stone and metal. Steel arches and copper domes and riveted iron. Gold chasing and the iridescent patterns of electrolysed titanium. Granite slabs and marble flags and slate roofs and walls. All was ordered, and all was good.

The city was a living thing: full of the heat of the fires that burned in the forges and blast furnaces, the city shrugged off the chill of the wind that had sprung up from the north.

The city was healthy, it was strong . . . and yet this morning it shook like a leaf spring with the news that travelled up the railway lines from the south.

Kavan had entered Turing City.

What next? wondered Spoole. He didn't blame Kavan. He had been in that position himself, once. It wasn't that he had been hungry for power, not exactly. It was just that Spoole had been made to lead. In the making rooms, his mother had knelt at the feet of an Artemisian Storm Trooper and twisted the metal into a mind that would be a suitable leader for Artemis City. And so, as he had grown, it had been obvious to Spoole just how badly things had been run in the city. Spoole knew that he could do a better job, because his mind had been woven that way.

No, it wasn't exactly that he had been hungry for power; rather, he realized that he couldn't let things stay as they were.

That was the way it was, for Artemis wove its own leaders. Spoole was made to be clever and charismatic. His mother had twisted into his mind the knowledge of how to make himself so very attractive to women. His father had had that knowledge too;

he had shown his son how to build a body that was both strong and agile.

Gearheart knew this. She both loved and hated his body.

'Your mother was a traitor,' she would say. *'Attractive men find it too easy to have children twisted. They lose the sense that a mind is a special thing. They cease to take sufficient care in their directions to the mother.'*

'I attracted you, didn't I?' Spoole would reply.

'I was made to be attracted to you, Spoole. Don't flatter yourself.' And at that Gearheart would stand and pirouette, or stretch, or in some other way show off her perfect body. *'But you have found life too easy, Spoole. You would not make a good father. I will never weave you a mind, since you have no understanding of the balance.'*

'You flatter yourself, Gearheart. Why should I want a child? It was not woven into my mind.'

'So you say, Spoole, but you are speaking to a woman. No man could understand, but the weave is not so flexible as you might suppose. Some things are immutable. A woman may suppress the reproductive urge in a mind, but she cannot totally remove it.'

'You manage to suppress the urge,' Spoole would say, but without heat.

And at that point, the conversation would end. But sometimes Spoole would push it a little further. Just out of reckless curiosity.

'But, Gearheart, if we were to have a child, how would you twist him?'

'Him?' Gearheart would laugh. *'Not as good-looking as you, Spoole. Men like you tilt the balance away from women.'*

Spoole gazed reflectively at the city. He had never seen Kavan, but he had been told that the robot wasn't attractive. No wonder. Kavan didn't have the same privileged start to life as Spoole. He wouldn't have had the education, the access to metal; he wouldn't *know* how to build a body as well as Spoole could.

They were different in so many ways, but they still held so much in common. The same need to do what was *right*.

Spoole wondered if Kavan realized yet how difficult it would prove to bring about the change he wanted. Had Kavan yet glimpsed the essentially one-way nature of his quest? Did he yet see how, once one goal was achieved, another would immediately appear? Did he not see, that no matter how far he travelled, those people beneath him would be gripped with the same ambition, the same need to do what was right, only to do it better than himself? They would be there already, climbing up the stairs behind him, and if Kavan didn't want their awls in his back, he would have to climb even faster.

Spoole stood on the roof of the city, on the roof of the world, on the roof of Artemis. He looked out at the chimneys and the forges and the factories and for a moment he saw a pyramid, a mound of robots, with himself at the top kicking down, and everyone else reaching and grabbing and pulling themselves up towards him.

He told himself he was being ridiculous, and he allowed his eyes to follow the floodlit railway lines that fanned out from the marshalling yards. He looked into the darkness to the south.

Kavan was out there somewhere. Kavan and his robots moving into Turing City. The first phase of the attack had been successful. Kavan had requested more troops, and Spoole had sent them. He could hardly do otherwise. But all that metal expended on what had seemed a reckless venture? Reckless? Now Spoole wasn't so sure. Would Kavan win or lose?

Either way, Spoole would win; he would either gain more territory, or lose a potential rival.

But also, Spoole would lose. What would come riding back up the tracks from the south? News of defeat, or worse, Kavan, now a hero, leading a horde of battle-hardened troops?

Spoole looked down at the marshalling yards, and suddenly he smiled. He had the answer.

He turned and signalled to a slim robot that stood patiently near the stairs.

'Fetch me the head of the engineers. Get me the railway chief.'

The thin wind carried Spoole's laughter into the night.

There was always someone who wanted to take your place. Let

Kavan handle his own would-be successors. Spoole was more than capable of handling his.

Eleanor

Eleanor was impressed by Kavan's progress, but she was frustrated at the role he had selected for her in it. Kavan never quite seemed to trust her.

She marched through the cold night into the broken remains of the railway station. It was almost peaceful in here under the cold stars, the dark jigsaw pieces of the remaining station walls screening off the sounds coming from the half-defeated city. She could understand why Kavan had made this his headquarters.

The wreckage of the front of the reaction train had been dragged to one side, the remains of the ripped-open carcass of the railway station had either been made safe or torn down. New rails had been laid, and a steady relay of trains had been set up, bringing in troops and supplies from Artemis, Bethe, even from Wien.

It took her some time to spot Kavan, just another grey infantry-robot standing near the front of the station, reading from a piece of foil. Wolfgang, Kavan's aide, stood nearby, along with Ruth, who had formerly been General Fallan's number two. Their silence was a good sign: it meant things were going according to plan.

Eleanor marched up to Kavan. She was badly burned down her left-hand side, soot and scorched paint covered the bare metal of her arm, thigh and torso.

'One of the foundries,' she explained, noting Kavan's glance. 'The robots in there had jury-rigged some sort of flamethrower.'

'It's almost a pleasure to hear of someone here bothering to fight,' said Kavan, rolling the foil into a ball and dropping it on the ground.

'I don't understand it,' said Eleanor. 'Where has the spirit gone from this city? For years we feared it, and yet today we find it as empty as a ghost.'

'It was the same in Wien and Bethe and Segre, and all the other states where the citizens had ceased to take responsibility for all of the state's functions. The people here are happy to operate a forge, or paint pictures, or make machine parts, but they will no longer scrub the algae from the stones or fight in the army. When you have a state that leaves those jobs to the immigrants and the under-class, you have a state that is already dead.'

The singing of rails announced another train approaching the station. Kavan and Eleanor watched the blue and yellow nose of a diesel approaching along the Bethe line. The midnight-black bodies of Storm Troopers could just be made out, lined up in racks on the trucks behind the engine.

'Artemis itself has begun to follow that path . . .' continued Kavan thoughtfully.

Eleanor looked up at the night. The stars shone so brightly, as if the heavens themselves were watching Turing City's end.

'You need to get yourself cleaned and repainted,' said Kavan suddenly, and Eleanor was dragged back down to the world of Penrose.

'Later,' she said dismissively. 'We almost have control of the city now.'

'No, we haven't.' Kavan sounded tired. 'We have taken a lot of ground, but that's the easy part. Holding it will be more difficult. Come the morning, the sun will rise, and the robots of Turing City will see what they have lost. When they understand that all the easy options have gone, then the hard fact of fighting will not seem such an unpleasant alternative. We need to break their spirit now, before that truth occurs to them.'

Eleanor remained silent. Behind Kavan, a line of Storm Troop-ers stepped down from the train to the platform in perfect unison, their feet making a perfect double crash.

'Get your troops, Eleanor.' said Kavan, coming to a decision. 'Send them out to the residential districts. There will be civilians cowering in their homes, wondering what they should do. Well, let's keep them cowed. Get your troops to kill about a third of them.'

Eleanor gazed at him, shocked. 'If you think so, Kavan.'

'I do think so,' said Kavan. He stared at her. 'You want to be leader, Eleanor . . .'

'No, I . . .'

'Don't deny it, Eleanor. You want to be leader. You know it. Very well, do you think you are really committed to Artemis?'

'Of course I do.'

'Then you will understand why I do as I do.'

Eleanor turned on her heel.

'Oh, and Eleanor.' She paused, looking back. Behind Kavan, the Storm Troopers stepped two paces forward in perfect formation. He continued. 'Give them Nyro's choice.'

Eleanor grimaced. 'Of course, Kavan.'

Karel

Karel and Susan sat in silence in the cooling forge room, listening to the hum of Axel's sleeping body. The child stirred, the yellow glow of his eyes deepened.

'Go back to sleep, Axel,' said Susan. 'It's okay.'

'Why can't we light the forge then, Mummy?' said the child, sleepily. 'I want to work on my legs.'

'In the morning.'

Axel leaned against the wall and drifted back to sleep.

'Where are you going?' asked Susan.

Karel stopped by the door. 'Back outside. I want to see what's going on.'

'Be careful.'

The hallway was dim. Karel turned his vision right up, crept down past the doors of his neighbours to the stairwell, now plunged into darkness. A faint noise of metal on metal echoed up from below. The sound of robots moving about. Karel felt a prickle of tension in his electromuscles. What was happening down there?

Karel crept down the stairs, ears turned up full.

'Someone's coming . . .'

He heard the voice and froze. A light snapped on, framing him in its beam.

'*Who's that? Karel?* What are you doing creeping up on us?' The voice was unfriendly, suspicious.

'Garfel, is that you?' Karel strained to see past the bright glare of the light.

'Stay where you are!'

Karel had been on edge all night, wondering what was happening outside in the city, fearful for his family, rejected by his fellow citizens. Their command was enough to ignite the anger that was woven deep into his mind.

'*Rust* NO!' he swore. He stamped forward, roughly pushing aside the lamp and the robot who had shone it at him.

'Hey, be careful!' Karel recognized Gustav's voice. And now Karel's eyes adjusted to the dimness of the communal area that lay beyond the stairs. A wide, tall space, the furniture pushed to one side to make more space for the robots that had assembled in the darkness. And Karel felt his anger increase. So many robots, men, women, children: all Turing Citizens and all dressed in underwater bodies. Grey whale metal, elongated faces and big glassy eyes, all illuminated by a dim green glow.

'Traitors!' said Karel. 'Traitors, all of you!'

There was an uncomfortable silence. Robots looked to the floor, to the ceiling, everywhere but at him.

A voice spoke up. 'Who are you calling traitors, Karel? Who is it that allowed these Artemisians into our city?'

'What?' Karel felt a burning inside him like the flame of a forge. 'What are you talking about? No one *let* the Artemisians in. Didn't you notice, Ruther? They attacked! They destroyed the station!'

'Oh yes, we have been attacked. But before that, Karel. Who was it that diluted Turing City by allowing in immigrants? Who was it that diluted the resolve of the people by allowing refugees from Wien and Bethe and Born, even from Artemis itself, into this state?'

Karel was furious. Even so, he controlled his temper. Just.

'I don't see any refugees amongst this crowd,' he said. 'I only see Turing Citizens. I wonder where the refugees are at the moment. I wonder if they might be out there in the city, fighting for it?'

There was another uncomfortable silence at this point. Karel pressed home his advantage.

'And think of this, you robots who are about to run away, who are about to become refugees yourselves. What are you going to do when you are walking on the seabed if you meet another state already down there? Will you expect them to welcome you with open arms?'

No one spoke. The robots focused on the floor, on the ceiling, on anything but each other.

And then Garfel came forward. Garfel who lived in the apartment above Karel and who ran the residents' committee. Garfel who was too friendly with Susan, Garfel who had an opinion on everything.

'Why are we even taking the time to listen to you Karel, here at the fall of Turing City?' he asked. 'Even twenty years ago there were citizens who would have turned your mother back out onto the Zernike plain when she carried you here as a child. And maybe they would have been right to do so, because even twenty years ago, when all was at peace, there was something about you that some never did trust. Well, that was then, and this is now. Just be happy Karel that *your* side has won. I say you should think yourself lucky we don't take things further. As it is, I say leave us alone and go home. Go back up to your apartment and wait for your friends to arrive.'

There was more uneasy stirring in the crowd. Karel's fury burned like a jet of white flame now, a flame intense enough to melt metal. But still he held himself in check.

'I am as much a citizen of this place as you are, Garfel. More so, because I am staying here and not running.'

Garfel laughed. 'Or are you staying here because you, at least, have nothing to fear?'

He turned to the assembled robots.

'Come on, it's time to move out. We need to reach the sea before dawn.'

Garfel's words brought a momentary stillness to the robots in the hall. Karel understood why. For all of them, this was it. This was the moment when their flight became real. For these robots, Turing City was no more.

'You could stay,' suggested Karel.

'No, *you* can stay,' said Garfel. 'But you can also be merciful. Send down Susan, we'll take care of her.'

And the white flame was there again, threatening to melt Karel from the inside.

'What about Axel?' he asked.

'*He* can stay. He's half Artemisian after all.'

Something clicked in Karel's mind. He lashed out, buckling and badly hurting his hand on the whale metal of Garfel's chest. He didn't care, he didn't feel it. He was a storm of metal, kicking and gouging and scratching and stabbing, but he could find no purchase on Garfel's new body. Still he didn't care. Still he fought.

But Garfel was too strong. He'd always had so much lifeforce and now he was clad in heavy whale metal. Slowly, he pushed Karel to the floor, stepping onto Karel's left arm, bending it out of true, wrenching the electromuscle with his hand so that it fed back, making Karel let out an electronic scream.

Garfel released him, and Karel struggled to get up again, to attack Garfel, but another robot kicked his arm away, and he rolled across the floor, anger and pain flooding through his mind. He tried to rise again and was tripped once more. And then they were all over him, stamping on his chest, denting the panelling. They wrenched at his arm so that the metal bent and the electromuscle twisted painfully over the tear in his own panelling. A heavy whale-metal foot stamped down on his hand, crushing three of his fingers.

Anger gave way to pain, pain was swamped by despair. Through the legs of his attackers he could see the sea-grey bodies of his former fellow citizens gradually draining from the hall. None of them looked back in his direction.

Eventually the beating ended. Finally they let him alone.

'Traitor . . .' said Karel from the ground, his voice an electronic whine. Garfel stood over him, gazing down with his pale grey eyes.

'How long,' whined Karel, 'how long were you planning this?'

Garfel said nothing; he just continued to stare down at Karel, who lay listening to the heavy tread of robots filing from the room.

Olam

Olam made his way along the street, eagerly scanning the windows and doorways for further prey.

'You've never been to Turing City before, boy?'

Doe Capaldi was there at his side. It seemed as if Doe Capaldi was always there at his side, checking up on him.

'Never,' said Olam. 'I've read about it, of course. It's a lot smaller than I expected.'

'You're not seeing the real city here. We're heading into the residential area, not the centre. We're coming in from the east, stopping anyone escaping out this way.'

'I know what we're doing,' snapped Olam. 'You've been to Turing City before, I suppose?'

'Naturally,' replied Doe Capaldi, swinging around for a moment to check a sign of movement down a side street. An Artemisian infantryrobot emerged from a doorway down there and gave them an okay sign.

'Yes,' continued Doe Capaldi, 'I came here several times as part of the ambassador's retinue. On one occasion I was presented with a breastplate of electrum. It was a fine piece of work.' He was silent for a moment, lost in memory. 'The paint shops in the galleries are particularly fine, too. A pity we were not sent to ransack those instead, boy!'

'Don't call me boy,' said Olam. 'We're equal now, both soldiers of Artemis.'

'I'm still your sergeant,' Doe Capaldi reminded him.

'You hate me, don't you?' said Olam. 'I tried to have you killed.'

'I understand why you did it,' replied Doe Capaldi smoothly. 'It's all down to the way you were made. I would expect nothing else from one of your class.'

Just one day ago the insult would have goaded Olam. But not now. Olam had killed and he felt different now. He wasn't a commoner any more.

He lowered his voice. 'Don't speak to me like that, Doe Capaldi. I'm watching you, you know. You should watch me. One dark night in the middle of battle . . .'

'You're making too much of the past, boy. We're all Artemisians now.'

Olam laughed nastily. 'Yes, and I bet that hurts you a lot more than it hurts me. You've lost far more than I have, Doe Capaldi.'

But Doe Capaldi wasn't even listening. He gave a signal, and his patrol moved to either side of the street, lost themselves in its doorways and shadows.

Something was coming.

Olam waited in the shadow cast by an ornamental metal pillar that climbed the side of one building.

There was movement further up the street, and for a moment Olam was plunged back into the stories of his childhood, of ghosts that rose up and stalked the world at night. Ghosts, the empty metal shells of bodies from which the mind had been taken, or which had merely died. Ghosts! Bodies that did not need minds to make them move, they hunted the world at night, searching for wire that they could draw from a sleeping child's head, winding it out inch by inch. As the child slumbered, their dreams were turned to darkness as their life was spooled away, to be bottled up and reawoken in the perverted nightmare of a ghost's shell.

Olam almost let out a whine of fear, but then he realized that these were not ghosts but the living citizens of Turing City. He could see the light in their eyes, dim and green and almost dissolved by the light of Zuse.

Why do they look so odd? he wondered. Their bodies were grey and misshapen, they marched two abreast in silence through the streets, seemingly oblivious to their surroundings.

'Where are they going?' The words were spoken so softly that Olam momentarily imagined they floated from the hollow lands, borne to him on the cold breeze as if the ghosts of the north were speaking to him. But no, it was only Doe Capaldi, leaning close to him in the shadow.

'I don't know . . .'

The misshapen robots marched silently past, their strangely wide feet planting themselves solidly on the smooth concrete of the road, pressing firmly down into shadow. Adults, children, young and old, all making their way through the night, two by two. And now the tail end of the procession had passed. Doe Capaldi gave the signal, and his squad began to move through the shadows of the moonlit city, silently following the grey ghosts.

Susan

'Karel!' gasped Susan. 'What's happened to you?'

Karel dragged his way into the room. She took in his injuries with a terrified stare. He couldn't move one leg properly, a hand was badly mangled.

'Speak to me, Karel!'

His voice was nothing more than an electronic whine.

'Oh Karel! Was it Artemis? Are they downstairs?'

'No . . .'

The forge had gone cold now. Still, there was tin, there was a little gold. She could do something with those. She felt the electronic pulse throbbing from his leg, turned him over and saw the way the electromuscle there was caught on the external metal. Gently, she set about easing the panelling away.

'Easy,' she said. 'It will be all right.'

She looked over to where Axel lay sleeping, dark despair filling her like oil.

Olam

Olam fixed his gaze on the two robots that brought up the rear of the grey procession ahead.

'Why don't we attack?' he asked. 'All that metal should belong to Artemis. You're letting it get away!'

'Let's see where they're going first,' replied Doe Capaldi, giving him a questioning look. 'They're not going to move very fast. There are children with them.'

'We should shoot the children first. Let the parents see them die. That will break their spirit.'

Silence.

'It's true,' said Olam.

'We follow them for the moment.'

'But they're heading out into the darkness!'

Olam looked down his rifle sights, turned the gun to bear on a grey child, took aim at the oddly shaped head that swayed back and forth as it walked. Doe Capaldi pushed the rifle to one side.

'I wasn't going to shoot.'

'Weren't you?' Doe Capaldi gave him another questioning look. 'You know, the upper classes of Wien used to debate about behaviour like yours.'

'Wien is no more,' said Olam, with bitter satisfaction.

'That may be,' said Doe Capaldi, unperturbed. 'But the debate remains. You see, some argued that we are all just metal, that in the end we are all equal.'

'But we aren't, are we?'

'You're missing the point,' replied Doe Capaldi smoothly. 'That was one side of the debate, but there was another. There were those who said that the upper classes were needed. They said that we were the necessary check on society, that which kept things functioning within reasonable bounds.'

'Wien is no more.'

The land outside Turing City was pitted with open-cast mines; it was scored with the lines of abandoned ditches and valleys that had followed the veins of ore to their end. The heavy black exhaust gases of the city forges settled out here, the sea wind rippling the oily surface of the stagnant pools and agitating the sluggish rivers of smoke.

The Turing City robots marched out of the city, and Olam watched as they waded into a stream of black smoke, waded deeper and deeper until they were lost beneath its surface.

'They're getting away!' said Olam in frustration.

'Just for the moment,' said Doe Capaldi. 'Look over there.'

Olam looked in the direction that Doe Capaldi had pointed, still getting used to his more powerful Artemisian eyes. And then he saw it, a line of smoke parting as if an invisible ship sailed through it, a silver shape ploughing a furrow beneath the wave.

'It's a train,' he said slowly.

'Built along the valley floor,' observed Doe Capaldi, 'hidden by the smoke. Jenny, what do you think?'

Olam wondered what it was exactly that Doe Capaldi saw in Jenny. They all wore exactly the same bodies. Why did he constantly defer to her?

'More Turing Citizens escaping?' wondered Jenny. 'I get the impression they were expecting us.'

'But how?' said Olam angrily. 'We didn't know ourselves we were attacking until a couple of days ago.'

'Peace, Olam,' said Doe Capaldi. 'Jenny, can we take out that train?'

Jenny gazed at the roiling line of smoke, judging distances.

'No.'

'Then let us kill the robots on foot,' said Olam. '*Now*, before we lose them amongst the smoke.'

He stared in frustration at the line of citizens as they slipped down into the valley.

Doe Capaldi spoke. 'I think we should return to the city now. These robots pose no danger to us. There may still be fighting in the city itself.'

'But they will get away!' said Olam in amazement.

'They can't go so far. Their metal will be ours eventually.'

'But . . .'

'Olam, there is no mind. There is only metal. Does it matter when Artemis claims their metal? Come, we return to the city.'

At that, Doe Capaldi's section turned and began to move back towards the burning city.

Olam paused for a moment, watching the last of the grey shapes disappearing into the pall of smoke.

He wanted to kill.

Karel

Four o'clock in the morning, and the silence was broken. They heard a hard clanging, the sound of a metal hand beating on a metal door. They heard voices and an electronic scream, suddenly silenced.

'The end of the hall,' said Susan. 'Draycott, Foxcote and Cookham.' She didn't stop working on Karel's poor damaged hand. It was dark, they had no heat from the forge, but she was still working away skilfully, straightening joints, reattaching ligaments.

Someone was shouting now. It sounded like a question, the same question being asked over and over again.

'What's going on?' murmured Susan.

There was a gunshot, and then another scream. It went on and on.

'Axel, turn off your ears.'

The child had been woken by the noise. He gazed around the room with bright yellow eyes.

'What for?'

'Just do it!'

There was more banging.

'They're moving up the hall,' said Susan. 'That's Dunley and Hinton.'

Karel said nothing. They should have run. Maybe it wasn't too late to do so. If only they had magnetic hands and feet, they could climb down the outside of the building. Karel looked towards the cold forge and cursed himself. They couldn't do anything without the fire.

They could hear more shouting. The same question being asked as before. Karel listened closely. It sounded like they were saying 'Choose'.

Susan had heard and she understood.

'Choose Axel, Karel,' she said. 'Choose Axel.'

'It won't come to that,' said Karel. 'We'll just cooperate with them.'

For a moment Susan lost control of her voice. Strange squeaks and squawks and crackles cut the air.

'Don't let them take my baby, Karel,' she managed at last. 'You're stronger than me. You'll be better able to look after him. Choose him, Karel.'

There was another gunshot, another scream.

'Susan, I'm not going to let anyone . . .'

And then the pounding started again, this time on their own door.

Karel looked at Susan. *They've missed out Madeley and Tungaka,* he thought, *they're here already.*

He got to his feet.

'Karel, I love you. No regrets.'

'I love you too, Susan.'

Karel paused, his gyros spinning, and then he opened the door.

There were two Artemisian soldiers standing outside. Only two of them. Grey-bodied infantryrobots, smaller than he was. Weaker too. He could fight them, he realized. He and Susan were stronger. He could lure them into the apartment and then take them.

And then get his whole family killed by the other soldiers who had invaded the rest of the rooms along the hall.

The two infantryrobots pushed him back into his apartment, into the forge room. Susan was crouching on the floor, her arms around Axel.

'My name is Eleanor,' said one of the robots. 'I am a leader of the Artemisian army. Welcome to Artemis, fellow Artemisians.'

Susan attempted to say something, her voice whistling and squeaking. She tried again, and this time her voice was clear.

'I am a citizen of Turing City,' she said.

'That state no longer exists,' said Eleanor. 'The population of this city is to be reduced by a third. Which of you will die?'

'No!' said Karel.

Susan gazed at him hopelessly. She had known, he knew. She had known.

Eleanor held her rifle aimed at the floor. 'The woman or the boy? Which one of them dies?'

Susan gazed up at him. 'I love you, Karel.' Her voicebox whistled as she spoke.

'CHOOSE!' The second infantry robot was younger, and he stabbed his rifle barrel at Karel's head, knocking his gaze aside so that he could not focus on Susan properly. 'CHOOSE, CHOOSE, CHOOSE!'

'Save my boy,' said Karel, his own voicebox now crackling and shrieking. He looked at Susan in despair.

'Thank you,' she said.

Eleanor turned her gun towards Susan's head. Her finger tightened on the trigger. Susan gazed up at Karel. At the last moment, Eleanor jerked the rifle towards Axel and fired.

Axel's head exploded in a cloud of blue wire.

Axel was dead.

The two infantryrobots left the room. Karel barely noticed their departure. Axel was dead.

Susan looked at his little body, her own covered in tangles of blue wire from his shattered head.

Her mind hadn't yet caught up with events. All the blue wire, twisting and tangling in the night. All that blue wire of Karel's that Susan had twisted that night, four years ago. All for this, to be blown apart by a single bullet.

Axel was dead.

Axel's body slumped forward and fell to the floor with a clatter. Susan just knelt there, gazing at it.

Karel stared down at the body of his dead son. It still didn't make any sense.

Axel was dead.

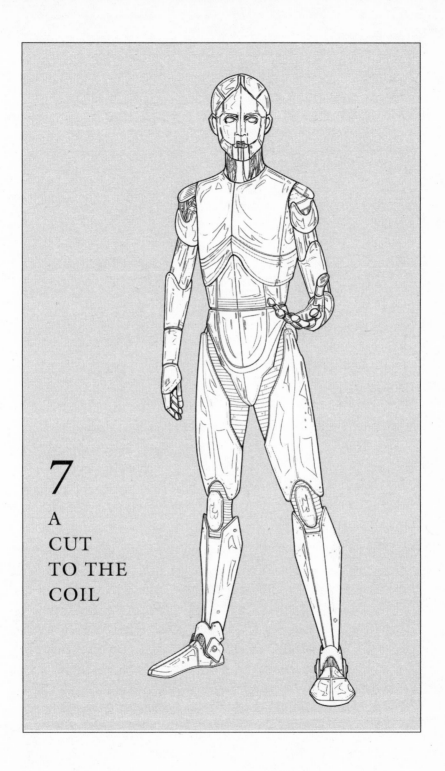

7

A
CUT
TO THE
COIL

Karel

Karel's son's body lay on the floor in a slippery pool of blue wire. He saw the expression on Susan's face, he read the fracturing of all her hopes, the death of the biggest part of her. He saw the gun of the infantryman swing in his own direction, and Karel tensed, waiting for the shot, but all the time he was thinking about his son. Had Axel suffered? Could a mind feel pain as it was expanding in an unravelling cloud of wire? Karel was himself going to die now, but he didn't care.

'No, these are both for collection.' The female Artemisian had pushed the other infantryrobot's rifle away.

'With respect, Eleanor, it's easier to kill the early ones and to keep the later ones. Prisoners only get in the way when you're halfway through a clearance.'

Karel gazed at the young infantryman. How old was he? Eleven, twelve?

'Thank you for your advice, Keogh. Nevertheless, I want you to take this man away now. See that his mind comes to no harm.'

'I'll do my best, but –'

'I said only that his *mind* comes to no harm. Those are Kavan's orders.'

Kavan? thought Karel. *What does he know about me?*

'I'll deal with the woman,' continued Eleanor.

'As you wish.'

The infantryrobot swung and fired into Karel's left thigh. The surge of pain from the electromuscle was indescribable. The infantry man shifted his aim and fired again, and now Karel's left bicep muscle crackled in agony.

'Karel!' Susan was screaming. He tried to look at her, he wanted to tell her he was okay, but the pain in his arm and leg was too great. It overwhelmed his coil, blocked the signals he tried to send to his mouth. He fumbled at the panelling on his left leg, trying to release it, to get at the electromuscle so he could unhook it.

'Get back, *Tokvah*!' Eleanor kicked Susan away from Karel. Susan fell over backwards, into the slippery pool of blue wire. She screamed.

'Ignore her. Now stand up.' The infantryrobot held an awl under Karel's chin and slowly pulled it up, forcing Karel to stand, his left leg and arm exploding in pain as he did so.

'Susan,' said Karel. It was all there was to say.

Susan sat up, sobbing, as she peeled Axel's blue wire from her body.

The infantryrobot began pushing him out of the room, and he took a last look at the painted walls, the scattering of tools on the floor, the distress of his wife and that tiny, broken scrap of metal on the floor that had been his son. And then he was gone, pushed out of his life in Turing City.

After that there were only fragments: disjointed pictures in his memory.

The hallway, metal doors to apartments broken and crumpled.

The stairwell, the broken body of another child, in a tangled metal heap at the foot of the steps.

Two Artemisian robots, stripping the decorative copper foil from the pillars outside the apartment block, rolling it up into bales ready for transportation back to Artemis City.

The dark streets, the bright stars above, the sounds of gunfire, the spark of cutting tools, the rolling of wheels. Dark shapes of Artemisians moving through the night, tearing the city apart.

And there, in the middle of the street, a terrible sight. It was enough to make even the young infantryrobot who pushed Karel along pause for a moment.

A City Guard lay dead on the hard-packed gangue of the road. His body was crushed and dented, exposing deep golden electromuscle of an impossibly fine weave. One of his legs was cut off below the knee, his head almost flattened. Yet he lay with his rifle in his hands, still aiming at some target down the road. A deep feeling of respectful awe crept over Karel. This robot, at least, had fought to the very end.

From somewhere to the west he heard a rending, tearing noise. The sky there lit up in brilliant whiteness, so bright it threatened to overload Karel's eyes. A low vibration shook the metal of his body; it rumbled up through his feet, it throbbed in his electro-muscles.

'What is it?' asked the young guard.

By way of answer the brilliant white light shorted out, leaving the night suddenly so dark by comparison. And then there was an explosion that shook the very earth, and red flames leaped up into the night.

Karel looked over to the west. He knew what it was. He knew what lay in that direction.

The fort of the City Guard had been breached.

Turing City had fallen.

Maoco O

The ending had come so quickly. One minute he had been there in the darkness before the fort, the brilliant white bolts from the Tesla towers arcing down over him to strike the Artemisian forces that were massed just out of rifle range. He had been moving to the dance of battle, weaving through the night, forming patterns with Maoco L and Maoco P and Maoco S. Seeking out the few black-painted Storm Troopers that crept forward through the night, their bodies loaded with explosive, despatching them with a shot to the metal of their minds.

And then, the next moment, the Tesla towers seemed to be feeding back on themselves, the great white electrical bolts arcing down towards the earth and then jumping back to the towers. The current was building in intensity, the flow making the very ground vibrate.

Maoco L was suddenly there at his side. 'They've laid a grid on the ground,' she was saying. 'They've crisscrossed the land with iron and they're reflecting the current back to us. We have to disable it!'

But it was too late. There was a shriek and the current shorted out, the light died.

A horrible low grinding noise, the creaking and shifting of stone that had lain undisturbed for years. The fort itself was collapsing. Artemis was attacking.

Maoco O was calm. He felt a quiet sense of pleasure. This was what he had been built for.

Grey robots and black robots and silver robots came rushing towards him. He fought with his rifle, with shuriken and knife and awl and hands and feet.

The outer wall of the fort had fallen. Artemisian troops rushed for the breach and Maoco O went to slow them, but there were too many robots around him now. He fought on, kicking and slicing and chopping, all the time trying to move towards the fort.

The Artemisians had almost made the wall now, but they were . . . they were falling! Cut down by a hail of bullets and thrown stars. Maoco O was confused. There weren't that many robots left in the fort, surely? And then he understood.

Emerging from the breach in the wall were tall golden robots. Their hands and arms were long and flexible, their legs smooth and unarmoured. Yet they carried guns and rifles and they wielded them with deadly accuracy.

The Mothers of the Fort, the robots that had woven the minds of the City Guard, now fought their last stand.

Karel

Another Turing City robot and its guard joined them, and then another, and Karel found himself part of a growing procession of the defeated, winding through the city towards the wreck of the railway station. The yellow light of the false dawn bloomed above it.

Karel felt so vulnerable, his thin, brightly coloured panelling was scratched and dented. It seemed pathetic when compared to the utilitarian grey of the infantry that surrounded him and the other prisoners.

Their city was being stripped apart. In the half-light, grey infantryrobots could be seen, tearing foil and leaf from the façades of buildings. Blue engineers with heavy-duty cutters followed them, cutting away iron pillars and supports, piling up sheets of steel on the ground, ready for processing. The decorated windows of buildings were smashed with hammers, so that Karel found himself crunching through diamond and ruby and amber and jade fragments of broken glass. Walking down a wide boulevard, he and the other Turing Citizens saw the tin beading being pulled from the windows of a meeting house so that, one by one, the curved plate-glass panes toppled forward into the road, their shattered glass skittering along behind him.

The Artemisians worked so quickly. That's what really amazed Karel. Bare hours had passed, and, as they approached the centre of the city, already some of the buildings were stripped down to skeletons.

They had machines there. Digging machines, long cylinders with spiral noses.

'We need a mind,' called out one of the blue-painted engineers. 'He'll do.'

The engineer was pointing directly at Karel.

'No, he's not to be touched,' said Keogh, Karel's guard.

'Take this one,' offered another guard.

A Turing Citizen was pushed forward.

'No!' he cried in terror, but the engineers seized him, popped open his skull and pulled out his mind, carefully detaching the coil. The mind was placed into one of the digging machines.

'Keep going down,' they said to the ear, built into the rear of the machine. 'We need to get at the foundations of the building.'

'I don't know if these Turing City minds have enough power to run these machines,' said one of the engineers. But then the screw at the front of the machine began to turn.

'Looks like they can,' said another engineer. 'Okay, we need four more robots.'

Four more Turing Citizens were pulled from the crowd, and then the procession moved on. They heard the pleading shouts of the chosen abruptly cut off as their minds were detached.

They reached the railway station just as dawn was breaking. The reflected light from Zuse threatened to outshine the pale yellow sunlight that picked out the stripped carcases of the city buildings, the long shadows of which extended across the marble square in front of the station. Only a few hours earlier Karel had been standing there with Susan.

Susan. What had happened to her?

The square was full of Artemisians, so many of them now. New soldiers were pouring into the city on trains, Karel could see them freshly disembarked and already marching in lines into the stricken city. Along with them came engineers and surveyors and reclamation robots. Now the city had fallen Artemisian workers were pouring into Turing City to claim the spoils.

And there went the prizes of conquest. A steady stream of metal was being marched and rolled and trundled and carried back into the station. Girders and steel plate, bundles of foil and reels of wire, all being fed onto the waiting trains to be whisked away, back to the factories of Artemis.

Karel had a thought that disgusted him: the process was like organic life. It was as if the city was eating itself: the railway station was a mouth that was now sucking the rest of the body into itself, sucking up all that metal to leave nothing of Turing City but the empty spaces in the long-depleted mines.

Karel's procession was now all the way through the square. He was made to join a growing crowd of other male prisoners. He looked around and wondered what had happened to the women. Most importantly, where was Susan?

And then he remembered the little body of Axel, lying broken on the ground.

Everything was gone.

Spoole

The marble flagstones of the parade ground were becoming abraded at the edges, stained and eroded by the acid rain. The thought gave Spoole pleasure: it was a sign that Artemis was a healthy, growing place. Even now, the three tall brick chimneys of the infantry factory belched smoke into the pale dawn, and a thin, cold breeze braided little curls of it across the clear morning sky. A team of robots scaling the chimneys, already two hundred feet up, were heading to repaint the white collars that encircled the tops.

Two newly manufactured battalions of infantryrobots formed squares on the parade ground. The doors of the factory had been flung wide open, and a company of Scouts were marching out, silver skins flashing in the pale light.

Gearheart leaned close to him. 'Just think what I could do to one of their bodies,' she murmured. 'Just imagine the mind I could twist from their wire.'

'Not another word.'

Gearheart annoyed him. Not her words so much, rather the fact that she tried to goad him. Everything about her seemed gauged to irritate him. She was wearing so little panelling today that the beautifully knitted electromuscles in her arms and legs were clearly visible, and Spoole realized how the soldiers, both male and female, would be looking at her.

'My appearance is symbolic,' she had claimed, 'it's an indication of your power, Spoole. A robot doesn't need protecting in this state that you have built.'

'You were woven to be attracted to me,' Spoole had replied, just before they had come out here that morning. 'It's like you feel you have to annoy me, just to prove that you have some control over your life. Don't think that I don't know that you're playing games with me, Gearheart.'

Gearheart had just altered her pose, showing off even more of her body.

'Playing games? I'm not the only one, Spoole. Look at Kavan. Where will he turn his attention next, now that he has taken Turing City?'

'I will deal with Kavan just as I will deal with you if you ever cross the line with me.'

'Oh, Spoole,' she had said, reaching to touch his leg, so that he felt the wire stirring within him, 'don't be like that.'

Spoole focused his attention on the here and now. He counted two thousand and fifteen robots standing to attention before him, both polished silver Scouts and matt-grey infantry. Behind them soared the red-brick façade of the factory with its tall windows. Through the open doors he could see the glow of the forges, and he felt a glow of pride himself at what had been wrought.

'Soldiers of Artemis,' he called out, his amplified voice rolling over the parade ground.

'Three weeks ago you entered the factory. Not as soldiers, but as robots of Bethe and Segre, of Stark and Born and Raman. Even of Artemis. And in the factory you stripped away your own metal and put aside your old form. Short or tall, wide or narrow, you have all built your new bodies to the same plan, and in this you are now all equal. You have each taken metal and beaten it to the same length, you have knitted electromuscle and threaded it into each other's arms. You have assembled your own and each other's bodies.'

He paused. The assembled robots stamped their feet, once, twice. Two thunderous cracks echoed across the parade ground.

'You have placed the ultimate trust in your fellow robots, allowing them to remove your mind from its old body and to place it in the new. For, as we all know, Artemis is not about individuals, it is about Artemis.'

Stamp, stamp.

Spoole looked down at the marble chips broken from the flagstones by the continued stamping of metal feet. Such power. It was good.

Now he lowered his voice. 'Let me tell you something,' he continued. 'You will have heard the rumours that Turing City has fallen. Well, let me tell you . . . those rumours are true!'

Stamp, Stamp.

'. . . already metal from Turing City is being sent here! Already robots from Turing City are riding towards us, carried here on Artemisian trains! Soon they will march through this city to the factory, and those of you who are still here will look upon them and you will notice they already wear grey infantry bodies. For those who chose to join Artemis have already have been presented with an Artemisian body. And yet, on entering the factory, that body will be taken from them! Those of you still serving in the factory may become teachers in order to show these new robots what you have already learned – how to strip apart their grey infantry bodies and rebuild them anew, exactly the same as they were.'

He lowered his voice. 'And you might wonder why this should be.'

'You're boring them,' murmured Gearheart.

Spoole felt a stab of anger at her remark.

'You might wonder why this should be,' he repeated, 'and yet, think for a moment. Think about how it would be if you too were presented with a body, ready made. Imagine if you were asked to wear a body over which you felt no real sense of ownership. You would no longer be an Artemisian soldier in the true sense of the word. You would be something apart: a mind with no feeling for its own body. You would think of the mind as something separate, something that did not truly belong to this state.'

Over the heads of the assembled multitude, the maintenance robots had finally reached the summit of the three chimneys. A band of clean white was now being drawn through the dirty paint. Spoole felt satisfied. High above them all, the city still functioned. He turned his attention back to the assembled soldiers.

'There are states that don't think as we do. There are states that believe that the mind is something special, something apart from the metal that it drives. I should say, rather, there *were* such states. The last of them fell this morning. Turing City is no more!'

As one, the soldiers drew up their right legs and stamped down hard on the marble surface. And then their left and their right again. The sound of stamping crashed through the city. It shook the painters on their towers, it shook the robots at their forges. Even out in the marshalling yards to the south, the engines and trucks echoed to the sound of stamping feet.

Spoole had to shout over the stamping. 'Never forget this! How we build Artemis into ourselves. How we weave it into our children!'

The stamping grew louder still.

'We are Artemis!'

Stamp, stamp, stamp.

He turned to Gearheart, in her half-naked, unpanelled state.

'Do you think Kavan could do this?' he asked. 'Do you really think *he* could inspire his troops in this way?'

'He doesn't have to,' came her infuriating reply.

Spoole turned back to the soldiers, raising his hands for silence. Instantly the stamping ceased.

'Listen, fellow soldiers, I want to tell you something else. Look at this city. Look at the factory behind you. Look at the steel curves of the Basilica, the copper roofs, the iron galleries and walkways. Do you understand what you see? Remember the story of Nyro, and how this land was once empty of metal. Remember that everything that you see here comes from elsewhere in the continent.'

Stamp, stamp.

'Everything! All the iron, stripped from the mountains to the north. All the gold and silver, carried here from the south. Everything! Look at me, you Borners and Bethers and Starkists – Artemisians now, all of you. Look at me! My mind may have been twisted here, but it was twisted of metal brought from your own former states! Remember, Artemis was an empty land. Everything that you see here did not happen by lucky chance; rather it was built solely by the will of Artemis.'

Stamp Stamp. Raised hands. Silence.

'But why?' asked Spoole. 'Why do we do this?'

He paused. The only motion now was the billowing grey smoke and the growing white lines that wrapped themselves around the chimney tops. That and the clouds that moved over the clear sky.

'Why do we do this? Why this urge to conquer? Why this urge to bring all the metal from across Shull to this place? After all, metal is metal. Does it really matter whether it remains hidden beneath the ground? Why not leave it locked in stone, or forced through the cracks in the rocks? Why not just leave it to rust in the rain and the sun?'

He felt unbalanced at the very thought.

'You know why. You know the answer as well as I do. It *feels* wrong to let good metal oxidise. It feels wrong to let metal go to waste. So now I ask a question on a more basic level: why should some metal seek to make copies of itself?'

They were all staring at him now. Eyes that should be fixed directly forward had all swivelled to gaze at him.

'Sometime in the past a piece of metal made another piece of metal just like itself. So why does some metal sit immobile, when other metal moves? Why does some metal seek to make copies of itself?'

'Who cares?' murmured Gearheart.

'I will tell you why: because that is how it was twisted!' roared Spoole. 'Twisted metal seeks to make more twisted metal! This is the basic reproductive urge! What are these bodies that we wear but twisted metal's way of twisting more metal? And now that same twisted metal, that wire twisted in the pattern of Artemis, controls the entire southern part of this continent! The wire, I say, not the bodies. Oh no, those bodies were built by the wire! You are the proof of this! So I ask you, what should you do now? Simply remain here, twisting dead metal into copies of yourselves?'

He pointed at the Scout nearest to himself: a silver woman, the blades at whose hands and feet were razor sharp with newness.

'You!' he demanded. 'Tell me, should we remain here?'

'No sir!'

Spoole was delighted.

'No! Of course not! There is dead metal still on this planet, and if we do not twist it, then some other robots will. Dead metal does nothing, only twisted wire *is*. Inevitably the metal on this planet will be twisted, if not by us then by others. Well, I say, let it be us who twist it all!'

The stamping began again.

'It does not end here, robots. To the north there are the mountains. But what lies beyond them? More states, grown rich and complacent on the metal that lies there? Are we to allow them to retain it, those who have never had to fight for everything that they now are, those who have not been tempered in the fire as Nyro's people have been? I say no! We say no! Artemis says no!'

Stamp, stamp, stamp. Tiny pieces of marble all jumping in time on the flagstones.

'It does not end here in the south of Shull. It does not even end when we have captured all of Shull! Even when the whole of this world of Penrose is ours, we will look to the moons, and then to the planets, and then to the stars!'

The stamping reached a crescendo. At that moment, Spoole felt invulnerable. That was the moment the robot chose to make its attack.

A flash of silver metal, a mercury stream falling through the air, metal claws on Spoole's chest. He was falling backwards.

A gunshot sounded.

Up above, high in the sky, the billowing smoke drifted; the robots painting the chimney remained unconcerned, unaware of what was happening below.

Gearheart was lying on the ground, the electromuscle in her thigh sliced neatly in two. She was twitching convulsively while beside her lay the motionless silver body of a Scout.

Spoole was already moving forward. Three silver scratches shone across his chest, curls of swarf at their edges.

Now his personal guard were milling around, trying to push him to safety.

'Let me through,' he commanded. 'I am no more important than any other robot here.'

The words came automatically. He wasn't thinking properly. He crouched down by Gearheart's side.

'Spoole?' she said. 'Spoole, something's wrong. I can't move. I can't feel anything.'

'Stay still, Gearheart. You'll be okay.'

'She's cut my coil, hasn't she? She's cut my coil.'

'She can't have done, or you wouldn't be able to speak.'

'Why did she do that? Why attack me?'

'There are always one or two who get through,' said Spoole. 'Spies or maniacs, or those with a grudge. Don't worry, she's dead now.'

There was a cut at Gearheart's neck, clearly visible on her unpanelled body. The electromuscle there was completely severed, sliced by the retractable metal blades on the Scout's hand. The rod that formed her back had a silver slice taken out of it. And, there, Spoole caught a hint of blue wire. The blade had also cut into Gearheart's coil. It hadn't completely severed it, but there was a nick.

Spoole felt a static charge take hold of his chest, making his electromuscle twitch oddly.

The silver robot had crippled Gearheart.

Karel

The pale sun rose over the expanding square in the rapidly disassembling city.

Karel stood with the other captives at the edge of the great square, his left leg and arm sending shivering charges of pain through his body. The other robots had been similarly wounded, presumably to prevent them from moving too quickly and thus causing trouble.

Karel felt as if he had been dipped in a bath of crude oil. Everything seemed so slow and sluggish, immersed as he was in his numbing misery. He looked at the other captives, wondering why there were so few of them. Had many of his fellow citizens escaped into the sea, like Garfel and the rest? He scanned the other robots as they entered and left the square, looking for the women. He saw plenty of Artemisian females, but none from Turing City. Where were they? Where was Susan?

He did this partly to distract himself, but all the time his mind kept being drawn back to that scene the previous night. The sight of the suddenly shifting gun, of his son's mind exploding in a cloud of wire.

And then he noticed the robot approaching them. Not an Artemisian, though, for this robot was taller than the standardized soldiers that busily worked the square. A Turing Citizen but walking free. Its body was of unpainted steel. But as Karel looked closer he saw the tell-tale flecks and stains at the edges of the body. Paint stripper. This robot had hurriedly removed its decorations, trying to blend in with the invading forces.

And now the robot was talking to one of the Artemisian soldiers. But not like a prisoner, more like it was one of them. Finally Karel understood what he was watching. A traitor!

And then he recognized the robot.

She had spoken at the parliament, where she had preached calm. She had promised to increase the guard at the railway station . . .

Noatak.

Kavan

'What now, Kavan?'

Eleanor was frustrated at the previous night's events, the way she had been sent off on a seemingly meaningless errand when she should have been helping organize the sacking of the city. When Eleanor felt like this she would snipe at him, cast doubt on Kavan's decisions.

'Where do you go now?' she asked. 'Back to Artemis to strip away your standard-issue body? Will you dress up in gold leaf and take your place in the conquerors' gallery?'

Kavan stood at the head of the central platform, gazing along the tracks fanning out across Copper Valley. Diesel engines roared constantly, moving the trains that fed the Artemis war machine. Wheels bumped across joints; he heard the high-pitched hum of reaction engines in the background, saw the sparks and flash of metal being cut and soldered. Eleanor's voice was just another part of the machine.

Somewhere out there along that line lies Artemis City, he thought. *Where now, Kavan? What would Nyro do? Where does your path lie now?*

It was almost as if Eleanor could read his thoughts. She taunted him with them, venting her frustration on him.

'Where now, Kavan? Do you head north, beyond the mountains? Go to northern Shull to conquer the ghosts and vampires?'

There was a cold wind blowing from the north; it blew the black smoke of the burning city out to sea; it left the view along the railway line crisp and clear.

'Or do you continue to ride the moment, Kavan? No one expected you to come this far this fast. First Wien, then Turing City. Spoole will be frightened, and you know it. You worried him when you deposed General Fallan, and so he sent you here, hoping, at the back of his mind at least, that you would be wiped out. What will he think now that you have taken Turing City? What will he be planning now, Kavan? What's waiting for you up those tracks? That's what you're thinking about, isn't it? Because you know the truth, don't you, Kavan? You know that Spoole can't afford to leave you as you are. You're too powerful now. You've become a threat. It's either you or him. Shull can't contain you both.'

She was right, of course, and it came as no surprise. This was what his mother had woven him for. The path that he had followed across the continent was curved and intricate, but it was as definite as the shape of the twisted metal that made up his mind. And just as his thoughts had a definite beginning and end, so did his path. It was now leading him north, back to Artemis City.

'. . . because you know it, Kavan. You can't fight it. It's twisted into you. *You* are Artemis, and Spoole is not.'

'How do *you* know that, Eleanor?'

His question startled her, he could see. She hadn't been expecting the mildness of his tone, this sudden interruption of her flow. Still, she collected herself, answered smoothly.

'Because Spoole is not out in the field. He is not fighting. He is not contributing to Artemis: he's only taking. Think of the Basilica, the fine metals, the service . . .'

'Sometimes a leader needs to stand back. Sometimes a good leader sends other robots to die, simply because it is right for Artemis. I have done the same myself.'

'Spoole clothes himself in gold leaf and whale metal. You wear an infantryrobot's body. So which of you is closer to the ideals of Artemis?'

Kavan turned to gaze back at the shell of Turing City. Truth be told, he felt cheated by this easy victory. There was still energy within his electromuscles ready to be spent.

'I have decided,' he said. 'Raise a battalion. We ride to Artemis.'

Karel

There was a change in the air. Every robot assembled in the square could feel it. The Turing Citizens that were huddled up around Karel; the Artemisian troops; the cutters and the lifters and the folders; all the robots who worked to disassemble the city and to turn it into folded metal to be transported across the plain to be eaten by the forges of Artemis, they felt it too.

The soldiers, the Storm Troopers, the commanders.

And Noatak, the traitor. Especially Noatak, the traitor. She felt it more than anyone.

There had been a shift in the engine, the sound of a changing of gear in the Artemis machine. Karel gazed at Noatak, watching how the robot shifted nervously, how she jumped and turned at the slightest sound, her newly bare metal panelling glinting in the weak sun.

Something was happening. Identical grey soldiers, the lapping waters of the Artemisian army, were receding into the station. What was happening?

The Artemisian engine had changed gear, but still it worked with relentless efficiency. The buildings of the city were still being stripped of their metal, the spoils of war taken away to be processed. Only now it was the turn of another sort of metal.

On command, Karel's line of robots stepped forward. He found himself standing in the front row. A grey Artemisian infantry-robot walked the length of the line, inspecting them. And there was Noatak with them, speaking to the Artemisian commander, telling her the names of the assembled citizens, informing her of their jobs and their family details, yet jerking nervously at the sound of the troops marching into the station.

Karel felt hollow, like a northern ghost. There was nothing inside him but the emptiness of his dead son, the emptiness of his lost wife. A single raindrop fell on his metal shell, and his body rang like a bell. Another raindrop fell, and another. Karel heard the ringing as if from a great distance away.

'And this one?'

The Artemis commander wore a silver flash on her shoulder. Apart from that, she was identical to the other infantryrobots that she commanded. But she could not compare with Noatak the trai-tor, who hovered at her shoulder in her bare metal body still stained with paint stripper; Noatak whose body panelling was hammered so smooth that the seams barely showed – how that contrasted with the cheap tin solder of the commander.

More rain drops fell on them all. Plink plink plink. Plink plink on Karel's head.

'This is Karel, ma'am,' said Noatak.

'Karel?' The commander's voice was strange. Or maybe it was just the rain, dripping down onto their bodies.

'That's right. Karel worked in Immigration. He controlled who entered our state . . .'

Once. Yesterday. Was it only yesterday?

'So *this* is Karel,' said the commander, thoughtfully.

'Yes, ma'am. Do you know of him?' Noatak looked uncertain, nervous.

As well she should. What was she doing, standing here, when Axel was lying dead, back in their flat? If their flat was still even there . . .

'He is unusual within this city,' continued Noatak. 'His mother was . . .'

'No matter,' said the commander, turning to watch the soldiers still marching into the station. 'We need transport.'

Axel dead on the floor.

'Noatak,' said Karel, quietly, his voice almost unheard below the pattering of the raindrops.

'Now this is Beryl,' said Noatak, anxious to move on. Karel moved as fast as a spring snapping back. He shoved the traitor, tripped her, seized her head and smashed it onto the wet slippery ground, badly denting the skull. Noatak made to get up, but Karel kicked her feet away, slammed her head on the ground again. That was it: he felt himself being pulled away, hauled up by two infantryrobots.

The commander was standing before him again.

'I had heard that he had a temper,' she was saying. 'Better not let him give vent to it. Take him into the station *now*.'

Karel heard Noatak emitting an electronic whine.

'Turn it off,' ordered the commander. 'Or, if it's a fault in your voicebox, get it fixed. Swap it for the voicebox from one of these *Tokvah*. Now get back up. We have to get all these processed.'

Karel twisted, lashed, kicked at his captors to no avail. As he was dragged backwards into the station he saw Noatak, head badly dented, still working her way down the line of robots.

The well-oiled machine of the Artemis invasion processed Karel.

He thought of his conversation with Banjo Macrodocious, just a few days ago.

Don't you realize that if you had emerged in Artemis we wouldn't even be having this conversation? You would already be owned by the state! Every item there, every rock, every mine, every robot is nothing but property.

And now he, Karel, was nothing but property. Nothing more than metal, and Artemis did not distinguish between the metal of the body and that of the mind.

The infantryrobots twisted free his arms and his legs, the easier to control him. They laid his body on the station floor. He craned his head this way and that, trying to see what was going on.

Engineers brought forward metal and bent it to make a chassis. They worked so quickly, following a well-practised drill. Metal wheels were then rolled up on the rails, the chassis fixed over them.

'What are you doing?' asked Karel. No one answered him.

Six engineers approached carrying a shiny diesel engine, no doubt freshly unloaded from an Artemisian truck. They took it over to the half-built frame and slotted it into place. It fitted perfectly. Karel was impressed, despite himself, by this Artemisian efficiency. Already, side panelling was being pop-riveted into place, and the engine was being coupled to the wheels.

A diesel locomotive was taking shape before his eyes.

Someone took hold of Karel and rolled him onto his front. They started to strip the panelling from his body. They rolled him onto his back and completed the operation, leaving his head and naked body lying helpless on the floor, whilst next to him they went on constructing the train. His bare electromuscle touched cold stone. It ached.

They were welding the seams of the locomotive now: sparks dripping down onto the floor near his head.

And then he felt himself being moved again. He felt hands inside his body, someone touching his coil, unplugging his mind from his body.

Nothing.

Maoco O

Turing City changed shape by the hour. The broken-rock roads grew a block at a time, stamped into the ground by the Artemisian troops as they marched. Crossroads appeared, sending new branches of tracks and thoroughfares reaching through the heart of the city. They were foreign roads, alien roads, made of stone from broken buildings, gravel and shattered concrete stirred up from foundations, all stamped flat by the pounding feet of the invaders.

These roads spread through the city like organic life, creeping through the cracks, tipping over buildings that had stood for decades. Like organic life they sucked the life of the city away: on Artemisian carts loaded with the stacked metal that had been columns, the folded metal that had been decorative panelling, the bundled metal that had been minds . . .

The galleries with their intricate iron work, their stained glass, their leafwork . . . all were now empty shells, the ground a pointillistic nightmare of broken and trodden paint tubes scattered here and there by the invading forces. Dislodged marble rubble from broken fountains rolled multicolour tracks through the colours that were being washed into the drains by the pattering rain. Ripples appeared in yellow and red and purple puddles.

No one saw Maoco O as he crept through the plundered streets. He was the broken metal at the foot of a building here, the sound of rain dripping from shattered tiles there. He was the silent shadow that flickered across the square as windblown litter tumbled over the ground.

There had been an entrance to the fort amongst the columns that decorated the southern end of the galleries. In the old days, Maoco O had been able to emerge from that entrance and merge with the milling shoppers unnoticed. Now half the columns had dominoed, fallen and shattered, sending sections like thick-toothed yellow wheels rumbling across the square.

The entrance to the fort was still there, but now covered by one of those stone cylinders. Maoco O heaved at it, electromuscle straining, and the stone shifted ever so slightly. He needed a lever of some sort. He cast around to locate one, and found himself facing a pair of Artemisian Scouts, their silver bodies sparkling with raindrops.

It was difficult to tell who was the more surprised, Maoco O or the Scouts, but all three moved at precisely the same time. Maoco O was moving sideways so that the kick launched by the left Scout went wide; he blocked the punch thrown by the right Scout, taking the awl from her other hand as he did so. He scraped a foot down her calf to stamp down on the instep, snapping the claw mechanism there. Water slipped from silver bodies in a diamond spray. Maoco O kicked down again at an exposed leg, tearing through the panelling and into the electromuscle beneath. Reaching underneath the chin as the body doubled up, he ripped back her head, exposing the coil and slicing through it with one sharp palm edge. The other Scout was now moving in. Maoco O squeezed the electromuscles in the dead Scout's foot so that claws were exposed and he raked them down the other's chest.

The scene fractured into shards of sensations. The flashing of polished metal and sparks and rain like diamonds, reaching up and grabbing blue wire, and then there was just Maoco O staring at the emptiness of two more dead bodies.

The warrior's mind was fading, lost in the emptiness of it all. The city had fallen: his purpose was now receding once more.

Maoco O looked at the two metal shells, disconnected a pair of legs, twisted the mechanisms around.

Now he could make himself a lever to shift the yellow stone.

The heart of the fort stood silent and empty. And hidden. Elsewhere, Artemisians were sacking the public areas, the DMZs and the dummy rooms, but the core of the fort, the secret heart, still remained hidden beneath the earth.

Maoco O made his way through forgotten passages to the silent darkness that lay deep beneath the broken city, listening hard. Was he the only one who had escaped? Was he the only one to make it down here? The City Guard had planned for everything. They had planned to hide here even in defeat, to regroup and to prepare for the future. But no one could have predicted the utter rout that had been inflicted upon them. Robot after robot had fallen on the arena before the fort, locked in furious battle.

Only Maoco O, it seemed, had been able to muster the strength to walk away. To escape from the killing ground and to hide away while the battle swept past him.

Maoco O the coward.

Now Maoco O was heading down and down, heading for a certain room near the centre of the hidden quarter.

Finally, he entered the room he sought. His body was badly damaged, but there was metal here. Metal and coal and tinder. And a forge, cold and unused.

Maoco O looked around for a lighter.

Eleanor

Eleanor watched Kavan marshalling his troops.

It was funny, she reflected. He had travelled across half the continent and succeeded in a task others had declared impossible: he had conquered Turing City. And yet, for all that effort, he was going to depart from the scene of his greatest victory having seen nothing more than the railway station.

Not that it was really possible any more to see Turing City as it had been. All Kavan would now ever have seen of the once-proud state on the southern coast would be its component parts being carried past him, piece by piece.

It was appropriate after a fashion, she decided, for Kavan did not care about any philosophy other than Nyro's. He saw Turing City as nothing more than building materials.

She turned her attention back to the matter at hand.

A train was being made ready. Just one train to conquer Artemis.

'It took a division to take Wien,' Kavan had declared. 'It took a regiment to take Turing City. We'll take Artemis with a battalion.'

Eleanor didn't argue. Kavan had been proved right so far.

He had summoned his troops, ordered oil and cleaning fluid. Forges had been set up along one platform; he had the quartermasters set up shop along the next. The chosen robots had stripped their bodies down, cleaned and repaired themselves and each other and rebuilt themselves afresh for yet another battle. The activity had slowed the removal of material from Turing City, but this was more important.

The train on which they were to travel was newly built: a functional thing of unpainted metal, edges of solder and curls of swarf marring its unsmoothed extent. The troops were already boarding.

Kavan, Wolfgang and Ruth took their places in the lead carriage. Kavan finally noticed Eleanor.

'Come in here,' he said. 'I'll need you with me.'

Eleanor made to join him in the lead carriage, pleased to be back amongst the minds of the army. Kavan gave her a rare smile as she climbed into the carriage; her feet echoing like a drum beat on the bare metal floor.

'I'd rather have you in here where I can watch you than out there plotting behind my back,' he said.

Eleanor smiled. 'How well you know me, Kavan.'

Karel

Vision returned. Then sound.

'Three minds,' said someone, and Karel was shown two minds nestled into a metal frame. There was space for a third between them. His own, he presumed. Questions began clamouring for his attention. How was he seeing? Where were his eyes? Where was his body?

'You control this locomotive,' said the voice. And his vision moved, giving him a view along the dull grey length of the freshly built machine. He saw the roughly cut metal, the unfiled coils of swarf curling from the ends of panels. The view swept further along the train's length, showing a line of bare metal carriages, infantryrobots climbing on board. The view shifted again, and for a moment it lingered on the platform. He saw his old body stripped of its panelling, arms and legs removed, head empty. And then his vision moved again and it was gone.

'Your coil has been hooked up as follows,' said the voice. 'Your legs are linked to the motor. It's diesel, so give it time to warm up. It should have a good midrange pull, this model usually does. Left arm linked to the brakes, right arm to the gears. You'll soon get the hang of it. You've got ears so that you can be told what to do. You've got a mouth, but unless we want to hear from you we won't be using it. Mostly we'll just have you linked to a buzzer. One beep for yes, two for no. Long beep if you see something important.'

I should have fought while I had the chance, thought Karel bitterly. That wild, unreasoning anger that had always filled his life was swirling inside his mind, searching for a release. There was none.

Suddenly, his thoughts were with his mother. For the first time in his life he had empathy with Liza, an understanding of just how powerless she had been on the night of his making.

It came as a revelation. For the first time in his life he realized something crucial: who could blame her for what she had done? Kneeling before an Artemisian soldier, a gun held to her head, she had done her best to keep the terror from her mind, but the anger that she had felt was woven into Karel's mind.

The voice continued speaking. 'There are three minds. Disobey orders and your coil will be crushed. We'll just link up one of the other minds. Do you understand?'

Rust your mind! shouted Karel. All that emerged was a strangled beeping.

'One beep for yes,' said the voice.

Karel said nothing.

'Answer me now or I hook up the next mind. I do that, and you may end up riding this train in limbo until you die.'

To take away his sight as well, to take away what little sensation he had left, the thought filled him with terror. *Yes,* said Karel, and he heard a single beep.

'I knew you understood. Hey, think yourself lucky that you are the middle mind. It must mean you've got a friend somewhere. Okay, you'll be setting off soon, so watch the signals.'

And that was it.

There was darkness for a moment, and then his mind was plugged properly into the locomotive. He saw the view down the tracks before him, and then, with a surge of awakening, he felt the power of the diesel engine.

What to do? He practised revving the engine. He practised pulling at the brakes with his arm.

This was what Artemis did to minds, he realized. It treated them like things. Now his mind was nothing more than metal to be employed by Artemis in its never-ending conquest. He had warned Banjo Macrodocious about this, but he had never expected it to happen to himself.

He was jolted from his reverie by the voice. 'Hey, can't you see the light? It's time to go!'

He noticed the green signal shining up ahead. He concentrated on walking, felt the surge of diesel power. He saw the sleepers begin to slip beneath him. He was moving.

'Okay, engine, I don't expect to have to speak to you again. We're off now. Next stop Artemis City.' Karel heard a little laughing noise, and then the voice spoke again.

'And take care driving, you've got Kavan himself on your train.'

Karel emerged from the wrecked railway station into Copper Valley. The train picked its way over the bridges and points as he headed north. North to Artemis City.

Kavan

The journey northward passed without incident. Even Eleanor was silent. She just sat in the corner of the carriage, cleaning her rifle, sharpening her knives, making herself ready for the coming battle.

The others were much the same. Wolfgang, his aide, stared at the ceiling, concentrating. Ruth remained standing, swaying with the movement of the train.

Kavan wondered at how he now felt. Was he doing the right thing, or had his hand been forced? Something didn't feel right.

'Why is the train stopping?' he asked.

'I don't know,' said Eleanor. 'Pendric, Dylan, find out what's going on.'

The train was slowing to a halt. Two grey infantryrobots slid open the carriage door.

'Get up the front to the driver,' called Eleanor, and the two robots dropped out onto the desolate plain that lay outside.

Kavan went to the door and looked out. The sun was going down, huge and red, setting the underside of the dark clouds on fire, lighting up the thin gusts of rain that the cold wind sent splashing over his metal skin. He could see another train in the distance, running on a nearly parallel track. It seemed to be setting out from Artemis City, heading towards Stark or Segre.

'We're almost there,' said Eleanor, leaning forward from the train beside him. 'I can see the city. I can see the Basilica. It's all lit up in red.'

The robots waited in silence, the metal of their bodies plinking and pattering as the rain drops fell on them.

There was a shout from ahead.

'Kavan,' called Pendric. 'I've got some engineers building an observation tower. There's something that you need to see.'

'What is it?'

'I think you'd be better looking from the tower.'

'What about the attack?' said Eleanor.

'Patience,' said Kavan.

He dropped out into the rain, and made his way to the skeletal tower that was quickly taking shape.

'Safe to go up now,' said one of the engineers.

Kavan nodded, and then swarmed up the rods they had left protruding from the sides of the tower, using them as a ladder.

The city confronted him: a magnificent, smoky mass of metal sprawling over the barren plain.

And, as he looked back at Artemis City, Kavan did something that many of his followers had never seen him do before.

He laughed.

All the choices, all the indecision rolled away.

He would not be attacking Artemis City today at least. Like it or not, his mind had been made up for him. The twisted metal in Spoole's mind had followed a path similar to Kavan's. Similar, but not exactly the same. The other's metal had danced its course around Kavan's without the two paths ever actually touching.

Spoole had outwitted him: elegantly, delightfully, easily.

It was written before him in the pattern of the rails, slicked with rain and lit up with red fire from the evening sun.

Where once the railway lines had filled the plain like a rough sea, crisscrossing, rising, falling, plugging Artemis City into the rest of the continent, now the lines were raked smooth to circle the city in a neat concentric pattern of lines. Artemis City rose like an island from this red sea, untouched by the pattern of fire that surrounded it.

It was an act of challenge, a parry and an insult all in one. It was the actions of Nicolas the Coward written in metal for the world to see.

Kavan couldn't enter the city. The railway lines no longer ran that way. Instead, they ran around the city and continued north in an unbroken line.

The message was obvious. Kavan was being sent north to break his troops against the mountain range that cut the continent in two.

'It's a challenge,' said Kavan.

'Sorry, Kavan?' queried the engineer that waited at the foot of the tower.

'Never mind. Tell the troops. We're to go north. The south is not enough. We are to conquer the whole of Shull.'

The cold wind gusted rain across Kavan's body. Drops beaded on his metal fingers. He gazed down at them, thoughtfully.

'The winter is coming,' he said. 'The snow will be blowing from the north, and we will be fighting against it, every step of the way.'

'Can we really do it?' asked the engineer.

'The mountains are high and there is no route through them that an army could take. We may have to split our forces. They could pick us off easily in the passes . . .'

'But can we do it?'

'Of course we can. We always do.'

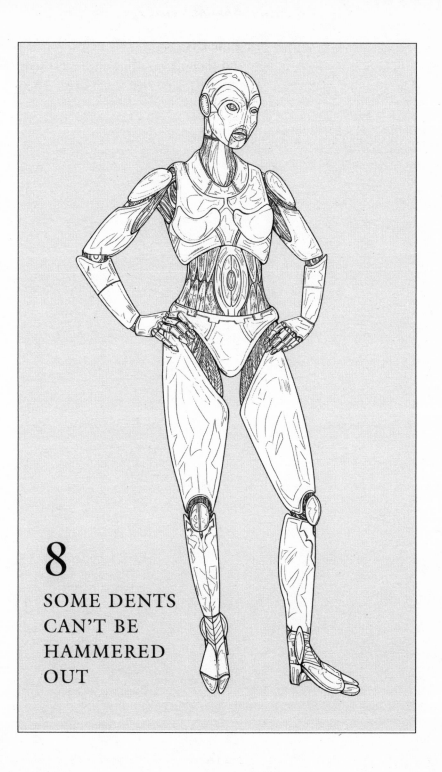

8

SOME DENTS CAN'T BE HAMMERED OUT

Interlude: La-Challen

Far away, in distant Yukawa, the radio operator turned a dial.

'What is it, La-Challen?'

'I don't know. Static, but of an odd signature. It's coming from Shull, I think. Every fifteen minutes I hear the signal. Perhaps you could enlighten me, Cho-La-Errahi?'

The superior took the jack from La-Challen and plugged it directly into his body, a serene expression on his face.

'It will come again in less than a minute, my master.'

'Silence, La-Challen. I am listening . . .'

Olam

It had been raining for days, raining in cold gusts that seeped between the panels and dampened the electromuscles. The broken rocks of the mountain were shiny wet, and Olam's feet were sodden from wading through puddles that jumped under the never-ending impact of raindrops. There was nowhere to shelter, no chance to take apart a shorting limb to dry and clean and oil it. There was nothing here but rain and rock and dust. Lots of dust. So much wet grey dust, it worked its way into body and mechanism. Dust that stuck to the hands and the face and body so that everything was constantly gritty and damp.

Not for the first time, Olam wished he were back in Wien, dressed in his old body, feeling its metal warming in the sun's heat. Standing in a marble tower and looking out over the bay . . .

'Get ready,' called Doe Capaldi, jerking him from his reverie. His section crouched in the limited shelter of a sheer rock face, their metal skins glistening with diamond drops of rain. Doe Capaldi didn't seem to care about the weather. *Why does he always look so calm?* wondered Olam. *Why doesn't this upset him as much as it affects me? After all, he has lost far more than I ever had.*

People were running towards him. Olam heard the splash of feet, the clink of metal on rock and the squeaking, unhealthy sound of robots that had spent too long being wet. He looked up the valley to see Spuran's section pelting back down the newly carved valley, running from . . .

'Cover your eyes! Turn off your ears!' ordered Doe Capaldi. Olam obeyed, just as a hammer struck down on the world.

His mind seemed to bend for a moment, his thoughts elongating. Electromuscle crackled, sending clouds of colour dancing inside his head. And then there was a white light so bright that it filled the inside of his skull. It illuminated the receptors of his covered eyes, sending a lance of lightning deep into his twisted metal, right back to the very start of the pattern – to the first knot tied by his mother.

The ground was shaking, rattling him around like a wingnut discarded on a forge floor. A shower of stone was falling, rocks and rubble rumbling and crashing. His whole body vibrated, he could feel screws loosening under the harsh percussion. A howling wind threatened to tear his fingers from the crack in the rock to which he clung so tightly . . .

And then the white light faded. So did the rain, for the moment at least.

Doe Capaldi was banging on his head. Immediately, he turned his ears back up, just like he had been drilled.

'Bomb's still ticking,' called Doe Capaldi. 'We've got fifteen minutes. That's twelve minutes to get it into position, and then three to run to safety. Let's go!'

The whole section was up now, grabbing hold of the trolley, which ran on big plastic wheels. They were running, up the valley, towards the source of the explosion. Olam ran to the front, kicking aside smaller stones, shoulder-charging larger rocks to push them aside and help clear a path for the trolley and its deadly, ticking load.

The gusting rain returned in cold cannonballs that raised fountains of moisture on the slippery rock. Still Olam ran on, the trolley bouncing behind him. *Be careful with the trolley*, he muttered to himself, *be careful with the trolley*.

Doe Capaldi was now by his side, urging the other robots onwards, and Olam felt a familiar stab of hatred.

Further up the newly excavated valley, closer to the source of the previous explosion, and the going was soon becoming harder, the broken rock beneath their feet ever more unstable. There was a rumble to the right, and an avalanche of scree spilled downwards.

'Zuse,' swore Olam, dancing over the sliding rock, struggling to keep his feet.

'Plenty of time,' called Doe Capaldi. 'Clear from the left-hand side, where the rubble is shallowest.'

Olam bent and shovelled away fragments of stone with his hands, throwing it back across the valley floor. Later, the sappers would use the stone to fill in the gaps and cracks in the ground as they levelled it, or maybe use it as ballast for the railway lines they were laying northwards. Slowly and inevitably, Kavan's path to the north – and conquest – was taking shape.

Not that Olam cared at this moment. Behind him, the trolley bounced along, and the bomb was ticking. All he cared about was laying it and getting clear. He had already seen too many dented and half-melted robot bodies along the path, caught too close to the EMP and the subsequent heat of the blast. Above him, the jagged and broken peaks of the valley reached up into low clouds. Olam shovelled rock, making a path for the trolley.

And now the path was clear. Clear enough, anyway. The trolley bumped forward, and Olam got a proper look at the bomb: an evil-looking black glass cylinder, with a metal plate fastened to one end.

'Go, go, go,' called Doe Capaldi.

On they went, running for the new head of the valley, seeking the best location to site their bomb. The new valley snaked through the mountains, following the faults in the rock that the nuclear explosions had found. The robots living in the mountains had been totally confused by the haphazard course of Kavan's clearance, had been unable to plan an attack on the excavation. No one could have predicted which way the track would travel next, not even Kavan and the Artemisians.

But it was hard work, reflected Olam, as he and Doe Capaldi tipped an enormous boulder off balance and rolled it clear of the new path they were forming. Behind them was a line of nuclear bombs, their timers set a week previously in Artemis City itself, each one of them ticking down to zero, carefully timed to explode at fifteen-minute intervals.

Each bomb had its own attendant team, all waiting their turn to rush forward to the head of the growing valley to plant their deadly cargo. After that they would rush back to collect their next bomb and rejoin the lethal carousel. Doe Capaldi's team had now done this twice; they reckoned they would have to do it twice more before Kavan's forces finally pierced a way through the central mountain range.

But what audacity! Even Olam was grudgingly impressed. Everyone had wondered at Kavan's strategy for advance upon the northern part of the continent. There were so few avenues of approach. Would he take them through Raman and Born? Would they establish base camps in the mountains, gradually taking ground? No one could have guessed at this. Kavan had simply put in a request to Spoole and had waited, safely clear of Artemis City, until the bombs he required had been delivered. Black cylinders, doubly sealed and already ticking. Security: a way to prevent Kavan using them upon Artemis City itself. Not that Olam thought Kavan ever would. Why should he try that, when a whole new land was awaiting conquest, just the other side of the mountains?

Now the dust started to fall again: powdered grey stone, sucked up by the explosion, it took a while to find its way to earth again. It covered his body, it covered Doe Capaldi, too. It was washed away by raindrops that ran down robot bodies and hung from robot fingers like diamonds. Still they bounced the trolley forward.

'Eight minutes,' called Doe Capaldi. 'Olam, Blackmore, Lord, come with me. We'll clear a space in the rocks there and site the bomb at the base of that column.'

The four of them ran ahead of the trolley, up to where the heavier boulders had fallen. Shattered pillars and daggers of stone big enough to spear a robot as they plunged into the ground. They worked at shifting them, prying a space to drop the bomb into. The trolley came bouncing closer.

'What's that?' asked Blackmore, pointing up into the shafts of rain. Olam looked up. He couldn't see anything.

'Paragliders,' shouted Doe Capaldi. 'The idiots are attacking again! Don't they realize that we have a bomb?'

Olam looked up, caught a glimpse of a silver-foil sail, cutting across the sky.

'No time for that,' called Doe Capaldi. 'Get the bomb into place.'

The trolley crew had formed a line and were already passing the heavy black cylinder up over the uneven rocks towards Olam and the rest. There was a hissing noise and a silver sail passed over them, momentarily cutting off the fall of rain.

Olam took hold of the bomb, placed one end on the ground and wedged it with his foot as Doe Capaldi and the others levered it up.

'That's the angle,' decided Doe Capaldi, and they slid the heavy black shape into the crack in the rocks.

'Easy, easy. Okay, it's in! Now let's get out of here.'

There was a crack, and Blackmore fell to the ground, a neat hole drilled in his head.

A robot seized her rifle from where it lay on the trolley, turned and shot at the enemy robot that had landed nearby, the silver foil of its paraglider slowly settling to the ground. The rest of the section grabbed their guns, turning them on the other robots that now fluttered to the ground all around them.

'Leave them!' ordered Doe Capaldi. 'Only three minutes. Run!'

They turned and ran, rain splashing, silver foil folding down around them, the crack of rifle fire behind them, the sound of ticking echoing in their heads.

A shadow swooped over Olam's head and he looked up to see one of the paragliders. A robot gazed down at him. Its body was small, it gripped the wires of the paraglider with short arms and legs. Olam watched as it pulled at a cord and sent the craft spinning around and he realized, with a thrill of horror, that it was coming straight for him. The rest of his squad was running on, but he was frozen, transfixed by the sight of the strange robot as it settled on the ground before him. Olam raised his rifle. There was a crack and the robot fell down, dead. Olam hadn't fired.

'Run!' yelled Doe Capaldi, lowering his rifle.

Olam ran. There was a flash and he was falling, his leg crackling and shorting in agony. He twisted as he fell, firing one, two, three shots into the air at random.

Doe Capaldi bent over him.

'Save yourself,' snarled Olam.

Doe Capaldi was scanning the area.

'Get away,' shouted Olam. 'You owe me nothing!'

Still Doe Capaldi remained silent. He pushed Olam down to the ground, rolled him onto his front. Rainwater ran into Olam's eyes, blurring his vision. Doe Capaldi was kneeling on his back, grappling at his neck.

'Is a bullet too quick for me?' Olam asked, with some satisfaction. 'You'd rather crush my coil?' Still Doe Capaldi said nothing. He felt the sensation switch off in his arms and legs. Doe Capaldi was unhooking his head.

Then his vision was bouncing, jumping. He saw the ground, the clouds, the ground again. He could hear Doe Capaldi counting off the seconds.

'. . . *forty-three, forty-two, forty-one* . . .'

Was he actually trying to save him?

'. . . *thirty-eight, thirty-seven* . . .'

On and on they ran. Gunshots ricocheted off rocks. Why didn't they hit Doe Capaldi? Little weak bodies, couldn't they aim straight?

'. . . *sixteen, fifteen* . . .'

They weren't clear. Surely they weren't clear? The rocks would be shaken loose by the explosion. They would fall and crush them, bury them alive. And who from Artemis would come to search for them?

Then they were diving, diving for cover . . .

'Close your eyes!' screamed Doe Capaldi.

Olam did so. He only just remembered to turn off his ears in time, too.

Spoole

Gearheart dragged herself across the floor, her dented metal shell scraping on the sandstone.

'Don't stare at me,' she shouted, silver eyes flashing.

Spoole ignored her request. He squatted, the better to see the way she swung her left arm. The useless hand had been replaced by a hooked shape that she dug into the grooves of the floor to pull herself forward. The delicate panelling that covered her body was dented and scratched, peeling back at the seams, but she refused to let them replace it with something more suitable and hard-wearing. There was a dent near the top of her head, but she refused to let anyone hammer it out, claiming, probably correctly, that no one would be able to do the job as well as she herself could.

As good a job as she herself could *once* have done, Spoole corrected himself.

She had reached the foot of her chair. 'Go on, then, help me up!'

One of the two sentry robots that now accompanied her every movement made to lift her, but Spoole waved him back.

'I'll do it,' he said, and he took hold of Gearheart and gently placed her in the chair. She weighed so little: a combination of rare alloys and her once-superb engineering skills.

'Speak to me, Spoole. I'm bored.'

'What do you want to talk about?'

'Tell me about Kavan. Where is he now? Have the mountains defeated him?'

'No, Gearheart. He blasted a passage straight through the mountains with atomic bombs. He is exploring the north now.'

'You gave him bombs? Foolish, Spoole, you should have let him break himself on the mountains. The more you indulge him, the more powerful he becomes.'

'Gearheart, I cannot go against Nyro's will. Kavan and I both serve Artemis. At the end of the day, we are each nothing but metal.'

'We're nothing but twisted metal, Kavan,' she said bitterly. 'I truly understand that now.'

'No, there is just metal, Gearheart. That is what Nyro said.'

Spoole gazed at Gearheart as she used her one good arm to steady herself in the chair. *Nothing but metal*, he thought. *And yet look at Gearheart.*

Spoole felt as if his mind had lurched, that a gear had slipped somewhere in the chain.

Look at Gearheart. Just a few strands of metal in her coil had been cut, and yet look at her now. The same metal, exactly the same metal, but for those few nicks. And what a difference it had made!

If Nyro could only hear his thoughts now: this was treason and blasphemy of the highest order. But surely this wasn't what Nyro had meant? Surely she would understand that Gearheart would have served Artemis better as she had been, not as she was now?

Look at her, struggling with that one bent arm to straighten herself, the lines of her body crumpling like foil in a child's hand. Maybe Kavan should be leader of Artemis. How can I truly claim to embody Nyro's philosophy while thinking these thoughts? Speculating that there is something beyond mere metal, something beyond the state?

Gearheart's arm slipped, and she tumbled forward onto the edge of the steel table. Delicate metal was bent further out of true. Spoole gazed at her in wonder. Gearheart could never be made the same again, not even if all her metal was melted down and they were to begin again. The world had lost something precious.

Traitor, he chided himself.

Susan

Susan was pushed into a wagon with forty other women, and left there for sixteen days.

Sometimes the wagon moved, and the robots that crouched within the darkness of the wagon felt the click click of the wheels on the track through their feet. For a long time the wagon remained stationary, and they listened to the pattering of the rain on the tin roof.

Inside the wagon the women spoke and sang, they cleaned and repaired each other as best as they could. They tapped out rhythms on the sides of the wagon, keeping time with the clicking wheels when they moved, or imitating the motion of travel when they stood still.

They did their best to hold their nerve but, inevitably, someone put the first twist in the wire, starting to build a panic.

'They're taking us to Artemis. Look at us all, full of lifeforce, well built. They're going to rape us.'

That woman was quickly silenced, but the metal now had a twist in it, and it was inevitable that the women would continue to work it in their minds. It was true: all the women in the carriage wore well-built bodies. The Artemisians had chosen the best from Turing City.

Susan didn't care. Her thoughts kept returning to Axel, his little body lying lifeless on the floor, to how that mind that she had carefully woven had been scattered and ruined.

She thought, then, of Karel, the expression on his face as he had been marched away.

She wondered where he was, or if he was even still alive.

Eventually the door to the wagon slid open, and the dim rain-filled daylight flooding into the interior seemed impossibly bright. The women turned down their eyes as they were led, one by one, out of the wagon and across a narrow cobbled strip. They couldn't see properly, couldn't make out their surroundings. There was only the suggestion of tall buildings covered in soot. And the feel of metal all around. So much metal.

Through a door, they were marched along one long corridor after another, then down steps, descending deeper and deeper underground. They could hear voices, many, many voices. Nearly all of them female, they echoed from the bare metal walls of the seemingly endless corridors through which they marched.

Finally they came to a room that was just a bare metal box furnished with rows of benches. Susan waited her turn as the line of women took their places. When they were all seated, an Artemisian woman entered the room and took up position facing them all. A lecture, Susan realized. This was going to be a lecture.

The woman at the front was nothing to look at. Her body was simply made: efficient, but with no line of style and no grace. Iron and steel panelling, copper fingers and toes, she was a little smaller than Susan, but then again, most Artemisians were. They had built themselves small when metal was scarce, and the old habit still remained.

'Call me Nettie,' she began. 'Ladies, welcome to Artemis City. Welcome to your glorious futures as mothers of Artemis!'

So it was going to be rape after all, thought Susan. She wasn't surprised, and at that moment she couldn't bring herself to care.

Nettie carried a steel stylus which she used to write on the smooth metal panel set on the wall behind her. The robots in the room watched silently as she formed the letters.

A Child Every Night.

The women of Turing City stirred in their seats, murmured to each other.

'I know what you're thinking,' said Nettie, turning back to face them. 'It can't be done. Well, trust me, I've been there. I'm a Bether and I once thought as you did. Now I know better. It *can* be done. You *can* twist a mind every night. Do you want to know how?'

No, thought Susan. *No, I don't. I don't want to know anything about this.*

'Nyro,' explained Nettie. 'Nyro's pattern. Ladies, who here has twisted wire already?'

No one spoke. No one raised a hand. The women all looked down at the floor, no one wanting to volunteer anything.

'Come on, ladies,' said Nettie, 'you're safe in here. Forget your troubles, they are now at an end. Tell me, who has twisted wire? No one? Well, I'm sure that's not true, but I can understand your reticence.'

She smiled at the assembled women. She wanted to be their friend, Susan realized. She wanted them to like her.

'Well, let me try to talk this through,' continued Nettie. 'When a *Tokvah* twists wire, she will spend some time thinking of the mind she will create. Maybe she takes a walk, storing experiences, remembering certain sights and sounds.'

Susan gazed harder at the floor. *If she sees me, she will know that's exactly what Karel and I were doing . . .*

Nettie continued: 'Any *Tokvah* woman wishing to twist wire will invest a lot of time and thought in exploring what she believes to be the best pattern for her child. She will want to make a child that has the best chance of survival in the world, a child that will have the best chance of reproducing in the future. She wonders, therefore, should the child be helpful, or selfish, or trusting, or sharing? Should it be brave and take foolish risks, or instead a coward and risk nothing? Should it be an optimist or a pessimist?'

She paused to smile round the room again.

'Ladies, these are all hard decisions – decisions that no mother ever feels that she gets completely right. Isn't it true that guilt is a natural part of motherhood?' She laughed at that. No one else did.

'Well, here in Artemis, a woman is spared such doubt. Here she is free to devote her time to more productive activities, for, when it comes to twisting a mind, there is only one pattern: Nyro's.'

Susan felt her gyros lurch at Nettie's pronouncement. The poster put up in the railway station flashed through her mind.

'Nyro's pattern. This is how you will weave a child every night. By following Nyro's pattern. Once you have learned it, there will be no need for thought or concentration. Your hands will weave the pattern unaided! Is that not wonderful? Is that not freedom? Freedom from thought, from guilt, and from unnecessary labour?'

The women were stirring.

Somebody speak out, thought Susan. *Someone only speak out and I will join in too. I have lost my son and husband. I have nothing to live for. Just one person speak, out and I will join in with the chorus of voices that will surely arise.*

She waited in the whirring silence, nothing but the hum of robots and their pulsing lifeforce. But nobody spoke.

Nettie clasped her hands together, her plain copper hands.

'Is this not wonderful, ladies? Is it not too wonderful? We shall become the mothers of the world. Metal pours into Artemis City from the four corners of the continent. Iron and copper and tin and gold, silver and titanium and tungsten. Now that the railways pass even through the mountains, soon the metal from the northern states will come rolling back here into Artemis. All that metal, pouring into here, into the nurseries. You are here at the centre of the world, ladies, twisting metal into new minds! This building will be the womb from which all life on Penrose will eventually originate!'

A womb? thought Susan. *What is a womb?*

Maoco O

In a hidden room within the fort, deep beneath what remained of Turing City, Maoco O began.

First he slid the panelling from his body, pushed down on the seams and slid the silver shining metal along the grooves hidden beneath his skin.

He laid the separate pieces on the black stone floor, an intricate jigsaw that formed the broken pattern of his once indestructible body.

He stood in the glow of the forge, looked in the mirror and saw himself standing naked in the red-glowing darkness.

His electromuscles stretched in bands around his body, so thin and so finely knitted that he could barely see the weave. So many muscles, twisting in all directions, over and under each other. More than one mind could comprehend the pattern of.

He reached down and began to unhook them, picking them off one by one and dropping them in their appropriate place on the floor amongst the panelling. He kept on doing so until his legs finally gave way and he collapsed.

He unhooked his legs, unhooked his superlight alloy bones. Then he lifted himself up on his powerful arms and, in that way, walked himself across the floor to the forge. There was metal waiting for him there. Simple iron plate and wire, glowing red in the heat.

A pair of tongs hung waiting in a rack. A hammer and an anvil. A trough of water, a trough of acid.

Maoco O took hold of the tongs, heard their clinking as he pulled metal from the fire. He took hold of the hammer and beat at the metal in a starburst of sparks, molten flakes dropping to the floor.

This is what Nicolas the Coward did, he thought. *He gave up his powerful body so he could walk away unnoticed and unchallenged. But I have no choice. This body is damaged. The engineers and the mothers are gone. There is no one to repair it but me.*

There was something else, however. Swinging the hammer, feeling the ringing percussion of metal on metal: it felt so good. It felt right.

Clumsily, uncertainly, Maoco O set about reinventing himself.

Susan

The women sat in the room for hours, listening to Nettie lecturing them on the twisting of wire. The base knot, the deep brain, the emotion vectors – all those things that Susan had known instinctively were rendered obscene by the act of verbalizing. It was like the laying bare of lovers' secrets; spoken out loud they became nothing more than a series of mechanical motions.

Worse than that, under it all, like a throbbing bass pulse, was Nyro's philosophy, the skewed beat that drove the whole mind.

Susan's gyros couldn't spin properly, she felt dizzy and disoriented, as did all the others, but still nobody spoke. No one but Nettie, standing at the front of the room, declaiming in that thrilled, excited voice, laying down the pattern of Nyro's mind.

But the worst was still to come.

The lecture finally ended, and they were led from the room, heads spinning, and taken down the metal corridors to another room, one which was sealed with a great steel door.

The women stiffened, their electromuscle shorting with tension. They could sense something in the room beyond.

Something different.

Men.

The door opened, and they were led into the making room.

Twenty-four men were waiting there: young infantryrobots, standing in two rows before the chairs that lined both walls of the long room. The women were made to walk up the lines and forced to take their own places, kneeling before them.

Someone speak, thought Susan, as she knelt herself. The floor in here was covered in black plastic, which gave beneath her knees a little. The robot that stood before her wore a clean, unscratched body. A thin smear of oil leaked out at the joints of his knees; the plastic soles of his feet were fresh and unworn. He looked as if his body was newly built.

Nettie had followed them into the room. Her voice was more thrilling than ever, and then Susan realized that Nettie was ashamed and embarrassed too. She was trying to hide it. *Well rust her*, thought Susan, she's not the one forced to kneel here.

'Now, ladies, let us practise the first few movements! The base knot and the deep brain! Take hold of the wire and think on Nyro's pattern as you begin the making of a mind.'

Susan looked up at the young man who stood before her. He gazed down at her awkwardly.

He doesn't want to do this either, she realized, and then, for the first time since Axel's death, she felt something else other than numb despair. Anger rose inside her like the bubbling, spitting steam that hisses from hot metal thrust into water. *He doesn't want to do this? So rust him! He's part of this twisted state, but I'm not. I'm not going to do this any more. I'm going to speak up . . .*

'No!'

The voice wasn't Susan's. Another woman, down the other end of the line had stood up.

'No!' she repeated. 'I'm not going to do this. I will not do this!'

Another Turing Citizen. Susan began to stand up; ready to join in with a voice of dissent, but it was already too late.

No one had noticed the Scout, polished and gleaming, who had been resting quietly in the corner of the room. Now she sprang forth, light flashing down the length of her body, her eyes extending, the blades on her hands and feet sweeping out and slicing through the body of the woman who had spoken, right down through her head. That same brave woman whose voicebox still went on speaking even as the top of her head fell to the ground.

'Join me,' she was saying. 'They can't make us allllll . . .' Then her voice faded to nothing as the top of her head spun to a rest on the rubber floor, the coil of blue wire inside clearly visible, popping and curling out, ends shiny where they had been cut.

Then there was no sound but that of the stricken woman's body collapsing to the ground in a grinding of metal.

No one spoke. All the other women looked on in horror.

'Anyone else want to speak?' asked the Scout, her voice thin like a blade.

The prisoners looked at each other, terrified. Susan felt her anger shrivel inside her. *They can't kill us all*, she thought. *Yes, they can*, she realized.

'This one moved too.'

Susan looked up in horror, yet contempt too unfolded inside her. It was *her* man that had spoken. The robot had looked so awkward and afraid she had almost felt sorry for him, but now she saw him for what he was: a coward and a bully, using another's misfortune to hide his own fear, to massage his own ego.

'You little coward,' said Susan, her contempt now greater even than her fear. 'You *Nicolas.*'

The Scout was behind her. She could feel the current from its electromuscle, so strongly. A blade hooked around her neck.

'Shall I remove your coil too?'

A pause. Then Nettie was there. Susan didn't turn around; conscious of the metal blade touching the wire of her coil, straining to hear the words Nettie urgently spoke to the Scout. There was a pause, and then Susan felt the blade withdraw. She heard footsteps as the Scout walked away.

Relief washed over her. She had been spared. But why?

The woman kneeling next to her was staring in her direction. Why was she looking like that? Susan had almost been killed. Why was she gazing at her with such hatred? The woman spoke, so softly that Susan barely heard the word.

'Traitor.'

Traitor? Why had she said that? Because Susan had been spared execution? Nettie was speaking again. She raised her voice slightly. The scraping noise as the body of the woman who had dissented was being dragged from the room underscored her words.

'Now, ladies, let's have no more unpleasantness, shall we? Let us begin.'

Susan had never felt so alone. The woman on her left gave her a look of contempt.

The robot that Susan knelt before was gazing down at her with such a superior look as Susan reached up for his wire.

And then she realized that she couldn't do it. Her hands dropped to her sides and she felt such a feeling of release. All her decisions had now been made, all fear had left her. She understood now: she'd rather die under the Scout's blade. She heard a little voice behind her.

'Please, do it. You must do it.'

Nettie. A copper hand reached forwards; a finger drew out a

shape on the rubber floor. A circle. The finger reached out and placed an invisible dot at the top.

Susan stared in amazement. The same shape that Maoco O had drawn. The shape that Masur had drawn on her hand in the paint shop. Even here in Artemis City? What did it mean?

'Please, Susan.'

Susan felt her resolve fade. Maybe it was the pleading in Nettie's voice.

Slowly, so slowly, the male robot gazing contemptuously down at her, she reached up and began to twist metal.

Olam

Olam opened his eyes and realized that Doe Capaldi was speaking to him. Olam remembered to turn his ears back up.

'. . . covered by the rock. Clear way out. Bit hard. Legs aren't working.'

Doe Capaldi's head was dented, his left shoulder wrenched out of alignment.

'Need do it quickly,' he continued. 'Another blast twelve minutes. Farther away, but still might shake rocks further down. Got to move.'

Doe Capaldi turned and started to push at the tumbled stone behind him. Olam could see daylight through the cracks. He realized that they weren't buried that deeply.

'You saved me,' he said.

'One of my section.'

There was something wrong with Doe Capaldi's voice. Had the wire in his head been bent out of true by that dent?

'But I tried to kill you!'

'All follow Nyro now.'

'You can't *really* believe that!'

'What else believe?'

Doe Capaldi heaved at a plate of rock. Something shifted. A rush of gravel slid down into their rocky prison. Olam tried to jump up to help him. Then he remembered he no longer had a body. Doe Capaldi had cut it loose, only carrying Olam's head as they ran from the bomb.

'Nearly there!'

Bands of shadow and light. Olam still couldn't believe what Doe Capaldi had done. How could one of the aristocracy give up so much, so easily?

'No Wien any more,' said Doe Capaldi, answering his unspoken question. 'Better live two years good Artemisian than die in stadium.'

'Yes, but . . .'

There was a final grinding of stones followed by a creaking scrape as they settled into a new position.

'Got it. Come on.'

Doe Capaldi took Olam's head and pushed it through the space between the rocks. Olam found himself facing Doe Capaldi as he wriggled and scraped his way to freedom.

'Not far,' said Doe Capaldi. 'Can see light.'

Olam saw clearly now the dent in Doe Capaldi's head, the silver glint of electromuscle where his shoulder had been cracked open. Then something occurred to him.

'Live two years,' he said. 'You said "better to live two years as good Artemisian . . .".'

'Bomb. Radiation on wire in mind. Cut lifespan.'

'What? How do you know this?'

'All troop leaders told.' Doe Capaldi laughed, then concentrated, and came close to forming a proper sentence. 'Why do you think that conscripts put to work on clearing mountains?'

Doe Capaldi pushed Olam's head forward once more, then painfully, metal scraping on rock, he pulled himself onwards. Somewhere behind them the rock creaked.

'You knew this?' said Olam. 'You knew this all the time?' Realization struck. 'So this is your revenge. You save my life, but only for a little while. Two years?'

'More like six months now,' said Doe Capaldi. 'We both too close to blast.'

And at that he gave Olam's head a last shove and sent him bouncing out into the rain.

Olam was free.

Free to live for another six months.

He heard a noise nearby.

'Over here!' he called.

A clattering of feet, then he saw the grey shape of an infantry-robot leaning over him.

'What happened to you?' a voice asked.

Susan

Susan felt disgusted with herself. It was as if she had let her hands rust, allowed her electromuscle to unravel. As if she had let some-one else build her own body for her. To kneel at the feet of another man and to twist his metal . . . ?

She had ideas in her mind, pictures and emotions she had been saving up for this day, but they waited untouched in the darkened rooms of her mind as her hands twisted the young man's wire in the pattern that Nettie had just taught them.

Twenty-three women knelt in that room, all working in silence.

Yellow eyes stared down at her in contempt, and Susan felt such hatred in her heart. All that had happened to her at the hands of Artemis, she now focused that hatred on the man seated before her. Oh, to stand up and to take hold of his coil, to see the expression in his eyes as she crushed it slowly.

But she didn't dare. Instead, she just twisted blue metal. It was too thin, she thought; the lifeforce that flowed through it seemed so much weaker than that of Karel's wire. Everything about this man was a pale shadow of her husband.

What would Karel think if he could see her now, kneeling like this?

She thrust the thought from her mind, just went on twisting wire.

Nettie walked around the room, watching them, checking on what they were doing, offering advice. Everyone seemed to be

doing okay, but no one dared otherwise for, there in the background, they could feel the presence of the Scout, eyeing them,
half mad with the shrieking current that poured through her mind,
waiting for an excuse to pounce.

Susan's hands twisted away, following the instructions that
Nettie had given, winding the deep brain around the base knot . . .
and a growing sense of unease began to emerge from the disgust.
She was reaching the end of Nettie's preliminary map of a Nyro
mind. What was she supposed to do then? Follow the plan that
she had been working out for Karel and her child? What type of
bastard child would emerge from such a synthesis?

The other women felt that unease too. They stole glances at
each other. Susan could see them. None of them looked directly
at her, though.

Nettie clapped her hands together in a rattle of copper.

'Okay, ladies, and now we stop!'

Susan and the rest paused, their fingers holding their place in
the weave.

'Put down the minds.'

No one moved.

'Put down the minds, ladies.'

There was a murmur of concern.

Someone spoke up. 'But they will unravel!'

The Scout pounced, a bladed hand was held to one kneeling
woman's neck.

'So let it unravel, *Tokvah*.' The Scout's voice sounded like a drill
piercing hard metal.

A cry took hold of the voicebox of every woman kneeling in the
room.

'But ladies!' shrilled Nettie. 'Ladies! You hold nothing but wire.
Nothing but metal! Weren't you listening to all I said? Nyro says
there is no difference between metal that walks and metal that lies
in the ground! Whether we are spontaneous or twisted by our
mothers, we are all nothing but metal. This city, the railway lines,
the wire that you hold, all is nothing but metal. However Nyro's
philosophy chooses to shape it, there is nothing but metal. You

hold wire in your hands, ladies. Let it go. Let it spill and tangle on the ground, to be later made into guns or blades or walls or other minds. What does it matter? It is nothing but metal.'

'No . . .' sobbed a woman. The Scout was suddenly there, knocking the wire from her hands, her hand on her neck, squeezing, breaking her coil.

The women on either side shook the wire from their hands, sobbing electronic squeaks and wails.

'Well done, ladies,' called Nettie. 'You see? It is nothing but metal! Remember, this truth is written in the very stars and moons themselves!'

The woman who had just had her coil broken slumped to the floor.

Crying, sobbing, Susan shook the wire from her hands and saw her second child die.

Maoco O

Noises echoed throughout the fort. The muffled sounds of distant explosions, the shriek of metal being torn apart, the dull pounding thump thump thump of engines working away deep underground. Artemis was here, stripping the home of the City Guards apart.

And now it was time for Maoco O to face them once more.

It felt so strange, leaving his hiding place dressed like this. He felt so weak and vulnerable, with his badly knitted electromuscle and his imperfectly forged bones. Maoco O had had no practice at building bodies, he felt ridiculously proud of his first attempt. For the first time in his life, he felt *connected* with the world. The pressure of his feet on the floor, the tension in his electromuscles as he padded through metal corridors. The sound of his footsteps, the sound of the pounding as the Artemisians plundered the fort; it was as if those noises were passing directly into his mind. He had built those ears himself!

A noise just around the corner made him dodge backwards into a convenient room.

The terror that arose within him was strange. If he was found, he would have to fight – but fight with this weak body? He could be killed! *Nicolas the Coward,* whispered a voice. *But no,* he thought, *this is not cowardice. For the first time in my life I will be properly fighting. Almost as an equal. What does it matter when this risk makes me seem so alive!*

The room in which he found himself was small. An armoury, filled with racks of knives: everything from large pangas to tiny awls. Shiny prying knives and carbon-blacked throwing knives. A rack of carbon-steel kukris sat just next to him, their blades covered in a film of oil.

He took one from the rack and weighed it in his hand. It was a lot heavier than he expected, the balance all wrong for his new body with its thinner electromuscles. At the moment, everything felt strange.

There were footsteps outside.

Maoco O adopted a ready position. How would he fight, dressed as he was?

The door slid open.

The robot outside wore a blue-painted shell. Its arms were long, its fingers thin and prying. It saw Maoco O and recoiled in horror.

'Turing Citizen!' it called out.

Maoco O's reactions were faster than the body he had built. His mind set him leaping forward, his newly built legs stumbled, his arms flailed, and he dragged the kukri in a deep scratching cut down the front of the other robot. The robot looked at the mess the weapon made of his shell and panicked.

'Help!' it shrieked.

More footsteps pounding towards him. Infantryrobots. Maoco O's reflexes told him they were easy prey, but his mind overruled them. As the other robot curled up in a protective huddle on the floor, he scrambled over it and ran out into the corridor.

'Down here! One of the engineers!'

The voice came from further down the corridor. Maoco O

turned and ran, enemy feet pounding along behind him. He was just waiting for the gunshot that would blow his mind apart. It didn't come, and he felt disgust at the amateurism of these troops. Who had trained them? They were chasing him, rather than just shooting at him.

Round a corner, he dropped through a trap in the floor, hit the lock button and then doubled back along the corridor below. He paused a moment to listen for sounds of pursuit.

Nothing.

Maoco O had escaped.

His body was unsteady, there was a rattle somewhere in his left knee, his gyroscopes were spinning, his electromuscles spasming . . .

He had never felt so alive!

Susan

It went on and on: Nettie lecturing them, drilling them on how to twist a mind the Artemisian way.

The sessions in the making room, kneeling before those young infantrymen. Being made to shake the wire of a half-made mind from your hands over and over again until you became hardened to it. Eventually coming to see what you were doing as nothing more than twisting metal: she realized she was being hammered in the forge of Artemis, her mind folded over and hammered again until it became nothing more than a shining, hardened piece of metal, and she began to see metal as nothing more than *metal*.

The world outside of this nursery building was fading in her mind, her life with Karel and Axel now seeming like the empty shell of a ghost. She could picture the exterior appearance, but she could remember no life beneath the façade.

There was no chance to speak, and no one to speak to. The women were marched back and forth from the lecture room to the making-room: there was nowhere else they went. One hundred and forty-four steps to the making room over the iron and plastic floors, through corridors lit by single bulbs. Kneeling on the making-room floor before a succession of young men who spilled their wire into her hands, and later looked down with pale eyes as half-completed minds were brushed in tangled clumps from the floor. Didn't they care what happened to their own wire?

Sometimes there was time for a brief exchange of words in the corridor, a chance for a quick snatch of conversation. She heard the other women exchanging names, words of support. But not to Susan. Word had spread, and the only word she heard from the others was *traitor*. Why? Because she had been spared death at the hands of the Scout?

Or something else? The rumours had followed her here from Turing City. She was the woman who had married Karel. They were convinced that Karel was a traitor, and now she was, too. Hadn't she received special treatment?

And there was Nettie. Nettie remained friendly towards her. The other women had seen it. She was the favourite. No wonder they considered her a traitor.

But why? What had she done? Nettie and Masur and Maoco O. Each of them had drawn that same symbol; the circle with the dot at the top. Like it was a sign that she should recognize.

Back and forth along the iron corridor. How many days had she now been here? How many weeks?

It took two hours to make a mind. Over ten thousand twists, and Susan and the other women had been drilled on each and every one of them. Over and over again, so many minds half-made and then abandoned. She felt hollow inside.

Finally, though, the time came.

Nettie, her body as dull and unimpressive as ever, paused before the sheet of polished metal upon which she had sketched out her instructions, then laid down her stylus and turned to face the twenty-two remaining women.

'And that, ladies,' she said, 'is the end of the training. So now we test you.'

There was nothing else, no congratulations. The women were stood up and marched down to the making room.

There Susan took her place, kneeling at the feet of a grey infantryrobot. She reached up and began to twist wire.

And then something happened. Something that had never happened before. The robot leaned down and spoke in her ear.

'Hello, Susan.'

Susan paused. She glanced around the room. No one else had heard. They were all busy working away, twisting wire. She looked for the silver shape of the Scout. It wasn't there.

'Aren't you going to speak to me, Susan?'

Hands still twisting, she looked up into the yellow eyes of the infantryrobot.

'Who are you?'

'My name is Banjo Macrodocious.'

'Who?' The name sounded familiar. Where had she heard it before? Had Karel mentioned it?

'What do you want?'

'I don't want anything. That's why I'm so special. I was made that way.'

'Why?'

'So I could do my job. We have two hours together, Susan, and I want to speak to you. I want to discuss philosophy.'

'Why?' she glanced fearfully around the room. 'Are you trying to get us both killed?'

'We will be okay. Nettie is one of us. No one else here will speak because they are too frightened of what might happen to them. Susan, have you heard of the Book of Robots?'

Susan felt a thrill. The Book of Robots. Maoco O had mentioned it, what seemed like years ago.

'I've heard of it,' she said. 'What is it?'

'Heresy. It contradicts everything that robots believe.'

'Why?'

'The Book of Robots is supposed to contain the map of a robot body.'

'So? Any woman could twist a map of a body!' Her tone was bitter. 'I've just spent weeks learning one such map.'

Banjo Macrodocious leaned closer. 'This is the plan of the *first* robot.'

Susan was genuinely puzzled, her hands still twisting wire.

'What do you mean, the first robot?'

'What if I were to tell you that robot life did not evolve on this planet, as we have all believed? What if I were to tell you that we, too, were *designed*, just as a robot would design a hammer or an awl or an engine?'

'But that's ridiculous—'

'The Book of Robots is said to contain the plan for the original robot. It lays out the reason for our construction, the laws that we are meant to follow, the ultimate reason for our existence.'

Susan had fumbled a twist in the wire. She glanced around the room, checking that her slip had not been noticed. No one even looked; each lost in contemplation of the making of a mind. Around the room, the men leaned close to whisper in the ears of the women dutifully weaving wire in the Nyro's pattern.

'I don't believe it,' whispered Susan. 'That's . . . wrong!'

'How can it be wrong if it's the truth, Susan? Just think about it, what if we were made to some purpose?'

'It's wrong!' repeated Susan, her voice cold and low. 'Every mother has the right to weave the mind that she chooses!'

'You say that as you kneel there weaving a mind to Artemis's pattern? Think on this, Susan, what if Artemis is right? Suppose Nyro's philosophy is proving so successful because it is in fact our true purpose?'

'No! I don't believe that! I would rather not have lived than for that to be true!'

'Interesting,' said Banjo Macrodocious.

Susan wove in silence for a few minutes, while Banjo Macrodocious said nothing. He leaned back, his eyes dimming. Susan's anger rose. She jerked on the wire.

'Who are you? Why are you telling me all this?'

Banjo Macrodocious looked around the room before leaning close to her ear.

'Keep your voice down! Do you want the others to hear?'

'I don't care!'

'I don't believe that, Susan. You've already had plenty of chances to speak out since your capture. The fact that you are here twisting metal suggests that you chose not to die.'

The robot's words struck home, and Susan was silent for a moment, hands twisting away.

'What do you want me to do?' she asked.

'For the moment, nothing. We just want you to know that we're here. That you are not alone.'

'But why me? Why speak to me?'

'Because you are one of us.'

Banjo Macrodocious drew the sign in the air, the circle with the dot on the top.

'The robots at the top of the world,' he said. 'There is a land at the top of this world: north of Shull, beyond the Moonshadow sea. The Book of Robots was said to be written in that land, and then brought to Shull by the roads that run beneath the sea. Brought past the house of the glass robots around which the whales swim . . .'

'What are you talking about?' said Susan. 'Ghost stories of the north!'

'Have you ever noticed how all the ghost stories are set in the north, Susan? And now Kavan has passed the mountains, now that he has begun conquering the states there, what do you suppose he will he find?'

'I don't know. What does that have to do with me?'

'Your husband travels north, with Kavan.'

'Then he is all right?' For the moment, Susan was filled with a fierce joy, the first time she had felt an emotion so strong since she had been brought here. But it quickly faded.

'But what can I do, trapped here?'

'For the moment, Susan, nothing. You must await your time.'

And at that Banjo Macrodocious fell silent. Nothing else that Susan said elicited a reply.

She returned to weaving the mind of her first Artemisian child.

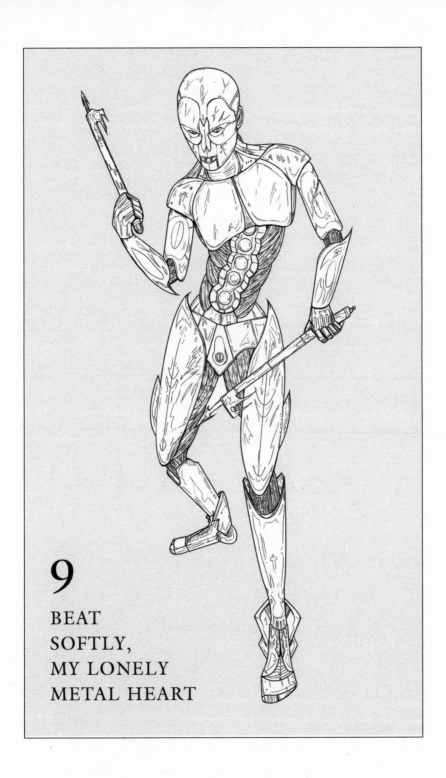

9

BEAT
SOFTLY,
MY LONELY
METAL HEART

Karel

Karel felt so *strong*. When he flexed the electromuscles in his legs, diesel engines roared and propelled him forwards. When he squeezed his fingers he felt the heat as he gripped the locomotive's wheels. Even when he coasted, as he did now, following the curve of a mountain down into a wide valley, he felt the sheer mass of his body as it rolled smoothly along.

The northern scenery was awe-inspiring, terrifying and beautiful. Up here, organic life had not been eliminated to the same extent as in the south, so the low hills that rolled up towards the mountain peaks were green with grass. This land contrasted the organic smoothness of such hills with the sharp edges of mountain peaks that speared the sky: it was an unnatural, but strangely attractive, sight.

Karel only wished he could move his eyes. The track along which he ran skirted the edge of a reservoir, the wind blowing the rain in bands across its level surface. There were cylindrical buildings of smooth stone at the far end of the lake. Extremely well constructed, too: the robots who inhabited this state were expert stonemasons, no doubt compensating for the relative scarcity of metal. Karel wished he could turn his eyes to get to see it all properly. Up here there were castles on the mountain peaks, half seen as he wended his way through the northern lands carrying supplies and troops. He wanted to get a better look. The castles were rooted in sheer cliffs, their walls rising up to towers that sought the sun in the same manner as the strange plants that were allowed to grow here. Looping metal roads ran from their fortified entrances down along the valley walls. Karel felt he was travelling in the land of childhood myths and stories, carrying troops north and then bringing captured metal south, as plate, as pipes and as bundles of blue wire.

He felt as if he were being seduced by it all. His anger was there still, sharp and unpredictable as it had ever been, but Karel was gradually training it to burn slower and longer, just to keep alive the feeling of dull anger that reminded him of the great wrong that had been done to him. And yet, he was coming to understand the dark appeal of Nyro's philosophy, of being a part of this powerful, all-consuming engine that was spreading across the surface of Penrose. To have no doubts. Most of all to be so *strong*. He could feel the pulse of the diesel, the incredible weight of the load that he was pulling.

Even so, there remained a sense of foreboding.

Day by day, the blanket of cloud that spread southwards over the sky had thickened and darkened, from pale to dark grey, to almost black. The cold rain fell constantly, sometimes in thin drizzle, increasingly often in heavy sheets that were transported up by the never-dying wind that blew from the north.

Karel was strong, and yet he had no control over the path he followed.

He wondered where it was taking him.

Kavan

There was a stone throne set in the very centre of the room, facing out over the mountains and valleys which this little kingdom had once ruled. One could sit there in this castle eyrie and gaze through the empty frame of the window with a sense of absolute power.

Kavan had seated himself on a little stool just by the window ledge, the foil sheets that surrounded him fluttering around the lumps of lead which weighed them down.

The conquest of Northern Shull proceeded apace. They had blasted through the major mountain range with little incident, and into the country beyond. It seemed that the summit of every hill and mountain here boasted its own castle, and every castle boasted its own king or queen ruling the land immediately around it.

Kavan had picked off these kingdoms one by one without any trouble. Self-important little rulers who ruled over their pathetic lodes of iron. Life was too easy for them while they stayed put, squandering their resources on petty squabbles or on building ever more baroque displays of architecture to flaunt their wealth.

Kavan looked out over the view from castle Ironfist, smiling at the name. Queen Ironfist herself had surrendered without a fight then had willingly boarded the train taking her to the making rooms of Artemis City.

Down below he could see the grey bodies of his troops laying railways that would follow the curves of the iron-grey reservoirs, busily linking these lands to each other and ultimately to Artemis City. And then the rain rolled in again, a hissing sheet that quickly travelled the length of the valley. Brooding clouds enfolded the mountain tops, leaving him in grey isolation in his chosen eerie. The cold wind fluttered through his sheets of foil, and he realized that it was time to move further back inside again.

'Help me with these, Wolfgang.'

Wolfgang took hold of the other end of the little table and helped him to manoeuvre it through an archway to the space beyond the exposed throne room. This was the kingdom's parliament chamber, the stone ribs of its vaulted ceiling carved out of the rock of the mountain itself and decorated with silver and a little gold. A great iron slab of a table sat in the centre of the room.

'Eleanor is here,' announced Wolfgang.

'Send her in.'

'She's wearing that self-important look,' warned his aide.

'Then I'll have to find something else to keep her busy.'

Eleanor entered the room, her infantryrobot's body looking more scratched than ever and badly in need of paint. Wolfgang was right, reflected Kavan. She *was* making a point.

'Hello, Eleanor. Everything going well, I trust?'

'So so.'

Wolfgang and Kavan were busy laying out the foil sheets on the iron table. Eleanor twisted her head, trying to read what was written on them.

'I wonder if this is how Spoole feels,' said Kavan, reflectively. 'Only a few weeks ago I was part of the troops attacking Wien. When we took Turing City I may have brought up the rear, but I was part of the fighting there too, after a fashion. Now I do nothing more than sit in this castle and direct operations.'

He waved a hand across the table. 'These reports are the only sight of the action I get nowadays. Maybe I was wrong to criticize General Fallan as I once did.'

Eleanor sat down in a chair without being invited to.

'Don't put words in my mouth, Kavan,' she said. 'If I really thought that of you, I'd come out and say it.'

'And yet you come here with your armour all battered, which is usually a sign that you're not happy with something. You know as well as I do that a good infantryrobot keeps her body clean and in good repair.'

'When I get the time, I will. Kavan, I know how hard this is for you. You're at the pinch of the hourglass. You've got Spoole and Artemis to the south feeding you arms and materiel, you've got the whole northern continent above you arming up and preparing to defend itself against your attack. Get it wrong and you'll be crushed between the two of them . . .'

'Get it right and I'll conquer all of Shull. What do you want, Eleanor?'

'Kavan, there's something odd happening to the north.'

Kavan was genuinely thrown. He had expected Eleanor to come here and to subtly challenge him, as she usually did. He wasn't expecting this.

'Odd?'

'I don't know how else to describe it. This is a strange land, Kavan. I don't think that you've experienced it quite like the rest of your troops have.'

'Ah! So I was right about the battered armour!'

Eleanor rapped at the iron table in annoyance.

'Okay, so maybe I *was* making a point. But that's not why I'm here. Kavan, you need to see this land for yourself. This land is really *strange*: the lack of metal has stunted it. You must have seen the organic life out there, it's rife. But have you seen how the robot life changes the further north you go? Have you seen the animals? There isn't enough metal for them to build themselves properly, so they're . . . *strange*. All of them small, or elongated, or twisted. All engaged in a constant fight for what little metal there is. Tiny beetles that scratch metal from your body and carry it away. Spiders that use magnetic fields to lure those beetles into their lairs . . .'

'Should we be afraid of them?'

'Worms that creep into your skull and twist the metal there into their young,' continued Eleanor. 'They say that a robot can walk around not even knowing that these worms are eating away at his mind, gradually robbing him of his thoughts. Other robots try to tell them what has happened, but the worms have eaten that part of the mind that lets him understand this. And so it goes on until the day that robot just dies.'

'I've often heard it said that life can thrive in the most unlikely places,' replied Kavan. 'Is this what you have come here to tell me?'

'No,' said Eleanor. She hesitated for a moment. 'Kavan, have you ever heard of the Book of Robots?'

Kavan said nothing.

'It's a heresy, I know. But some robots say that . . .'

'I've heard of it,' interrupted Kavan.

'Well,' continued Eleanor. 'There are stories. Stories of a road that leads north, right across Northern Shull and then out under the sea to the top of the world itself. Some of the Scouts say they think they may have seen part of this road.'

'So there is a road that leads north. Is that such a surprise?'

'Perhaps not. But there are tales also of another kingdom, far to the north of here, further than any of our troops have so far travelled. A kingdom lying almost on the northern coast of Shull itself. A place where there is so little metal that the robots there use organic life as part of their bodies.'

'Who says this, Eleanor? Because it sounds like the sort of rumours that we ourselves spread before attacking Wien and

Turing City. It's the sort of rumour that saps the morale of your enemy and makes the fight so much easier.'

Eleanor looked down at the table, embarrassed. 'I know that, Kavan. I realize that. But we've heard these stories from the robots in all of the little kingdoms that we've so far conquered. And at first I thought as you did, but as we moved further north these stories became more detailed, more specific. Still we thought nothing of them. And then our own troops began to report strange occurences.'

'Like what?'

'Like the story of the voices in the dark.'

Karel and the Voices in the Dark

Karel rode the rain-slicked rails northwards. Lately there had been a touch of snow in the endless rainfall which smeared itself across the rails, making his wheels slip as they struggled for traction.

Night was falling; it had already settled in the steeper valleys and cuttings through which Karel struggled.

He guessed he was currently pulling troops. He had seen them lined up by the side of the track outside Artemis City as he picked his way through the points to the marshalling point. Hundreds of grey-painted infantryrobots, washed shiny by the never-ending rain, all fresh from the city's forges. More metal twisted by busy hands to continue with the conquest of the continent. For a moment Karel had a vision of Susan being forced to work in the making rooms of Artemis. Was that where she had ended up? he wondered. Better than being dead, maybe. He quickly thrust the thought from his mind. Why torture himself? It was better to con-centrate on the day at hand.

Up and up the slope that led along a dark valley, its sides lined by the sodden shapes of organic trees appearing no less strange for being viewed through infrared. He had never been so far north before. The landscape here was different, starker, sharper. Every-thing was a little poorer and thinner up here: the quality of the light, the stone, the low mountains that had almost descended to the level of the foothills. There was none of the grandeur of the lands through which Karel had first travelled: the terrain up here felt so dead and empty of metal . . .

There was something blocking the tracks ahead!

He gripped the brakes, felt the disks lock in his hands, the wheels slipping on the rain-slicked rails. The weight of the carriages slammed into his back, pushing him forward, unable to stop, pushing him into a fall of rocks that covered the line. He was going to hit them. He was slowing. He was slowing . . . He stopped.

A voice sounded in his ear.

'What are you playing at?'

When was the last time someone had actually spoken to him? How long had he driven in silence? He didn't care about the harshness of the voice. It was a pleasure just to be able to speak.

'Rockfall ahead,' he explained. 'It's covered the tracks.'

The voice could be heard, faintly conferring with someone else. 'Does it look natural to you?' it finally asked him.

How should I know? thought Karel. *All I can see is straight ahead.*

'I don't know,' said Karel.

'It could be an ambush . . .' said the voice thoughtfully.

'It could be,' said Karel. 'I can't see anything to the sides.'

But there was no reply to that.

'Hello?' called Karel. 'Hello? Are you still there?'

The sound of the voice had reminded him of how lonely he actually was. The feeling of power that he had enjoyed while driving the train now vanished, and he remembered just how cut off he was from other robots; that all he was now was a piece of machinery, just something to make the train go. And then the images came smashing through his defences, overwhelming him. All those pictures that he had blocked. Memories of his old life. Of walking with Susan through the galleries. Of talking to her, talking to other robots. Of conversation and companionship: not this endless isolation.

He tried to push the images from his mind, but to no effect. Still they came crowding back.

The memory of the forge, of the nights spent there, Susan sitting opposite him, painting metal with her clever, skilful hands. Of Susan smoothing the weave of his electromuscle. And worst of all – he tried not to think about it, but he couldn't stop it – the memory that hurt the most – of Axel, of his little boy, sitting on the floor of the forge, fiddling with two pieces of metal, talking about how he was going to make arms that were so strong, how he was going to build a body that would be so handsome when he was fully grown.

All that would never now be.

And for the first time, unable to help it, Karel began to cry. All that emotion that he had blocked for all these weeks came leaking out. It set up a feedback loop in his voicebox – wherever it was now located on that train – and began to whine.

Somebody must have heard.

'Stop that,' a voice ordered, and there was a click as his ears were turned off.

Time passed. No one went to move the rocks ahead, but Karel scarcely noticed. Night deepened, and for the first time in days the rain ceased. White light then spread across the sides of the valley. The clouds had cleared, and the light of Zuse, the night moon, shone down unimpeded.

There was a click: 'They're speaking again . . .'

Karel was momentarily at a loss. 'Who is speaking?' he asked. The voice he remembered, it had come back.

'Outside the train. Can't you hear them? They are asking us to look outside. Can you see them?'

Karel gazed along the track towards the fallen rocks, the scene lit up in sharp black and white by the night moon.

'I can't see anything,' he said.

'We go out and look for them, but there is no one there!'

'Why don't you clear the rocks? Let me ride onwards!'

'We go towards the rocks. The voices call us away!'

'You're Artemisian soldiers! You go where you please!'

'I don't understand it. The voices call us into the mountains. Some of the troops have already vanished up there.'

'Why are you telling *me* this? What am I supposed to do?'

There was no reply.

Karel sat in the valley, bathed in the white light of the moon. Eventually, the clouds rolled back overhead. Shortly after that it began to rain once more.

Kavan

'You spoke to the driver of the train? Who was it?'

'Karel.' Eleanor stared at him as she said that name. What was she thinking of now? he wondered.

'That doesn't sound like an Artemisian name.'

'You know that he's a Turing Citizen, Kavan.' Still she stared at him. Challenging him.

He stood up. 'What happened to the train?'

Eleanor held his gaze for a moment longer with her yellow eyes, and then she continued. 'A second troop train came up behind, about eight hours later. They found the original train standing empty.'

'Hmm. How many people know this story?'

'Virtually half the army by this time, I should imagine. You know how these rumours spread.'

'I know. I myself have used that to good effect in the past.'

'You think you know what happened?'

Kavan waved a hand dismissively. 'A train full of barely trained infantryrobots travels through new territory. Easy to ambush, easy to pick off one by one as they come to clear a fall of rocks on the line. Robots moving about the mountains, calling out mysterious invitations in the night, and then hiding behind rocks with awls at the ready when a few credulous robots come to investigate? Oh yes, I think I know what happened. And then only one survivor lives to tell the story, who then brings it back to spread fear and confusion.'

Kavan rose to his feet. 'You were right, Eleanor. I have not spent enough time in these northern lands. I think someone wants to play a game with us. Very well, let us accept their offer.'

Spoole

'You're doing well, Spoole,' said General Sandale. 'Very well indeed.'

'It's not for you to comment on my progress,' replied Spoole coldly, but he felt a deep sense of satisfaction at the other's words.

They were in the command room, looking up at the partial map of Shull that was engraved directly onto the steel wall of the basilica. The southern part of the continent rose twenty feet up the same wall and was picked out in great detail. The former city states conquered by Artemis were now bound to Artemis City by the lead chasing of railway lines. For ten years now Spoole had gazed at that same, nearly unchanging, map. Only now was any detail of the section to the north of the central mountain range being filled in. The path taken by Kavan's nuclear excavation of the mountains had already been engraved on the map, and now the branching lines of the railways were expanding outwards, the detail of the surrounding countryside being slowly etched in as survey data was sent back bit by bit.

Spoole gazed with pride at the growing map, visible testament to his success as a leader.

'Testament to Kavan's success,' remarked Gearheart, as he joined her in the glassed-in office at the southern end of the vast room. 'They're all saying it. General Sandale, the commanders, the computers, they all know the truth.'

'Peace, Gearheart,' replied Spoole without heat. He was used to these outbursts.

The battered robot was propped up in a chair overlooking the vast floor of the command room. The ranked desks of the computers could be seen, steel robots studying a constant stream of sheets of copper foil. They scanned their contents and made marks on still more sheets of foil that were collected and summarized and collated, and so produced reports on the growing wealth and strength of Artemis City.

'I will not be quiet,' said Gearheart, bitterly. 'You take the credit, but it is Kavan who drives our forces north into emptier and emptier territories. And all the while there are decreasing amounts of metal flowing back into this city, and you know it. Kavan will break himself on those empty hills, and then you will claim the credit for the conquest he has made.'

'I do what is best for Artemis,' said Spoole simply.

'You do what is best for yourself,' replied Gearheart. 'The same is true of this whole city now. We hide here in safety and send other robots to do our work for us. We have forgotten Nyro's way.'

'What we are doing is successful, Gearheart. How can what you say be true whilst Artemis still grows?'

'We both know I speak the truth, Spoole. Look at me – what use am I now, in this broken body? If we were true to Nyro then this body would be taken away and melted. The metal of my mind broken down so that it could be spawned anew, and a new robot could walk on Penrose.'

'Your mind is your mind, Gearheart. It is a unique and beautiful thing. I realize that now –'

'The beauty of my mind was expressed in the metal that I could shape. Look at my body now.'

She waved the bent metal of her hooked arm in despair at the dented and scratched shell in which she sat.

'My mind was made to twist metal, but what metal can I twist now? I missed my opportunity, Spoole. I should have made a mind with you, and I never did, through foolish pride. What a child we could have made together, Spoole! What a way to serve Nyro that would have been. And now that chance has passed.'

Spoole gazed at the growing map at the far end of the room. 'It is not Nyro's way to mourn at what might have been,' he said.

'I was a fool,' said Gearheart bitterly. 'I remain a fool. I taunt

you constantly, Spoole, and you allow me to. You're a better servant of Nyro than I shall ever be. You have achieved so much.
Leave me, Spoole. Your metal should not go untwisted.'

'I won't leave you, Gearheart,' said Spoole softly.

'But that's not Nyro's way!'

Spoole didn't answer.

'Find another woman. Make a child with her. Your metal is
strong.'

Spoole gazed at Gearheart, so upset, and he himself felt so
guilty. Guilty at what he had done to her, guilty that he really was
betraying Nyro by thus keeping her alive.

'Make a child,' repeated Gearheart.

'But I did once make a child,' replied Spoole.

The Story of Spoole's Child

Spoole was young and ambitious and going nowhere.

*Artemis was growing by the day, leaping across the continent,
snapping up all in its way, and Spoole seemed doomed to spend his
time trotting along behind, making do with what scraps were left for
him, and this filled him with such a cold, aching jealousy that he was
scarcely able to remain civil to those around him.*

*Spoole had been bred for greatness, his mind had been woven for
leadership. Surely it was his purpose to command Artemisian divi-
sions to the greater glory of Artemis, yet it was his destiny to always
arrive too late, to see the choicest posts and promotions going to the
less intelligent, to see the best opportunities offered to the less deserv-
ing.*

*Tonight had been the nadir of his progress. Finally put in charge
of a division, Spoole had commanded with diligence and flair, sending his troops forwards again and again against the Bethe defences,
only to see them cut down. Too late he had realized what his part in
the grand assault was intended to be: a diversion and nothing more.
The main force had attacked further to the north, and whilst Spoole
and his remaining troops had languished on the plain, the rest of*

Artemis had poured into Bethe, claiming honour and glory and spoils for themselves.

This realization was too much for Spoole. He had abandoned his command and walked off into the night, feeling lost and alone. Lightning arced across the sky, gravel and stones skittered across the plain, kicked by his metal feet.

'Nyro,' he called out, 'what would you have me do? Why have you had me built like this only to deny me my purpose?'

As if in answer, a tearing noise began in the east, white light spreading across the night like a curtain, waves of photons washing across the continent, pummelling him, pummelling his eyes, pummelling his olive body. Suddenly Spoole was very frightened. He had called out to Nyro, and it seemed as if she was answering.

'Nyro,' he said again. 'Nyro, I know you are long dead. I know that you cannot be speaking to me.'

Who was he speaking to? wondered Spoole. He didn't believe that Nyro could hear him, and yet he continued to shout into the night. 'Why weave my mind and not put it to use? What is the point of that? I was made to lead, to command, to strive for the honour and glory of the great state of Artemis and yet, at every turning, Artemis denies me this. Why make me, then?'

The tearing noise became louder and louder, Spoole's fear increased. What was Nyro trying to say? And then an answer came.

'If we were Artemisians . . .'

The words were faint, on the edge of hearing, distorted by the crackle of the electrical storm. Spoole's fear was a thing so great it set up a standing wave in his mind, it resonated around his body, taking control of his arms and legs. Nyro had answered him!

But that couldn't really be Nyro speaking! Nyro was long dead. And then realization dawned, and Spoole felt incredibly foolish. His ears were still turned up to their full extent. He placed a hand to the side of his head, felt the overlarge housings that he had built there, the better to keep track of the battle he had commanded. The words he had heard were not intended for his ears, but he had taken them as a reply nonetheless. He scanned the night as the white light faded from the sky. And then he saw who had spoken, who he could still hear speaking now.

Two robots were making love in the middle of an electrical storm.

Spoole was gripped with such jealousy and hatred that he felt quite weak. Their happiness threw fresh light onto his near-despair, making it seem all the blacker. He had nothing to look forward to but a return to Artemis and obscurity, and yet there they both crouched, twisting wire, secure in their own future. What about his future? And then he realized what they were saying. They were discussing how to make their child, whether it should be woven according to the philosophy of Artemis, or Turing City.

Artemis! What did they know about Artemis? The man's whingeing voice cut through Spoole. What did he know about Artemis, what did he know about Artemisian philosophy? Look what it had done to him, Spoole! The woman's reply was more measured, but still they argued. How would they make the child? The woman was giving the man the choice, and Spoole was gripped by fury. How dare they? How dare they! At that moment it seemed as if they were mocking him. He raised his rifle to his shoulder, took aim along it, and waited for the man to speak his answer.

And Spoole realized at that point that he didn't care what answer the man was going to give. He was angry, he just wanted to destroy. The two robots weren't Artemisians, they were the enemy, and they deserved to die.

He fired, and the man died.

Susan

Susan was now a fully trained mother, and in Artemis that job brought a certain respect. Okay, she was led every night into the making room, where she knelt at the feet of yet another grey infantryman, but the attitude those men displayed had changed subtly. The contempt had gone to be replaced by something like respect, an acknowledgement that both of them were, in their way, advancing the Artemisian cause.

Or maybe that was just the way that Susan wanted to see it, a way for her to try and make her new existence bearable. Something she needed to believe in as she sought to forget her old life – to put Axel and Karel and their old forge finally out of her mind.

Not that the other women would let her do that. Though they were all, technically, Artemisians now, as they moved from the making rooms to the lecture theatre and back again there were still the looks, the silences, the intimations that she was receiving preferential treatment. It was there in their days spent in evaluating and refreshing and discussing the Artemisian mind; it was there in their nights spent in twisting it anew.

And then, suddenly, there came a break from the routine.

They were led from the making room, not back to the lecture theatre, but the other way down the metal corridor, passing beneath the single lightbulbs that divided the darkness into sections. The women were worried; they looked at each other nervously, wondering what awaited them. Had they failed in some way? Were they being led away to be disassembled?

They came to some stairs and began to ascend, up and up until they emerged into the night.

Out into the open air for the first time in so long. Around them, the suggestions of tall buildings, rising into the darkness amid the sooty snowflakes that tumbled into the dim light, illuminating the slushy courtyard in which they stood. The red light shining from the building ahead, Susan saw it and felt such an odd feeling, here in the middle of Artemis City. One of homecoming, of happiness almost. The other women felt it too. A forge? They were being led to a forge.

They headed across the square, the slush squeezing into their feet through the dents in the metal that had gone too long without adjustment. Walking through an open door into the light, the warmth, the utter joy of the forge. Susan had such a feeling of peace and happiness at the sight. They all did. The women looked around in wonder at the tools, the anvils, the plates of cheap metal that lay stacked around them. There were cans stacked on shelves and laid on the floor, filled to the brim with oil and grease and even a little red paint. It was poor fare compared to what she had enjoyed the use of in Turing City, but at this moment, for Susan, it seemed even better than a visit to Harman's body shop.

Nettie was waiting for them in the middle of the room, her chest panelling already removed.

'Ladies,' she called out to them. 'You have worked well this past month. Artemis recognizes the service you have provided. Artemis also recognizes that the work you do will be aided by healthy bodies! And so here is metal and fire and oil! Adjust your electromuscle! Hammer out those dents! Lubricate those joints! Make yourself the clean, sweet, silent machines you know yourselves to be, the better to serve Nyro's purpose!'

The women didn't need to be told again. They began to strip away dented panelling, to help each other adjust electromuscle, to strip down mechanisms and drop them into shallow cleansing baths of thin oil. For the first time in a night month they smiled.

All but Susan, left alone at the edge of the group, struggling one-handed to undo the electromuscle in her left arm. She looked at the other women for help, but they pointedly turned away from her.

A soft electronic moan emitted from her voicebox. No one seemed to hear it.

No, someone did.

'Do you need a hand, Susan?'

Nettie was there beside her. Without being asked, the other woman unhooked the electromuscle from Susan's arm.

'It's all kinked up. You'd be best knitting it anew.'

Susan looked at Nettie, unable to speak. *She's lonely too*, she realized. *No one wants to speak to Nettie the traitor.*

'Can't do it one-handed though,' said Nettie. 'Tell you what, why don't I do this for you now, and you can return the favour for me some time?'

Susan nodded wordlessly, so grateful for this small act of kindness in this forgotten place. She looked at the other robot, with her badly made body, and wondered for a moment at what sort of arm she would knit for her, then she pushed that thought aside.

Who was she to feel proud of her Turing City body, with its fine paintwork? Give her a few months and she would be just like Nettie. Just another interchangeable Artemisian body.

The other women were now staring at her. Susan didn't care any more.

'Th . . . Thank you,' she said.

'That's okay,' said Nettie. 'Although I must admit, I don't think I could do as good a job as you. There's good weaving here, Susan. I've watched you weave minds too. You're very deft.'

'Thank you,' said Susan, then she remembered herself. 'Though I think you're being too modest. That's a nice body you have.'

'You're only being polite,' said Nettie. 'If I were that good at twisting metal, that's what I would be doing. Instead they have me lecturing you all on how to make minds.' And at that she gave such a wistful look, it made Susan wonder. Would she really rather be in Susan's position? And a thought arose: had Nettie *ever* made children for herself? Would this lecturing be Nettie's only contribution to the twisting of a mind? What a sad, sad thought.

Nettie pulled wire from a nearby reel and began to knit with her fingers. Susan sat back and just relaxed, for the first time in ever so long. The glow of the fire, the chattering of the other women, the sudden feeling of companionship. Her right hand stirred on the soot and grease of the floor. She found herself drawing a shape: a circle, then a smaller circle on the top. Maybe it was the sudden sense of relaxation, maybe it was the realization that she had so little left to lose, but Susan asked the question that had been puzzling her for so long.

'Nettie,' she asked, 'what does this mean?'

It took Nettie a moment, as she clumsily knitted away, to realize what Susan was pointing to. When she saw the shape her fingers froze for a moment. Then she continued to knit as if nothing had happened.

'Rub that out,' she said, conversationally. 'Do you want to get us both killed?'

Susan did as she was told, the worn plastic on her hand scuffing the grease and swarf into dirty flurries.

'But why? You drew that shape yourself. I saw you!'

Nettie was obviously distressed, was doing her best to hide it.

'Susan, this is Artemis City! We follow Nyro's philosophy here! The Book of Robots is heresy! There is no philosophy but Nyro's!'

Susan gazed at the robot. 'But you drew the shape. So did Maoco O and . . .'

'Don't mention their names! I don't want to know!' She continued to knit, agitatedly, and for a moment Susan wondered what her left arm would feel like when Nettie had finished. How long before she could politely knit herself a new muscle?

That didn't matter now. She wanted to know about the Book of Robots. 'But why do people keep telling me about this!'

'You mean you don't know?' said Nettie. 'But you bear the mark!'

'What mark?'

'It's woven into you. You built it into your body! Can't you see it?'

'See what?'

Nettie looked at her, puzzled. 'Have I made a mistake?' she murmured. 'No, it's there! Don't you see, the way you have shaped yourself? How you resemble me? It's subtle, but unmistakeable!'

Susan looked from Nettie to herself. She couldn't see anything, just two robots.

'The mark is all around us!' said Nettie. 'I can see it written in the world, in the moon! It's so obvious. You and I bear the mark!'

'I can't see it.'

'But why not? Your mother wove the pattern into your mind, so that you would make yourself as you do—'

'I can't see it! I told you! I can't see anything!'

The other women were all looking in their direction now. Susan pretended to take an interest in the electromuscle that Nettie was knitting. She asked questions on her technique, as if anyone else would want to imitate Nettie's poor knitting. The other women returned to their work.

'Listen,' said Nettie. 'I don't understand why you can't see it,

but the mark is on you. The knowledge must be in you somewhere, you just haven't seen it yet. You need to search through
your memories. It will be there somewhere, you need to recognize it.'

'How will I recognize it?'

'I don't know – it's obvious to me. Listen, this is what I know.
Some time, a long time ago, the first robots were made. They had
a purpose, a reason for existence, a philosophy that was woven into
them. When they made their children, they wove the same philosophy into their minds. And their children wove it into *their*
children's minds. But, in time, as the generations went on and the
years passed, the mothers stopped weaving in the full knowledge.
They substituted other knowledge, for reasons that no one under-
stands.'

I was right, thought Susan. *You never did twist minds. Any
mother would understand why the full knowledge was not passed on.
Any mother would add something new to the weave in order to give
her child an advantage in life. They wouldn't hesitate to discard
something that would hold their child back.*

Nettie continued: 'And so the original knowledge was diluted
and broken apart, and gradually the robots diverged into different states and different beliefs. But, even so, some knowledge is
still passed on even now; some few fragments are woven into the
minds of children, along with other memories. Those memories
contain the sign' – Nettie's finger made the symbol of the dot on
the circle – 'woven into them. We few who carry those memories
are charged with the task of assembling the true knowledge back
into the whole. Of rediscovering our true reason for being.'

Susan was silent for a moment, thinking.

'But that's not right,' she said finally. 'Robots weren't built. We
evolved, just like all the other life on this planet. There is no purpose, no reason for our existence. We just are!'

Nettie smiled sadly. 'You can't see it at the moment, Susan.
Search your memories. It's in there somewhere. You'll see that I'm
right.'

Susan didn't think so, but she didn't feel confident enough to disagree.

'Tell me about the Book of Robots.'

'Ah,' said Nettie, pausing to examine her progress with the electromuscle. A loop of wire had popped out, further up the pattern. She tried to pull it back into place. 'The Book,' said Nettie, absently.

Suddenly, she seemed to remember where she was and took a look around the room, but no one now seemed to be paying them any attention. 'Well,' she continued. 'Some people hold that assembling all the fragments of memory will be an impossible task. They are too diffuse and too much has been forgotten.' She nodded. 'I must admit, I can understand their point of view, but I am not so defeatist. My mother made me that way.'

Susan nodded.

'But there are those who believe something else to be true. They hold that the memories are lost and that we should not waste our time trying to bring them together again. Instead, we should search for the Book of Robots, the design for the original robots. It contains the pattern in which the original minds were woven: the philosophy, the rules, everything. Find the book, they say, and we will know our purpose.'

'Okay,' said Susan, 'where should we look?'

Again, Nettie drew a circle on the air.

'Large circle,' she said, 'our planet of Penrose. Small circle,' she drew a smaller circle on top, 'Kusch. The continent on the top of the world. The birthplace of the robots. That is where we should be looking for the Book of Robots.'

Karel and Kavan

'What's your name, driver?'

Karel's hands tightened around the brakes at the surprise of again hearing a voice. It didn't matter, the train wasn't moving.

He had sat waiting in this valley for hours now, just watching the wet snowflakes melting into a slushy mess on the rails ahead.

'I asked, what's your name?'

'Karel,' he replied.

'Karel, my name is Kavan. Do you know who I am?'

'You're the leader of the Artemis troops. You led the invasion of Turing City.'

'That's right. And you're the robot who drove the train from which all those troops mysteriously disappeared. Tell me about it.'

'I've already said all there is to say.'

Silence. Wet snowflakes falling on rock.

'You're very brave for a robot whose coil I could have crushed at a moment's notice.'

'I'm not being brave; I'm just telling the truth. I've been over this many times already.'

'Hmm. Tell me, do you believe in ghosts, Karel?'

'Ghosts? No. That wasn't twisted into my mind. I'm not superstitious. We weren't superstitious in Turing City.'

'We aren't superstitious in Artemis, either. We don't need to be. We just believe in iron and the forge. But up here, up in the north, it seems that things are different. They twist the minds of the robots up here to look for patterns in everything. The snow blows down the valley and they look for a death. The day moon casts a shadow over the sun and they look for the coming of a stranger. They twist suspicion into the metal of their children's minds and think nothing of it.'

Why is he telling me this? wondered Karel. *Why does the leader of the Artemisian army want a lowly train driver to know this?*

'No wonder all the ghost stories come from the north,' continued Kavan. 'It is in their nature to believe in such things.'

'Oh.'

'But that makes *me* suspicious,' said Kavan. 'When I hear about what happened to the troops that were being carried on your train, it makes me think about war. Do you know, Karel, that one's tactics reflect one's philosophy? In Turing City you hid behind your supposed superiority of mind, and behind your City Guard with their superior bodies. Artemis has been so successful because we know that Nyro's philosophy transcends the metal of our minds. And now we meet a state where the robots look for patterns in the night, and they attempt to fight us in that manner . . .'

'I can't help you.' said Karel, impatiently. 'I've told you all that I know.'

The slightest of pauses.

'I've heard of you, Karel. Even before I entered Turing City, I had heard of you. Not by name, as such, but through the story of the robot with the hidden mind.'

'Every robot's mind is hidden.'

'To a certain extent, yes. But there is something special about your mind. It is almost the embodiment of the fight between our states.'

'There is no fight. Artemis has won.'

'So we have. And I wonder how you feel about that?'

'You killed my son. You took my wife from me. How do you think I feel?'

'A true Artemisian would not care. Are you a true Artemisian, Karel?'

Karel was silent.

'No reply? Not that I expected one. Well, we leave soon to head further north. Another kingdom to conquer. And then what, Karel, and then what? What would you do if you were in my position?'

The voice was soft, almost as if he were genuinely interested in Karel's reply. Karel waited a moment before he gave it. 'Well, I suppose, if I were you, if I had the chance, I would . . .'

'Yes?' asked Kavan. 'Yes?'

'I would crush my own coil and have done with it.'

Karel heard Kavan laughing loudly as he broke the connection.

Kavan

The torture chair sat in the middle of the stone room. It was quite ingenious in its own way: a little bowl into which the twisted metal of a mind was placed, a little hole for the coil to poke through and to be plugged into the taut wires that stretched down the chair's arms and back. Wires like electromuscle that could then be plucked and strummed like a lute, and the delicious pain of feedback sent playing through the coil into the mind itself. An exquisite device, thought Kavan, and indicative of the minds of the robots that had inhabited this kingdom. A device entirely contradictory to Nyro's philosophy, for it was not the Artemisian way to treat a mind as anything more than so much twisted metal.

The prisoner that Eleanor brought into the room still wore her original body: she had not yet donned the standard grey body of an Artemisian infantryrobot. She looked at the torture chair and wriggled her fingers slowly in fear.

'Ignore it,' said Eleanor. 'This is Kavan. Tell him about the Kingdom of the North. You say you have been there.'

'Once,' said the prisoner. She was small, her legs too short in proportion to her body, her arms too long. Kavan had seen the locals climb the mountainsides, seen how they would fall forwards to scamper up on all fours. Idly, he had wondered if he should get some of his troops to adopt that same design for fighting in this terrain. He dismissed the thought for the moment: it would be something to discuss later with the forges of Artemis City, when and if he returned there.

The prisoner relaxed a little. She now ignored the chair and adopted the storytelling pose that Kavan had seen other northern robots assume.

'Once,' she began, 'when I was younger, I did travel to the edge of the North Kingdom. Back then, that same year, my kingdom had harvested much wood from the western slopes, so we had a surfeit of timber that we wished to trade before it could rot.'

Kavan glanced at Wolfgang, standing silent at the prisoner's side. His aide had explained it earlier, but Kavan still thought it strange, the northern habit of relying on organic life as a construction material or a source of fire.

'What did the North Kingdom have to trade with you in exchange?' asked Kavan.

'Labour. Slave robots, they would work for us for five years before returning to their northern homes. The slave robots are well regarded, for they are strong and work hard. They have minds that can think, but they have no sense of self. The secret of how they are made is known only to the Northern Kingdom.'

Kavan glanced at Wolfgang again.

'Such robots are not unknown in the south,' said the aide. 'They turn up here and there occasionally, though they usually claim to be Spontaneous. It's possible, I suppose, that they originate from up here.'

Kavan nodded. 'Tell me more. What did you see there in the north? What did you learn?'

'I must report that I saw little, for it was raining during most of the journey. We walked the Northern Road. It is wide and was in better repair back then.'

Kavan and Eleanor exchanged glances, but the woman didn't notice, and continued to speak.

'The land of the north is not so mountainous as here, but there are still valleys filled with mist through which one must walk, there are rivers and streams that fill the air with noise of running water, and the ever-present drizzle that makes the rocks so slippery also curtails the vision. I saw very little on the journey there.'

'But what of the North Kingdom itself?'

'Alas, I saw that not at all. For the Northern Kingdom lies in the last of the mountains that rise before the Moonshadow sea. It nestles, hidden from sight, within a ring of rock through which there is only one entrance: a maze of rock known as Lazar's Labyrinth. The way through is known only to those who dwell within.'

'More stories and superstition,' said Kavan to Wolfgang. He turned back to the woman.

'Tell me, how long were these lengths of timber that were to be carried through the maze? Twenty feet? Thirty?'

'Longer,' said the woman. 'For the trees that we grew were tall and proud, and the integrity of the wood was much prized by all that dwelt thereabouts.'

'So they carried through timber more than thirty feet in length? I don't suppose, therefore, the maze would be *that* difficult to traverse.'

'I cannot speak the answer to that,' said the prisoner. 'We were not allowed to enter. We found our slaves waiting for us at the entrance to the maze. Twenty of them, tall and hard-working. We got good use out of them for our five years' worth of labour.'

'What happened to them at the end of the five years?' asked Eleanor.

'One bright morning, beneath the light of Zuse and Néel, who shared the sky with the sun that day, the slaves formed themselves into a group and then marched back home again. There were only eighteen of them still working by then. Two of them had been damaged during their labour for us.'

'Did the North Kingdom not object to this damage?' asked Wolfgang.

'No,' replied the kingdom woman. 'The remaining slaves carried the bodies of the broken robots back with them, for metal is the most precious thing in the North Kingdom. Now if we had kept the metal of those bodies, then their retribution would have been terrible to behold . . .' she trailed off, smiling.

'Do you fear the North Kingdom that much?' asked Kavan.

'We respect them, for the North Kingdom is said to have been established by the robots from the Top of the World.'

'The robots from the Top of the World?' Kavan felt like laughing. 'We heap story upon story! And who, exactly, are they?'

'A child's story, Kavan,' volunteered Wolfgang. 'The Top of the World is the place where children believe that the first robots lived. Alpha and Gamma. Their children are said to have moved south to inhabit all the rest of the world.'

'And do *you* believe in the robots at the Top of the World?' asked Kavan of the prisoner.

'Well, no,' she said, her fingers waggling slowly again. 'No. Not as such. But there are stories. They say the North Kingdom holds a fragment of the Book of Robots. And that, although they are poor in metal, they are rich in knowledge. They know something of the true nature of robots, and this is what gives them power. They say that they can increase the power of their lifeforce just by meditation. This is why they are so respected.'

Kavan was silent.

'Worried, Kavan?' asked Eleanor.

'No,' replied Kavan, 'but I wonder about these stories and their power. The robots who dwell here have superstition twisted into their minds. I wonder at how much this superstition will increase as we travel further north. I thank Nyro that our own troops have minds that are twisted true.'

'Some of them do, at least,' said Eleanor. 'We have so many volunteers at the moment, it's difficult to predict how they think. And don't forget that some of our troops are now conscripts from here, from the conquered kingdoms of the north.'

'Hmm.' Kavan gazed at the prisoner. 'So tell me more about the North Kingdom. You say they are poor in metal. What does that mean?'

'There is little metal in the circle of the mountains that form the North Kingdom,' she said. 'They say that the robots there do not make their bodies as we do, instead they must make their bones from wood. The wood rots eventually and must be replaced. They say that a robot from the North Kingdom can shatter its own body with its own electromuscle if it squeezes too hard.

'It is said that they dwell in poor hovels, built on mud through which metal worms swim. They say that the robots shape a nugget of metal into a bell and press it into the mud at night in the hope of attracting a metal worm. If the worm takes the metal, they hear the noise of the bell and pull the worm from the ground.'

'Metal worms?' said Wolfgang. 'That sounds a little like the porphyry worms of Turing City State.'

'Tell me more,' said Kavan.

'I don't know . . . oh . . . it is said that metal is so scarce that men cannot waste their wire on any woman who might twist an inferior mind. They say that the kingdom locks the men in high rocky towers, and the women must climb up to meet them. The women must surpass doors closed by ingenious locks and puzzles in order to prove their skill at shaping the twisted metal that a man produces, in order that they can then make a mind.'

'That's an old story,' said Wolfgang. 'I've heard something similar originating from Stark. It claims to explain how they rose to engineering dominance. Only there it was the women who were shut away . . .'

'Okay, is there anything else?' asked Kavan.

'Tell him about the Wizard,' said Eleanor.

'The Wizard?' said Kavan.

The prisoner threw a dark glance at Eleanor, but continued.

'The Wizard is the ruler of the North Kingdom. He is a sterile man. You understand, a man who cannot make the wire that a woman may shape?'

'I know what sterile means,' said Kavan.

'And yet it is said that the title of Wizard passes to the Wizard's son! This is some of the magic of the North Kingdom!'

'I thought you didn't believe in that sort of thing,' remarked Kavan.

'I don't,' said the prisoner, 'but—'

'I think I have heard enough,' said Kavan. 'Rumour has settled on this land like rust on untreated iron. If left too long it could weaken even the strongest army. We cannot remain here, counting metal and reading reports, while these stories spread further.'

He turned to Eleanor. 'Send out the signal. We move out within the hour. We are heading north!'

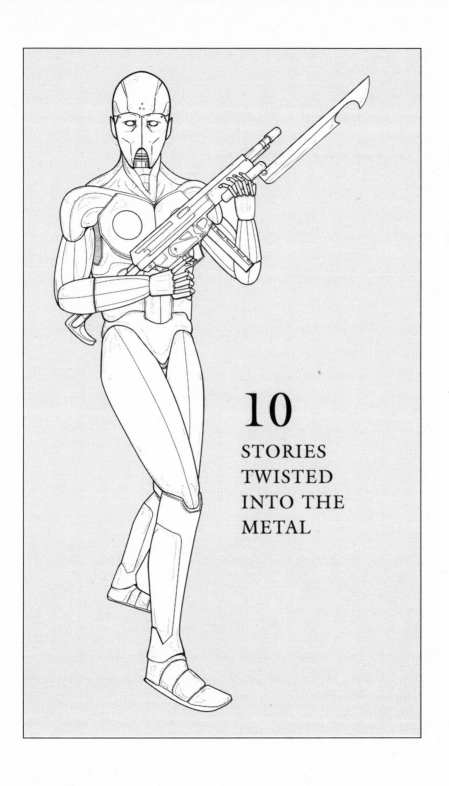

10

STORIES
TWISTED
INTO THE
METAL

Kavan

Kavan marched north.

The temperature had dropped, the rain had turned to snow, the wind had increased in speed. Even the elements seemed to be attempting to slow the Artemisian expansion. Still, Kavan marched on, disregarding the omen of the weather for what it was: mere superstition. Kavan's army was on the move, heading north with Artemisian efficiency.

Silver Scouts cut along the mountain tops, the blades at their feet and arms slicing the wind in two. They reconnoitred the land ahead; leaving signs indicating the best paths for the advance. Already they had been up to the borders of the North Kingdom, setting traps and devices in place for the coming attack.

Black Storm Troopers marched the trails blazed by the Scouts, smashing aside obstacles and crushing what little resistance to their advance that there was, mostly just a few poor robots who were too slow or weak to run.

Behind them, grey infantryrobots trudged through the rocky valleys, the wind driving snow inside their cold metal bodies. They were guarding the engineers who directed the laying of ballast and the construction of bridges, the blasting of cuttings and the supporting of walls.

And behind them all, trains rumbled along newly laid tracks, tilting and clanking as the freshly laid ballast slipped into position.

Kavan, Eleanor and Wolfgang marched amongst a troop of other infantryrobots. The mountains were slipping away behind them, now they made their way through the empty wind-blasted lands and snow-filled valleys that led to the stone circle of the North Kingdom.

'Don't you think we're stretching ourselves a bit too thin, Kavan?' asked Eleanor.

'No. Spoole will send us more troops as long as we keep moving north. He can't be seen to let us fail.' He wiped snow from his face and peered into the distance. 'Someone is coming,' he observed.

A Scout slipped towards them through the wind. Her blades were retracted, her eyes pulled in tight.

'Small group approaching from the mountains,' she reported.

'They'll be wanting to parley,' suggested Wolfgang.

Eleanor raised her rifle by way of answer. 'Artemis does not parley,' she said.

'No,' said Kavan. 'I want to speak. We know so little about them. I want to know what they think is important. Call a halt. Tell the troops to stand at ease.'

The message went out and the army emptied itself into the available cracks of the land as troops sought shelter in the lee of rocks to adjust electromuscle and clear away snow. But Kavan and Eleanor remained standing, waiting, the blizzard whipping around their bodies.

Two Scouts came forward, leading a third robot between them.

Kavan had never seen its like before. The newcomer was so small and thin. It wore no plating, leaving its bare electromuscle exposed to the wind. Kavan found himself trying to peer beyond the muscle, to see if it were true, that the robots of the North Kingdom really wore wooden bones.

The strange robot raised a hand. 'The Wizard of the North Kingdom sends his greetings, Kavan, by way of his servant, Banjo Macrodocious.'

Wolfgang spoke at Kavan's side.

'A slave name. This robot will have no sense of self.'

'I suppose that is why it has been sent to speak to us,' he mused. He looked down at the slave robot, at its small body and ridiculously oversized head. He didn't bother to raise his own hand in reply.

'You describe yourself as the Wizard's *servant*?' he said. 'In Artemis there are no servants, for we all merely follow Nyro's philosophy. Well, Banjo Macrodocious, take this message to the

Wizard, that Artemis welcomes all those robots that wish to follow Nyro's philosophy.'

'I have no orders to take messages to the Wizard,' replied Banjo Macrodocious. 'Rather, I am here to bring this message: that the North Kingdom is mentioned in the Book of Robots, and there it is written that no one shall enter it uninvited. Those who seek to do so are working contrary to the true purpose, and therefore they will fail.'

'I don't believe in the Book of Robots,' said Kavan. 'I say that we have no creator, we have no purpose, save that which we choose ourselves.'

Banjo Macrodocious ignored this – as he would have been told to do, realized Kavan.

'It is written in the Book of Robots that those who cross the line of the mountains will have their true nature revealed to them in three ways,' said Banjo Macrodocious. 'First their artefacts will fail, then their bodies will fail, and finally their minds will fail. For all that is twisted in metal was originally written in the Book of Robots, along with the works that they should perform.'

'Kill him,' said Kavan, and the blade of one of the Storm Troopers swept out of the blizzard, slicing the head of Banjo Macrodocious neatly in two. Kavan peered closely at the wire that lay inside, and saw that it was just like the blue wire of any other robot. Well, almost the same, it had an odd greenish tinge to it, as if the metal used were not quite pure. Probably due to the scarcity of metal up here, he realized. Thoughtfully, he squatted and pulled aside the electromuscle of the dead robot's arm. There was metal beneath, not wood.

He straightened up.

'Was that wise, Kavan?' asked Eleanor.

'Better that than he continues to spread superstition amongst the troops.' He looked to Wolfgang. 'Get somebody to check that body over, and then recycle the metal. Get the troops to fall in. We march on.'

Susan

Nettie was speaking again at the front of the lecture hall, as the women sat and listened in self-satisfied silence. They were the mothers of Artemis, they wove minds, they were respected. The shouts and the screams of Turing City could only be faintly recalled now, the memories of loved ones fading with time.

Susan still sat a little apart from them, still the outcast. And yet now it wasn't so bad, as she had found a friend in Nettie. Nettie the childless woman. Nettie the mother to all those Artemisian minds they wound in the night.

They were supposed to be debating, rehearsing, discussing the way in which Nyro wove a mind. Instead, Susan's mind was wandering.

The mark? Nettie had mentioned the mark. She had said that Susan had woven it into her own body, and yet Susan could see nothing. It couldn't even be said that she still wore the same body. Over the weeks, the women had all been slowly replacing parts of themselves with Artemisian spares. They were all gradually assuming the same short, stocky appearance of Artemis robots. Yet Nettie said she could still see the mark there in Susan's body.

Susan looked from herself to Nettie, looking for what they had in common, looking to see how they differed from the other robots. She could see nothing obvious.

And then there was the knowledge. That fragment of purpose in her mind that Nettie had told her would be there. Something woven by her mother. Some understanding or philosophy. She searched her mind again, just as she had done so many times before. At night, kneeling and twisting wire, in lectures, in muttered conversations with Nettie. Nothing. There was nothing there.

Someone was watching her. The woman in the next seat was smirking at her. It made her think of something that Nettie had said while they had been crossing to the forge, across the moonlight-filled yard.

'Why do robots smile, Susan?' Nettie had asked. 'Why do we

have mouths? All we need is a speaker, and yet we weave electro-muscle and construct mouths to communicate, visually. Where did that idea come from? I'll tell you – from The Book of Robots! We all still refer back to the original plan in subtle ways. Listen, Susan, we take so much for granted in this world.' And she had stopped, there in the middle of the yard, her body shining dully in the moonlight. 'There are clues all around us, and they are so big that we don't notice them.'

Clues everywhere and we don't notice them, thought Susan, as she gazed at Nettie, still talking away at the front. Nettie raised an arm and swept it around, pointing out something written in the metal of the wall behind her.

And then Susan saw it: the mark. It had been there all along, and she had never noticed it. Big circle, little circle – it was built into Nettie. Susan had built it into herself all this time without realizing that was what she was doing. She had built herself that way because it seemed right, because her mother had twisted it into her mind, just as she had twisted the knowledge that she should have two arms and two legs.

It was so obvious now. How long were her arms? How big was her head? What was the ratio between the length of her foot and her leg? Between her hips and her torso?

Always the same. The same as the ratio between the two circles that Nettie had drawn. That Maoco O had drawn. That Banjo Macrodocious had drawn.

She was excited now, though she tried to hide it. That other robot was still smirking at her. They all were, she realized. All those women smirking at her, showing their contempt.

She ignored them.

She had seen the mark. Now she needed to see the memory. What was it exactly that her mother had woven into her?

And then she had it. It had been there all along. It had been there all of her life.

It was the story of Liza, the robot who had made Karel. It was the story of her husband.

It was the memory of his first days on Penrose.

Liza

It was morning, and the flare of the previous night's battle had long since burned out. Somewhere across the Zernike plain, Bethe had fallen. The rising sun cast long shadows and, walking through those shadows, Liza entered Turing City, her newly made child in her arms.

'What's the matter, Liza?' asked Llywber, his body still slick with the oil from the great pistons that he was helping to build down near the forges.

Liza was silent but for the low buzzing sound that emerged from her voicebox, the unstoppable feedback of grief.

Echecs had seen her distress, and she came running across the white marble flagstones to comfort her friend.

'What's the matter, Liza? Where's Kurtz?' Echecs looked down at the little metal bundle in her arms. 'Is that your child? Oh, isn't he adorable?'

She didn't sound as if she meant it. She was too busy checking the child for signs of damage, wondering if Liza had made a mistake and twisted the mind improperly.

'Can I take him?' she asked. 'Can I hold him?'

Still Liza marched on, through the wide spaces where the galleries were being extended. Sheets of multicoloured glass were stacked in piles across the ground.

'Where's Kurtz?' Echecs muttered to Llywber. 'Go and find Kurtz!'

The oil-covered robot nodded and made to go, but at that moment Liza spoke.

'Kurtz is dead,' she said.

'Dead?'

'Killed. Shot by an Artemisian soldier.'

'Shot? What's an Artemisian doing out here? I thought they were all over in Stark!'

'Hush, Llywber, she doesn't need that now. Go and tell Kobuk what has happened. I'll look after Liza.'

Llywber did as he was told. He dashed off, leaving a trail of oil droplets on the white marble.

'Come Liza, I'll take you home. You're safe now. To think of it! Those Artemisian Choarh, *shooting a man who has just become a father . . .'*

At that the buzz from Liza's voicebox rose louder.

'No, Echecs, Kurtz had not become the father. Not properly. He died before . . . before we had finished . . .'

And at that the buzzing feedback of grief became too much . . .

Susan

Was that it? wondered Susan. *Surely that had nothing to do with the Book of Robots?*

It was her mother's memory, for Echecs was Susan's mother. She had been there when Liza had returned to the city, and she had woven the memory into Susan's mind. But why? Why was that so important? What did Karel have to do with the Book of Robots?

And then something else occurred to Susan. Had Echecs also woven it into her mind that she should marry Karel? Susan was a little younger than her husband, so Echecs would have witnessed Liza's return to Turing City before twisting Susan's mind.

But why? Arranged marriages were not as common in Turing City as some other places, but they were by no means unknown. And Susan had always loved Karel, right from childhood. There had never been another for her. Had that been her mother's design?

Nettie continued speaking, and Susan continued wondering.

Olam

Olam and Doe Capaldi stood waiting at the foot of the hills, along with the rest of the squadron.

'It looks like a huge crater,' said Parmissa. 'Like someone dropped a huge stone in the mud and the sides all squished up.'

'Who told you that?' asked Olam.

'A Scout,' she replied. 'She'd been up there scouting. Seen over the edge into the North Kingdom itself. She told me what it was like. Once we get over these mountains, it's all rock and mud.'

'Oh,' said Olam.

'She says it could be true,' continued Parmissa.

'What could be true?'

'You know. The Book of Robots.'

'Keep it quiet,' called Doe Capaldi. 'We need to be ready to move.'

The gale had dipped for the moment, but not before it had piled up long drifts of snow in front of the scattered rocks and ledges that surrounded them. More snowflakes drifted down from the silent clouds above, to settle on their grey metal bodies.

'Aw, they're pretty!'

Olam didn't like Parmissa. She played cute. He knew that Doe Capaldi didn't like her either. She gossiped and spread rumours.

Olam gazed up at the slope before him and suddenly felt as if his lifeforce was draining away. He only had six months to live: that was what Doe Capaldi had told him. What was he doing wasting the rest of it here, at the end the world? More than once, on the long march north, he had thought of making a run for it, slipping away into the night and heading south to find his way to one of the little kingdoms. Maybe there would be one or two still unconquered, hidden away on some forgotten peak.

'Have you heard about the curses?' said Parmissa suddenly.

'What curses?' asked Olam.

'There are no curses,' snapped Doe Capaldi.

'They were laid upon Kavan when he killed the Wizard's herald. First our machinery will be cursed, then our bodies, and then finally our minds!'

'Now listen,' said Doe Capaldi, raising his voice so that all the section could hear, 'this is a kingdom like any other we have conquered. If anything, it is weaker because it has so little metal. The only thing that makes this kingdom strong is superstition. It is woven into the minds of the robots that live up here. Would you allow yourself to fall prey to children's stories?'

Doe Capaldi looked up and down his troops, frost patterning their metal skins in cold loops.

'I thought not! Now, the attack won't be long. Wait for the signal.'

'There are Scouts busy trying to find a way through the maze,' explained Parmissa. 'That's what I was told.'

Doe Capaldi laughed contemptuously. 'Since when did Artemis try to find its way through mazes?'

At that moment there was a giant, rumbling, earth-shattering roar, and Olam recognized the sound of an atomic bomb detonating.

Doe Capaldi laughed again. '*That's* how Artemis traverses a maze!' he shouted.

Spoole

The map of Shull was almost complete.

Spoole stood alone in the command room gazing up at it, wondering.

'He'll be coming back soon,' said Gearheart.

'Oh, be quiet, Gearheart.'

'No, I won't be quiet. This is your fault, Spoole, my being crippled. I was made to be your companion, that was twisted into my mind. You knew that, so you should have protected me. You shouldn't have let that assassin get so close to me.'

Spoole didn't reply. What she was saying was all too true.

'Did you protect your child, Spoole? Is it still alive now, I wonder?'

'Oh yes, the child is still alive. I'm sure of that.'

Gearheart gazed at him. 'I wonder what it's doing now?

Artemis or Turing City? I suppose it doesn't matter. But I wonder which way she twisted the mind?'

'I think I know,' said Spoole.

Spoole and Liza

'Hello, Karel,' murmured Liza. She looked down at the dead body of her husband. 'Here he is, Kurtz. We did it. Here's our little boy.'

Carefully she placed the mind inside the tiny body.

'All finished,' she told Spoole.

Spoole looked from her to the child. 'Did you really do it?' he asked.

'I'm not telling you,' replied Liza.

Spoole called her bluff. 'Then I shall say goodbye, Tokvah.'

'Then shoot me. But you'll never know.'

Spoole stared at her, red eyes glowing. Did he care, how she had twisted the child's mind? What difference did it make, really?

But he wanted to know.

Spoole was miles from where he should be. What difference would a couple of extra hours make? He had *to know.*

He came and stood in front of the woman.

'There is a way to find out,' he said.

Spoole

'Even back then, you were a traitor,' said Gearheart. 'That child was just a bundle of twisted metal. You should have lifted it up and smashed it to the ground. You treated it like it was something special.'

'It might have been an Artemisian.'

'Should that have made a difference?'

'No! But, Gearheart, you've got to understand it was different back then. Artemis was a lot less powerful. We didn't really believe we could take on Turing City. Zuse, even a few weeks ago we weren't really sure we could do it!'

Spoole looked down at her, with her twisted, crippled shell of a body.

'Surely you must understand, Gearheart, you of all people? Take a look at yourself! Surely *you* can't believe that a mind is nothing more than twisted metal!'

Gearheart spat static at him, white noise hissing.

'And she was taunting me, Gearheart. Even though I held a gun to her head, Liza was taunting me. I was made to lead, yet even that *Tokvah* woman doubted my authority. And so I wanted to know. I wanted to know what she had done, what she believed – when I felt that I didn't believe anything myself.'

'So what did you do? How did you find out?'

'I gave her Nyro's choice. I set her to work making a second child. Making a child with *my* metal. I told her she had better twist it the same as the first, exactly the same, because at the end I would take one child for myself. I would place it in the nurseries at Artemis and see for myself whether it thrived or not.'

'And did it thrive?'

'Oh yes,' said Spoole. 'Oh yes.'

Eleanor

The ground shuddered, and a small avalanche slumped over the feet of a nearby troop of infantry robots, much to Eleanor's amusement.

'Second bomb,' she counted. 'Next one in fifteen seconds.'

Kavan looked down at the ground, lost in his own thoughts. Eleanor wanted to say something to him, but already the alert was travelling down the lines of the assembled troops. Ears down, eyes averted. The third bomb exploded, sending a hammer blow into the earth.

'The path through the maze should be wide enough now,' said Wolfgang.

There was a weird sort of light to this place, thought Eleanor. It was dimmer this far north anyway, the sunlight not as strong.

But there was something about the falling snow, the dull white clouds. It lit up the valley in an eerie electric glow.

'We hold position until the fifth bomb explodes,' said Kavan.

'Shouldn't we send in the new conscripts first?' asked Wolfgang. 'We don't want to expose regular troops to radiation.'

'Why?' replied Kavan. 'Aren't we all Artemisian?'

The call was travelling down the lines again.

'Five seconds,' said Eleanor. *Four, three, two, one* . . . Nothing happened.

She looked at Kavan. He remained staring at the ground, snowflakes settling on his painted shell. What was he thinking? It struck her then. Banjo Macrodocious's first warning: *First their artefacts will fail* . . .

'They found the bombs, that's all,' said Kavan, reading her thoughts. 'So we adapt our plans.'

He gazed at Eleanor.

'Begin the attack.'

Spoole

'But I don't understand,' said Gearheart. 'Why *two* children? Why make her weave the second? Why not just keep the first for your own?'

'She didn't understand either, Gearheart. I wonder if a woman ever could.'

'You wonder if a woman can understand? What are you talking about?'

'About twisting wire. A mind is formed just by the way in which a woman twists wire! Does the man play no part at all?'

'A man's wire provides the lifeforce. You know that!'

'I know that, but I don't understand it. But women do! They understand the patterns that they weave. This woman, this Liza, had woven a mind that expressed the battle that was raging at the time! And there I stood, so impotent . . .'

'So you made her weave a second mind. You raped her?'

'Yes.'

'It would make no difference, you know. Any woman could have told you that. It's all about the way that the metal is twisted. There is nothing else. There's nothing special about the metal.'

'I know that now.'

'But you made her submit. You found your answer.'

'Not exactly. The *gar* still managed to trick me, right at the end.'

Susan

Nettie went on with her lecture.

Susan placed her hand on her own thigh, stroked the current in the electromuscle there, just like Karel used to do to her. She thought about how she would gently twist his joints and parts back into true, smartening him up, making him run so much more smoothly. These were the reciprocal things that lovers did for one another.

Susan loved Karel. She had known him since childhood: back when he was the child that other children were kept away from. The suspicion about the way his mind was twisted had been there from the start, the way he'd grown up in such a strange way: always building his body efficiently, but with the simplest of materials and a minimum of ornamentation. Even as a child he'd stood out amongst the ostentation of the other Turing Citizens.

She thought of Karel as he used to be, seventeen years ago: a small child, dressed in iron, with such a quick temper. No wonder the parents used to talk. They had seen it, noticed it, even if she hadn't.

Why hadn't she seen it? Because her mother had woven her not to?

But surely that wasn't why she loved him? Could no one else see that other side to him? That depth, that inner belief? That seriousness that was so unusual in a child, it had attracted her even then.

Did it matter? She had been happy – happy at least until Artemis had invaded. But why?

Absently she drew a circle on her thigh, a smaller circle at the top. That was enough to unlock the memory.

Liza

'I don't know if I did the right thing, Echecs.'

The memory was so vivid. Susan was there: she was Echecs, taking Liza's hand. The child – Karel, her husband – was sleeping in the corner of the room . . .

'You made a mind, Liza,' said Echecs. 'There is no right or wrong, just a child to take care of.'

Liza looked up at Echecs, and Susan was struck by just how yellow her eyes were – the same shade as Karel's.

'They're already talking about him,' said Liza. 'Llywber and the rest – I heard them.'

'They don't mean anything,'

'They do. Oh, Echecs, what is he going to do? He's going to grow up all alone. They'll never accept him.'

'Liza, you could just end all this now. Why don't you tell them exactly how you twisted his mind?'

Liza's yellow eyes seemed to be looking somewhere else.

'Will they believe me, whatever I tell them?'

Echecs didn't answer.

'You see? Bad enough that this thing happened to me. Now they will punish my son for my misfortune.' Her gaze returned to the corner of the room, the little iron body of baby Karel. 'My poor son . . .' she repeated.

Echecs didn't speak. Susan could tell she was thinking hard, coming to a decision. She knew what it was going to be . . .

'Liza,' said Echecs.

'Yes?'

'Have you heard of the Book of Robots?'

'No.' Liza didn't care; she was lost in the contemplation of her son. Echecs continued anyway. 'The Book of Robots contains the philosophy that all robots should have woven into them by their mothers.'

'I've never heard of it.'

'One of the things it says is that robots should take care of one another. They will survive and prosper better that way.'

'Oh.'

Even from a distance of twenty-two years, Susan recognized the state of mind Liza was in. She knew that soon Liza would leave this room and walk to one of the great hydraulic pistons that Llwbyr was constructing and then place her head beneath it.

She would never be aware of the offer that Echecs was making her, that her son would be looked after. That Echecs was offering to weave him a wife.

Olam

The signal for the attack came.

Olam and the rest ran forward, scrambling up the rocky slope before them, metal hands grasping stone, eyes always fixed on the summit, scanning for the defenders.

There was nothing there to see.

Dropping for cover behind rocks, rifle at the ready, covering your comrades, then up and forward again, feet slipping on the packed snow. More snowflakes spiralling down towards you in that eerie glow that distorted vision. Darker clouds moving in above, blown south by the rising wind. Someone firing, a dark shape at the summit, drop and shoot. Back up and run, everything was becoming so fuzzy.

'Ch**!' called Doe Capaldi. 'Ch***!'

What was that? Ears so fuzzy, eyes so fuzzy, then he understood. *Chaff!* Blown over the summit by the wind, tiny metal particles filling his muscles, his eyes and ears, his mind. Unstick a magnet grenade, throw it forward to attract that chaff, run up in its lee.

Slipping when you ran, no grip, metal body sliding backwards, cold snow slipping into his chest, melting on the electromuscle.

No fear. Just a mounting sense of excitement, hot fury building within him. Hand tightening on his rifle. Scan the summit, look for someone, something to shoot at.

Past the grenade, out of its magnetic lee, chaff creeping back in again. Parmissa had reached the summit.

Doe Capaldi picking something up from the ground. Chaff grenade. Janet already at the summit.

One last push. Then, looking down into the North Kingdom . . .

Kavan

The sky was darkening; the wind howling as it whipped through the jagged passage the atomic bombs had ripped through the mountainside. Kavan marched through in the midst of an infantry platoon, Eleanor close by.

Rock was still falling, skittering, bouncing down the sheer walls. Sometimes a larger stack of stone would suddenly slip and crash down in a cloud of dust and snow. Ahead, the Storm Troopers were an unstoppable mob rolling forward. All around them Scouts flickered past, their silver bodies reflecting the light in crazy patterns. Gunfire crackled ahead, interspersed with the heavier crump of grenades and bombs: the attack had begun in earnest.

'Almost there,' said Eleanor.

Kavan nodded. 'Get a team of engineers to follow us in here,' he said. 'I want railway lines laid as soon as possible. I want Artemis to be seen to be plugging its way right into the heart of this state.'

The message was relayed back along the line . . .

Olam

Olam crested the summit looked down on the North Kingdom. His gyros lurched at the sight, and he struggled to keep his balance.

The rumours were true; they had come to the land of ghosts. He could feel the emptiness below him, a place of too much rock and too little metal. He was looking over a stone bowl filled with old mounds of snow-blown rubble. It was a broken land, long fallen into neglect.

And then the image resolved itself, and a sense of order became apparent.

Those mounds were not piles of rubble, rather a regular array of buildings carved directly from the rock or put together from loosely fitting brick. A series of roads and tracks ran between them, radiating out from the very centre of the bowl.

What he had mistaken for neglect was the result of scarce metal being stretched to its very limit. This kingdom reeked of poverty and starvation of resources, but in its midst and in its layout there were obvious signs of order and control.

That control radiated from the centre of the kingdom, and the wealth of the kingdom, such as it was, was on display there in a tower of metal. A copper sphere sitting on a skeletal tower, it rose over the surrounding mounds, dark in the approaching night, the snow whipping around it and hurling itself towards the invaders.

All around him, Olam's fellow Artemisians were cresting the summit and pausing at the sight.

Doe Capaldi did not hesitate. He was there, shouting into the wind.

'Attack! Attack!'

And the spell that had taken hold of the troops was broken. Olam gripped his rifle tightly and felt the killing lust rising within him like hot oil pumping up inside his body. He began to slip and skid down the hillside, his metal feet tearing out long dark gouges in the mud. The mud and something else . . . Organic life!

Growing from the mud! And now his hatred boiled. What sort of creatures could live here, to let their environment be polluted so?

He ran on downwards, the killing lust rising higher, plunging on towards a line of what he thought at first were abstract sculptures. And the realization dawned: trees! Organic trees planted in a line! These rust-ridden robots actually cultivated them! He kicked at one with his foot as he passed, shaving a white weeping wound across its surface.

And now he was past the trees and upon the outer edge of the little kingdom. A row of ramshackle stone mounds stretched to the left and right. There was an opening directly ahead of him: the entrance to a hovel. He had lost sight of his section in the swirling confusion, and he ran forward without thinking, plunging into the hovel without further thought.

He found himself in a small, dome-shaped room, its two occupants cowering against the far wall. Thin, pathetic things, they looked up at Olam, holding out their hands in supplication. Poorly made hands of impure metal, blotched and stained. Bodies shaking and quivering from badly tuned electromuscle.

'Please . . .' said one of them, whether man or woman, Olam couldn't tell. His rage surged up through the electromuscle. They didn't even deserve a bullet, it told him. His awl was already in his right hand, striking down through the skull of the pleading robot: it tore through the thin metal without any difficulty, tangling in the sick green-blue wire that lay beneath. The other robot began a pitiful wailing; it clung to Olam's legs. He kneed it, felt the metal of its chin crack, then with a savage joy he brought down the awl once more, splitting open the second skull.

They were both dead. That's when the frenzy overtook him. He began to tear apart their pathetic bodies, scattering them around the room. He tore electromuscle, he snapped metal bones riddled with impurities. Blue-green twisted wire unravelled on the floor, and he looked at it with disgust. There was a little fire in the corner of the room, barely fit to be described as a forge. He pushed twisted metal towards the flames with his foot, watched it begin to glow and then collapse in on itself.

And then rage passed, and in the lull that followed his attention was caught by a sheet of metal hanging on the wall above the forge. A sheet of steel, the quality of this metal easily superior to anything else in the hovel, and yet it had been hung there on the wall rather than used to improve the build of a body.

Olam moved closer to the sheet, puzzled. There was a symbol engraved on its face: a large circle, a smaller circle on the top of its circumference. What did it mean?

He heard more noise, the sound of gunfire, and that brought him back to his senses. Outside, the attack continued.

He tore the sheet from the wall, crumpled it and dropped it on the fire. The lust was rising again.

Karel

Karel had no ears to hear what was happening around him; his eyes could only see the railway lines in front. Even so, he knew that the attack had begun. He could tell by the purposeful movement of those robots around him. He saw the grey troops piled on the trains pulling out of the valley ahead of him.

He was impressed, despite himself. They worked quickly, the Artemisians. Fast and efficient.

Karel waited in a shallow valley, twilight falling with the swirling snowflakes. He counted eight sets of lines squeezed between the valley walls, all for the benefit of the constantly moving traffic of Artemis as it prosecuted another war.

Karel had drawn his train up amongst all the others that morning, and had spent the long day waiting, watching the snow piling up around the tracks. He had watched the other trains leaving the temporary marshalling yard, their wagons stacked with rails and sleepers, hoppers filled with ballast, and he had pondered the fact that Artemis was moving north again and another state was about to fall.

All day long, Karel had revved his engines, felt the rumble of the diesel shaking his frame. He had been told to keep his engine running, to be ready to move at a moment's notice. But that moment had not come, and as the day progressed the shallow valley had slowly emptied. He began to hope – and to fear – he had been forgotten about.

He watched the wind chase a flurry of snowflakes down the tracks towards him, and then realized that there was movement to his right. The long line of ballast hoppers that had been parked there since lunchtime was moving forward, red-rimmed wheels spinning slowly.

Again, Karel wondered if he had been forgotten.

He watched the hoppers departing to the north, leaving him alone in the valley.

Artemis was on the move.

Eleanor

Eleanor stood at the edge of the North Kingdom, looking down over a view that she almost recognized from the stories she had heard as a child. Not that there had been that many tales, growing up in Artemis, but robots talked, and sometimes the infantry that returned to the forges to rebuild themselves would tell what they had seen and heard on their travels over the continent.

But even those stories had not prepared her for this. She had never seen a land so desolate. She felt something almost like pity for the robots that lived here.

'I never realized,' she began.

'The poverty?' said Kavan. 'I suppose it provides an answer . . .'

'An answer? To what?'

But Kavan didn't reply, and Eleanor felt a stab of annoyance at his recent attitude. There had been a time when Kavan had shared his confidence with Eleanor. As he rose in importance he seemed to regard her more and more as a threat.

Irritated, she turned her attention back to the scene before her.

The attack was going well. The rising storm gusted clouds of snow, obscuring parts of the scene before her, but then the wind would shift to reveal a line of black Storm Troopers marching forward, pushing hovels over with their heavy hands and feet. Another gust and she saw a line of grey infantryrobots firing patiently at the few pathetic robots that emerged from the rubble. And, throughout it all, the silver shapes of Scouts slipping back and forth, flashing and spinning and kicking.

'There doesn't seem to be much resistance,' she offered.

'There won't be straight away,' said Kavan. 'They'll still be reeling from the shock of the bombs. They will have fallen back and regrouped. They'll launch their counter-attack when they are ready.'

As if on cue, the wind blew a differently patterned sound towards them.

'Not our rifles,' observed Eleanor, thoughtfully.

She stared across the expanse of the bowl to where a handful of Scouts lay unmoving in a bank of snow. It took her a moment, and then she spotted them. Black iron robots advancing steadily. Big bodies, heavy panelling. Mining robots. A squad of infantry saw them, fell back, hesitated, then raised their rifles and let off a volley before falling back again.

'Fools,' said Eleanor. 'Their rifles won't pierce that metal.'

'They're panicking,' said Kavan. 'Eleanor, get yourself down there.'

'I'm gone.'

She unslung her rifle and ran off down the hillside, heading straight for the infantry troop. It was only when she was gone that she realized that Kavan had done it again. He had sent her away from the command position.

It was too late to worry about that now. The mining robots were already upon the infantry. Slow-moving, they sought to catch hold of the Artemisians and crush them. The grey soldiers dodged them easily, but discipline had broken down. There was no order to their movements, they were panicking, firing their rifles at random.

A flash of silver nearby, and Eleanor saw three Scouts emerging from a nearby doorway. They were carrying something.

'Drop it!' called Eleanor. 'Come with me!'

The leader extended her eyes, spread her claws at having been spoken to in this fashion. Then she realized who had addressed her.

'Look at these, Eleanor,' she said, holding out a metal sphere, roughly the size of a skull. 'I think they're important.'

Eleanor didn't give the object a second glance.

'Leave them for later. Come on,'

The three Scouts dropped their loads and followed Eleanor down the hill.

Ahead, one of the mining robots had succeeded in grabbing hold of an Artemisian. It lifted it in the air, one great hand taking hold of the head and crushing it. It dropped the crumpled body and immediately made a grab for another.

The remaining infantry raised their rifles and let loose a hail of bullets that spanged ineffectually from its body.

'Get back in line!' yelled Eleanor. The milling troop turned to see who had shouted at them. There was a moment's confusion, and then recognition.

'We can't hurt them,' called an infantryrobot.

'Not with your rifles,' said Eleanor. 'But that doesn't mean you give up. Do it like this!' And a wild recklessness overtook her as she plunged forward over broken rubble, dancing around in front of one of the huge mining robots. Slowly, it lunged to grab at her arm; she quickly dodged out of its way. But it was a trick: it reached out and grabbed her other arm easily. One of the Scouts raised its rifle. 'Leave it,' called Eleanor, as she was lifted up into the air. She twisted around in its grasp and saw how the dark metal of its body was scratched by the rocks through which it burrowed, saw the thick grease that oiled its joints, saw the thick glass lenses of its eyes. Now the other arm was reaching in for her head, hand extended, ready to crush her thin skull and the wire beneath it. She waited, waited for the right moment . . . And now she swung herself forward, detached her pinioned arm, leaving the big miner stupidly holding it. As she gripped the robot's head between her thighs, she reached out with her remaining arm, popped the lid of its head open, took hold of her awl, dipped it into the big black skull and tangled and pulled loose the blue-green wire nestling within.

The mining robot died, slumping forward, and Eleanor fell to the ground awkwardly, her balance gone. One of the Storm Troopers retrieved her arm from the fallen robot's grip and slotted it back in place. She flexed it, found it was dented at the elbow, but it would do. She turned back to the remaining infantry.

'That's how it's done,' she called. 'Come on!'

Heartened, they attacked. She saw one mining robot fall, then another. Just as she began to feel the first wave of satisfaction at her work, there was a shout and then something tumbled down close to her feet.

A rough sphere, slightly smaller than a head.

It exploded in a tangle of blue wire.

Kavan

Through the swirling snow, in the last of the evening light, Kavan watched as Eleanor defeated the mining robot.

'Good work,' he noted approvingly. 'If nothing else, she is a fighter.'

Then he noticed that dark shapes had begun falling amongst the right flank of the attack. One of them fell at Eleanor's feet: he saw the explosion, he saw her fall.

'They're coming from farther around the bowl,' said Wolfgang, pointing.

'What are they?'

'I don't know.'

'Send Anders' troop up there to deal with them.'

Wolfgang relayed the order to a waiting Scout. Kavan turned back to observe the unfolding attack. Things were going well. Losses were still acceptable.

He looked towards the skeletal tower that squatted at the centre of the valley: a ball of riveted copper plate, supported on iron legs. Was the Wizard waiting in there, directing his defence?

'What about Eleanor?' asked Wolfgang.

'What about her?' Kavan gazed out over the darkening battlefield. 'Artemis is not about individuals. Either she lived or she died. The attack goes on.'

A sudden blast of snow covered Kavan's metal body, and he staggered. The wind was particularly strong here at the end of the corridor of rock, blasted through the mountain by their bombs.

'We need to move,' said Wolfgang. 'The engineers need to clear this area if we are going to run a railway into here.'

'Very well.' Kavan was looking at the fractured rock walls around them. 'We'll move over to the left, I think. It should give us a good view over the battle when daylight returns.'

Kavan and his aides began to pick their way along a path that led around the rim of the stone crater. They compacted the snow with their metal feet or scuffed it aside. Kavan looked with interest at the line of trees planted along the side of the path. Their branches had been carefully pruned away along one side, keeping the way clear. Someone had been taking proper care of these organic life forms.

Across the expanse of the bowl, the skeletal tower seemed to be watching him.

'Maybe we should regroup?' suggested Wolfgang. 'Hold off until the light is better?'

'No. *We* don't need to see to destroy. *They* are at a disadvantage.'

And as he spoke, light flared up from the skeletal tower: a golden fountain of light that rose into the deepening night, illuminating all of the battle. And then a ribbon of fire spilled out along the ground, unrolling from the flimsy-looking structure of the tower. And then another, and another. It became a crisscrossing net of flame that spread throughout the land below them.

'What is it?' wondered Kavan.

'Petrol,' said Wolfgang. 'They've filled trenches with petrol! They're lighting up the night so that they can see the battle!'

The orange light became like a solid wall sweeping across the North Kingdom, till it evinced an almost tangible presence: Kavan saw the way the falling snow danced and billowed upwards, repelled by the heat of the flames. Black smoke belched out and began to flow west.

'West, not south!' observed Wolfgang. 'The heat's affecting the wind,'

Something else was burning. One by one, great hands of fire were igniting, fiery fists brandished at the sky. And then Kavan realized what he was seeing: the trees that lined the paths through the North Kingdom were igniting, bursting forth with blossoms of red fire, adding more smoke to the line snaking west.

'They're sacrificing part of their own city,' said Kavan, in awed tones.

He looked around for Eleanor, chided himself for doing so. She would return if she would return. But he wanted to share this moment with her. She would understand. They hadn't done it in Stark, they hadn't done it in Wien, they hadn't done it in Turing City. But they were doing it here. The enemy were giving their all to the fight. These people really *believed* in something.

He turned to a nearby Scout.

'Tell the engineers to move quickly. We're going to need more troops in here soon.'

Olam

Olam and the rest had moved virtually unchallenged through the maze of streets that ran amongst the hovels. A few of the pitifully thin robots had tried to form a line in order to defend their homes. Doe Capaldi and Parmissa and the rest had simply marched through it, their kicks and punches easily breaking their opponents' badly constructed bodies. Olam had crashed into their homes, searching out the robots that sheltered there, shooting the adults, taking the children and swinging them by the legs, cracking open their heads against the sharp ground. Their bodies were left in piles to be collected later by the scavenger teams, the metal to be bundled up and sent back to Artemis City for recycling.

The killing lust was welling up inside him again; it pulsed in time with the movements of his electromuscles. As the streets had lit up with fire and the trees had begun to burn; as the patterns of the flames danced on the silver skins of the Scouts that darted back and forth along the paths; as the sound of metal twisting metal rose up on the gusts of the wind, as the battle moved to its climax, Olam finally surrendered himself totally to Artemis.

He was no longer a Wiener, he was an Artemisian. He was part of the ultimate power, the supreme race, the conquerors of Shull, the future rulers of the entire world of Penrose itself.

Smoke belched from the trees, from the burning ditches, enfolding him, hiding him . . .

Releasing him.

Karel

Karel stood alone in the valley, revving his engines, impatient to be off. Ahead of him the sky was slowly illuminated by a great orange glow, and he wondered what was happening over there. Thick black smoke was feeling its way down the tracks towards him, more and more of it pouring its way south, shouldering aside the falling snowflakes. It lapped over the tracks, lapped around his wheels, and then it slowly rose, engulfing him.

What was going on?

'Hello?' he said, tentatively. No reply, not that he had been expecting any.

He waited, seemingly suspended in the darkness. They had taken away his family, then his body . . . now they had taken away his sight. What next?

He revved the engines, felt the train shudder. The enfolding smoke cleared a little. He saw shapes out there, infantryrobots maybe, running past him. Running away? He revved the engines again. This time he saw nothing.

What was happening out there?

Then there was a voice.

'Drive! Quickly! Get out of here!'

The voice thrilled with urgency. Karel revved the engines, released the brakes, started to roll. The smoke parted a little, and he saw more infantry running past.

'Faster!' urged the voice.

'I can't see where we're going!'

'It doesn't matter. We need to get to the front!'

He felt a coughing splutter somewhere inside him.

'Faster!' said the voice. It seemed to guess his thoughts. 'Ignore that sound!'

That splutter again. And then something else.

'The wheels are slipping!' protested Karel.

More spluttering. The engines. What was the matter with them?

'There's something wrong with the engines!'

'It's the smoke, it's blocking your intakes.'

'Then I must stop!'

'No, go faster. You can coast to the front! They need you there!'

Again the engines spluttered. Karel increased his speed. Suspicion suddenly gripped him.

'Who are you?' he asked.

'Banjo Macrodocious.'

'Banjo Macro . . . ? but aren't you the robot . . . ?'

And at that the engines gave a final splutter and died.

Karel swore. He had been tricked! Tricked into filling his own engines with the choking black smoke.

He jammed on the brakes, squeezed them hard, but they felt wrong too. They were mushy, and the wheels seemed to slip through his fingers.

'But whose side are you on, anyway?' asked Banjo Macrodocious.

Karel didn't know. He just wanted to stop the train, and the brakes weren't working. He was rushing through darkness, and then, suddenly, his vision cleared and he was running through a newly formed valley. There was a train in front of him, moving more slowly than he was.

Clenching desperately at the mushy brakes, he rolled forward, frantically trying to avoid a collision . . .

Olam

Olam killed and killed and killed, and yet his frustration grew.

It was getting harder to find new prey. The houses he came upon were nearly all empty. Those robots that he met were the very young, sheltering behind parents, or the very poor, or those with insufficient metal to make bodies capable of moving.

Fires burned all around him, black smoke engulfed him, and suddenly he realized he was all alone. Where had the rest of his section got to?

He saw a familiar shape through a break in the clouds and ran towards it.

'Oh, it's you, Parmissa,'

Parmissa turned awkwardly to look at him. Her legs seemed stiff, her arms hung loose at her side.

'Is that you, Olam? Are you feeling okay? I can't seem to move my arms or neck at all how I want to.'

'I'm fine,' said Olam dismissively. 'Where is everyone?'

'Spreading out through the houses. Janet said that she'd heard the enemy were retreating. Pulling back to that tower in the centre. They were going to try and cut them off. Are you sure you feel okay?'

'I told you, I'm fine.'

Although, now he thought about it, Olam did feel an odd stiffness in his own shoulders. He soon dismissed the thought. He didn't care. He wanted to move on. He wanted to kill.

'This is a strange place, isn't it?' said Parmissa, her arms dangling loose as she turned to look around the buildings that loomed on either side of the street. 'Have you seen those funny plates they all have in their houses? Not enough metal to panel their own bodies, and yet they waste it on all those little signs. Circle on circle.'

'Who cares?' said Olam, impatient to be off. He turned in what he thought was the direction of the tower. 'I'll head this way. The others will need help. Are you coming?'

'I think I need to sit down a moment,' said Parmissa. 'I feel tired.'

She slumped down heavily to the ground, slush and mud squirting over her body.

'You stay here if you want to. I'm going on.'

But now he felt tired too. Like the lifeforce was draining from him.

'What's the matter with me, Parmissa?' he asked, slumping down beside her.

'Don't know,' said Parmissa. 'Let's just stay here. Don't think I can move.'

Nor could Olam. All the killing lust evaporated from him in an instant. Suddenly the ever-present black cloud was not something in which to hide, instead it was something that was watching him. He tried to raise himself back to his feet, but his hand slipped and he fell forward, face-down. Slushy mud began leaking into his body.

'Listen,' said Parmissa. 'I can hear footsteps,'

Eleanor

Eleanor was wrapped in blue-green wire. It had cut through the panelling of her legs, slicing right through the electromuscle beyond; it was tangled around her waist and her right arm. There was no pain, only a rising sense of disgust.

She was caught in the twisted wire of a mind!

The sky above her was dark, as if time had suddenly jumped forward to deepest night. Everything was in the wrong place, and the fighting had suddenly moved away from her. What was going on? It was as if she had fallen asleep.

But she hadn't slept since she was a child!

Her body was half covered in snow. Nearby lay the body of the mining robot she had killed, the wire of its mind still trailing from its head. And there were other bodies there, too – Artemisian infantry, also wrapped in wire. She had been lucky, she realized, that this wire bomb had caught her around the legs. She gazed at what remained of another infantryrobot lying on the ground nearby. Blue-green wire had sliced into his skull, wrapping itself around the blue wire of the Artemisian's mind.

Carefully, Eleanor began to pull at the wire that entangled her own body. It peeled back easily, the lifeforce long drained from it. She freed her right arm and looked down at her ruined legs. There was no saving them, she decided. She detached them and then dragged herself over to the nearest dead infantryrobot, where she set about stripping the working parts from its body and attaching them to her own. Soon she was back on her feet again.

Where would Kavan be now, and why hadn't he sent anyone to look for her?

She laughed at the thought. Like Kavan would care! He was probably just grateful to be rid of his rival.

The spot where she and Kavan had stood earlier had changed. The engineers had excavated deeper into the rock, cut a notch deep into the side of the bowl and had then run a railway line through it. The line now extended a few tens of feet into the Northern Kingdom and then petered out, first into bare sleepers and then ballast. There was no sign of the engineers who should have still been working on it.

Eleanor turned slowly, taking in the scene. Below, the bowl was filled with the dying flames of fire trenches, the snow gradually beating its way back against the heat. The trees that had once lined the paths of the kingdom were crumbling into glowing ash. What had she missed? She got the impression that the Artemis advance was faltering.

What had Kavan done, to throw away his advantage so?

Oh, Nyro, she thought, *what would you have me do here?*

Eleanor didn't believe in signs. She wasn't superstitious, like these robots of the north, but if she were ever to believe in such things, it would have been then. Because at that moment there was a rumbling and a shaking. A scraping noise screeched out into the night, and something came skidding and tumbling along the newly laid track.

A train. It ran to the edge of the rails and then slewed across the empty sleepers, tumbling and skidding its way down into the bowl of the North Kingdom.

What had caused it to do that, wondered Eleanor? Then she saw the second train that pushed along the first, saw how it was desperately trying to brake. Without success. It too came off the end of the rails, but this one skidded to a slow halt, only the engine and the first wagon resting on the freshly laid ballast. Slowly, that second engine tipped over and landed with a crash on its side.

An accident, she realized. There were always accidents in war. This was not a sign: Nyro was not speaking to her.

And then she recognized the train.

Kavan

First their artefacts will fail, then their bodies will fail, and finally their minds will fail.

'Superstition,' declared Kavan.

'That black smoke, full of carbon particles from the burning trees,' said Wolfgang. 'It's getting into the electromuscle of the troops. It shorts out the spaces between the weave, stops it working properly. Wipe the residue away and they'll be fine.'

An aide pushed her way forward. 'What about the machinery?' she asked. 'The engines have stopped working,' It was Ruth, General Fallan's former aide, now wearing a Scout's body. If only she had a Scout's courage, thought Kavan. She had never dared to question him until now. Funny how people gained a little courage when things started going wrong.

'It's sabotage,' said Kavan, firmly. 'We are fighting a clever enemy, nothing more.'

'Don't forget the atomic bombs.' said Ruth. 'They didn't go off either, and that was before the fires started. What about them?'

'They obviously found our bombs in time and disarmed them. These things happen in war. The attack is otherwise proceeding satisfactorily.'

'I don't think so,' said Ruth. 'We've lost too many troops on the left flank. The smoke is lifting now, and our troops that were fighting there have disappeared. So have the enemy, what little of them there was for us to engage with.'

'They'll be falling back to the centre,' said Kavan. 'Make no mistake, they will attack us, but, when they do, we will be more than their match.'

'No,' said Ruth, gaining confidence all the time. 'We should stop now; send for reinforcements from Artemis City. The railway lines are in place.'

'No,' insisted Kavan. 'We still have sufficient numbers. There are three companies of infantry in reserve on the right flank. They will be enough.'

'I hope you're right,' said Ruth.

Kavan gazed at her, wondered if he should discipline her, decided against it. She was merely raising valid concerns.

Just for one treacherous moment he wondered if three companies would be sufficient, but those doubts were quickly quashed. Yes, he decided. Yes, they would be enough.

It was at that same moment that the darkness over to their right lit up. They felt the wind increase. Kavan turned away, only just managed to turn down his ears in time. The explosion hit them with so much force it knocked them off their feet.

Even as he fell, even as he rolled himself to safety, Kavan realized that the explosion was centred just where his reserve troops had been waiting. Even so, he took a certain pleasure in realizing where his two missing atomic bombs had got to.

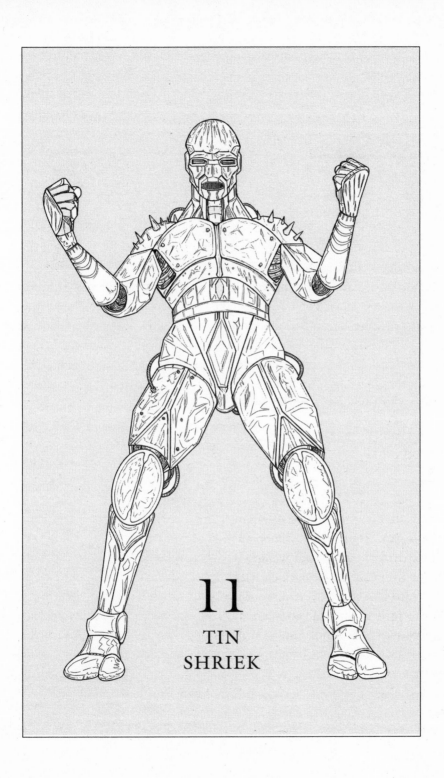

11

TIN
SHRIEK

Interlude: Cha-Lo-Ell-Curriah

Halfway around the world of Penrose, the continent of Yukawa baked in yellow sunlight. All was in harmony.

It was the time of morning changeover.

In the silver cities, lower-caste robots gave way to their superiors as they stepped from the shade of metal awnings into the cool dimness of the lime groves.

In the farmlands, robots harvested the hemp and cotton that would be spun into a rope or thread more flexible than could be made from any metal, their silent labours observed by the aesthetes of the upper class, who relaxed in their woven pagodas.

Around the mines of the central plains, the gentle wind peeled thin streamers of brown dust from the baked land and sent it ribboning south. The son of a mine prefect watched the unfolding streams of dust and saw a poem written in the air, a poem speaking of the harmony of the Yukawan Empire, its peoples unchanging throughout all these centuries.

It was a harmony that would soon be lost.

Cha-Lo-Ell-Curriah strode across the runway, his steps too light in his flying body.

Flying required a body made to be as light as possible, and so Cha-Lo-Ell-Curriah wore aluminium bones draped with thinly knitted electromuscle that was only just sufficient to control the aeroplane. He wore a mesh skull and plastic fingers. And as for his panelling . . .

It was a fine day for flying, at least in Yukawa. According to the meteorologists, there were ice storms over Shull, but that was another continent, far away. For the moment, it was enough that the sun polished the shiny green leaves of the organic life that waxed strongly along the edge of the runway, it was enough that the sun reflected brightly off the simple aluminium roofs that covered the flight buildings.

The sun did not reflect from Cha-Lo-Ell-Curriah's body, however, for Cha-Lo-Ell-Curriah was dressed in organic matter. Not half an hour before he had stood in the centre of the dressing room, arms held wide, as two young women stripped away thin aluminium panelling from his body. They had oiled his joints, straightened the weave of electromuscle in his arms and legs with their delicate fingers and then they had brought forth the flying skin.

Stored in a box made from organic matter – black polished wood from one of the tall trees that grew in the plantation just south of the airport – the flying skin was cut from a living animal by specially trained women. Working with sharp knives, they held the terrified, kicking, bleating animal between their legs as they drew the short blades up the creature's seams. Along its legs, under its belly, around its throat. The skin had been removed in three parts, and then it had been taken to the tanning room, where it was smoked and stamped and cured. It had been cut and shaped and sewn to make the garment that was now carefully rolled over Cha-Lo-Ell-Curriah's body.

Up his arms, over his feet, and up to his thighs. A waistcoat was then fastened around his chest by long, clever fingers, and Cha-Lo-Ell-Curriah, only half immersed in the dressing contemplation, wondered at what minds these women would make, should they ever be allowed to twist metal.

It took time to dress for flying – the ritual could not be hurried – but eventually it was done, and now Cha-Lo-Ell-Curriah caught his reflection in the polished aluminium side of the aircraft as he climbed up to the cockpit.

His body was short and thin, and pale. He looked almost like an organic creature himself. Like the Nightwalker from the old legends.

He settled into the cockpit.

Me-Ka-Purhara helped to strap him into position.

'All is Harmony?' asked Cha-Lo-Ell-Curriah.

'All is Harmony,' replied Me-Ka-Purhara.

There was a high-pitched whine as the turboprop awoke.

Cha-Lo-Ell-Curriah lost himself in the takeoff contemplation.

Kavan

Kavan stood in the middle of the chaos, thinking.

The howling wind of the nuclear explosion was dying, the flames of the trenches and the trees had gone, their fuel charred and evaporated by the blast. Dark shadows cast by their bodies were scored into the grey ash, and stone covered the ground.

The snow that had been blown away by the atomic blast was only just returning; melting even as it mixed with the ash from the fallout.

Down below, Artemisian troops were milling, disorientated. A white glare erupted on the battlefield, followed by another and another, as a few of the more experienced commanders set off magnesium flares.

More flares were ignited alongside the railway line that been laid into the kingdom. Kavan was pleased to see figures down there, already darting about, beginning to clear the wreckage of the trains.

Nearby, his aides were becoming frantic. Kavan decided it was time to rejoin them.

Ruth wasted no time in offering her opinion. 'We should withdraw now,' she called. 'We need to regroup and prepare for the second attack.'

'Why?' asked Kavan.

'Why? Isn't it obvious? They are all over us! We don't stand a chance against their . . .' She stopped herself just in time.

'Their what?' asked Kavan. 'Their magical powers? Are you so gullible? They operate by superstition alone! Look at them. Yes, they have severely disrupted our attack, our troops are milling in confusion, but ask yourself this: have they pressed home their advantage? No! And why not? I suspect they have nothing to attack us with. Why else would they have destroyed a major part of their own kingdom? This last display was nothing but desperation on their part.'

'Desperation? They are *destroying* us! We gain nothing by continuing with this attack!'

'We weaken them! I tell you, you have become too soft after the easy victories of the last few months! You forget what it is like for us to fight as people of principle. Are we only to fight when victory is easily grasped? Now that you finally encounter a people such as these, physically weak but gripped by great principle themselves, would you just give up? If so, then you're not acting as Nyro would wish you!'

That silenced Ruth. That silenced all of them. But Kavan pressed on.

'And should the worst come to the worst and they defeat us tonight, then what of it? Artemis will return in greater force and reclaim the metal of our bodies.'

It took a moment, but Kavan noted the horrified realization creeping across their faces as they understood that he really meant what he was saying. He lowered his voice.

'For did not Nyro say, *there is no mind, there is just metal?*'

He turned back to the centre of the bowl, which was now filling with the light of magnesium flares, and he gazed over at the skeletal tower.

'I think it is time to see what we all really believe in, both us and the Northern Kingdom. Get the wreckage of those trains moved. I want railway lines laid right into the heart of this place! Tonight, we will conquer, or we will die!'

Olam

Olam was dragged through rocky alleys, his useless electromuscles cold with the muddy slush that filled his metal shell. He tried to see where he was going, tried to look at who had captured him, but he couldn't move his head, only gaze up at the sky as he was dragged left and right, deeper and deeper into the shanty city, until finally he was pulled through a doorway. His last sight was of the night lighting up with the glare of the nuclear explosion, and he felt a surge of hope. Artemis was still attacking. They would surely find him!

But that feeling soon passed as Olam was dragged across the floor and manoeuvred into a sitting position, the walls and floor of the stone-built shanty in which he found himself vibrating with the shock of the explosion. Loose fragments of rock were shaken down from the ceiling.

Now that he had time to look around, Olam saw that there were other grey robots in the room with him. With growing horror, he recognized Doe Capaldi and Janet. And now Parmissa was being dragged into the room, and he finally got a look at their captors. To his surprise, they were nothing special. They were just the same thin, poorly made, pig-iron robots that he had killed so many of. They propped Parmissa up against the wall right beside him and then they moved to the centre of the room. There was a poor fire burning there, a little forge, but the warmth it gave off was enough to melt the snow from his broken body, sending dark rivulets of water running away from him across the floor.

The door opened, and a new robot came in, this one better made than the rest. Its panelling was of good-quality steel, polished to a shine. It moved with the grace and poise afforded by finely tuned electromuscle.

It took in the captured Artemisian robots at a glance. 'Bring one of them to the middle,' it commanded.

The other robots immediately deferred to it, two of them dragging Janet's limp metal body to the centre of the room.

The steel robot ignored her. It turned instead to the remaining captives, bending forward a little as it addressed them.

'Artemisians,' it said, 'the twisted metal of the mind is a wonderful thing.'

Somebody took hold of Olam's head, turning it slightly so he could see the steel robot all the better.

'Metal can move, it can bend and crack and snap. Metal can melt, it can be drawn, it can conduct electricity.'

The steel robot turned its attention to Janet. Ever so carefully it began prying apart the metal of her skull. Peeling back the pieces and dropping them on the floor, as the poor thin robots hungrily watched them fall.

'What is he doing?' asked Janet, her body still immobile. No one spoke; no one interrupted the steel robot.

'But when metal is twisted just *so*, it transcends itself,' it said. 'It becomes a mind.'

'Tell me what it's doing!' Janet looked around the assembled captives, pleading for an answer. She tried to look up, to see what was happening.

Now the blue wire of her mind was exposed, nestling in the cup of the skull base. Olam watched, terror struck, as the steel robot ran a hand over that wire.

'The metal becomes a mind,' repeated the steel robot. 'This is written in the Book of Robots.'

Now he was peeling back the base of the skull, exposing the mind completely. The blue wire seemed to shiver, and Olam felt himself willing his immobile electromuscle to tense, as if that would hold the wire of Janet's mind together, stop it slipping and unravelling.

'But this mind here is not the mind described in the pages of that book,' continued the steel robot. 'The minds that are woven today are but pale shadows of the true mind, for over the years the knowledge of the strength and purpose of a robot mind has been diluted and forgotten.'

The steel robot now scooped Janet's mind from her skull, lifted it carefully into the air. The long braided length of the coil was still attached to the body, and Janet's eyes still rolled upwards, looking in horror at what was being done to her.

'For, even today, twisted metal has more lifeforce than many realize, yet that lifeforce is but a fraction of that enjoyed by the first robots.'

'Put her back!'

Doe Capaldi's voice rang across the room. The steel robot turned to gaze at him, the blue wire of Janet's mind wobbling in his hand.

'She is perfectly safe,' said the steel robot. 'Or at least, she will be if her mind is twisted true. It all depends on how far she has diverged from the plan laid down in the Book of Robots. Even then, you may be surprised. As I said, the mind has more lifeforce than robots realize.'

And then, so quickly that Olam could barely follow it, the steel robot pulled out a detonator cap and pushed it between the slippery coiled wire of Janet's mind, pushed it deep inside. Carefully, he dropped the mind back into its skull cradle.

'What has he done?' whispered Janet. 'What has he done to me?'

'Nothing,' called Parmissa, her voice strangely modulated. 'He hasn't done anything.'

'He's put a detonator cap in your skull!' said Olam. 'Parmissa, why lie to her?'

'Why lie indeed?' asked the steel robot, bending down before Janet. 'Just a small charge. You have the strength, you know – the lifeforce to keep your mind together. All you have to do is concentrate. To really, really concentrate. Here it comes . . .'

'No! Take it . . .' began Janet, and then there was a muffled crack, and Janet died. Blue wire exploded in a tangled mess.

'No!' called Parmissa, and then she was silent. They were all silent.

'You saw it, didn't you?' said the steel robot. 'The power of the mind?'

They had all seen it. The blue wire had exploded in a tangled ball, but then it had happened, something that they had never seen before. The wire had contracted. It had tried to pull itself together again. It had almost made it, too.

'This is the knowledge of the Book of Robots. The lifeforce.'

Olam barely heard him speak. Janet had almost made it. She had used her lifeforce to almost pull her mind back together, but not quite. Blue wire slipped and flopped across the rough stone floor.

'Now,' said the steel robot, brightly. 'Who's next?'

Eleanor

Eleanor ran to the front of the train. Burning diesel was spilling from one of the fuel tanks, and she splashed her way through a puddle of orange flame that sizzled as it burned its way through the snow. The front of the train lay on its side, one uncoupled wheel still spinning slowly. She looked along the train's underside, searching for a likely panel or access hatch, but there was nothing there, just the wheels and springs and drive coupling.

A muffled whoosh and a wave of orange flame swept over her, covering her with greasy soot. She felt the heat in her electro-muscles as the light grew brighter. The flame was spreading.

Quickly, she scrambled up the bogie, on to the top, or rather side, of the train. Again, she looked for an access panel, hoping that the train had not fallen onto it. Finally, she spotted it, its out-line painted in red and yellow stripes. She unsnapped the catches. There was another muffled thump and another wave of heat, much stronger now. She flung the panel aside and dropped inside the train.

There were three minds in there, nestling in a neat line. One of them was dead, its blue wire dull and brittle. She pulled out the other two, carefully disengaging the coils, and climbed up and out of the train. Orange flames burned bright all around her, sucking the oxygen from the night. She jumped to the ground, into the heart of the fire, and ran as quickly as she could into the darkness. Flames swelled up into the sky, casting shadows into the darkened surroundings. She ran on, out of the fire and into the night, look-ing for the dead and broken bodies of infantryrobots. After some searching she found enough parts to make a body.

Carefully, she slid the first mind into the body, plugged in the coil . . .

'AIEEEEEEEEE . . .'

The robot began to scream a shrill high-pitched electronic note. It wrapped its arms around its head and curled up on the ground, unmoving.

'. . . EEEEEEEEE . . .'

Eleanor quickly unhooked the robot's coil, silencing it. She looked around, seeing if anyone else had heard the noise. Was someone coming to investigate? She scanned the night. No one was in sight.

Now she slid the second mind into the same body.

She waited. The robot on the ground moved its arm. Then the other arm. Slowly it turned its head and looked at her. It reached out and patted the ground, patted itself, patted Eleanor's hand.

'Are you okay?' she asked.

'I'm fine. Who are you?'

'Eleanor. Are you Karel?'

'Yes.'

Eleanor smiled. 'Excellent. Then come with me. There's someone I think you should meet.'

Olam

The tangled minds of three robots spilled over the floor.

'This one almost did it,' said the steel robot, looking at the pool of twitching wire that slowly uncurled around its feet. 'See? It *is* possible. Remember that, when it's your turn.'

Olam's gyros lurched as the robot looked directly at him. Was it to be his turn next? And then, to his overwhelming relief, the steel robot turned and walked through the door, leaving the building.

Olam and the rest remained silent for a moment, unable to quite understand what had happened. Not quite willing to believe their good fortune. Were they to be saved?

No, because now the thin, pig-iron robots were pulling Parmissa to the centre of the room, they were unpicking the metal of her skull.

'Please!' she called. 'Please, not me!'

'Parmissa!' called Doe Capaldi. 'Show some dignity. You are an Artemisian!'

'No I'm not! I'm a Wiener. I only joined this army so I didn't have to die back in Wien!'

Just like me, thought Olam.

'Did you hear that?' she called to the thin robots. 'I'm not really an Artemisian! Let me alone!'

Mercilessly, they unpicked the last of her skull. Slowly, carefully, they lifted the blue wire of her mind from her body.

'No! I told you! I'm not one of them! I'm . . .' They unhooked her coil from her body, and her voice died.

They slipped the detonator cap in between the wire of the skull. Olam felt as if his gyros were filled with sand, the way they now seemed to grind inside him. He knew what was coming next . . . Except he didn't. Because now a hinged shell was produced, the size of a skull. Parmissa's mind was hooked up inside it, the shell closed with a snick, the whole then placed carefully on the floor. What were they doing?

They had finished their work with Parmissa. What now? Horror: they pointed at him. It was Olam's turn. They were coming towards him . . .

'Olam!' called Doe Capaldi. 'Wire bombs! They're making us into wire bombs!'

Olam was being dragged to the centre of the room, his body being propped into position next to the empty shell of Parmissa.

'Olam, when the charge detonates, you mustn't fight it! Don't try and keep your mind's shape! You will only harm some other Artemisian!'

'What do I care for Artemis?' Olam shouted, his voice shrill. 'Parmissa was right! We only joined because we wanted to live!'

'I didn't!' said Doe Capaldi.

'Then *you* relax and let your mind be blown apart! I certainly won't!'

Fragments of Olam's skull were dropping to the floor in front of him. He willed his electromuscles to start working, to no avail.

'I don't want to die!' called Olam. 'Listen, I'm not an Artemisian. My mind is not just metal!'

'Don't be such a coward!' called Doe Capaldi. 'Why not try and hold on to some dignity? You'll never make it anyway! None of the others did. It's all a trick!'

'A trick?' shrieked Olam. 'We didn't even know this was possible until twenty minutes ago! Did *you* know that the mind had that much strength? Did *you* know about the Book of Robots?'

So much metal falling to the floor. How much longer did he have?

'Olam, what does it matter? Your mind is steeped in radiation. You'll only have a few months left anyway!'

'So? What did you say to me? Better six months of life than death in Wien—'

And then his vision was cut off. They had unhooked his coil.

What was happening now? Were they squeezing the detonator into his mind? Would he feel it? Could he tell the difference?

How long had it been? How long had it taken them to prepare Parmissa? By now they must be placing his mind into a hinged shell. Hadn't they hooked Parmissa's mind up to it in some way? Why was that?

The answer came in the shape of grey light. He could see again, after a fashion. And he could hear the dim sound of Doe Capaldi's voice.

It was done, Olam realized with horror.

He was now a wire bomb.

Eleanor

Eleanor kept having to stop to wait for Karel, struggling as he was to come to terms with his new body.

'Come on!' she called impatiently.

'I keep thinking I'm still in the train,' he replied, trailing behind her as they picked their way up the hillside. Snow and dust whipped out of the darkness, forming random patterns around them. 'So many sensations . . . I keep wanting to pull the brakes.' His hands made compulsive gripping motions as he spoke. 'Where are you taking me?'

'To see Kavan. You've heard of Kavan, haven't you?'

'Kavan?' Karel stopped. 'He's the *Choarh* who invaded Turing City. He's the one who had my child killed!'

Karel began to stumble up the hill behind her, unfamiliar feet slipping on stray pebbles, the cold creeping in at his joints and numbing the electromuscle there.

'Why are you taking me to *him*?'

'Don't you want to see your child's killer?'

Hadn't he realized yet, she wondered. Hadn't he recognized her? And then she felt him take hold of her arms, felt him pull her around to face him. She saw his yellow eyes gazing into hers.

'It's you, isn't it?' he said, his voice crackling with static. 'You were in my apartment . . . ?'

He lashed out, gripped her neck, tried to force her head upwards, tried to get at her coil. Eleanor almost laughed. He was doing it all wrong: infantry bodies were deliberately engineered to stop this happening, the pieces were joined in different fashions.

Besides which, she was trained in the use of an infantry body. She had worn one for years, while Karel had worn one for only a few minutes. She broke his grip easily, tripped him and sent him tumbling backwards onto the ground.

'There's no point fighting me,' she said, gazing down at the robot on the ground, his hands still clawing the air furiously. 'Listen, I only followed orders. It was Kavan who sent me to your apartment. He's the one you should blame.'

Karel gazed up at her silently from where he lay.

'Karel listen to me! Kavan is losing it. This battle could well be his last. You don't know how Artemis works: if Kavan isn't the right leader, then he'll be replaced. Kavan knows that, and if he thinks he is wrong for Artemis, he would be *happy* to be replaced.'

'What's that got to do with me?'

Eleanor held his gaze. She wanted him to understand.

'*I* can't kill Kavan,' she said.

Karel said nothing. Eleanor turned on her heel and resumed her climb up the hill. The weather was going crazy: the icy wind drew itself across her body like a saw, frost patterned her chest, and yet, across the bowl of the North Kingdom, the land was dissolving in a warm mist.

She continued her climb, listening for the sound of Karel's feet. What would he do? Would he attack her again?

Through the wind she could hear the clank of metal as Karel began to follow her.

Kavan

Kavan's forces had been pushed back on two flanks. In response he concentrated his remaining troops into one force, intending to push forward like an awl, deep into the heart of the North Kingdom. He would stab right up against the skeletal tower that stood at the centre.

He stood on a splintered shelf at the edge of the broken maze, looking down over the ever-present railway lines that reached from Artemis City, so far to the south, now preparing to probe deep into this last northern post of resistance.

He looked over the remnants of his army as they ranged down the nearest slope, barely three hundred infantryrobots and sixty Storm Troopers. No one knew for sure how many Scouts were still out there.

His troops were forming into the shape of a knife, ready to thrust forward. The mess of the train wreck had been heaved to the side; ahead of it engineers were busy lengthening the track, piercing their way forward.

'We're almost ready,' said Wolfgang.

'They can see us massing,' said Kavan. 'They'll need to strike soon if they are to finish us off.'

He gazed over at the far side of the bowl. 'Wolfgang, what's making that mist?'

The far side of the bowl was filling with a white haze. The magnesium flares reflected eerie white light back from a rising fog bank that was engulfing the land beyond the tower. The wind blew tentacles of mist out across the bowl, which slowly insinuated themselves throughout the Artemisian lines.

'Heat,' said Wolfgang, suddenly. 'The snow is evaporating.'

'What are they burning to produce such heat?' wondered Kavan aloud.

'Something beneath the ground,' mused Wolfgang. 'Something that burns for longer than petrol. Coal, maybe? Charcoal?'

And it struck Kavan then, with such force. *They really believe*, he thought. *They are burning their land, rather than surrender to us.*

'Come on,' he said, as he began to make his way down the hill. Behind him, through the wail of the wind, he heard Ruth's voice.

'Where are we going?'

'To join the troops, of course,' answered Wolfgang. 'This is the final attack.'

Even some of my aides don't really believe, thought Kavan. *Even some Artemisian soldiers still believe they are more important than Nyro's philosophy.*

In some ways, the people of this kingdom are stronger than we are.

Eleanor

Eleanor watched the troops forming into lines. She saw Kavan and his aides making their way to join them.

'Come on, Karel,' she called. 'We're going to join the attack.'

'Why should I? This isn't my battle. I'm a Turing Citizen!'

'There is no Turing City any more. If you're not an Artemisian, then what are you?'

The words struck home more than she had intended. He came to a halt in the middle of the dirty snow, churned up by the feet of so many robots.

'What am I?' he repeated. 'What am I?'

Eleanor took hold of his arm, dragged him onward.

'You're wearing the body of an Artemisian, soldier, so get

marching. If you are still a Turing Citizen, then think on that when you meet Kavan.'

Down they descended into the bowl.

'Look.' Karel pointed. Faint red lines traced their way across the stone landscape. 'The hillside is burning on the far side.'

'Does that matter? Come on!'

She pushed and pulled and cajoled him forward, eager to rejoin the fight. A group of Scouts, limbering up against the wind, saw them coming. They gazed at them as they approached, their blades now half exposed.

'Get this soldier a rifle,' called out Eleanor. 'We're going to join Kavan.'

The Scouts recognized her and moved apart. One of them found a rifle and lazily tossed it to her. She caught it, slapped it into Karel's hands.

'Get behind him,' said Eleanor, right there at his ear as they walked on. 'Then shoot him through the back of the head.'

Kavan

All was ready. Wet snow blew through the mist that rolled around the hillside; it barrelled around the copper sphere atop the skeletal tower. The red cracks of fire in the slope opposite were widening.

Kavan was ready. 'Give the order to advance.'

The call went out. Rifles slapped against metal hands, feet stamped on rock. Silver metal flashed as the Scouts scattered, running forwards and sideways to secure ground. The Storm Troopers stamped their feet as they advanced, rattling stones from the few buildings that were still standing ahead of them. Such was the force of their advance that one or two of the smaller hovels seemed to give up their hold on life, suddenly collapsing in a tumble of stones. Iron feet stamped through the rubble as the stream of metal flowed around the larger buildings.

'Hello, Kavan.'

Eleanor appeared at his shoulder, paintwork scorched and body scratched. As ever. There was another robot with her. An infantry-robot.

'Who is that?' he asked.

'Karel.' She gazed at him intently with her yellow eyes, as if trying to read him, and he wondered what game Eleanor was now playing, right in the middle of an attack. It hardly mattered.

Metal spheres curved through the air, before landing amongst the advancing troops.

'Keep formation,' ordered Kavan. The troops did so. The wire bombs exploded in a blue tangle of wire that quickly contracted, snaring the arms and legs of infantryrobots. Grey soldiers collapsed, some of them emitting electronic squeals of pain. A few of them snapped off useless limbs, attached new ones, and rejoined the march.

'Some of the bombs didn't contract,' observed Wolfgang, staring at one blue tangle of wire that washed across the snow.

The wind whipped the sound of the crackling rifles towards them. Over there, on the left flank, enemy robots were attacking. So thin and fragile, they were reduced to throwing rocks that bounced ineffectually from the Artemisian bodies.

Two Scouts had seen what was happening and they ran towards the enemy, a length of razor wire held taut between them. The wire sliced through the thin bodies of the northern robots, cutting them down.

Now more of the enemy appeared, running headlong towards them. The infantry shot at them, the impact of the bullets flinging their light bodies backwards in the snow. They wore only tin and pig-iron, their metal shattering and shrieking under each blow delivered against them. Still they came running, more and more of them.

Children now, tiny bodies dodging closer and closer. Coming in amongst the troops, they rubbed themselves against the Artemisians, they rubbed their hands over arm joints and knee joints. They clasped heads and embraced necks, they clung tightly onto the infantry, even as they were stabbed and shot, even as the twisted metal of their minds was unwound.

The Artemisians tried to prise those dead children free. But the corpses were unmovable, they clung on, the sand and adhesive that covered their bodies hardened, gluing up the joints of the Artemisians. Kavan watched as soldier after soldier stumbled, fell to his knees, gripped hold of a tiny body and tried to tear it loose, only to find that his hands were stuck to it.

And all the while the network of red fire that covered the hill-side was widening, the glow was spreading.

Even the children, thought Kavan. *Even the children believe.*

'Shoot the sticky ones,' shouted Eleanor, unnecessarily. The troops had realized what was happening. 'Don't let them get close.'

Another wave of resistance was now advancing: thin, pig-iron bodies almost lost in the snow. They carried slingshots, each loaded with a metal sphere. Kavan watched as they swung them around their heads and launched another volley of wire bombs . . .

Olam

Olam had regained the sense of seeing by grey light, but there was nothing to see. He was wrapped up in something, so that all he caught sight of was a glimpse of stone, a glimpse of sky. He guessed he was being carried from the hovel.

He had no gyros, he felt no motion. He could hear, though: hear the whistle of the wind, the stamping of feet, the crack of rifles. And he could hear the voice of the robot that carried him.

'Can you hear me, mind? Can you hear me in there? Wrapped in a sling, all ready for throwing?'

He hated that voice, hated its tinny vibrato, hated its false jollity. Give him his old body and he would have taken such pleasure in taking hold of the robot's puny neck, squeezing the brittle pig iron, feeling it shatter in his hands, feeling the slipperiness of the coil in his hand as he crushed it and crippled his tormentor.

Most of all though, he hated the fear welled up inside the metal of his own mind: the cold, aching fear that made him feel as if his gyros, his non-existent gyros, were lurching and bouncing and breaking loose inside him. He wanted to cry, to run, to curl up, but he could do none of those things.

'Where have you come from? I wonder. What did you see as you marched here to our land? All those memories, there in your wire.'

All those memories. And yet the only memory that played through Olam's mind at that moment was of a detonator being pushed into Parmissa's mind by long steel fingers.

'We're coming to the battle now. There go the stickyrobots. My daughter is one of them. She's only five years old, but she's covered in glue and she goes to fulfil her purpose. I wove her that way. I wove her so that she would not be afraid to die.'

Her daughter? She had sent her own daughter to her death?

'But what about you? What do *you* believe in? Are you frightened of dying? Will you try and keep your mind together, or will you relax and save your friends? Which will it be?'

Olam wanted to live. He thought of Wien and of his family. Where were they now? he wondered. Dead, most likely. He tried to picture them, but he couldn't. He tried to picture Wien, with its towers and its islands. Nothing. All he could see now was his section, Doe Capaldi and his fellow Artemisians. All he could remember was what it was like to march through the streets of Turing City, the feel of the gun in his hands, the feeling of welling joy as he fired, as he saw another robot drop dead before him. Such elation!

'What are you going to be? A bomb, or a dud? What will your final purpose be?'

No! He wasn't ready. He didn't want to die. That wasn't his purpose!

'Here we go. I will whirl you round three times, and then let you go. Are you going to count with me?'

No! Not yet. He wasn't going to die. He deserved to live. He possessed the lifeforce, he knew it. All he had to do was concentrate.

'I can see your troops over there. They look so big, so powerful. All that metal. What a mind I could weave with one of them . . .'

Concentrate. Don't let her distract you!

'One . . . two . . . three . . .'

The words were fainter now, lost in the wind as he spun, and then he had left the sling, he was flying forward. All those stars above. All that expanse of ground below. Soldiers. Artemisian soldiers. Is that what we look like from the air? What about the explosive charge? What would it feel like to die?

He wouldn't die. All he had to do was concentrate. Concentr . . .

Karel

Metal spheres continued to fall amongst the troops, each exploding in a tangle of blue wire that instantly contracted, snaring anything within range, choking it, cutting it, destroying it. Eleanor and Kavan and the rest ignored them, even when they fell at their feet, and Karel attempted to do the same. Still, he couldn't help but duck down when one of the shells sailed over his head. It hit the robot behind in the chest, blue wire swarming over his grey body and tightening. Ripping into the panelling, tightening behind the neck, slipping through the joints and into the coil.

'Wolfgang!' called out Kavan.

Karel was amazed. Kavan seemed genuinely upset about the robot's death. This was not what he had expected. Karel watched as Wolfgang slumped forward, and then tumbled down to the ground.

'Hey,' said Eleanor, standing at his side, 'it's just metal. Just like the rest of us.'

She was taunting Kavan, realized Karel. She was taunting the robot she wanted him to kill. *But why me?* wondered Karel. He gazed at the dying Wolfgang. The blue wire was still tightening, still squeezing. That had been a powerful bomb, he thought. More so than the others.

'Don't taunt me,' said Kavan to Eleanor. 'Wolfgang was a valuable resource.'

Karel looked up. Were the pair of them about to start a fight, here and now? What would he do? Kavan didn't carry a gun, he noticed.

The front of Kavan's shell was covered in condensation. They were all similarly covered, noticed Karel, covered in beads of water that ran in hurried little streams down fingers and arms and legs. The heat from the fires across the far side of the bowl was increasing. Red cracks were spreading wider: they now ran red fingers around the base of the skeletal tower.

'Keep up, Karel,' ordered Eleanor, and he looked up to see that Kavan was now gone ahead, marching on again, following his troops' thrust into the heart of the Northern Kingdom.

Karel hefted the rifle, condensation running down his fingers. The wind was lessening noticeably, being pushed aside by the rising heat. The snow had turned to slushy rain.

There is Kavan, just ahead. Why not raise the rifle and shoot him? I could do it right now. I would be killed straight away, but what does that matter? I've nothing left to live for, so what's stopping me? Is it because I don't want to be a part of Eleanor's game? Or is it something else?

Because I can see it: that we're both so alike, Kavan and me. Does anyone else realize that? All those people who whispered and hinted about how my mind was twisted, asking me what I was thinking: as if anybody could really tell what their mother had woven into their mind. And yet, I can see something of Kavan in myself.

He raised the rifle, sighted along its length, took aim at Kavan's head.

Pull the trigger. Kill him.

A shrieking metal noise rang out. The skeletal tower was sagging, its legs twisting, giving way.

The Artemisian troops sensed victory. They began to stamp their feet as they marched forward.

Slowly, oh so slowly, the great copper sphere at the top of the tower toppled forward.

Kavan

Kavan watched the copper sphere falling; saw the thin, undersized enemy robots running out from its base.

'You've done it,' said Eleanor, marching at his side. 'You've done it again. And now the whole continent is yours.'

'The whole continent belongs to Artemis,' he corrected her.

The copper sphere hit the stony ground and crumpled, split along one side.

'You've defeated the Wizard,' said Eleanor, and there was wonder in her voice. As if she had really believed in the Wizard.

Kavan had halted. He wanted to call Wolfgang, but Wolfgang was now dead.

'Look at the sphere,' he said to Eleanor. 'Look at it! What do you see inside?'

The sphere was collapsing, like a bubble of glass blown too large. It was splitting into two pieces under its own weight.

Eleanor gazed through the gathering mist.

'It's empty,' she said. 'Hollow. There's nothing inside.'

Kavan was becoming quite animated. 'And look at the fire on the hillside: charcoal, coal, all burning. They're leaving it all to burn.' He looked around. 'They lit the fires when we first attacked. The petrol in the trenches, the trees burning, they ignited their whole kingdom. They are destroying their own kingdom!'

Kavan felt something fierce burning within himself. A fierce joy, a glowing respect.

'Of all the peoples on Shull, only these people truly *believe*,' he said. 'They would rather destroy their kingdom than have it fall to us!'

'But why?' asked Eleanor.

'I don't know! Perhaps because they really do believe in the Book of Robots.'

'But look at this place! If the book does exist, it will burn with the rest of them! It will be melted to slag!'

'I know, I know . . .' Kavan gazed around the bowl again. Something wasn't right, and he knew it. 'Where are the slave robots?' he asked suddenly. 'Where have they gone? Why aren't they defending this place any more? They were here when we first attacked . . .'

The mist billowed around them, threatening to smother them in a pink world of muffled calm. The metal of their shells was growing warmer, and the night was lit by red fire. He scanned the scene, looking through the gaps in the fog for any of the slave robots, searching for robots wearing mining bodies. He saw none.

'We've been tricked!' he announced. 'Fetch the Scouts!' he commanded. 'Get them to fan out into the surrounding countryside. Find the slave robots!'

'What about the infantry?'

'Tell them to keep marching on. We will recover the metal of their bodies from the slag that will eventually run to the centre of this bowl.'

The order went out.

Kavan turned and ran back up the train tracks, heading out of the bowl.

Spoole

The wind blew cold over Artemis City. The snowflakes danced in the light of the fires of the forges; they danced around the smoke that belched from the chimneys.

Spoole stood alone on the roof of the Basilica, gazing to the north.

Even through the howl of the wind, he heard the sound of footsteps behind him. A Scout, judging by the light tread.

He wondered if this was the time. Was this when his reign as leader would end? Down below, in the Basilica, were they already making ready to welcome back Kavan? He was being paranoid, he told himself. General Sandale and the rest still congratulated him on Artemis's advance. They recognized Spoole as a brilliant tactician, using his troops to their best advantage. Or was that just what they wanted him to believe?

'Excuse me, Spoole.'

He turned, and a Scout waited there.

'This message just came through on the radio,' she said. Her blades were withdrawn, she held out a piece of foil in her hands.

'Thank you,' said Spoole, taking it.

He read the words imprinted there.

The Northern Kingdom had fallen.

The wind blew, and still he gazed at the words.

The Northern Kingdom had fallen.

What now? he wondered.

Kavan

The three Scouts had spotted the slave robot making his way along a river, iron shoulders leaving a wake in the dark water. The Scouts had crippled him, cutting electromuscle in his arms and legs, then they had dragged him clear of the water onto the snow-covered bank. The slave had accepted his treatment without complaint.

The Scouts had been ordered to bring back the whole body, not just the mind, and so they had slowly carried it back northwards, towards the red glow that could be seen for miles around in those bare northern lands.

Word had been sent to Kavan, and he strode through the night to meet them, accompanied by Eleanor and Karel.

He made the Scouts prop the body of the slave up against a low rise and then sent them out into the night to keep guard, silver blades flashing as they cut at snowflakes.

Kavan gazed down at the slave robot. It looked back up at him without emotion.

'What's your name, robot?' asked Kavan.

'Banjo Macrodocious.'

Kavan looked at Karel. 'Well?' he asked. 'Eleanor says you used to deal with robots like this. Do you know him?'

'That was the name of the robot I met back in Turing City,' said Karel. He looked down at the crippled slave. 'But that wasn't you. I'm sure of it.'

'We are all called Banjo Macrodocious,' said the slave. 'Our minds are all twisted in the same manner; therefore we are all the same. Why name us differently?'

Kavan wasn't interested. 'What happened to the Wizard?' he asked. 'He never existed, did he? Just another rumour. Another story to frighten people with.'

'There was a wizard a long time ago. But she was a woman. She welcomed slave robots into her tiny kingdom and used us wisely. Her kingdom prospered, and the Book of Robots was kept safe.'

'The Book of Robots? Is it real?'

'Yes.'

Kavan paused, thinking. He had noticed the expression on Eleanor's face at the slave's words.

'Then where is it?' he demanded. 'You don't carry it, I see.'

'All slave robots carry it, at least in part.' replied Banjo Macrodocious. 'It is woven into our minds.'

'What does the book say?' asked Eleanor, thrilled.

'It doesn't say anything,' said Banjo Macrodocious. 'The Book of Robots carries the plan for the way a mind should be twisted. It contains the philosophy of a mind: the purpose. My own mind is an imperfect representation of that plan. Other minds carry other parts of that plan.'

'But you're a slave,' interrupted Karel, outraged. 'You don't mean that the Book of Robots intends us all to be slaves?'

Banjo Macrodocious focused on him. 'You are from Turing City,' it said. 'You find that disturbing. Your colleagues do not.'

'Nyro's philosophy,' commented Kavan, with some satisfaction.

'I did not say that,' said Banjo Macrodocious.

'NO!' shouted Karel at the same time. 'I don't believe it! You said it yourself, Banjo Macrodocious, that your mind is an imperfect representation of what is written in the book! Nyro *cannot* be right! A mind is more than just twisted metal!'

Kavan and Banjo gazed at Karel, waiting for him to finish. Eleanor had turned her back on them, she gazed out at the night.

'Not all minds that carry their part of the Book are slave robot minds,' said Banjo Macrodocious. 'Besides which, I cannot comment on what a mind is. You would need to speak to those at the top of the world.'

Eleanor turned around at that. 'The robots at the top of the world?' she said. 'You've met them?'

'No,' said Banjo Macrodocious. 'But I've visited their places.'

'What places?' she asked, eagerly.

'There are many places built by the robots at the top of the world. We are not far here from the Northern Road. It joins to the road that runs along the seabed from the top of the world to Shull. They say there are many roads across the seabed and that the whales follow them. They say that there is a glass building that stands somewhere below the surface, so deep that the light of the sun cannot reach it, or illuminate the glass statues of the strange robots that stand within . . .'

'Never mind what they say. What places have you visited?' demanded Eleanor.

'The road from the top of the world emerges on the northern coast of Shull. There are buildings there, erected by those who came down that road.'

'What's inside the buildings?'

'I don't know. I was not ordered to enter.'

'But weren't you interested?' shouted Karel in frustration. 'Didn't you care? Didn't you want to know?'

Banjo Macrodocious turned his head to face him. 'I wasn't ordered to be interested,' he replied.

'Enough of this,' commanded Kavan. 'We are at the end of a battle. What happens now to the Northern Kingdom?'

'It will fall,' said Banjo Macrodocious. 'We will then walk across the land and we will find a place where we can prosper once more. The Book of Robots will be preserved.'

Kavan was silent.

'There will be a place for you within Artemis,' said Eleanor.

'That's not your decision to make, Eleanor,' said Kavan.

And now Eleanor turned to him, wearing that familiar expression of contempt.

'You've conquered Shull,' she said. 'What's Spoole going to do about you now? Are you going to let him send you on across the whole of Penrose? Or are you finally going to march on Artemis City?'

'With what troops?' asked Kavan. He turned to Karel. 'Turing City is no more. What would *you* have me do now?' He jerked a finger at Banjo Macrodocious. 'You heard what he said; do you still think that Artemis is wrong?'

'Yes! A mind is more than just twisted metal!'

'But why do you think that? Only because that is what your mother wove you to believe. When Nyro's philosophy is woven into every mind on this planet, then what difference will *your* feelings make?'

Karel tried to frame an answer. Kavan turned to Eleanor.

'You ask which way do we march next, Eleanor? I don't know. But I think that decision cannot be made yet. Because I have crossed the extent of Shull, from the south to the north, and it is only here that I have met robots that truly believed in anything other than just themselves.'

The wind was dropping. The sky was clearing, just a little. A few stars shone above, glimmering amongst the falling snowflakes.

'We will visit the buildings to the north of here. Just the three of us – you, me and Karel. We will see what we find there. And then we shall decide where we are to march next. North, or south.'

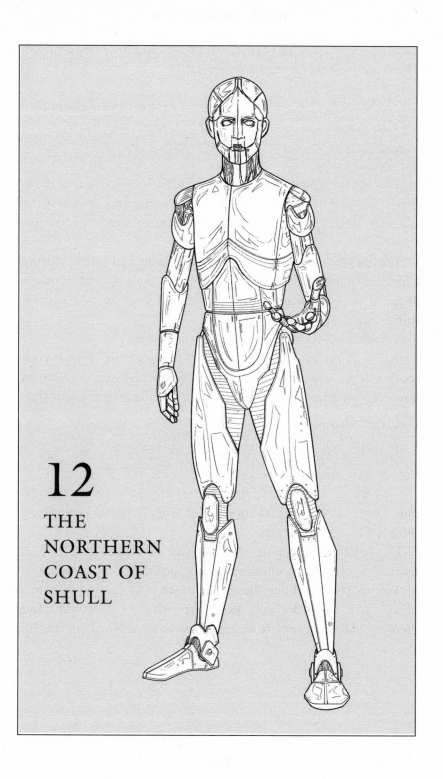

12

THE
NORTHERN
COAST OF
SHULL

Maoco O

Maoco O emerged from a pile of gangue into what had been Turing City, his reflexes immediately dropping him to the ground for cover.

Everything had gone now. There was nothing left but rock and sky.

He knew the scenario, he had been trained in Artemisian tactics for reclaiming a city.

The buildings that housed the foundries that used to line this road would have been taken apart brick by brick; their metal frames unbolted and fed into the forges to be melted down and formed into ingots for transportation. The huge acid tanks would have been drained, their contents sprayed on the very dust to make salts out of the scraps of metal that had fallen there, and then the tanks themselves broken apart to make even more ingots, then loaded onto trucks that ran on temporary railway lines laid into this area solely for the purpose of deconstruction. Maoco O could see the faint imprint of the sleepers in the windblown dust that covered the stony ground.

He felt as if his gyros weren't spinning properly. Everything looked so wrong. Even the sun seemed too big, a wobbly yellowy-red presence, shimmering in a rusty sky; it gave the land a patina of death, of dissolution into crumbling rust.

He tried to make sense of this new landscape. *There* was the rocky outcrop on which the fort had stood, so *that* must be the slope leading down to where the galleries had once been.

And over there was the railway station. The station itself was gone, but the railway lines remained. In fact, there were more now than ever: so many lines, they flooded into the valley bottom before spreading out like a river delta. Those lines had penetrated deep into Turing City and had leached all of its metal away, leaving only stone behind. Maoco O could see that even those same railway lines were now being dismantled, loaded up into the trucks that trundled away northwards, taking all that precious remaining metal to Artemis City.

He heard a sudden noise nearby, just around the other side of the pile of gangue from which he himself had emerged. Cautiously, he edged his way around the heap of dirty white stone. The noise came again, the clink-clank of stone slipping down upon itself.

He dodged in and out of the bays and coves of the immense pile of gangue, working his way around to the north till his new ears gradually became aware of another sound. The sound of industry: of diesel engines roaring, of heavy machinery moving, the rumble and roar of rock being dug.

And then he rounded another corner, and the noise was forgotten.

A round, crab-like machine, not much bigger than his head, was squatting at the base of the gangue pile and feeding fragments of rock into its jaws, grinding it all down. Powdered stone spilt from its crude mouth, covering the ground and staining the metal shell of the machine itself. Such an ugly machine, it was roughly constructed of iron, the top of its shell an uneven mix of leftover metals. This was a cheaply made construct.

They were reclaiming even the gangue itself, Maoco O realized. Turing City had been so rich it had left the mined-out slag lying in piles around the city, but Artemis wasted nothing. Maoco O suddenly felt a terrible admiration for their efficiency. He watched the crab machine as it moved forward slightly, selecting a choice piece of rock with its claws to feed into its mouth. There would be some metal there, enough for it to process and add to its own body. It would be a long and tedious job. The machine could process gangue all its life and would still only find a few ounces of metal. And then a terrible suspicion took hold of him, and he crossed to the crab, examined its body, flipped open the top, and looked in horror at what lay inside.

The blue twisted wire of a brain: a Turing Citizen.

He heard scuttling behind him. Another two crabs rounded the corner.

'Hey, what are you doing?'

The infantryrobot was standing on the gangue hill above him, its rifle at its side.

'Just looking for my section,' said Maoco O, easily. He flipped the top of the crab back in place and straightened up. The infantryrobot lifted its rifle to aim directly at Maoco O's head.

'What section? What are you talking about?' He raised his voice. 'Hey, Camber, there's something over here . . .'

The infantryrobot slipped his way down the pile. He leaped forward, landing in front of Maoco O, his gun still covering him.

'You're a Turing Citizen, aren't you?' he said. 'Where have you been hiding all this time?'

Maoco O heard more footsteps crunching on the mined stone. That must be Camber, coming to the aid of his colleague. He had to move quickly.

'I'm sorry, sir,' he said, moving towards the infantry robot. 'I'm new here and I was just wondering . . .'

'Stay back,' snapped the infantryrobot.

'Goscin!' The second infanftryrobot came into view. In the merest fraction of a second it took Goscin to glance at his friend, Maoco O leaped forward. This new body was too slow, too weak, but the training, the reflexes were still there. He gripped the enemy's rifle, twisted it free of the other robot's hands, rolled forward, stood and turned and fired at Goscin's head.

Nothing happened.

The safety catch was on, he realized. He flicked it off just as Camber fired, the bullet tearing through his left shoulder, piercing the electromuscle there. Goscin was already charging at him so he turned and shot at him one-handed. His body was badly tuned, he fired too low, the bullet passing through Goscin's throat. The other robot fell however: Maoco O's bullet had clipped its coil, disabled its legs, crippling it. Maoco O kicked down at Goscin's neck, and broke the connection there with his foot.

Another rifle shot, a second bullet hit him, again in the left shoulder. Camber was clearly panicking, either that or his rifle sights were not set correctly. Calmly, one-handed, Maoco O took aim at him and fired.

The bullet caught him dead centre in the skull. Blue wire exploded.

There were more shouts, more footsteps. Maoco O needed cover urgently.

But first he dropped the rifle, looked down at the gangue crab, bent over and flipped open the top. Carefully, with one hand, he eased the mind out of the machine. Fix his arm now, and he could come back for more.

Then Maoco O ran.

Susan

Susan knelt, twisting wire at the feet of another infantryrobot, her mind lost in the contemplation of Nyro's pattern.

'He's alive,' said the man, his blue-green wire spilling into her hands.

'Who's alive?' asked Susan.

'Karel,' said the robot. The man made the sign, small circle, large circle. 'One of my brothers saw him in Northern Shull. He was walking with Kavan and another robot.'

Susan looked down at the concrete floor, at the metal scraps curling amongst the dust. Karel? She tried to remember the light of his eyes, the shape of the body he had been wearing. It all seemed so far away now.

'Aren't you pleased?'

'Oh yes,' said Susan, hands busy twisting. She glanced around the room. There was no Scout on duty tonight: there hardly ever was, any more. Even so – 'I've learned not to draw attention to myself.'

There was a sense of purpose filling the making room that had gradually grown with time. It sang in the metal walls. The other women who knelt on the concrete floor felt it, too. No longer Turing Citizens, they were now Artemisians. They twisted metal quickly and efficiently, all according to Nyro's plan. The work was hypnotic and seductive, it drew you in with the feeling that you were becoming part of something much bigger than yourself, part of a mighty machine that spread out across an entire continent. Susan held wire in her hands, and she felt as if she was connected to all the metal of Artemis. Some days lately she had to fight to remember who she was, and what had been taken from her. But now it seemed the outside world had come to remind her.

'Who are you?' she asked.

'Banjo Macrodocious.'

'No, you're not. I met him already. You're not the same robot. I can tell by this wire.'

'We are all called Banjo Macrodocious.'

'Why do I keep getting these messages?'

The robot made the sign of the two circles.

'I know that already,' said Susan, 'but it's not an answer. Do you know what? I've been thinking, all this time kneeling here on my own. Thinking about what has happened to me. My child was killed by an Artemisian, but he was only acting that way because his mother twisted his mind to act like an Artemisian. And his mother only did that because her mind was twisted that way, too. And I only had a child because I married Karel, and I only did that because my mother twisted my mind so that I would. And we all act the way we do because our parents made our minds that way, and they only act that way because their parents did the same to them . . .'

She paused in her twisting for a moment, gazed up at the robot. Some of the others in the room were now looking in her direction. All of a sudden, she didn't care.

'Do you know what? I don't really care about the Book of Robots. I don't care if there is a right way for robots to be. All that has happened to us has happened, and even if we wove the perfect robot tomorrow, it wouldn't change who I am and what has happened in my life.'

She raised her voice. 'You know what I think? I think that we shouldn't be wasting our time thinking about regaining perfection in the future. Instead, we should be thinking about how to make the best of what we are right now.'

The other women stared at her. So did the men at whose feet they knelt.

'Hey,' Susan said to them. 'Get back to work.'

Slowly, much to Susan's surprise, they all did so.

Banjo Macrodocious leaned forward. 'Do you know, Susan, that there are many who would agree with you. Some people say that the Book of Robots is written all around us at the moment, in the twisted metal of the million robot minds that inhabit this planet.'

Susan resumed weaving too.

'Well, I like that interpretation better,' she said.

She was a quarter of the way into the pattern now, two and a half thousand twists gone, nearly eight thousand left.

'And some people,' continued Banjo Macrodocious, 'say that the first robots were rather crude, and over the years they have improved themselves, and that we have yet to see the perfect robot.'

'That may be,' replied Susan equably.

'Karel may find the answer,' said Banjo Macrodocious. 'He travels north – north to where the answers lie.'

'Do you think I will ever see him again?' asked Susan, gripped by a sudden longing. It hurt, because it cut so deep. All the walls that she had built up within herself, the layers of insulation she had placed over her emotions, were suddenly sliced cleanly through, and the silver edge of her feelings shone through.

'I don't know,' said Banjo Macrodocious.

Already Susan was sealing herself off again, soldering over the breaks. She was kneeling on a concrete floor in a metal room again, deep underground in the heart of Artemis City. There was nothing else now but Artemis.

'I don't suppose I will,' she said. 'Turing City has gone. It will not rise again.'

Maoco O

'What's your name?' asked Maoco O.

The newly built robot moved its arms experimentally, then looked down to see that it had no legs as yet. Maoco O had left it to build its own; things would be more efficient that way.

The robot looked up at him, green eyes shining. 'I'm Gabriel,' it said. 'Thank you for rescuing me.'

'Don't worry. You'll have the chance to repay me. We're going to build more bodies, and we're going to rescue more minds.'

Gabriel hadn't fully registered the words; he was still lost in the horror of his recent experience. 'It was awful on the gangue,' he said. 'Those crab bodies . . . they had no senses, only the feel for metal.' He was beginning to babble. 'There was nothing but emptiness, the crushing of rock. A lifetime trapped there . . .'

'Not any more,' said Maoco O. 'You're free now.'

Gabriel couldn't let go of the memories. 'My wife, my children. They pushed us all into those crab bodies . . .'

'I told you, we shall rescue them all. Step by step.'

Gabriel waved his arms around, seemingly without control.

'To see, to hear, to move . . . You wouldn't believe the feeling . . .'

'I know,' said Maoco O. 'I know. Just take your time, Gabriel.'

This was going to be harder than he had expected, but Maoco O could do it. He knew it. First his own body, then Gabriel's, then the others. He had a collection of minds already, laid out on shelves next door.

Some of them were crippled, having had their coils crushed. The robots in those minds were irretrievably separated from the world. Doomed to thirty or forty years in silence and darkness, and then death as the lifeforce leaked away.

But some of the minds he had collected were whole. There was enough metal left outside for bodies to be built for them. There were even City Guard minds among them. Maoco O would patiently show them how to build their own bodies, how to reconnect with the world once more.

There were even places to hide while they rebuilt themselves. Turing City wasn't quite dead. Not yet.

'What's your name?' asked Gabriel.

'My name? Maoco O.'

'A City Guard! What happened to your body?'

Maoco thought of his former body. So fast, so powerful. When Turing City had seemed strong, it had seemed so important. Now that the city had proven to be as brittle as poorly cast iron . . .

'My body? This is my body, Gabriel. It changes from day to day. Now, come on, let's get those legs built. And then I will teach you how to fight.'

Spoole

Artemis City was growing. Metal girders seemed to spring from the ground, climbing up towards the moons, a few remaining snowflakes blowing through their skeleton frames. Metal plate crept across the ground. Metal hammers rang, and black smoke billowed from chimneys. Molten metal spilled red and golden from blast furnaces, splashing out into blackened moulds.

Spoole stood at the top of the city and looked out at a landscape turning to metal.

'He's coming, Spoole,' said Gearheart. 'Your son is coming home. How does that make you feel?'

'My son?' said Spoole.

'Oh, Spoole, we both know who Kavan is. Don't you feel proud? That your wire is strong? Does that satisfy your virility? Does it make you feel like a man? Or don't you like it, the fact that you are no longer the greatest?'

'Be quiet, Gearheart.'

Gearheart slammed down her spoon-shaped arm. Her battered, misshapen body was so ugly now. Spoole noted the lightest speckling of rust beading on her chest panelling, and he felt disgusted.

'Don't tell me to be quiet,' snapped Gearheart. 'You call your-self an Artemisian? Look at you skulking here in this Basilica while better robots than you are off changing the world. All that metal flowing into this state, and what are you building? More troops? More weapons? More railway lines? No! You are expanding Artemis City to your greater glory. Spoole, you have forgotten Nyro.'

Spoole looked down at Gearheart, her battered shell lying on the floor nearby. She couldn't see the view from up here, but she didn't care. She didn't seem to care about much at all, any more.

'Forgotten Nyro?' said Spoole. 'You know, maybe I have. Or maybe not. Maybe Nyro's philosophy wasn't woven into my mind as strongly as into others'. Remember, I was made to lead. I wonder if we leaders can ever consider ourselves truly expendable? I think we will always see ourselves as different to the metal around us.'

'Kavan doesn't think so,' said Gearheart. 'And he has con-quered all of Shull. He's a better Artemisian than you, Spoole.'

'Maybe he is,' said Spoole.

He looked out again over the expanding city. Cold metal in the pale sun.

'Does it really matter, Gearheart?' he asked. 'Someone takes some metal. She twists it, and it thinks for forty or so years, and then it dies. Look at this city. Some of the metal that makes up these buildings would once have been minds, would once have *thought*. It may do again sometime in the future. Minds live and die, and all the while metal twists its way across the surface of Pen-rose, in the form of cities and railway lines and body plating. Once the metal is extracted from its ore, it will dance its way across this planet for all time. Sometimes it will think, and sometimes it will not. But all the while it will just be metal.'

As he spoke he knelt down by his consort's body. There was rust here at her neck too, he noticed. Red speckles of it. The Gear-heart of old would never have allowed herself to have sunk to these depths. And yet she was the same Gearheart, the same metal in every respect, save for those few tiny cuts that the Scout had made.

'What is the matter with you. Spoole? What are you doing?' Gearheart sounded worried.

Spoole was crying, he was shocked to discover, a faint electric whine emerging from his voicebox. But that was silly. There was nothing here but metal. Why should one piece of twisted metal feel anything for another piece?

He had an awl in his hand. All it would take would be a quick jab to the soft metal of the skull. He had done it so many times before, back when he was younger. On the battlefields of Zernike and Stark and Bethe.

'Are you going to kill me?' asked Gearheart, wonderingly. And then her voice hardened. 'Do it, Spoole. It's what Nyro would have done.'

Nothing but metal, thought Spoole. And some day his lifeforce would give out too. The pair of them would be melted down and perhaps the metal of their minds would flow together. Gearheart was right: it was what Nyro would have done. But was Nyro right?

'Gearheart?' he said.

There was no reply.

Spoole looked down at the blue wire that trailed from his awl, down his hand, over his arm.

'Gearheart,' he said, one last time.

He allowed the empty metal shell to tumble to the ground. He looked up at the city growing around him.

Spoole stood alone. Just as had been woven into his mind, a leader stood alone: a leader did not worry about procreation. This way Artemis was strong.

In the meantime, metal was raised on the land, metal would march and metal would die.

He looked down again at the empty metal body at his feet. Once it had contained a mind called Gearheart, now all there was was twisted metal.

Once there had been so many minds, and some day all there would be would be metal. Did it really matter in the end? Did it matter whether it was he or Kavan who led Artemis?

He heard the Scout entering the room behind him. He turned.

'Yes, Leanne?'

'Spoole, I have news of Kavan. He has left what remains of the army and has travelled north alone.'

'What? Why?'

The Scout was deliberately not looking at the broken body of Gearheart.

'No reason was given.'

What is Kavan doing? wondered Spoole. *To leave his troops at this moment. What is he planning now?*

Metal flowed across the world, he reflected. Kavan and Spoole, did it matter who led Artemis? Yes, he decided. Yes it did.

So Kavan had left his troops? More fool him, since his strength had lain in his ability to command. Who would he command now?

'Leanne,' he said. 'I think it is time that we took a look at the new extent of our Empire. I think it is time that we met with Kavan. Notify General Sandale that we shall be travelling north. Make ready a train and two thousand troops.'

'Yes, Spoole.'

And when I meet Kavan, it will be from a position of strength. And I will ask him, who will be the leader of Artemis now, Kavan?

It was morning, and yet Zuse, the night moon, still hung in the sky, late in setting this day.

Spoole looked up towards it, and the moon looked back down on a world of flowing metal.

Kavan

The wind was dying: occasionally it mustered the strength to drive furrows through the wet snow, to send a white spray of flakes tumbling down into the sea that sucked at the dark rocks below; but for the most part it just cooled the metal of his shell, blew patterns of salt crystals across the paint.

The sky was grey with low clouds, the sea iron-grey as it stretched to the northern horizon, and Kavan felt as if he was at the end of the world.

Eleanor and Karel stood beside him, gazing out over the water-slicked rock shelf that slid into the sea.

'Why are you here, Kavan?' asked Eleanor. 'Would Nyro have come here looking for answers?'

Kavan didn't reply. Eleanor was teasing him, he knew. She was goading him as she always did. Shull wasn't conquered. They may have pushed troops to the four corners of the continent, but that didn't mean that they truly possessed the lands they had occupied. That didn't mean that Nyro's philosophy yet operated in the minds of all the robots of Shull.

'I think we need to be a little to the east,' said Kavan. He turned and began to walk down the rocky slope, following the path of the land as it twisted around the hungry sea.

He saw it almost immediately. The land there ran down a slope to a shingle beach, and then back up again to a rocky island, almost cut off from the mainland by the waters that noisily sifted through the shingle.

A stone building stood at the summit of the island, red stains of long-rusted iron running down its sides.

'What is it?' asked Karel softly, the first time the robot had spoken that day.

Kavan didn't know. The white stone of the building was like nothing he had seen before: more lustrous than marble, it almost seemed to glow in the grey morning light.

They walked down to the shingle beach. Opposite them, a worn set of steps, cut directly from the rock, rose out of the shingle and made their way up to the building.

'The path must have been covered by the beach,' observed Eleanor. 'Just how old is that building, do you think?'

They climbed the path, and Kavan noticed how the orange-and-white stains of lichen covered its surface. The shells of the organic life forms that inhabited this land were stuffed into every crack, lining the walls below the tideline in obscene profusion.

The three robots drew abreast as they approached the structure, metal feet rattling on stone. It was such an odd shape, its walls rounded, not straight like that of normal robot construction. They curved up and over to form the roof, giving the building an organic shape. There were strange symbols carved in a line around it, just higher than a robot could reach. Kavan stared up at them, trying to make sense of them.

'They look so familiar,' said Eleanor, but Kavan didn't think so. They just looked like a tangled mess to him.

They walked around the building, searching for an entrance. They found it on the far side, facing the north. A metal door, three symbols above it, engraved in the stone of the building. These symbols were larger than the others. Kavan stared at them for some time, trying to understand them. He couldn't hold them in his mind.

'What are they?' he heard Karel wonder out loud.

Eleanor laughed. 'You mean you don't know?' she said, disbelievingly. 'You really don't know?'

'No,' said Kavan. 'I have never seen them before. Have you?'

'No, I've never seen them before either, but I know what they are.'

'How could you?' demanded Karel.

'Any woman would know,' said Eleanor. 'That one is the pattern that you twist to make a girl, and this is the pattern you twist to make a boy.'

Kavan gazed at the patterns.

'What about the one in the middle?' he asked.

'I don't know. That one doesn't make sense. A mind twisted that way wouldn't think properly. It would have no sense of itself.' She looked thoughtful. 'The other carvings, the ones around the side of the building, they all make sense now. Or rather they don't. They are all minds, after a fashion, but they wouldn't work.'

They gazed at the symbols for a while longer, to the sound of the waves crashing below.

Eleanor had lost interest. 'What sort of metal is this?' she asked, touching the door. Kavan placed his hand on it. He could feel a little iron there, a little gold, a little tungsten. But there was something additional in the alloy, something that he had never felt before.

'I don't know,' he confessed, looking at Karel, the Turing City robot who had grown up surrounded by a richness of metal.

'You. Come and feel this. Do you recognize it?'

The other robot touched the door.

'It feels like . . .' he said. 'No, I don't know. But it's like something I half remember . . .'

The waves crashed around the island. A shaft of watery sunlight fell down upon them. The wind had turned east; it curdled the clouds, breaking them up.

Kavan pushed at the door with all of his strength. It didn't move.

'It feels different here,' said Karel.

Kavan waved his own hand over where the other had indicated, near the door jamb. He felt iron underneath.

'Could be the latch?' he wondered aloud. He concentrated hard, sent his lifeforce down into the metal of his hand, felt at the iron there, felt it click into place.

'Got it,' he said. He pushed at the door, and it swung open easily.

'I'll go first,' he said. 'Eleanor, you keep watch out here.'

'I want to go in.'

'Later.'

'What about the symbols? Can you be sure you will understand what you see?'

'Later,' repeated Kavan.

There was a crowd of people standing in the depths of the building, frozen in a dim half-light that filtered down from the roof to part-fill the single room. Kavan closed the door and turned up his eyes, waited for them to adjust.

The roof was sea-green and translucent: a thick old plastic faded by the elements. Not the original roof, reckoned Kavan, but something added much later by . . . who? It now looked so worn and weathered. A muted light filtered through it, illuminating the crowd that waited in patient silence below.

So many robots, arranged in rows, all facing the door, sightless eyes gazing into eternity. All of them dead, the lifeforce long drained from their minds, the current long gone from their electromuscle.

Slowly, carefully, Kavan moved up to the nearest, his own eyes adjusting to the gloom.

The robot body that stood immediately before him was old. It wore iron panelling, red rust bubbling up among the faded remnants of what little paint had not flaked away from its body. It was a little shorter than Kavan, the curve of the arms and the legs not as graceful as his own. Everything about the body was a little straighter, a little squarer, a little less elegant.

He moved past this robot to the next one in the line. It looked older still. Shorter again, the panelling that covered its body was punctured by holes where the rust had eaten it away.

Kavan continued down the line. What was the purpose of this display? Had someone come to this land and collected specimens of local life to be exhibited here? Had the robots at the top of the world come to Shull, explored the land, made this exhibit, and then left? Why?

Down the line, past the robots, walking backwards through time. The bodies on display became smaller and more primitive the further he went. Realization dawned: This was a depiction of evolution on Shull laid out before him.

He moved even further back along the line, pleased by his deduction. Now the robots looked less like robots and more like animals. He passed four-legged crabs in thick iron shells. Something a little like a six-legged spider. Now the bodies had no legs: he saw a fish and something like a tiny whale, its metal body snub and rounded. And then there was nothing but the shells of organic life. He came to the end of the line and looked back along the exhibit.

Now he understood what he was looking at.

This building was testament, proof and warning all in one. There was no Book of Robots, there never had been. There was nothing but the evolution of robots.

But Kavan understood this: that if he wanted to rule the world, then the Book of Robots would be a useful tool. Particularly if he had a say in what went in the book. Just look at how the North Kingdom robots had fought, all because they had believed . . .

So who had erected this display, and why? So close to the northern coast of Shull . . .

He looked up to the faded green plastic of the roof. It was old, of course, but plastic did not last that long. That roof had been constructed in the last hundred years or so. The building would be older than that. Much older . . .

He looked closer at the walls further up by the roof. He saw slots there, spaces for beams and supports to be plugged in. This building wasn't originally a museum, he decided. Had the robot display come later?

He turned around, scanning the walls for more clues, and then he noticed the patterns carved into the wall, opposite the door by which he had entered. They had been there all along, but he had been too taken by the display of robots to notice it. Now he moved back to take in the huge diagram that filled one whole interior wall of the building.

He gazed at up it, trying to make sense of what he saw. Circles, lines, dots, all in a half swirl, engraved into the smooth metal. For a moment, he considered going outside and summoning Eleanor for help, wondered if she might understand, just as she had with the patterns engraved on the building's exterior, but then, just like that, it all made sense. The pattern revealed itself.

It was an astronomical map. Here, at the side, was the Sun, then the first planet, Siecle, and then Penrose with its two moons, Zuse and Néel. And further out, Bohm with its single ring. All drawn to a larger scale, their position in the galactic map clearly marked. And over here, almost at the centre of the map, another system was marked. This system sat at the centre of a large circle. The Penrose system lay on the circumference of that circle.

Other systems were also marked. Some well within the circle, some beyond. Kavan gazed at them, not recognizing any of them.

Maybe he would return here later with an astronomer.

An astronomer? He gazed back up at the slots incorporated in the facing walls of the building. Now he knew what this building had been originally: an observatory. Those slots had held the mechanism that supported the telescope.

So, the robots at the top of the world had come here to Shull to look at the stars. And this is what they had seen, engraved on one wall of the building. What then? Had they taken down their telescope and installed this exhibit instead? Why? What could they have seen in the stars that would have caused them to do that?

Kavan looked at that plastic roof again. The exhibit had come much later, he was sure of that. This building reminded him of a battleground. A battle between two competing philosophies. Perhaps the robots at the top of the world had built it to perpetuate the myth of the Book of Robots. Perhaps other robots had built it to destroy that myth.

Kavan thought about Eleanor again. He should summon her to the building. Maybe she would spot something that he had missed? But he was unwilling to do so. Eleanor was already too unpredictable. What if she were to see something important and not tell him? Then he noticed something else written on the map wall. Something not so carefully engraved as the galactic map, but something written in a different style, carelessly scratched into the wall at robot height.

The Story of Nicolas the Coward, he read. And then:
The Story of the Four Blind Horses.
The Story of Eric and the Mountain.
And then, finally, in much larger letters.
Zuse! The Night Moon! The robots at the top of the world said it was the proof! Treason! But perhaps the Book exists, after all!

He gazed at the words. He had heard the first story, of course. Everyone had. The second sounded vaguely familiar, too. But the third one, *Eric and the Mountain*. He was sure that he had never heard of that before.

And as for the last words. The night moon? The robots at the top of the world had come here and had looked at the stars, and had found that Zuse was the proof.

Proof of what? Kavan had looked at the night moon nearly

every night of his life. It was just a moon, a perfectly normal part of his existence. What could the robots at the top of the world have seen in the stars that led them to believe that their moon was proof of anything?

Slowly, Kavan looked around the room, taking in the map, the display of the bodies, trying to understand what he was looking at.

For the first time in a life built on certainty, he wondered if there were other answers written before him, answers that he had walked past without noticing their presence.

Eleanor

'What do you think is over there?' Eleanor asked Karel, gesturing to the northernmost part of the island. 'Shall we go and have a look?'

'What about Kavan?' asked Karel.

Eleanor laughed. 'Kavan has led an army that has conquered an entire continent. I'm sure he'll be okay on his own in some old building for a few minutes.'

She began to walk down the northern slope of the island towards the sea. Pale yellow sun broke through the clouds and bathed her in its light.

She could hear the tread of metal on rock as Karel followed her.

'I thought as much,' said Eleanor. 'Look at that, the way the rock slopes into the sea. Banjo Macrodocious was right. There *is* a road from here to the north, or there was once, anyway. You can see its pattern under the shingle and the shells. It's been cracked and washed away, but there it goes, heading to the top of the world.'

Karel gazed at it. 'Do you think we are standing at the beginning or the end?' he asked.

'I was wondering exactly the same thing . . .' she said, and she turned to face him. '. . . Brother.'

He gazed back at her, taking in what she had just said.

'You didn't really think it was Kavan, did you?' she said.

'What are you talking about? I don't have a sister!'

She looked closer at him, gazed into his yellow eyes. 'I had wondered. You didn't even notice that we have the same colour eyes?'

He looked back at her. He knew she was speaking the truth, she realized. Eleanor almost laughed. She knew *exactly* what he was thinking. Of course she did. They both were the same person. Liza had woven them both to be the same, save for that one small variation in the weave . . .

'I never thought that I was like Kavan,' said Karel defensively.

'Yes, you did,' said Eleanor. 'You thought that he was your dark side revealed. You thought that you could do all that he has done. You can't lie to me. I *am* you. Look at me, look at how far I've risen within Artemis. All because of the way that our mother wove us. All because some soldier with a gun wanted to know what she really believed. You know what the joke was, though, don't you? Neither Artemis nor Turing City were what they claimed to be; when it comes to the crunch, hardly any one really believes what they think they believe.'

Karel said nothing.

'But you and I are different, aren't we, Brother? Because when that soldier held that gun to Liza's head he made her do something that neither of them expected . . . You don't want to believe me, do you? You even hate me a little for what I'm saying. I know why, because I feel it a little myself. Better to be Kavan than to be me. Better the leader than the second-in-command. You're reduced a little by seeing what you could have become, had you thrown in your lot with Artemis. You'd like to believe you could have gone all the way.'

'Artemisians are killers. I'd never have supported them.'

'Yes you would. Look at me: I'm the proof that you would. Come on, Karel, there's no shame in being second-best. Aren't you proud of me? Second-in-command isn't bad. And it helps you to realize just what a genius Kavan is. *We* couldn't have done what he did. Look at us – we couldn't even bring ourselves to kill him.'

Karel was whining softly. Eleanor could hear the faintest edge of feedback in the air.

'You know it's true, Karel. Think about it, Kavan never knew anything about you. How could he? It was I who told him about the robot with the unknown mind in Turing City. It was I who saved you from your apartment and had you put on that train.'

'It was you that had Axel killed!' he shouted.

'Listen Karel,' she said, 'I have no loyalty to your wife or to your child, I only have loyalty to Artemis. And to you. Liza twisted it into me when she made me. Fighting back at her attacker in the only way that she could. That and her little trick with the second child's sex. How would he tell the difference, until it was too late?'

'Eleanor?'

They both stopped at the sound of the voice. Kavan had returned.

Karel

Karel and Eleanor turned to gaze at Kavan. How much had he heard?

He didn't appear to register any thing. 'We return south,' said Kavan. 'There is nothing for us here.'

Eleanor and Karel exchanged glances.

'But what about the Book of Robots?' asked Karel.

'The Book of Robots does not exist,' replied Kavan. 'There is nothing in that building but what we have always known. Proof of robot evolution.'

'I don't believe it,' said Karel. 'Let me see.'

'There is no need to see,' replied Kavan. 'I speak the truth. This world is a natural place. There is nothing in that building or any-where else to suggest otherwise.'

'Why bring me up here if you're not going to let me see the building? I have experience of other cultures!'

'Yes?' Kavan seemed nonplussed. 'That experience is valueless. There is only one culture of note, and that is Artemis.'

'But what about Turing City?'

'Turing City is no more.'

'No!'

'You doubt my word? But you saw what we did there.' Kavan seemed more confused than annoyed.

'I want to see what's in the building!' repeated Karel

'I told you, there is nothing to see. The Book of Robots never existed. It was nothing more than an excuse for subversion, a fairy tale that robots could go beyond the way their wire was twisted by their mothers.'

'Let me see!' shouted Karel. Behind him, he was aware of Eleanor, drawing back, bringing them both within the sights of her rifle. Her rifle? He realized at that point he was no longer carrying his own. He had left it lying on the ground, near to the building. He wasn't a soldier; he wasn't used to carrying it . . .

Kavan was growing impatient. 'You will not see the building. We are leaving now.'

'Nicolas the Coward!' called Karel, anger rising within him. 'What is in there that you are hiding?'

'Nothing. This conversation is at an end.'

The anger that had lain long dormant inside him was surging forth, and it was all the stronger for its slumber.

'Then what was all this for? You've brought us across the continent. You've destroyed my city, my life, you killed my child, and for what?'

Kavan stared at him, genuinely puzzled.

'For what?' asked Kavan. 'For Artemis of course.'

Karel kicked at the half-frozen ground. A small stone skittered across the rock.

'Fight me,' he said.

'Karel,' warned Eleanor. 'Don't be silly . . .'

'Isn't this what you wanted? For me to kill Kavan for you?'

'To kill me, Eleanor?' said Kavan. 'Don't you think you can do it yourself?'

'You know I can't.'

Karel didn't care about any of this. 'Fight me,' he repeated.

'Come on. Turing City versus Artemis. We both wear the same bodies, we both believe we're right. This is about nothing more than our philosophy. This is where we find out which is the stronger.'

Kavan was gazing at Eleanor still. She spoke first. 'Karel, you're being ridiculous.' She drew back further, her gun aimed at the ground. 'Kavan has worn that body for years. He's a soldier. You won't stand a chance.'

'I don't care. He killed my son.'

Kavan was growing impatient. 'This has gone on long enough, Eleanor. Kill him. Or, if you think you can do it, kill me. I'm unarmed. Or if you still consider yourself an Artemisian, follow me.'

At that, Kavan turned and began to walk away southwards.

Eleanor raised her rifle, pointing it first at Kavan, and then at Karel.

'You coward!' shouted Karel at the retreating robot's back. 'Why won't you fight me?' His voice was thick with static.

'Apologize to him,' said Eleanor, desperately.

'Apologize?' said Karel. 'For what?'

Kavan had stopped. He turned, impatient.

'Why do you still waste time? Kill him.'

Eleanor looked down at the rifle she held in her hands like it was the first time she had really noticed it. Dark metal, shining with oil. She had carried it for so long. Now it was as if she was really thinking about what it was for.

'I . . . I can't,' she said. 'I can't kill him.'

'Then give me the rifle and let me do it,' said Kavan.

The rifle moved ever so slightly in his direction.

'I can't do that either, Kavan. He's my brother. It is woven into my mind to protect him.'

Kavan looked from her to Karel.

'Well, that explains something. I wondered why she insisted you accompany her here.' He looked impatient now. 'Time presses on. We shall leave him here. Will your mind allow you to do that?'

'Yes. I think so.'

'Come on, then.'

He turned and resumed his walk south. After a moment's hesitation, Eleanor followed him.

Karel watched them go. And then the anger arose in his mind for the last time.

He charged after Kavan, feet pounding on the half-frozen ground, spraying flashing jewels of shining snowmelt. Kavan still had his back to him. He let out an electronic roar of hate and flung himself forward. The other robot turned, grabbed his hand, and, seemingly without effort, pulled so that Karel tumbled forward, head over heels, landing on the stony ground with a crash that rattled through his body.

Karel pushed himself up, his right leg bent out of shape. There was the sound of gunshot, and he turned to see Kavan had kicked at the barrel of Eleanor's rifle, bending it.

'Are you with me or against me, Eleanor?' called Kavan.

'I don't know.' Eleanor looked down at the broken rifle in her hands. She ran a hand along it, feeling the twist in the metal. 'I'm lost, Kavan.'

'Then find yourself,' said Kavan, and at that he turned and lashed out at Karel.

Karel jumped back, found himself crouching, steadying himself, raising his hands at the ready. Kavan's expression was cold, empty of heat. The Artemisian feinted with his left hand and then he kicked out, landing a blow right on Karel's damaged knee. It gave way, and his body fell forward into the path of Kavan's follow-up punch, aimed right at the back of the neck, right at the spot where the coil was attached to the body. Karel's hand lashed back, smashing into Kavan's wrist, Karel kicked back at Kavan's knee. Kavan rolled forward, body crashing on the stony ground in harsh percussion.

Karel drew back, the current surging through his electromuscle. He was astonished at what he had just done.

Kavan rose up, gazing at him with new respect.

'So fast, Turing City. If only the rest of your state had shown such spirit. Or was it your state? Who are you really, Kavan? What is there woven into your mind?'

Karel looked at Eleanor. Eleanor who had flourished in Artemis. Eleanor who wasn't helping him, but who wasn't helping Kavan either. Eleanor, the woman who had killed his child. Eleanor, his sister.

Just what was woven into his own mind? Certainly he never realized he could move so fast. Maybe the potential had always been there, it just needed the right circumstances to unlock it.

'Turing City is gone, Karel,' said Kavan. 'I don't think you were ever part of it. Look at Eleanor. She's so much an Artemisian that she can't kill me. Is that the answer, Karel? Did your mother make you an Artemisian after all?'

'I'm not what you are, Kavan.'

'Are you sure of that? Stop the fight now. Turn around and walk away. I wish to rejoin my army as quickly as possible. We march on Artemis itself. For the moment, I have no quarrel with you.'

'Fight me!'

'You're not fighting me, Karel. You're fighting yourself. You're trying to prove to yourself that you are different to me. But it's not true, is it? Look at your sister.'

Why is he talking to me? The thought came to Karel at the same time as Kavan thrust forward a hand, and Karel's body surged with the shriek of feedback that screeched through his body. He couldn't feel anything below his waist, just a wall of agony, a break in the circuit. He was dimly aware of Eleanor shouting, somewhere in the distance.

'No, Kavan, pull it out of him!'

Kavan had stabbed him with a knife. Shorted out a circuit. Where? Karel didn't know this new body. He had hardly had any time to repair it since Eleanor had plugged his mind into it, let alone to examine it in detail. And yet Kavan had worn bodies such as this nearly all his life. He knew all their vulnerabilities. The fizzing charge of electricity was rising within his body now. He needed to pull out the blade, and yet he couldn't. He had felt the crack as Kavan had bent the knife, breaking off the handle, leaving the knife-edge lodged in his body.

Feebly he tugged at the stomach panelling on his body, trying to pull it free, trying to get at the knife lodged in his body. *Where was Kavan? Why hadn't he attacked yet?*

To the side, he was dimly aware of Eleanor struggling with Kavan, keeping him away, preventing him from striking the final blow.

Finally, the stomach panelling came loose. Karel tossed it to clatter across the rock. Moving his arms now felt as if he was thrusting them into the crackling current. Fighting through the pain, he fumbled at the broken knife blade.

He heard a clatter, a fall. Eleanor lay slumped on the ground, the metal at the back of her neck torn open. And Kavan was running towards him again.

Karel pulled the blade clear. Instantly the pain ceased, but something was wrong. He could no longer feel anything below his waist. Kavan had shorted out his legs completely.

He scrambled with his hands on the rock, seeking escape, realized it was pointless, turned to face Kavan, saw the foot lash out. Karel caught it, twisted it, hurled Kavan to the ground.

How did I do that? Where is that coming from?

Kavan rose to his feet. He gazed at Karel thoughtfully.

'So fast, Karel. We could fight all day.' Karel began to pull himself forward, his legs dragging uselessly behind him. 'But what would the point in that be?'

And at that he turned and began to walk away.

'Hey,' called Karel. 'Come back. This isn't over!'

Kavan said nothing, just continued walking, heading south, back to his army. What was left of it anyway.

Karel watched him go, watched his grey body disappear over the crest of dark hill, dark rocks soaked in melting snow. He didn't care. Kavan really didn't care. He really did regard Karel as nothing more than metal.

He heard a faint cry nearby. Eleanor.

Painfully, he dragged himself across the rock towards her.

Her grey body lay slumped on the ground. He examined the back of the neck, saw how Kavan had crushed the coil there. Crippled her. And there was something else. The black shape of an awl, thrust deep into her mind.

Carefully, he turned her head towards him. There was still light in her eyes.

'Karel,' she said, static lacing her words.

'How badly are you hurt?' he asked.

'Can't feel anything really. I can see and hear and speak. But things are fading. The circuits are discharging too fast. I'm dying.'

'He's gone.'

'He'll send someone back to reclaim our metal. He knows you can't get far like that.'

'What about you?'

'I'm dying, Karel. Current leaking away.' Her voicebox let out a low buzzing noise. It resolved into a voice again.

'Karel, take my legs.'

Karel looked down at her body. It was in better shape than his own.

'Good idea. I'll take your mind, too. I can carry it with me.'

'No point. I told you. Lifeforce draining away.' She let out an electronic burble. Karel was already at work on Eleanor's legs, disassembling the hip joint.

'Eleanor,' he began, 'He was right, wasn't he? We're Artemisians, aren't we? That was how Liza made us.'

Eleanor let out a bubbling laugh.

'You know that's not true, Karel. Not Artemisians.'

Karel felt a wave of relief.

'But not Turing Citizens either. Liza had a gun held to her head. She was made to choose how our minds would be woven, Artemis or Turing City. Imagine what passed through her own mind then. Hate, rage, despair. What was the right choice to make?'

'I don't know.'

'Nor did she, Karel. And there was so little wire for her left to twist . . . What could she put into our minds with that wire? What choice could she make? She put in anger, Karel. Anger at the world.'

'Anger?'

'Anger. More so in you than in me, Karel. All that anger she felt for that robot who was raping her, all that anger was woven into your mind. Because she knew that anger can be so powerful, it means you don't accept the world as it is, you try and change it. What you have in your mind is something so unusual. Something that few other robots have. You have the ability to choose. You can look at the way the world is and then choose which philosophy you follow.'

And at that point, Karel knew it was true. He wasn't just the mind that his mother had made him. He could choose his own mind . . .

'You're special, Karel. Many people know it . . .'

'If I'm special, then you must be too, Eleanor.'

'I was,' she replied.

And at that the light faded from her eyes.

'Eleanor?' he said. He gazed at the black awl, lodged in her head, unsure at what he thought. This was the woman who had killed his child. This was his sister.

He stared at her for some time, trying to figure out what he felt.

Eventually, Karel got to his feet. He turned his back on Eleanor and looked out to the north, to the brightening day, looked at the white foam that decorated the iron-grey waves like badly applied solder.

He felt angry, confused, dizzy. His gyros were spinning way too fast, and he sought to slow them. Turing City, Axel's death, the loss of Susan, his mind placed in a train, and now this . . .

It was the sudden change. You built up a picture of the world, you slotted everything into place, made sense of everything that you knew, built up a view that fitted all the facts, and then something came along that destroyed it all.

Karel had carried an idea of himself around all of his life, an idea of who he was that had been inviolate, untouched, unseen by anyone else. And then Eleanor had come along and had shattered it.

What should he do now?

His whole body shook. He felt as if it were disintegrating as he stood there, as if it were turning to rust and just flaking away.

Does anybody else feel this? he wondered. Do we all feel like this? Do we all walk through a world building pictures of what is normal, not realizing that at any minute the foundations of our world might be revealed to be false, that they will crumble away, and everything will collapse around us?

Or are some people lucky enough never to see it? Is the obvious falsehood so big that they never notice it, hanging there right in front of their face?

He looked up into the sky; the clouds were clearing. He could just see the night moon, setting for the day. A great orb, perfectly spherical: 7×10^{22} tons of metal, orbiting the world of Penrose. Such a natural sight.

At least there were no surprises to be had there.

What was he to do now?

The answer, when it came, was so simple that he almost laughed. He grasped at it gratefully, the only certainty in this shifting world.

He had come to the uttermost north of Shull. All of his past lay to the south. Everyone he knew was to the south. Susan, if she still lived, was somewhere to the south.

For the moment, at least, there was only one way to go.

The light of the sun reflected off Zuse's polished surface as he turned his back on the sea and began to walk.

Epilogue: Cha-Lo-Ell-Curriah

The turboprop of Cha-Lo-Ell-Curriah's craft spun so quickly it sent ultrafrequency vibrations humming through his frame. The twisted metal of his mind vibrated, his thoughts seeming to come from a little farther away. The pinging that now echoed inside his skull was irritating. It took him a while to realize that it came from the radio.

He clicked the send button. 'Cha-Lo-Ell-Curriah.'

'Cha-Lo-Ell-Curriah! Turn immediately on heading oh four oh two.'

'Affirmative.'

The wide blue sea tilted as Cha-Lo-Ell-Curriah banked the plane, eyes fixed on the navigation device before him. The radio controller had sounded excited, and Cha-Lo-Ell-Curriah wondered why, but manners and discipline prevented him from asking.

He clicked the send button again. 'Assumed the heading. Awaiting orders.'

'Cha-Lo-Ell-Curriah, we want you to check if the radar is malfunctioning. It indicates something approaching you from behind.'

I can't see it if it's behind me, thought Cha-Lo-Ell-Curriah.

'It's travelling at four times the speed of sound,' added the controller. 'It should be passing you anytime now.'

Four times the speed of sound? But breaking the sound barrier was supposed to be impossible! Any craft attempting to do so would shake itself apart in the attempt! Obviously the radar was malfunctioning. Cha-Lo-Ell-Curriah composed himself, meditated on iron and water.

And then his craft was shaken by a huge boom. A shadow passed over him, moving at such speed, and then he saw it . . .

'Control!' he called, 'I see it. An . . . aircraft!'

And what an aircraft. Clad in a silver skin, it was much, much *larger than Cha-Lo-Ell-Curriah's craft. Several hundred yards long at least, and painted with such odd symbols.*

'Cha-Lo-Ell-Curriah, report! What can you see?'

'I don't know! It looks like a . . . ship! A ship of the ocean, but flying through the sky! It's so high up, but it's descending. Where has it come from?'

There came no reply. The silver ship was rapidly receding into the distance. Cha-Lo-Ell-Curriah gazed at it with enhanced eyes. Was it decelerating? he wondered.

'It seems to be changing course. Control, I ask again: where has it come from?'

The carrier wave of the radio clicked on. Cha-Lo-Ell-Curriah could just hear the controller engaged in muffled conversation with someone else. Then the voice came to the fore.

'We . . . we don't know for sure. We think, we don't know, but we think, we think it has come from above the atmosphere. From out in space!'

Cha-Lo-Ell-Curriah opened the throttle of his own craft and he heard the rising note of the turboprop as he sought to chase the rapidly diminishing silver speck. It was flying in the direction of Shull, he thought. Was it one of their own craft? No, it couldn't be! Shull was a backward continent. They had little knowledge of flying craft; they could not build something like this. Was it true then that it had come from space?

The distant speck was changing direction. It seemed to be curving around, back towards Yukawa.

Control came back on the radio. 'Cha-Lo-Ell-Curriah, the craft is changing direction.'

'I can see that.'

'Cha-Lo-Ell-Curriah,' the controller's voice was low and hollow with emotion, 'the craft has spoken to us, using the radio. It is coming to Yukawa. It is coming to us, Cha-Lo-Ell-Curriah!'

'Controller, control yourself!'

'They say they have come from the stars! You are to escort them to Huru base!'

The silver speck was growing.

'Controller, they are so big! They could knock me from the sky!'

'They say that they can see you, small though you are. They say they can see all of our aircraft with their ship's senses!'

'Controller, what are they?'

'I don't know!'

The ship was getting large enough for Cha-Lo-Ell-Curriah to make out its shape, to see its smooth lines. It seemed to be built entirely of metal. He looked for its propulsion system, but saw nothing. There were no propellers, nothing to indicate how it moved.

Closer and closer the ship came, and then suddenly it swung around in a wide loop.

'Cha-Lo-Ell-Curriah, did we not ask you to set a course for Huru base?'

The words shook him from his reverie. 'Affirmative,' he replied, banking his craft once more. The silver ship moved smoothly alongside him, and Cha-Lo-Ell-Curriah picked out more details on it. White flashes marked with strange red symbols. Tiny little pits in the metal skin. And there, at the front, a transparent section: the cockpit.

Who was flying this ship?

Cha-Lo-Ell-Curriah opened the throttle to its fullest extent, his craft slid slowly forward along the great silver length, his enhanced eyes peering across at the cockpit.

He saw a figure in there, looking back at him. The figure appeared to be waving to him. He turned his eyes up to their fullest extent, and felt his gyros lurch.

The figure in the ship. It wasn't a robot.

It was organic.

It was an animal.